# desolate

AUTUMN
GREY

# playlist

"Ending"—Isak Danielson

"Bumper Cars"—Alex & Sierra

"Edge of Desire"—John Mayer

"Hunger"—Ross Copperman

"Say You Won't Let Go"—James Arthur

"Belong"—Cary Brothers

Full playlist on Spotify

# Sol

*Present - Thanksgiving Day.*

THERE ARE ANGELS AND DEMONS AT WAR INSIDE MY HEAD, and the demons are winning.

I'm sitting across the table from Grace, the only person who has the power to silence the chaos in my head, and at the same time cause mayhem in my heart. I can't stop staring at her. Her lips highlighted in deep red lipstick, the way her rich brown skin glows when the soft lighting from the lamp above us hits at the right angle, her curly hair banded at the nape of her neck, displaying a heart-shaped face that makes me question my calling.

I should be heeding the advice of my spiritual director to remove myself from temptation. Instead, I'm wondering if she still tastes and smells like vanilla waffles.

I wonder if this is God's test of my loyalty to him. How long will my resolve hold before everything falls apart?

I'm home from seminary for Thanksgiving. Grace's mother, Debra, invited my uncle and me for dinner.

I should have politely refused the invitation and avoided placing myself directly in the path of wickedness, so close to the one person who makes me want to sin ten ways from Sunday.

Instead, I accepted, then spent the next few hours alternating between meditation and praying feverishly to God for strength. Then I threw on a pair of running shorts and a T-shirt and went for a run, hoping the chilly November weather would help me focus.

By the time we left the rectory, I had steeled myself with resolve and patience and strength. That is, until Debra opened the door and stepped aside, inviting us into her home, and my eyes landed on Grace, standing beside the table with her hands clasped primly in front of her.

She smiled sweetly my way, and it hit me—coming here was a big mistake.

As we eat, conversation flows easily, but in my mind the same words keep playing, crowding my thoughts. *I hope my hard-on is not that obvious. God, give me strength to get through this dinner without embarrassing myself.*

It's hard to function when your mind is in turmoil. Hard to breathe when your heart is in your throat.

I'm not sure whether I love her or hate her. I don't know if it's myself I should hate for allowing her to occupy my mind, or if I should thank God for giving me the ability to love her so much that I've made an altar in my head of the memories we shared.

My gaze strays every so often to Grace. Hers briefly meets mine, sending a jolt of heat—*again*—straight to my groin before she looks away. Her eyes stay firmly on her plate as she lifts the fork to her mouth.

*Oh, God.*

Her sin-worthy lips part and close around the forkful of mashed potatoes, and I groan inwardly, picturing that mouth on me.

I quickly drop my gaze to my own plate and subtly shift in

my seat, desperate for relief. I tug down my napkin on my lap, hiding the visible bulge in my pants. Squeezing my eyes shut briefly, I mutter, "Forgive me, Father. Forgive me, Father. Forgive me, F—"

"You okay?" Luke asks in a low voice.

My eyes fly open and my head makes an awkward jerk meant as a nod. From the corner of my eye, I see him assess me with those knowing eyes of his. Judging by the look he's giving me, the answers to his curious thoughts are written all over my face for the world to see. He turns away, frowning, and continues chatting with Debra.

*The heart is weak, greedy, and reckless. Selfish,* my spiritual director advised while staring intently into my eyes during our last session together before I left St. Bernard Seminary for Thanksgiving break. *Stay away from temptation. If something or someone leads you to consider sinning or to have impure thoughts, then it is wise to remove yourself from that situation.*

The words are clear in my head now, yet, here I am. Unable to remove myself from this situation without looking obvious.

I could drag her to her room.

I could kiss her.

I could—

*Stop.*

Guilt cuts through my conscience, causing my stomach to twist painfully. I shut my eyes tight again, trying to rid myself of those thoughts.

I don't even care at this point if I look like the veins in my forehead are about to burst with effort. If I don't block her out, if I don't block Grace out, my restraint will snap. When I close my eyes, it's easier to see the face of my spiritual director staring down at me with such disappointment at my thoughts. It helps. A little bit.

Even though my gaze is on the plate in front of me, I know Grace is watching me innocently from under her lashes. I can *feel* her eyes on me. But they don't fool me. There's nothing innocent about the body beneath that pretty red dress. Everything about it is sinful and dangerous.

And no matter how hard I've tried to forget the feel of her skin against mine, both our smells mixed with the distinct smell of sex, it all seems to be imprinted in my very being. Those memories are a part of me. *She's* a part of me.

Two months ago, I renewed my pledge to God and myself. I promised not to let myself get easily swayed by memories of Grace. I purged all carnal thoughts from my mind. I was cleansed, and my faith and purpose renewed.

I was at peace, that is, until I found out where I'd be spending Thanksgiving dinner.

I wonder if today will be the day I break my vow.

# one

## Sol
*Ten years old*

SUNRAYS FILTER THROUGH THE STAINED GLASS, CASTING SHADES of color on the walls and floors. Specks of dust surround the light in a mesmerizing dance, and I can't stop staring, hoping if I stare too hard the rays of sunshine will reach the pew where I'm sitting and pour warmth inside me.

My mother once told me beauty can be found anywhere. All I needed to do was look for it.

I'm searching for it now, trying to find the beauty in my life, in this old church, in *anything*. But I can't. Not when I feel cold and empty inside.

Uncle Luke pauses in delivering the homily, his eyes moving to where I'm sitting with my shoulders hunched forward. He's been darting glances at me since Mass started twenty-five minutes ago. His electric blue eyes, the same as my mother's, pierce my similar ones. I take in his neatly combed brown hair and clean-shaven jaw. Other than these two things, he's the spitting image of my mom, down to the small indent in his chin.

He's trying hard to hold himself together in front of the congregation, but the worry lines bracketing his mouth and the slight furrow of his brows betray him.

He adjusts the white collar around his neck subtly with a finger as if it's too tight, then looks down at the open Bible in front of him. His gaze meets mine again before moving to the parishioners, then back to me.

His head slants to the side just like Mom's used to do when she imparted a morsel of advice. It's awfully familiar, the pain squeezing inside my chest still fresh.

I turn and stare at the windows again to avoid his eyes and dig my mom's rosary from my pants pocket. The feel of the smooth beads between my fingers soothes me. I can almost hear my mom's voice, see my dad as he smiles down at her with teasing eyes.

If I could go back in time two months ago before my parents were brutally taken from me, I would.

My gaze is pulled toward the cross on the wall. I can't breathe, and my chest feels like it's on fire as anger pushes through the numbing coldness in my veins.

I want to yell at the top of my lungs. Instead, I narrow my eyes at Jesus with his head bowed and arms nailed on either side of the two bars.

*I hate you,* I whisper angrily inside my head. *I hate you. Why didn't you take me too? Why not me? Why not me?*

I close my eyes, hoping the pain will recede, but it's too much and too loud. It's almost as loud as the booming sound that woke me as our car crashed against a tree on the Fourth of July. We were driving back from watching fireworks over the Charles River like we did every year, and the accident claimed my dad and mom.

I fell asleep in the car, so I'm not sure what happened exactly. According to the police report, a car swerved into our lane, causing my dad to twist the wheel to avoid a collision. But it was already too late. The two cars crashed into each other, causing our car to veer off the road. It rolled a few times before crashing into a tree.

Blood rushes in my ears at the memory of being jolted awake to the deafening sound of the crash. I remember the awful rasping as Mom struggled to breathe. Then everything went oddly silent, and terror filled me. My parents were dead, both of them, and I was still here, alone. Part of me died along with them at that realization. Later on, I learned that Dad had died on impact. I'd narrowly escaped death, somehow coming out of the ordeal with only a few broken ribs and a concussion.

Luke's voice snaps me out of my thoughts, and I gulp for air desperately to keep the pain from swallowing me alive. Maybe I should just let it consume me.

He repeats the words I've heard many times during the past few weeks. I want to rip my ears from my head so I don't have to hear them again. "Cast your burden onto the Lord, and He will . . ."

My head bows in defeat before he can finish that sentence.

I want to tell him I tried. I tried very hard to let God handle my problems. My pain. But the crushing weight of my loss still sits heavy in my chest. I'm tired of feeling angry all the time, tired of reliving the accident over and over, tired of missing them, tired of *everything*.

What if what if I walked out of the door and disappeared?

*What if you stayed?* a voice whispers in my head or my ear. I can't tell. It seems to come from everywhere at once.

I bolt upright in the pew, looking right and left, and then over my shoulder. All eyes are focused on my uncle at the front of the church, his voice resounding across the walls and domed ceiling.

The back of my neck burns as if someone is watching me.

I scan the church, wondering if my mind is finally giving in to the grief and pressure. First, I hear voices, and now, I feel as though someone is watching me.

I'm about to face forward when my gaze meets a pair of eyes staring at me with curiosity. The eyes of a girl with brown skin and curly hair that glows like a halo around her head, an effect from the sunrays streaming through the window. A pink flower is tucked into her hair. She's leaning her head against the arm of a woman with matching features.

We stare at each other for a few seconds, then I look away, my cheeks heating with embarrassment. She must think I'm crazy or whatever.

I jump to my feet, ready to flee. From the corner of my eye, I see the panic cross Uncle Luke's face. But I can't stay. I need to go.

I need to breathe.

"Excuse me," I mutter to the woman on my right at the same time as I push my feet forward, but they're stuck on the floor. Something is holding me in place. I can't *move*.

My vision suddenly blurs, and a loud *boom, boom, boom* fills my ears. Then I'm falling sideways. I grab the pew in front of me for support, but my hands miss it by inches, and my head smacks on something hard. My eyes fall shut, unable to take the pressure behind them. The last thing I feel before darkness claims me is a pair of strong hands grasping my shoulders.

☩

I blink my eyes open and stare at what looks like a white ceiling. I'm lying on a hard surface, and my head feels as if it's about to split open. I move my head to the side and take in the bookshelves filled with books and several framed photos.

There's a cross above the shelves and a picture of the Pope hanging beside it.

"Is he going to be okay?" a woman's voice asks softly. I tilt my head and see two women hovering at the door. The one with brown skin looks awfully familiar. My brain clears a little, and I realize she was sitting next to the girl with a pink flower in her hair.

"I don't know. I . . . he has to be okay. He just has to." Luke's voice cracks as he whispers those words.

No one says anything for a few seconds. I hear feet walking in my direction. Then small fingers—smaller than mine—wrap around my hand and squeeze gently.

"You're awake," a voice whispers in my ear.

I turn my head and meet the same eyes I saw earlier. Up close, they remind me of maple syrup. My gaze darts to the door, to the women speaking with my uncle, then back to the girl hovering above me.

"That's my mom over there." She jerks her thumb over her shoulder in the general direction of the door, then leans closer to my ear and says, "You're going to be okay."

I blink twice and croak out, "I am?"

She nods confidently. "Just a small bump here . . ." She taps a finger on her forehead. "It will heal. Everything will be okay. I promise, okay?"

Her big eyes watch me patiently. I want to believe her, but I'm having a hard time. My parents once promised me nothing would ever take them away from me. And where are they now? Dead.

A broken promise.

I turn my head to face the wall as another torrent of tears floods my eyes. Finger tips brush my skin, wiping the tears as they spill from the corner of my eye, and I can't help it. I bring my gaze back to this girl who's showing me kindness instead of shying away from the sadness.

She purses her lips as if she's in deep thought, then says, "My mom once told me tears are like rain for our souls. They wash away the pain and sadness in our hearts so we don't drown."

I wipe my cheeks with the sleeve of my shirt, my mouth curving into a reluctant smile at her attempt to make me feel better. "Your mom sounds awesome."

At that, she smiles wide, and I notice the little gap between her two upper teeth. Something jolts inside me, and a part of me melts a little.

"She's really amazing." She sing-songs the last word. "What's your name?"

"Solomon Callan," I reply without hesitation.

"Grace Miller." She opens her mouth to say something but then shuts it when the conversation behind us stops. Feet move in our direction, and she pulls her hand from mine. Immediately, I miss the comfort and warmth. She reaches for the pink flower in her hair and pulls it out, then puts it in my palm. I feel the sharp edge of the metal clip nip my skin.

I'm so confused. Why did she give me this? Is she expecting me to put it in my hair? "I don't . . . it looks better in your hair."

"It's a good luck charm, silly." She giggles, reminding me of the wind chimes that used to hang from the porch ceiling at my house in Boston.

Fresh pain slices through me. My mom and I loved to sit on the porch swing and wait for my dad to come home from work. Then he'd join us, and we'd rock back and forth on the swing, simply being a family while the wind chimes blew softly in the breeze. And now my family is gone. I wipe my wet cheeks with my free hand.

"I didn't mean to upset you," Grace whispers worriedly. "It's just a flower. I'll take it—"

"No. It's pretty. Thank you." My fingers curl around the silky soft fabric in my palm. She flashes me a relieved smile.

Before I have a chance to say another word, she says, "I have to go." She gives me a small wave, then turns and skips away.

"Sol?" my uncle calls out as he appears in my line of vision. I drag my gaze from Grace Miller and meet his. He sighs in relief and reaches for my hand, covering it with his larger one. "How are you feeling?"

I glance to the side again, searching for Grace, but she's already gone. I bring my gaze back to my uncle's.

"My head." I touch the spot on my temple. When I fainted, I must have hit the pew in front of me before someone caught me.

I wince as Luke sweeps the hair off my forehead with his hand, resting it on my neck. He sighs wearily. "I know you're hurting, bud. If I could turn back time, I would. I'd give your mom and dad to you." His voice is shaky with emotion, and his palm on my neck squeezes in comfort. "I miss them so much. But if we keep the good memories here"—he points the spot where his heart is—"they will always be with us."

"They will?" After the past few weeks, I want to believe him so badly. If there is a way to relieve this numbing pain, I'll take it.

He nods and smiles. His eyes fill with tears, but I can't tell if he's happy or sad.

I push up to my elbows and press my forehead into his chest. His arms circle my shoulders, and he pulls me close.

"You have me, Sol. I've got you."

# *Grace*

*Ten years old*

I can't stop thinking about Solomon Callan, the boy with sad blue eyes.

*Beautiful sad blue eyes.*

Right after dinner, my mom asks me to brush my teeth. She'll come to my room shortly to tuck me in, so I do as I'm told.

When I've finished, I run back into my room and head for my desk. I grab a blue notebook and tear out a small piece of paper, then pick a pencil. I quickly scribble today's date and Solomon's name. I fold it, open the glass jar wrapped in pink lace and white ribbon, and drop it inside. My Beautiful Memories Jar was a birthday gift from my mother on my sixth birthday. On the last Sunday of each month, I empty it and read the notes as a reminder of the beautiful things that happened over the past few weeks.

I skip to my bed and straighten the pink and purple sheets before climbing on top and getting on my knees like I do every night. I pray for my mom, thanking God for giving me such an awesome and beautiful mother. I pray for Solomon to find peace and ask God to heal the large bump on his head so he doesn't suffer from the awful headache for long. Then I pray for school holidays to come quicker so I can sleep longer in the morning and help Mom at the diner and eat as many vanilla waffles as I want without getting sick.

Mom comes into the room just as I finish praying. I crawl between the sheets, pulling them to my chin, and wait for her to read my favorite storybook from the nightstand.

She looks at the jar, and her mouth lifts in her smile. "More beautiful memories?"

"Yep." I beam, thinking about the boy with blue eyes and wavy dark hair.

"Good." She smiles and tucks several locks of hair behind my ear. "I noticed you didn't have your good luck charm flower on your hair."

"Solomon needs it more than I do."

She nods, her smile turning gentle. "He does, doesn't he?"

When she opens the book, she lies next to me, resting her head on the pillow beside mine. My eyes follow the slight sway of the paper cranes floating on a string suspended from the ceiling. I make a note to make more tomorrow to fill in the empty patch in the corner.

As soon as Mom picks up from where she left off last night, my eyes start to droop, lulled by her soft voice. My last thought before I fall asleep is that I wish I had the power to make people smile.

# two

## Sol
*Thirteen years old*

SATURDAY MORNING IS MY FAVORITE DAY OF THE WEEK. NOT only do I get to sleep longer, attend morning Mass where I'm part of the altar servers, but my uncle also drives us to Boston to visit my parents at the cemetery. Then we drive back to the house I grew up in and he cooks dinner for us. Later, we drive back to Portland. This has been sort of a tradition since I moved here to live with him three years ago.

After blacking out during Mass that day, Uncle Luke and I started attending grief therapy. It took me a long time to stop resenting God. I started to believe there was an actual reason He had let me live. I joined the altar server team a year later. At first, it was something for me to do. I wanted to feel useful. Then I realized I really liked being part of something as big as Mass. Something that offered peace and refuge to me and a lot of other people.

Then I started assisting Eric Beck—the youth ministry leader—with the youth group. I finally felt as though I fit in. I felt as if I was needed.

I glance at the digital clock on the wall that flashes 10:15 a.m., then I watch as the recreational room fills in slowly for youth group, which begins in fifteen minutes.

A group of kids ranging from ten to fifteen years old stumble through the door. They shove each other and laugh out loud. A few other kids, some of them around my age, walk in and sit down. Several come from troubled family backgrounds, and being here gives them a chance to experience a completely different perspective about life. I know I'm only thirteen, but I love seeing them transition from troubled teens to God-fearing youths. Even though they're a loud and rowdy bunch, I enjoy being a part of it.

A few weeks ago, my teacher—Mrs. Albright—asked each of us what we wanted to be when we grew up. It took me a while to figure out where my heart lay. Every time I attend Mass, an incredible peacefulness fills me like no other. Each time I minister the youth group, I feel surer about my decision. Then visiting the sick with Luke in their homes, I see how much hope and peace he gives them. When I told my uncle, he seemed concerned because I was too young to make such a decision. What he doesn't realize is that I know myself very well. Sometimes losing someone you love makes you grow up fast.

Ivan Alvarez swaggers into the room. He's only thirteen, like me, but he's so confident and sure of himself, the other kids turn around to look at him. Girls giggle and fan themselves with their hands.

We first met at Lincoln Middle School when I moved here. We hit it off, and we've been best friends ever since. He's half Korean and half Spanish and doesn't attend Mass as much as his father would like. He attends youth group, though, which makes things a little better between them.

Ivan stops in front of me, and I roll my eyes. "You're such a show-off," I mutter under my breath with a small laugh.

He grins and shrugs. "Bet you wish you were me."

"No." I laugh and shake my head. "I'm good."

"Eric not here yet?"

"Soon," I answer. His head slants to one side as he studies me, his eyes turning serious. "What?" I ask, running my fingers along the smooth cover of my Bible to stop the nerves from taking over. I can deal with Playful Ivan. Serious Ivan, on the other hand, makes me nervous.

"What's going on with you? You look so peaceful and happier than usual."

The nerves I was feeling vanish, and I smile at his question. This one I can answer. I've been waiting for the right time to tell him the news. I pull him to the less crowded side of the room. "Remember when Mrs. Albright asked us what we wanted to be when we grew up?"

"If you still plan to be a stage magician, I'm all for it."

I laugh. "I'm going to be just like my uncle."

His forehead scrunches up in confusion. "A priest?"

I nod.

"Why? I mean, Luke is cool and all, but a priest? Like, you'll never get married or have a girlfriend or . . . oh my God. You'll die a virgin because you'll never have sex. I hear that's some mind-blowing stuff right there." He scratches his head. "Dude. I'm so confused. You're thirteen."

I shrug. "I know that, you dork. It doesn't mean I'm not capable of deciding what I want to be, you know. I've never been more sure about anything in my life."

"But what about pulling rabbits out of hats or whatever?"

"I can still do that and be a priest."

He studies me thoughtfully. Then slowly, a big smile takes over his face. "This means more ladies for me, eh?"

I shrug his hand off my shoulder. "Could you be a little bit more supportive?"

"Could you be a little bit less goody two shoes?"

I sigh. He laughs. Then he glances around the room and says, "Wait. You blindsided me with your news. I forgot about him."

He points his chin to the door. I follow his gaze to where a boy stands in the doorway. He must be three years younger than me at most. His guarded eyes scan the room before cutting in our direction.

I glance at Ivan. "Who's he?"

"Seth. I found him in the hallway. I told him we serve cookies. You better dish them out."

I laugh again. "I can't even with you." I start to walk toward Seth to welcome him to the group but freeze when Grace Miller appears at the doorway. She mumbles something to Seth, and he steps aside to let her pass without saying a word.

My breath hitches when her eyes meet mine. She looks away first, tucking stray curls of hair behind her ear, and then sits on the chair nearest to the door.

Ivan groans. "Come on, Callan. Pick up your jaw from the floor and go talk to the girl."

I snap my gaze from Grace and face Ivan. "Uh . . ." I close my mouth, my cheeks burning at being caught staring.

He rolls his eyes. "She's only a girl, you know. Girls don't bite. Besides, it's not like you want to go out with her, right? Not when you want to become a priest."

I don't know what to say to that. I shove my hand inside my jeans pocket and scowl. Where the heck is Eric? "Let's talk to Set—" The boy at the door is already shuffling away.

Ivan follows my gaze and yells, "Seth! Wait up!" and takes off after him.

My eyes drift to where Grace is sitting. She's watching me again. We look away at the same time. My mouth tips in a smile. I risk a glance at her from under my lashes, and I see the corner of her mouth pulled up in a smile, as well.

My knees feel a little weird, as if they can't hold me up. I sit down on one of the free seats and stare at the floor. Grace and I don't go to the same school. The only time I get to see her is at Sunday Mass or youth group. Yet I feel this sensation in my stomach whenever I do see her. I wish I were brave enough to talk to her. I wish she could talk to me like she did the first time we met.

My fingers fumble with the rosary in my pocket, rolling the smooth beads with my fingertips.

When someone claps their hands twice, I lift my head and see Eric stroll into the room. He's carrying a white folder tucked under one arm, and the room falls silent at his presence.

After the usual prayer, Eric sets the folder on his lap and flips to the first page. We listen as he highlights the points of the upcoming fundraiser to help the local orphanage headed by Sisters of Mercy.

At some point, I notice Grace is no longer in the room. The more I sit here, the more I want to leave and look for her. Usually, she waits until the session is over. She's always the first person out of the room. I have a feeling that's the reason she sits close to the door.

I excuse myself and leave the room. My steps falter when I turn the corner to the hallway that leads to the washrooms and see her sitting on the floor. Her body is half-turned to a younger girl with curly blond hair sitting across from Grace.

I've seen the girl in church with her mother. She must be around eight or nine years old. They're both talking in low tones. It's rude to listen in on conversations, so I backtrack, but stop when I hear Grace say, "My mother always says we're all stronger than we think. All we need to do is believe, and we can do anything."

"You think I can do it? Those kids at school are . . . they're awful."

Grace reaches forward and hugs her. "Of course! The kids in my school are monkey poop. And you know what? I try not to let them get to me."

The girl giggles and pulls away from Grace. I press my lips together, fighting a smile.

Feet shuffle on the floor, followed by the sound of the swish of fabric. The last thing I hear before fleeing back to the recreational room is Grace saying something about a Beautiful Memories Jar her mom gave her for her birthday. I sit in my spot, my heart beating fast and eyes on the floor, waiting to hear the sound of her feet the second she walks back into the room.

Seconds turn to minutes, and she doesn't appear. And one hour later, I leave the room with disappointment hanging like a dark cloak around me.

# three

## Sol

*Thirteen years old*

GRACE DIDN'T SHOW UP TO YOUTH GROUP LAST SATURDAY, and today is the last weekend of the month. The fundraiser is planned for next week, and so far, everything is going according to plan.

I leave my uncle's office and head to the recreational room. It's empty save for Seth, who's staring blankly out the window. After he showed up here two weeks ago, he too disappeared. Until today.

"Hey," I greet, setting my Bible down on one of the chairs and stepping in his direction.

He blinks and looks at me. His eyebrows furrow in a scowl. He looks out the window again without saying anything.

"Whatever," I mutter before I can stop myself, turn, and head to my seat.

"So, Father Foster, is he your dad or something?"

I spin around to face him, surprised by his words and that he decided to talk to me. He's still facing the window. "He's my uncle."

He grunts something under his breath.

I sigh and grab my Bible and sit down.

"Seth Kruger," he mumbles without turning to face me.

"Solomon Callan."

We fall silent. I tug the ribbon attached to the Bible and open to the last page I read last night so I can catch up with my reading, in case Luke decides to spring Bible verse trivia on me during dinner. He has a habit of catching me off guard, but I love a good challenge.

The sound of feet shuffling causes me to lift my head. I watch as Seth takes a seat across from me, then stares at the ceiling.

"Dude, is everything okay?"

He sighs and drops his chin to his chest. "I don't really want to be here."

"I kind of figured that out."

His head snaps up, his gaze sharp and angry on mine.

I clear my throat and think of something to say.

"You have to want to attend youth group, you know. Otherwise, it doesn't really make sense to force yourself to be here."

"My mom asked me to come."

"Okay," I say.

"She says being here will be good for me. I don't see how this is good for me. The church is the reason why—" he stops abruptly, his fists clenched.

I perk up and sit straighter in my chair. "The reason for what?"

His jaw grows tight as he tries to control his anger.

"My mom . . . she was in love with this dude at our church back in Baltimore." He frowns, his eyes staring off in a distance.

"Um, that's a good thing, right? I mean, unless your mom was still married to your dad or this guy—"

"He was a freakin' priest." His gaze cuts back to me, his

lips curling into an angry sneer. "They loved each other. At least that's what Mom used to tell me and my twin brother, Sam. I think someone found out about them. He denied ever having anything to do with my mom, which broke her heart. We became social outcasts, and Sam took it very hard. He died . . ." Seth makes an angry sound in the back of his throat, and his hands clench in his lap. "The church refused to give him a proper Catholic burial."

My mouth is dry. I don't know what to say, but I need to come up with something. I need him to keep talking to me. "Why would they do that?"

"Because he killed himself." His cheeks are wet now. He swipes a hand down his face as if he's annoyed to show such weakness. "I hate the church. I hate how they treated my brother even though the priest responsible played a part in causing his death." The words rush out in a broken whisper. "I hate them so much. I don't know what to do . . ."

I stand and go to him. What happened to him and his family is so awful. Even at my age, I understand that priests shouldn't have girlfriends or wives. They promise to be faithful to God and God only. My uncle explained to me one day when I asked him why he wasn't married and didn't date.

"I'm so sorry," I tell him, placing a hand on his shoulder to comfort him. My instincts are pushing me into giving him a hug, but a part of me knows he might not be ready for that kind of comfort. "Can I do anything to help?" I blurt out, desperate to make things better for him, but I know nothing in the world can help. "My uncle, he's an awesome listener. He's really good at solving problems, too."

He shoves my hand off his shoulder and jumps to his feet. "No!" he yells, pressing his palms into his eyes. And then he seems to run out of steam, and his shoulders slump forward. "I just want this pain to stop. You don't understand how it feels to lose someone."

"Believe me, I do," I say quietly. "I lost my mom and dad three years ago. I know exactly how you feel, Seth." I pause, gathering my thoughts. "After my parents died, I wanted to die too. I begged God to take me. I was ready to give up. Then one day during Mass, a voice spoke to me. Maybe I imagined it, I don't know. But I'd like to think it was Him." I shrug. I've never told anyone this before. It sounds silly now that I've said it aloud, but for some reason, I need Seth to believe things will get better.

He stares at me with red-rimmed eyes. "How . . . when does the pain stop?"

I shrug. "It never really goes away. My uncle helped me a lot."

He looks so small and beaten down. Even though I don't know him, seeing him suffering like I did three years ago makes my stomach hurt. I can't stop from pleading with him one more time. "Uncle Luke is the best, I promise. I can go with you to see him, and you can leave anytime you feel uncomfortable."

He shoves his hands inside his pants pockets and walks to the door with dragging feet. The hope I was feeling before vanishes.

He stops at the doorway and looks at me. His green eyes pierce mine like he's searching for something. Then, he inhales deeply and says, "Will you come with me tomorrow? I mean, if he has time or whatever."

"Yes," I answer, hope washing over me once again. "I'm here for you, Seth. You can always count on me." I pause, suddenly feeling even more sure about who I want to be. "When I become a priest, I'll make sure something like this doesn't happen in my church," I say with conviction.

He looks up at me, frowning. "You want to be a priest?"

"Yeah."

He just nods and then walks out the door with doubt in his eyes. Of course, he doesn't believe me, given what went down in Baltimore.

I go back to my seat, thinking about Seth and how I can make his life better. *If* I can make it better at all. Being a kid sucks sometimes.

The room starts to fill, the kids being loud and shoving each other as usual. Then the familiar scent of vanilla waffles drifts into the room right before Grace steps through the door, quiet as always, prettier than ever. She's wearing black shorts, black Converse and a sky-blue shirt with those frilly lace thingies around the collar.

She sits at her usual place near the door and scans the room until her eyes meet mine. We just stare at each other, like, for hours. It feels like hours, anyway. I lift my hand and wave, offering her a half-smile. Her lips lift at the corners. She gives me a quick wave, then ducks her head.

I look away, her smile playing on repeat in my mind. Eric enters the room and I sit up straight, trying hard not to sneak another look at Grace. Or think about her. But I fail miserably. It's like someone stuck the image of her pretty face in my brain with Krazy Glue.

# four

*Grace*
*Eighteen years old*

TODAY IS THE MONDAY-EST MONDAY EVER.

The clock on the nightstand stares back at me, blinking 6:30 a.m. over and over. I wipe the beads of sweat off my forehead, then sit up on the bed. It's only the first week of June, but it's already hotter than hell. Well, not that I know how hot it is down there, but from what I've read from the scripture and heard Father Foster preach in his sermons, I can only conclude it's a shitstorm of fire and brimstone.

It's been a week since summer vacation started. I should be sleeping in. Instead, I'm wide awake and wondering about my future. I'm wondering what my next step should be.

My skin feels too tight against my bones, and my mind is racing with excuses, possibilities, and plan As and Bs. Most people my age have already figured out what they want to study in college. I thought I did, too. Seeing my mom smile proudly at me when I got accepted at Brown University made me drunk with happiness.

Then something in me changed. I realized I was trying to please my mom instead of doing what was best for me. I want to go to college and do something I love, not go to Brown just to fulfill Mom's dream. I love my mom a lot, and if we lived in a world where people were thrown in cages to fight lions or tigers, I'd volunteer to trade places with her in a heartbeat, Katniss style. But I can't live my life for her.

I need to talk to her about my decision soon. I can't continue to pretend everything is okay. I don't want thousands of dollars to be spent on my education if I don't even know who I am, what I want, or what I like. I'm tired of feeling so lost. I want to carve my own path and find my purpose on this earth, but the thought of confronting her makes me sick to my stomach. Brown University was her dream, a dream she never got the chance to experience because of me.

I hop down from the bed and head to the kitchen to get a glass of cold water. The scent of coffee greets me right before I walk into the room. Mom is already sitting at the small kitchen table, her fingers curled around a large mug. She's staring blindly ahead, her forehead creased in thought as one finger taps the rim of the cup. Sometimes I wish I could get a peek inside her head. I have a feeling there's this other big part of her life I don't know about.

I always take a few seconds to study her whenever she's distracted; her shoulder-length dreadlocks tied in a high ponytail atop her head, a clear, smooth chocolate-brown complexion, round cheekbones, stubborn chin, and a generous mouth. Even though she's thirty-six, she could easily pass for twenty-six years old. I may be biased since she's my mom, but just look at her. She's a beauty.

She and I have similar features down to the dimple in our chins. My skin is a few shades lighter, though. It's only been me and Mom for as long as I can remember. The only thing I know about my father is that he was Caucasian. Mom never talks about him, so I've made peace with it. I mean, why dwell on something that'll only end up hurting me in the end?

I have more pressing matters to think about, thank you very much. Like how the heck am I going to tell Mom I won't be attending Brown in the fall?

Just thinking about her disappointment makes me want to run back to my room and hide under the sheets like I used to do after I got upset when I was a kid. Then she'd trail after me with a cup of hot chocolate and make me smile again. God, being a kid was so much easier.

"Morning, Mom." I force my feet to move toward her and give her a hug from the side.

Her body tenses like it always does at unexpected hugs or touches. She blinks several times, then focuses her dark brown eyes on me. A smile quickly spreads across her face as she reaches up to brush the wayward curls off my face. "Aren't you supposed to be sleeping in until God-knows-when o'clock?"

"It's too damn hot. I couldn't sleep."

"Watch your language, young lady," she scolds.

"Sorry," I mutter, dropping my arms from her shoulders.

She hands me the coffee. "Everything okay, Grumpy?" she teases.

I'm not really a morning person. The Brown issue is making me even grumpier. Maybe I should just tell her, rip off the Band-Aid and get it over with.

I take a sip from the offered cup, then set it on the table in front of her. I head to the sink to buy time, silently praying for strength and also to avoid her knowing eyes until I'm ready to tell her. I swear some days I think she is a mind reader. Either that or she has a special antenna—programmed just for me—set to receive signals whenever there's a lot of activity in my head.

Like now. The heat in her curious eyes warms my back. My heart starts racing, causing this loud thudding in my ears.

Oh my God. I'm not ready to tell her.

Maybe tomorrow.

Definitely tomorrow.

"I'm . . . um . . . going to church. Morning Mass." I'm such a coward.

"Now?" she asks, surprise clear in her voice.

I spin around and smile so wide my cheeks hurt from the effort. "Yeah. I mean, I'll jump in the shower first, then head out."

Her eyes narrow with suspicion, but all she says is, "All right." I turn to leave, relieved I've narrowly escaped "the talk" when she adds, "You better finish writing a list of whatever you need for college so we can start shopping early."

I almost miss a step in my haste to escape her scrutiny. "Yes, Mom," I say without looking back at her. "Love you!"

"Oh, by the way, can you do me a favor? Could you grab some yarn for me from that shop downtown? I promised to purchase some for my next visit at SMU."

"Sure." Mom volunteers at Single Moms Unified every month. Growing up, she drummed into me the importance of paying it forward to the community. If it wasn't for the kindness and support she received when she arrived in Portland, she wouldn't be here today.

"Love you," she says just as my feet hit the small hallway.

Twenty-five minutes later, I'm sitting on the fourth pew at St. Peter's Church, blissfully basking in the cool interior. Father Foster's voice drifts in and out of my thoughts as he delivers his homily.

My gaze wanders around my surroundings. About fifteen people, at most, are attending Mass. Someone snores in the back, making Father Foster pause and lift his head a little with a small twitch of his lips.

Then I see him. Solomon Callan is occupying one of the

seats where the altar servers sit during Mass. Locks of wavy dark brown hair fall over his eyes, and his hand reaches up to brush the hair away. I can't stop staring, fascinated by that movement. Sol and I went to different schools in middle schools, then we attended the same high school at Winston High. It's just so weird how we never really spoke even though we ended up in the same class.

I guess we moved in different circles back then: me, the quiet girl trying to fit in with the popular crowd while he hung out with Ivan and a bunch of other soccer guys from their team.

Three years ago, Sol was this awkward teenage boy with a tangle of long legs and arms and a shy personality to match. Time has definitely been kind to him. His limbs have finally grown to fit the rest of his tall frame, and all the soccer practices back in high school have left him in great shape.

And God, Solomon Callan is glorious. He's known around town as Father Foster's nephew, the town's good boy and every parent's dream kid.

Too bad all that gloriousness won't be here long enough for us to drool over. Sol will be heading to seminary in the fall to become a priest. Otherwise, I'd totally break the promise I made to myself after things went south with my asshole ex-boyfriend, Gavin, to steer clear of boys.

As if sensing me, Sol's eyes lift and meet mine. One side of his mouth curls up in a subtle half-smile. I grip the bench I'm sitting on and drop my gaze to my lap, feeling hot and cold at once.

Well, that's an interesting turn of events. Sol has always been the cute boy from church who I met eight years ago. The boy I always wanted to talk to at youth group but wasn't brave enough to approach. I don't even know why he intimidated me. Maybe because he was so pretty and looked like a dark-haired, blue-eyed angel through my thirteen-year-old eyes.

I'm not sure what I'm feeling right now, though.

It's all in my head, even this stupid shiver that came out of nowhere.

I shouldn't be thinking about tall boys with cute smiles and messy hair who are bound to become priests, albeit very hot priests. I should be thinking of sorting out my own life.

When I glance up again, Sol's eyes are still on me. I wonder what he sees when he looks at me like that.

I force myself to look away, reminding myself that boys break the ever-loving shit out of your heart.

## Sol

The scent of frankincense and myrrh surrounds me as I extinguish the candles with a snuffer after morning Mass. When I'm done, I glance across the room at Seth as he shuffles around collecting the song books and placing them on the table in the back of the church.

Last summer he and two other boys attended the altar server training class. He's come a long way from the boy I met years ago. He's still a bit skittish about the Catholic Church at times. He attends Mass more often than he used to, so I consider that a win. Joining the altar server team is a big step for him. The other two boys prefer serving in the evening and Sunday Mass.

"I gotta run. Mom's waiting for me outside," Seth says when he's finished with his task.

I nod, giving him a two-finger salute. "Stay out of trouble, okay?"

He rolls his eyes and smiles. "Where's the fun in that?" His sneakered feet drag across the worn-out concrete floor as he heads toward the sacristy to remove his alb.

I chuckle, shaking my head, then drop to my knees in the first pew. I make the sign of the cross and clasp my hands in front of me.

Instead of filling the silence with a prayer, I choose to enjoy the quietness. I stare at the altar in front of me and let the tranquility of God's presence wash over me.

This is my thing. I like to take a few minutes after Mass to absorb the beauty my mom used to discuss. I think about how far I've come. I think about my path ahead. Over the past few years, my uncle has repeatedly asked me if being a priest is what I really want. I understand his concern, I really do, because I know what I'm giving up. I also know what I'm gaining by wholeheartedly giving myself to God. Life is too short. I want to make the most of it by having a positive impact on people's lives.

Okay. I'm going to be honest for a second. I'm not going to pretend I haven't entertained thoughts of having sex with someone special. I have, many times. I mean, I'm not a saint. I'm a teen with raging hormones, but I've learned the art of restraint to a science. Sometimes I get so wound up I feel like I'm about to shatter into pieces. I end up taking cold showers after rubbing one out. Guilt mixed with pure relief rides me hard after that, so I grab my Bible and read the scripture to force those thoughts out. Or play my guitar while wearing headphones as Linkin Park or Green Day blare into my ears.

My gaze lands on the cross. I wonder if Jesus had these feelings and if he acted on them by locking himself in a room and riding it out. I don't remember reading anywhere in the Bible about him having carnal thoughts.

I sigh and pray to God for forgiveness for putting Jesus and carnal thoughts in the same sentence. I pull out my mom's rosary from my shorts pocket, running the tips of my fingers over the smooth surface as I recite the Lord's Prayer. I mutter, *"For thine is the kingdom, and the power, and the glory, forever and ever. Amen."*

After pocketing the rosary, I step away from the pew. I'm about to head down the aisle when I see a familiar head with a riot of black curls to my right.

Grace Miller.

I groan inwardly when my stupid, *stupid* body heats at the sight of her. And instead of heading to the sacristy to remove my alb, I glance in her direction, taking in the way her hands are clasped in her lap, her eyes fixed on something in front of her. Despite the way her fingers keep flexing, her face is set in a calm expression. She tilts her head as if she senses me, and our eyes meet, sending a shockwave of awareness down my spine.

I nod my chin in her direction and let my lips curl in a smile. Her brows lift as if she's surprised I acknowledged her. She nods back at me hesitantly.

My feet move forward, intending to go sit next to her. A bold idea coming from me. I've never acted on my interest. And sure enough, as soon as I try, my feet refuse to move. I just stand there with my hands clenched into fists at my sides and give my body time to calm down.

"You're hovering," she says quietly, the words traveling across the empty church. I can't tell if she's angry or irritated. When I don't say anything, she continues talking without looking at me. "Dude. I'm kind of trying to talk to God here. You're making it difficult."

I clear my throat. Irritated it is, then.

"Yeah? About what?" I officially want to kick my own ass. What kind of question is that? Conversations between someone and God are private.

She's quiet for a few seconds, and when I think she's about

to bite my head off, she mutters, "Important life decisions." She shrugs absentmindedly. "But I think He's left the building because I'm not getting much of an answer sitting here."

Her head falls back, and she stares at the domed ceiling as if expecting the Big Guy to materialize from above. My gaze can't help but fall to her throat, tracing the curve of her smooth, delicate-looking skin. I swallow hard and rip my gaze away. "I assure you, He's listening."

She just shrugs again and continues to stare up. I want to add something more meaningful and encouraging, but I can't form any words. Her presence has stolen all of them, like always.

I sigh, feeling dismissed, and head for the sacristy. After carefully hanging my alb and putting away the snuffer, I grab my blue baseball cap from the shelf and head to Luke's office. I shut the door and lean over the desk, bracing my fists atop it. Bowing my head, I inhale deeply, my starved lungs greedily sucking in air.

What is it about Grace that makes me so nervous? What is it about her that steals my breath when I'm close to her, leaving me high-strung and speechless?

Where God appeases me, makes my soul lighter, Grace is like an electric shock jump-starting my dormant body.

The door opens behind me, and I jolt upright. Luke pauses at the door, eyeing me for several seconds before rounding his desk and sitting on his padded leather chair. Dressed in his usual black pants and clerical shirt with a white collar, he looks like the man I aspire to be. The man who inspires me, my confessor. The man who's been my mentor from the moment I chose to follow in his footsteps.

"I thought you were heading straight to work after Mass?" he asks while rearranging the already impeccable desk, straightening the pile of papers. "What are you doing here?"

"Do I need a reason to drop by?"

His hands stop moving. He sits back and levels me with a stare. Often, when he does small things like smiles or looks at me in a certain way, it's like I'm looking at my mom. It's a little unsettling at times, dredging up painful memories of her loss. Other times, I'm grateful I have someone who reminds me of her.

"All right. Talk to me," he prompts, taking me out of my thoughts.

He ducks down and pulls out a chessboard from one of the drawers behind his desk and sets it in front of us, then gestures for me to sit down. I stare at it, a reluctant smile creeping on my face as he stares at me expectantly. For Luke, playing chess is a ploy to make people at ease so they can open up.

I sit across from him and prop the cap on my knee. "Talk about what?"

He starts arranging the pieces on the board. "We both know you're here to talk about something that's bothering you, Solomon."

I blow out a breath and drag my fingers through my hair. "I'm not in the mood to play today."

"You need a haircut," he points out, pushing the board to the side.

"Yes, *Mom*," I shoot back playfully.

He chuckles, laughter lines fanning the corner of his eyes. "Smartass. I like seeing this side of you where you behave like a teenager instead of acting like a forty-year-old."

I roll my eyes and his grin widens.

We fall silent for a few seconds. My leg bounces, and I'm trying hard not to look nervous, but Luke's probing stare is my undoing. Although he might have a rough idea of what's got me tied in knots, he doesn't force it out of me. He's patient, always giving me all the time I need to speak my thoughts.

Eventually, I give in. "She was in there." I jerk a thumb over my shoulder in the direction of the door.

His head tilts slightly to the side as he continues to watch me. He doesn't need to ask who. He knows about Grace. "Did you talk to her?"

I shake my head. "I couldn't. I'm a mess whenever I'm around her. I don't know. It's just . . . frustrating. It's not like I want to have sex with her or anything."

His brows shoot up. "Sex, huh? So you've been thinking about it." There's no judgment in his voice, only curiosity.

God, he probably thinks I'm undecided about being a priest. I wonder if other guys who've chosen this path go through the same thing. It's messing with my head.

"I should be stronger than this. I *am* stronger than this." I rub my hand down my face and jump to my feet. "Look, can we pretend this conversation never happened?"

"Solomon." He pauses, leaning forward and aiming those all-knowing eyes at me. "It's not too late to postpone going to seminary. You can take some time to think about this. You'll be starting a journey that requires giving yourself wholeheartedly to serving God. A vocation that comes with a lot of challenges—"

"I'm aware, Luke. I'm an eighteen-year-old boy who has mastered control, remember?" I flash him a smile. He once told me he was quite surprised by how I'd managed to discipline myself from bowing to temptation and 'carnal pleasures' as he put it.

His lips twitch. "Okay. But you realize you've been a big influence on Seth. That kid is like a hawk. He notices everything. His faith in the Church was restored when you took him under your wing. He and the other kids at youth group look up to you like a big brother." His brows shoot up. "See where I'm going with this?"

I nod. "I know. My mind is made up. I'm okay, I promise. It was a moment of self-doubt, but I'm fine now," I'm quick to reassure him.

I don't want to take a break. The first time Seth told me why they moved here from Baltimore, I was outraged. I started to pay more attention after that. I did research and read articles online about priests accused of doing really awful things. I got even more furious and determined.

Why couldn't these priests be like my uncle, huh? Be the shepherd who guides people back to church. I knew I'd made the right decision then. This is my calling.

Doubt is such a fickle bastard.

Luke observes me thoughtfully for a long second, then nods, rising to walk around the desk. Resting his hand on my shoulder in a comforting gesture, he says, "Okay. If you need to talk later, I'll be here."

I nod and smile. "I know."

He's always there for me, never wavering, which makes me want to be more like him. Be there for others just as he is for me.

I head out the door. Grace is no longer where I left her when I fled the sanctuary in an attempt to clear my thoughts.

Seconds later, I exit St. Peter's Church and stride to my beat-up red Chevy that once belonged to my dad. I hop inside, and within minutes, I'm on my way back to work at Joe's Auto Body Shop.

# five

## Sol

I T'S BEEN OVER A WEEK SINCE THAT SPLIT SECOND OF DOUBT AFTER seeing Grace. I've actively avoided going to her mom's diner, hoping to repair my fragile resolve. Deb's Diner serves the best vanilla waffles, so I've been jonesing for them, but I've managed to be strong.

Until today.

Ivan insisted we grab lunch there during our work break, and after my many attempts to talk him out of the idea, telling him we could grab lunch elsewhere, I caved. My best friend can be very relentless. Plus, it's so freaking hot outside, my resolve shattered in the presence of scorching heat and Ivan's nagging.

And besides, what's the harm, right? If you don't look directly at the sun, chances of getting blinded by its rays are very slim. That's what I plan to do. Not look at Grace any more than I need to.

We've been helping with repairs at the Rosemary Inn. The summer storms can be quite brutal on Maine's coast, and the gazebo was torn apart by a storm two nights ago. Beverly, the co-owner of Deb's Diner, is getting married there on Saturday to her fiancé, Mark. So when my uncle approached a few of the guys from church, asking if we could help with the hasty repairs, we all agreed immediately.

"Let's grab a quick lunch and head back. Seth will be here soon. I don't want to keep him waiting," I tell Ivan when he stops walking for the tenth time since we left the gazebo. He pulls his phone out of his pocket to reply to a text from MJ.

He grunts. "You spoil that kid. No wonder he looks at you like you hang the moon, man." He finishes texting and shoves the phone back into his pocket. "Why don't you ask him to meet us there?"

"Because."

"Because why?" My best friend looks at me, one brow raised. "Let me guess. Grace."

I frown. "What about her?"

"You don't want your little protégé to see how much she affects you."

I start to shake my head, but Ivan cuts me off.

"He has you on a pedestal. He looks at you as if you're a saint."

I wince and shove my hands in my pockets, contemplating Ivan's observation.

Does he really? I mean, I love Seth like the little brother I never had. I see the way he looks at me with respect. It's something I take seriously because it means I earned it the hard way, given how broken he was when we first met.

But a saint? Ivan is prone to overdramatizing things sometimes. This is one of those times.

"Listen, liking a girl is not a weakness," Ivan says quietly, falling in step with me.

I roll my eyes. He's officially gone into Yoda mode.

"It doesn't mean you won't make a good priest, man. I support your choice one hundred percent."

I rub my neck with one hand. "So you're going to stop

pushing me to getting laid?"

"Of course not." He laughs. "Everyone needs to get laid at least once in their life. God gave you a dick for a reason other than to take a piss."

I chuckle, shaking my head as we step into the diner.

My eyes roam the space as if they can't help but search for *her*. They finally land on Grace sitting in a booth at the back. My whole body sighs at the sight of her, but whether from relief or losing a battle I've been fighting with my heart and mind, I can't tell.

Her shoulders are hunched forward as her fingers fly over the keyboard of her laptop. She pauses long enough to pull a pencil from behind her right ear, then scribbles something on a paper in front of her, brows furrowed in concentration as she starts typing again.

I don't realize my feet have stopped moving until Ivan slams into me from behind, propelling my body forward and wrenching me out of my trance.

"Dude. Stop it," he says, voice amused as he follows his words with a painful jab to my ribs.

I wince and face him, rubbing my smarting ribs to soothe the ache away. "What the—"

His eyes glint with mirth, lips turning up at the corners. "You're staring at Grace with that intense, creepy look again. Looks as if you're plotting to kidnap her. Wait, are you planning on *kidnapping* her? Because we could totally lock her up in the basement at my mom's shop." He lowers his head, eyes dancing as he whispers conspiratorially, "The next shipment doesn't arrive from Korea for two weeks, so Mom won't be down there for a while."

Dropping my hand from my side, I roll my eyes and tug the baseball cap lower onto my forehead, mumbling a quick, "Shut up," before walking away.

Three steps later, Ivan's large hand drops onto my shoulder, stopping me from going any farther. Slowly, he nudges me in Grace's direction. "Stop it with the longing and just talk to her, altar boy."

"Easy for you to say," I mutter as my feet make quick work of propelling my body in the opposite direction. I've never had an easy time approaching girls or talking to them. And Grace—

I shake my head, mildly terrified at the thought.

I slide into an empty booth, close enough that I can still look at her without being obvious but far enough that it's not too creepy. Ivan sits across from me and lets out a loud sigh.

After a beat, he shakes his head, scrubbing a hand down his face. Even frustrated, he still manages to look calm and collect-ed. "Aren't you exhausted from having a crush on this girl for ages? Why won't you talk to her?"

"It's been eight years, jackass," I retort. "And I'm not crush-ing on her. I'm just . . . intrigued."

"Sure looks like a crush to me, dude." He laughs, but from the look on his face, I can tell he knows more than he's letting on.

"What do you mean?"

He stays silent for a heartbeat as if he's debating if he should continue talking, then shrugs nonchalantly. "I've heard you pounding one out more than once. Moaning her name."

My face heats from both embarrassment and guilt. "Is noth-ing private anymore?"

He grabs one of the laminate menus, corners twisted from use, and smirks. "Our apartment has thin walls, Sol. It's a guy thing, you know," Ivan says. "God won't smack you upside the head for showing the guy down there some much-deserved attention."

I groan, rubbing my hands down my jaw. "Oh, God. Do you have to be so—"

"Right? Awesome? Wise?" He grins.

"Annoying," I finish, exasperated.

"It's normal, man. You don't need to feel guilty every time you think about boning Grace. She's fucking hot."

"Can we talk about something else?" I'm already getting hard just thinking about *boning* her.

He smirks. "You need to get her out of your system once and for all."

Do I? How is that even going to help me? Even if I could *get her out of my system*, Grace has never shown any interest in me.

And why am I even thinking about this?

I glance at Grace, her head bent as she types on the laptop in front of her. I follow the curve of her neck and swallow hard. Even back in high school, I found myself studying her.

I memorized everything about her, subconsciously cataloging each little detail. The way her eyes crinkled at the corners when she laughed, the way she smelled—like vanilla waffles. Sometimes she'd stare out the window, lips pursed with a far-away look in her eyes. Those were the times I wanted to talk to her the most, to find out where she went when she looked like that.

Then three years ago during our sophomore year in high school, everything changed. I remember it as though it was yesterday. She and that jackass Gavin Bachmann had been going out for a few weeks when everything fell apart after the pep rally. The only people who know what actually went down after the rally are Grace and Gavin. But rumors started to fly among the students that following Monday about her sleeping around with a bunch of guys in Gavin's crowd. In less than four hours, Grace Miller became an outcast. Gavin did nothing to defend her, and in fact, he actively avoided her. They broke up after that. She became withdrawn and quiet, as though she was trying to erase herself from the world around her.

I'd never wanted to hurt anyone as much as I wanted to hurt Gavin. I remember the surprise in his eyes when I strode toward him as he was about to get in his car, fists clenched, and socked him in the jaw.

I'm not a violent person. In fact, I abhor violence.

But something in me just snapped that day. Grace was hurting. The girl who had told me everything would be okay when I was ten with such wisdom and sincerity. I believed her. And Gavin stole the hope in her eyes.

"So what do you say?" Ivan asks, bringing me out of my thoughts. The teasing in his eyes is gone, replaced by a serious look. "It's not like talking to her will alter the path you've set to follow."

He's right.

I remove my baseball cap, smoothing my fingers through my disheveled hair before pushing my cap back onto my head.

"Jeez, you're like a dog with a bone. I'll go talk to her just to shut you up. Happy?"

"Tickled pink." He grins. "Remember what I said. Eye contact is key. And smile. Don't forget to smile. That frown of yours makes you look closed-off and shy."

I *am* closed-off and shy.

"Eye contact and smile. Gotcha," I mumble.

"All right. Break a leg. It's your time to shine, man." He sits back and stretches his arms, draping them over the edge of the booth.

I stand and take a deep breath before walking in her direction.

# six

## Sol

WITHIN SECONDS, I'M STANDING NEXT TO GRACE, watching her anxiously. I shove a hand inside my pocket, my fingers curling around the rosary and rubbing the smooth surface of the beads. If she senses I'm there, she doesn't bother to look up.

Shit.

Maybe this isn't such a great idea.

I glance over my shoulder and see Ivan leaning out of our booth.

His eyes widen, and he jerks his chin in Grace's direction and mouths, "Talk to her."

I clear my throat and—

"Do you plan to cast a shadow over me for a while or . . .?"

My heart stops beating for a second, then jump-starts painfully the next. With only her voice, she has managed to knock the wind out of my lungs. I open my mouth and close it, repeating the action a second time as I try to come up with words.

It's as if I've lost them all. Instead, I settle for a laugh followed by a croaky, "A shadow?"

"Can I help you with something?" She lifts her head, brows raised, but her mouth quickly forms an O when her gaze meets mine. She quickly recovers from the shock. "Oh, hey, Solomon. I'm starting to think you enjoy hovering a lot."

When I don't answer immediately, she sits up and squares her shoulders. Her mouth tightens in a scowl, but I know what she's doing. She's reinforcing the wall she's built around herself to keep people away, just as she's been doing since the incident in high school.

Honestly, this girl makes me nervous, and she's a distraction. One I can't afford to have right now. Or ever.

Yet, here I am, standing next to her anyway.

I had a plan. It was simple—graduate high school, attend the seminary, and become a priest.

Thinking about Grace always made me feel a bit guilty. During one of our talks, I'd told Luke about the situation.

His smile had been warm and endearing as he'd told me I needed to experience the world outside the rectory. He'd said I should spend my teenage years being a teenager. That I should figure out who Solomon Callan truly was before making any big decisions about my future. Know my options. Last winter, I moved into the apartment owned by the diocese two blocks away from the rectory. And after a long talk with Ivan's parents and Luke's reassurance he'd keep an eye on us, they agreed to let their son move in with me.

Grace and I live in the same town, so I can't avoid her forever. Once I'm ordained as a priest, I'll return to Portland. We'll most likely meet and interact—if she doesn't move away. I need to get used to talking to her without feeling as if my heart will burst through my chest and land at her feet. I need to get rid of this curiosity that has had me in its talons since the day we met.

"I saw you sitting here and thought I'd stop by and say hi."

Seriously? Did those words come out of my mouth?

So. Lame.

"Uh-huh," she murmurs and returns her focus to whatever she's doing. This is a dismissal if I ever saw one. Regardless, I forge on. I've no idea where all this courage is coming from, but all of a sudden, I find myself determined to crack her cool façade.

I take advantage of our proximity and drink her in. Her features have matured with age. Her cheekbones are more defined, her nose turned up at the tip. Her full lips turned upward at the corners as if she's holding back a secret smile, a contrast to the frown bunching her eyebrows. She bites her bottom lip between her teeth and huffs a frustrated breath.

Wondering what's made her so angry, I lean forward and catch a glimpse of a spreadsheet filled with numbers on the laptop screen.

Her head snaps back, her eyes narrowing with suspicion.

"Need help?" I ask even though math makes me want to rip my eyes out. Her brows dip even further.

She ducks her head, but not before I see her lips twitch. "Oh, puh-leeze. We both know math isn't your strong suit, Solomon."

Seeing that small smile she's trying to hide fuels me forward. With my gaze fixed on hers, I slide onto the seat opposite her, leaning forward to prop my elbows on the table.

"What do you think you're doing?" she asks, sounding panicked and no longer pretending to be detached.

At that moment, I see fear in her wide eyes before irritation takes over, but it's enough for me to realize that the need to ward off people with her attitude might actually be due to fear and anxiety. Apparently, she's more like me than I realized.

Suddenly, I don't feel as nervous around her as I was before.

# seven

*Sol*

HER LIPS FORM A THIN LINE, AND SHE EXHALES A FRUSTRATED breath. "Don't you have a gazebo to finish repairing?" She jerks her thumb over her shoulder in the direction of the square.

I press my lips together to stop from grinning. She probably doesn't realize that she just unknowingly let it slip that she knew my whereabouts even though she's trying really hard to send me running from the booth.

Has she been watching me?

I sit back and watch her as she squirms under my gaze.

"I don't have time for this." She pulls the laptop forward and starts to type, dismissing me for the second time.

"I'm really trying here, Grace." *Why the heck am I bothering anyway if she's just going to bite my head off?*

"Trying to do what, Sol?" One brow goes up in question, her eyes still on the screen.

I rub the nape of my neck with a hand. "Look, can we start over?"

Her fingers freeze in the air on top of the keyboard, and she looks at me. "You don't want to do this." All of a sudden her eyes narrow with suspicion. "Did someone put you up to this?"

Good God. Why does she have to make it so hard for someone to talk to her? I can see why people choose to keep a safe distance. "Wow, Grace. Your reputation precedes you," I say before
I can stop myself.

Her head jerks up, her eyes wide in panic. The look vanishes
as soon as it appeared.

Her nostrils flare, and she bites out, "You'll have to be more
specific than that."

I blink at her, confused.

"So which one is it?" After a beat, she adds, "My reputation.
The one that says I'm a bitch or the one that says I'm easy?"

*Wait, what just happened?*

Understanding dawns on me and dread quickly follows
behind. I want to kick my ass all the way out of Deb's Diner.
"Grace—"

"So you're here to see if you can get lucky, aren't you? Jesus.
I thought that shit would stay in high school after graduation."
She slumps back in her seat and drops her gaze to her laptop.
"Leave."

I study her for a few seconds. "Shit, Grace. That's not what
I meant."

"*Leave*," she bites out, but I can hear the pain she's trying so
hard to hide through the anger.

I scoot out of the booth and stand in the aisle, but her gaze
remains on the table in front of her.

"I'm sorry. I didn't mean to upset you." I glance around
the restaurant before taking a step in her direction and stop.
"You're terrified of anyone getting close to you. I get it. But
don't slam doors in the face of someone who's just trying to
be your friend. Not everyone is like those guys back in high
school." I lean my head closer. Still, her head stays down. "I
know you try so hard to be forgotten, Grace, but I see you. And

now I know you see me, too."

With that, I pull back and spin around without waiting for her response. But before I can get far, she calls my name. I stop and face her once more. Her gaze meets mine.

"Fuck you, Solomon Callan."

I flinch at her words. "All I want is to be your friend," I say again.

She smiles, but it doesn't reach her eyes. "Haven't you heard? Talking to me or being seen with me is enough to tarnish the reputation of a good boy like you."

Wow, this conversation went south real quick. From the looks of it, there's no way of repairing the damage I've caused with my careless words.

I walk back to our booth where Ivan is still seated, feeling like a monumental asshole.

"Looks like you made quite an impression," he muses as soon as I settle across from him.

"You think?" I retort.

It rubs me the wrong way that she thinks so low of me. Clearly, she needs some sort of enlightenment. I might rub one out every now and then while thinking about that elegant curve of her neck—God, forgive me—but getting in her pants is *not* what I had in mind when I approached her.

I grab the menu and pretend to peruse it. "Let's order; I'm starving. If I have to wait one more second, I might end up eating my own foot."

"She's probably just having a bad day," Ivan mutters, obviously trying to excuse her behavior.

I shrug. "Maybe."

"Or she's PMSing," he muses thoughtfully. "MJ turns into a foul-mouthed beast when she's going through that." He pauses. "Speak of the devil . . ." He trails off as the sound of a door squeaking closed joins the diner's hubbub.

I look up and see MJ, Ivan's girlfriend, scoot in next to him on the seat and plant a kiss on his mouth. She and Ivan have known each other since childhood, before her parents packed up and left Portland for New York. They only started dating after graduation a few weeks ago when she came back to Portland to visit her grandmother.

She leans back and focuses her green eyes on me, smiling. "Did you finally talk to her?"

"Hello to you, too, Mary-Jane," I say, shooting Ivan a lethal glare. I should have known that nothing is sacred when it comes to these two. Of course he'd tell his girlfriend everything.

She tucks her brown locks behind her ear, unmoved by my sarcastic tone, and grins at me while pulling out a yellow paper from her front shirt pocket. She lays it flat on the table and presses her palm on it to remove the wrinkles, then slides it in my direction.

"Sublime Chaos will be playing at Mike's Bar as part of the Fourth of July entertainment. You should totally ask her to go with you before someone else does."

Ivan and I share a look. We both know the chances of someone asking her are quite slim. MJ spent most of her high school years in New York and only came back here to visit her grandmother during the holidays. She has no idea about the rumors that followed Grace through high school.

All of a sudden, I *want* to ask Grace to go with me—strictly as friends—if only to prove to her that not everyone from high school is an asshole.

My gaze flickers to the booth at the back, only to find Grace watching me. Before I can read her expression, she ducks her head and starts fumbling with the papers scattered across her table.

"So plan B," Ivan says, and I focus on him again.

I raise my eyebrows. "There's a plan B?"

"If you're planning to go to war, you always need a plan B." I start to protest, but he waves his hand, dismissing my words. "Anyway, as I was saying . . ."

I tune him out as my mind wanders back to Grace. That girl needs a friend. I saw her, saw the fear written all over her face that I've never noticed before today. There was bitterness and loneliness there, too. For just a second, she reminded me a little of Seth when he first joined the youth group. I hate that life has changed her from that ten-year-old girl with an optimistic smile and encouraging words.

She's like a rose whose petals have been trampled on so many times that the only form of protection she found was to build a fort of thorns around herself. Keep everyone at arm's length.

I'll find a way to get through those thorns.

I'll show her I can be the friend she needs, even if she doesn't realize it.

# eight

*Grace*

STUNNED INTO SILENCE, I WATCH SOL'S LONG LEGS COVER THE distance back to the booth where Ivan is sitting. In mere minutes, he literally tipped my world upside down with just a few words and managed to take my mind off my current predicament of tackling the Brown issue with my mom.

I sigh, reluctantly admiring the way his gray T-shirt stretches across his broad shoulders, his narrow waist, and the way those shorts hug his hips.

I shiver involuntarily, my eyes squeezing shut in an attempt to squash the sight of him still haunting my vision.

Wrong move.

The mental image of his eyes is all I can see behind my closed lids; the way he looked at me—still a bit shy, but there was also playfulness in them and a hint of . . . something wild. Something that wanted to be let loose.

To explore.

In all the years I've known him, I've never seen him look at me like that.

He probably doesn't realize what's simmering inside, but I can see it clearly because I recognize those same things inside myself. Every time I look in the mirror, my reflection stares back at me, and I see a yearning for freedom in it, the need to run wild.

My eyes open, and I take a fortifying breath before focusing on Sol. Regret slams into me.

Why am I so paranoid? Sol was just trying to be friendly, and I treated him as though he's the enemy.

*This is what happens when you are so busy trying to keep everyone at arm's length.*

I learned early on that boys hurt you and break you. I love living in my own world and ignoring everyone. Ignoring the twinge of loneliness I sometimes get when I see couples holding hands and sharing tender smiles and sweet kisses.

Admittedly, ever since the pep rally at Winston High three years ago that brought my reputation crumbling down around me, I kept my head down. I chose to ignore everyone at school and bide my time. I knew they talked behind my back and actively avoided me like I was contagious. The people I thought were my friends dropped me like I was garbage. Something nasty they couldn't stand to be near. So I armed myself with confidence and disinterest and stopped giving a shit about anyone but myself. It was like surviving a jungle filled with snakes and creepy-crawlies.

I bite my cheek to smother a reluctant grin when he looks over his broad shoulder at me. And when he slides back into the seat across from Ivan, a gust of air rushes out of my mouth, the weight of it knocking me back in my seat.

*Wow.*

I force my gaze back to my laptop.

I can't remember the last time anyone was as determined to talk to me as he seemed to be. I want to ignore the fluttering inside my belly and brush him off, but his words cut through me like a well wielded sword. I want to go back into my little bubble where I feel secure from my own insecurities, but I'm not sure it's even possible now.

Something fills my chest. Something warm and foreign. I bite my bottom lip when a goofy smile threatens to split my mouth into two.

On a scale of one to ten, Sol is definitely a fifteen—a tall, lean-muscled giant of a boy-man with a mop of longish, dark hair he keeps hidden under a baseball cap. A strong, square, scruffy jaw, broad shoulders, trim waist, and narrow hips giving way to long legs. When he put his elbows on the table, I almost licked my lips at the sight of all the veins running up his arms and hands.

My breath catches in my throat as I realize I've memorized so much of Sol without even trying or meaning to. And now I'd lumped him with the rest of the assholes in school.

Part of me is desperate to believe he wants to be my friend. I want to believe he can be trusted. The way he watched me with rapt attention sitting across from me, those blue eyes made me feel like I was free-falling into the wide-open sky. Even though he seemed nervous, it didn't stop him from approaching me and talking to me.

It'd taken him *eight* freaking years to gather the courage to finally *talk* to me.

Oh my God. I'm such a bitch.

My thoughts are interrupted when a familiar girl with dark brown hair enters the diner and glances around. She seems to find what she's looking for, and a dazzling grin takes over her face as she heads to the booth Ivan and Sol are occupying. Even from here, I see her cheeks flush across her tanned face.

Mary-Jane Walker, known around town as MJ, is stunning. She's slightly taller than me. I'm shorter with a body full of curves. She walks with purpose and confidence as if she's already figured out her whole life. I can see why Ivan can't take his eyes off her. He is just as confident as she is. I like him. He and Sol were the only people in Winston High who were always kind and smiled at me, even when my only response was a sour look of disbelief.

"Okay, you're officially freaking me out."

Those words snap me back to the present. I jerk upright in my seat and look up at my mom leaning over the table with both hands planted flat on its surface.

I clutch the silver pendant attached to my necklace nervously and stare at my laptop's screen to avoid her gaze. "I'm almost done working on—"

"Grace, sweetheart."

I stop talking and look up at her.

"Smiling looks good on you."

In her voice, I hear wonder and hope. In her wavering gaze, I see shadows swirling in the brown depths. There are bags under her eyes, evidence that she hasn't slept in days.

Her fingers twitch as they sweep back a dreadlock from her forehead. She sits down across from me, momentarily swaying sideways before righting herself and smiling reassuringly. Even from this distance, I can smell it. The faint smell of alcohol slams into me.

My stomach twists as realization hits me. She's been drinking even though she's trying to hide it by smiling at me. Then the *reason* she's drunk hits me, sending panic through my body. I've been so busy freaking out about my own issues I completely forgot how sad she gets around this time of the year.

Alcohol seems to numb the pain. On most days, my mom is one of the strongest people I know, but not today. And not for the next few days.

I hate my father for turning her into a mess after he left

when she was pregnant with me. Hate the cloud of hopelessness that hangs over her and the sudden fear that shadows her eyes. She must have loved him so much that the memory of him cripples her emotionally. It's actually terrifying knowing I probably have the same capacity to love someone that much and that it could destroy me in the process. Which is why I don't blame her or beg her to stop. I believe we all experience heartache in different ways. Some have it worse than others, and if alcohol dulls the pain a few days every year, I won't stop her.

"Are you okay, Mom?"

Instead of answering me, she lays her hand on the table between us with the palm facing up. Instinctively, I place mine atop hers. She grasps it firmly, then fixes her gaze on mine. I watch the fear in them recede. Does she think I'll abandon her too?

"You know you're stuck with me, right?" I tell her. "Nothing will ever separate us. Never gonna leave the way my—"

She nods quickly. "I know, sweetheart." She falls silent, her eyes losing focus for a few seconds. Then she shudders and blinks several times, her grip on my hand becoming desperate. "I want to tell you so much. So much, Grace. . ."

My heartbeat accelerates in my chest. The sudden change in her scares me, and I'm not sure I want her to tell me whatever it is that has her looking so destroyed.

She takes a deep breath, and the distressed look vanishes as quickly as it had appeared.

"You're a godsend," she says, her words speaking her truth. "You know that, right?"

She gave up everything for me. When I look up into her eyes, the blinding love shining in their depths comforts me.

"I know," I whisper, still shaken from the change in her seconds ago.

"I wouldn't trade you for anything, Gracie."

That much is true. I'm alive and breathing because she traded her dreams to keep me. Yet I'm about to burst her bubble about the Brown issue.

"I want you to be happy," she says, and I see and hear the truth in her words.

"I *am* happy," I reply, but the words sound forced in my ears.

She studies me for a few moments in silence, then finally sighs. She pats my hand and stands up, swaying on her feet. And even though she's drunk out of her mind, her words are steady as she says, "Go talk to Sol."

My eyes widen in surprise. "But he's a—"

"Boy. He's a boy, I know." She swallows hard, washing away the words burning her tongue. "Gavin hurt you, but that doesn't mean all boys will treat you the same."

I want to tell her the same thing. I want to tell her just because my coward of a father walked out on us doesn't mean all men are bad. But I suspect that won't go over very well. Sometimes I get the feeling there's more to the story than my father simply leaving. Even my grandparents haven't been able to shed light on what happened eighteen years ago.

Mom avoids men like the plague—except Father Foster and Mark, Beverly's fiancé—which is why I'm surprised she's pushing me to talk to Sol. I wish she had someone who loved and cherished her like she deserves.

She wets her lips and whispers, "I haven't seen you smile in a long time. Until now. He made you smile." She pauses, eyes turning misty. "It pains me to see you hurting."

*It breaks my heart to see you hurting, too, Mom.* I swallow those words and just nod.

From over Mom's shoulder, I see Beverly—Mom's best friend and the other half of Deb's Diner—heading for us. She eyes me with sympathy, understanding clear in her eyes before turning to my mom. She angles her body, partially shielding us from the growing lunch crowd, and I'm so grateful. Sol keeps sneaking looks in my direction. I'm not sure how long I can keep my shit together as I watch my mom.

Beverly is a year older than my mom. They've known each other since Mom arrived in town eighteen years ago, pregnant and almost penniless. Beverly took her in and gave her a place to stay in her family's home until Mom could stand on her own two feet. I have a feeling she knows more than I do about my mom and her life in New York.

Beverly slides one arm over my mom's shoulder. "Why don't we let Grace finish the bookkeeping, Debs?"

Mom's gaze darts to my laptop, then back to my face, eyes swimming with tears. I breathe through my nose slowly, trying to keep my own tears at bay. I hate seeing her like this, but I just have to remind myself she needs this and that in a few days, it will be over.

"I have a little surprise for you later," I tell her, eager to tell her anything to cheer her up. "After we close the diner."

Immediately, her eyes light up, and she gives me a wobbly, teary smile. "I love surprises."

"Good." I exhale, relieved, and grin at her. "Love you, Mom."

"Love you, sweetheart."

Beverly raises a brow at me in question, and I subtly nod to let her know I'll tell her about my plan as soon as Mom's out of earshot. My mom suddenly grips Beverly's arm, halting their progress, and leans forward to whisper something in her ear. Her friend nods vigorously and tries to pull her past the counter to the back office.

Mom wipes her cheeks with her free hand. This time, the words are much louder when she says, "I don't think I can tell—I . . . I can't lose her, Bev."

"You won't," Beverly reassures her, then murmurs something as she leads my mom the rest of the way.

The second they walk away, I let my shoulders drop and bury my face in my hands.

What the hell is she talking about? And why would she think she's going to lose me, even after I reassured her?

*Fuck you, Dad. Fuck you very much for turning Mom into this version of herself.*

Does he ever think about me? Is he married? Does he have a family, maybe a daughter? Could I be replaced so easily?

My hands curl into fists against my eyes, and I breathe in deeply.

*Just a few more days, Grace, and she'll be back to normal.*

I drop my hands from my face, but the hairs on the back of my neck are tingling like crazy. My gaze, like a compass pointing to a destination, zeroes in on Sol. He's watching me with a troubled look on his face. He's always *watching* me, but I've never given it a second thought. I used to brush it off back in high school, never holding his gaze for too long. But after our little chat today, his glances feel more tangible, and they seem to hold more meaning.

I summon the energy to put on a blank face, then look down at the laptop, ignoring the heat building in my cheeks. I'm about to grab my earbuds when I catch movement in my peripheral vision. I look up and see MJ marching in my direction.

"Hey," she greets with a wide grin. She stops at my booth. "I'm Mary-Jane, but you can call me MJ."

*I know who you are.* That's what I want to say, but I'm still trying to process the fact that she's here, talking to *me*.

"Grace, right?" She reaches down and takes my hand,

shaking it in greeting.

"Um . . . yes." I return her handshake, then take my hand back. "Sorry. I'm just a little shocked."

"May I?" She points at the seat across from me, and I nod, then watch her as she scoots in. "I just thought I'd come by and introduce myself. Maybe we could hang out sometime."

Wait, what's going on?

My heart is beating fast now. "Yeah . . . sure. I'd love that."

"Great!" She digs out a flyer from her pocket, leans forward, and grabs the pen I was using, then scribbles something on the paper. She slides it forward and taps her finger on it. "Sublime Chaos will be playing downtown on the Fourth of July. And that's my number in case you want to join us or just, you know, hang out or whatever. Just think about it, okay?"

I nod, watching her face for any signs of . . . I don't know. Insincerity, maybe? But I'm met with genuine interest and kindness.

I don't know what's happening. First Sol came over to talk to me, then MJ.

Feeling curious, I glance at the booth where the two boys are sitting. Ivan smiles and waves at me as if we're long-lost friends. I want to look behind me just to make sure he's not waving at someone else, but I don't. Instead, I give him a small, hesitant wave and face MJ.

"Thank you. This is very sweet of you."

She stands up and surprises me again when she gives me a hug. "We're practically friends now. Call me, okay?"

I nod again and then watch as she heads back to where the two boys are sitting. Then it hits me. She didn't ask me for my number in return. I'm not sure what to think of that. And I'm feeling overly emotional at the moment. Given the fact that I'm seriously lacking in the friendship department, I'm suspicious and hopeful at the same time. But mostly *hopeful* and it's terrifying.

Before I can overanalyze everything, I rip a piece of paper from my notebook, then quickly scribble today's date. I write MJ's and Sol's names under it, then add "Dare to hope. Here's to new friendships."

I fold it and slip it inside my shorts pocket to put in my Beautiful Memories Jar. Then I plug the earbuds into my ears. Scrolling through my Play It Loud playlist mindlessly, I select a random song, and then "Sweet Child O' Mine" by Guns N' Roses streams through my ears, and I get lost in my work.

# nine

## Sol

BY THE TIME WE STOP WORKING ON THE GAZEBO, IT'S ALMOST nine o'clock at night. It's fully repaired and looks just as good as it did before the storm ripped it apart two days ago. My uncle has been a bit fussy about getting it ready as soon as possible because he'll be officiating Beverly's wedding on Saturday. The celebrations are to take place under it, so I took two days off my summer job at Joe's Auto Body Shop to help.

After the catastrophe, Beverly had been considering changing the venue, stressed we wouldn't be done in time for the wedding. So we had to hustle, our small group of guys coming together to tackle the mess. Luke was adamant that we inform Beverly the second the gazebo was rebuilt and ready so that the anxious bride could cross one stressful thing off her list.

So when we're done, I try calling Beverly on the phone, but it just keeps ringing. Doesn't she have voicemail?

"Why don't you head to the diner to check if she's there?" Ivan asks.

"Uh. . ." That's all I've got because Grace.

Even though I plan to ease her into friendship, I wasn't counting on seeing her again today. Or tomorrow. Or the day after. My nerves are still raw from earlier today. Her words still haunt me and make me sick to my stomach. I know she didn't mean what she said, given the contrite look on her face after those words left her mouth, but still.

Ivan looks up from his cell phone, his eyebrows shooting up. "What? I can't go. MJ and I have a thing."

"What thing?"

"Not suitable for priestly ears." He smirks, and Seth barks out a laugh.

I glare at them while rubbing the back of my neck with my hand. Seth's mom is picking him up any second now, so he's out of the picture.

I bite my cheek to stop myself from thinking or saying something that will have me asking God for forgiveness.

"Fine. Go do your thing." I head to the parking lot with Seth in tow.

"No hug? Come on, darlin'," Ivan says with a pouty voice.

I chuckle and shake my head, my irritation fading away fast. I can't even hold a grudge against my best friend. That's Ivan for you.

I shove my hands in my shorts pockets and glance at Seth. He's been a little more quiet than usual since arriving at the gazebo this afternoon, but I didn't have a chance to ask him what's wrong. He's come a long way from the broken boy he was when he arrived in Portland five years ago.

He kicks the gravel with his big-sneakered toe, his hands inside his pockets.

"You okay there, kid?" I ask, reaching over and ruffling his straight blond hair.

He jerks his head and scowls up at me. "You realize you're only two years older than me, right?"

"Yeah. Still older than you, *kid*." I grab him in a headlock. He wiggles and tries to slip away.

"Ugh. You stink, asshole."

I laugh, releasing him after letting him struggle for a few more seconds. He tries to swipe my foot with his, but I side-step, causing him to stumble forward. He laughs and mutters something about one day kicking my ass. At least he doesn't look sad anymore.

"So what's up?"

He scratches his head and looks away as we head to the parking lot. "Mom wants us to drive to Baltimore for my brother's memorial. I don't want . . . I can't go back there."

I study his hunched shoulders and the frown on his face. "Have you told her how you feel?"

He nods, then sighs. "My grandparents still live in Baltimore. I haven't seen them in a while. They are too old to travel, so they couldn't fly here."

His shoulders fall, and he lifts a hand to wipe his cheeks. "What do I do? I don't want to tell her I can't go back there . . ."

This sucks. I don't even know what to say to make things better. I clear my throat and give his shoulder a comforting squeeze with my hand, then drop it back to my side

"Sometimes we have to do things that make us uncomfortable and we're forced to face them head-on. It's okay not to want to go back there, Seth, but you know what you can do? Remember why you loved Baltimore before all the bad things happened. Remember the good things."

He looks away, staring off in the distance. "That could work, I guess."

The sound of a car horn interrupts us, and we both look up. Seth's mom, Beth, waves at us with a smile, then signals her son over. Seth sighs again, and he starts moving toward the car. He stops abruptly and swivels to face me.

"You're kinda awesome." He smiles, his eyes shining bright.

Ivan's words come flooding back. It's very humbling and terrifying at the same time to have someone put so much respect and trust in you, to be honest. I want to be worthy of these gifts he's giving me so freely. I want to do what I promised him five years ago and make people believe in the Catholic Church again.

"You're not so bad yourself." I give him a two-finger salute as he turns and jogs to the car.

"Hey, Beth." I greet his mom with a wave.

She smiles back. "Thanks for letting him hang out with you and the other guys."

"We had fun, right, kid?"

Seth scowls. I smirk, and Beth laughs. She knows how much her son hates being called kid.

"Have a great evening, Sol."

I watch his mom pull away, then head toward Deb's Diner across the street, my head brimming with thoughts of Seth, his brother, and his mom.

I'm a few feet away from the diner when my heartbeat accelerates at the thought of seeing Grace. I don't know what it is about her that hijacks my brain and shoves any other thoughts in the background. I need to rein it in. Maybe I can see Grace and talk to her without making a fool of myself.

*Talk to Beverly, give her the news, and head out, Callan.*

Easier said than done.

The closer I get to the diner, the shakier my legs grow. I know I'm being ridiculous about the whole thing, but I can't seem to help how my stupid body reacts to Grace.

*Please, God. My heart and body are yours to use as an instrument. Nothing has changed since I chose this path. I knew what I was getting into when I made this decision. Help me uphold the promise I made to you and to myself. And to Seth. Give me the power to resist.*

I repeat these words three more times until I feel a sense of peacefulness rest over me.

As I approach the door, I frown, remembering the look that had crossed Grace's features when her mom had approached her. I've been feeling like something is wrong ever since. And the way Beverly took charge of the situation, despite her anxiousness concerning the wedding, tipped me off some more. I don't think I'll ever be able to forget the sheer sadness on Grace's face as she watched Beverly steering her mother away in a gentle embrace.

What was that all about? Grace's mom is one of the strongest women I've ever met. She'd looked so unlike herself, hunched over, stumbling. Almost as though she was . . . drunk?

I take off my cap and run my fingers through my sweat-soaked hair, then put it back on, tugging it down my forehead. My hands are growing sweaty, and it's not from the work I've done all day.

*Calm down.* I need to calm down.

I climb the three steps leading to the door, grip the handle, and pull. Nothing happens. I glance up and notice the blinds are down and a piece of paper is taped to the glass door.

*Closed for business. We will be back as usual tomorrow morning.*

I sigh, but whether from relief or disappointment, I don't know. I'm totally not in the right headspace today.

I turn to leave, pulling my phone out of my pocket to try Beverly's number again. She picks up on the third ring.

"Please tell me the gazebo is ready," she prompts, bypassing greetings.

"It's ready." I smile when she squeals in excitement.

"Oh, thank goodness. Have you boys already left? You

should come over to the diner, free food to celebrate as my thank you."

"Everyone already left."

I glance at the closed door and scratch my head, suddenly feeling even more exhausted. I need to go home, take a shower, and get some sleep, but the thought of being in the same space as Ivan and MJ as they paw at each other isn't very appealing.

Laughter sounds in the background. I hear Debra's voice, but the words are barely decipherable. Then I hear Grace speak up. And just like that, my body fires back to life. "I'm actually standing outside—" *What the heck, Callan?*

The door flies open, and within seconds, Beverly's dragging me inside the diner, her phone still pressed to her ear. She flings her arms around me and hugs me tight.

"Mark, we're getting married!" she yells as she tosses her phone on top of the closest table, then turns around to face her fiancé, who's walking in from behind the counter, grinning.

He claps my shoulder and mutters, "Thanks, kid," but I'm too busy scanning the room for Grace.

I swallow hard when I see her standing behind the counter crammed with a variety of alcohol and snacks, enough to feed a small army. She's staring back at me with a blank look on her face. Her hair is pulled on top of her head in a ponytail, highlighting her cheekbones and neck. We gaze at each other for a few seconds longer, and just when I think I can't take it anymore, Debra appears from the back room.

Her eyes light up as soon as she sees me. "Sol, hi!" She splits a glance between her daughter and me and says, "Grace invited you too?"

I have no clue what she's talking about, so I shove my phone inside my shorts pocket and look at Debra.

"No, I—"

"I did!" Beverly yells as she disappears through the door Debra just walked out of. "Grace. Get the poor boy a drink, will you?"

Within seconds, the guitar riff of "Satisfaction" by The Rolling Stones throbs through the diner's speakers, the lights turning considerably dimmer. That's when I notice a small disco ball attached to the ceiling spinning in eternal circles as it casts shiny dots all over the room.

Beverly returns and joins her fiancé. The three adults start their celebration, chatting and dancing together. I stand there awkwardly, watching them laugh and throw their heads back and forth. Grace's mom looks much better than she did earlier today.

Mentally, my fingers caress the guitar strings, and my foot taps to the beat. The Rolling Stones are the shit.

"You play guitar?" Grace's voice is so low, so soft, I would have missed the question if my senses weren't so attuned to her every move.

I give her a sidelong glance, and I can't help it as my eyes take in her white Chucks and the way her blue shorts frame her thighs to perfection. When my gaze reaches her off-the-shoulder polka-dot top, it stays a little too long on the soft swell of her breasts. When I catch myself, I quickly jerk my gaze away, guilty and appalled by my inability to keep my eyes in check.

I clear my throat and ask huskily, "What gave me away?"

Unaware of my wayward thoughts, she looks at my hands, and sure enough, my fingers are strumming an imaginary guitar. There's a faint smile on her lips as she says, "You look like you're dying to play the song."

"Oh, I didn't realize I was doing it," I say, curling my hand into a loose fist. "I love this song."

We fall into this weird silence as we both scramble for

something to say.

Eventually, she breaks it. "So I was a bitch to you earlier today."

I raise a brow at her. "Is that your way of apologizing?"

"Sort of." She looks down at the floor, then at the three adults dancing a few feet away, avoiding my eyes as usual. "Yes."

"You could at least look at me, Grace. It's only fair when apologizing for trying to run me off," I tease.

She rolls her eyes at that and looks up at me with a smile. I smile back, pretending her eyes aren't shredding me to pieces from the inside.

"Apology accepted. I shouldn't have pushed you the way I did. I'm so sorry."

Her eyes widen as though she's surprised before she nods and smiles. "Apology accepted."

The song ends and another one picks up with a faster beat, worthy of a good hip shake. I'm definitely out of the loop with this song. Her mom waves us over, but I shake my head.

"She'll eventually come for you," Grace says with a laugh. "She can be very persistent."

The thought alone terrifies me because I don't have any moves to brag about. I've been to a few parties with Ivan over the years, but I always end up standing next to a wall somewhere, far enough away that it's clear to everyone I have no intentions of dancing.

"So, want a beer? Vodka?"

My eyebrows hit my hairline, but the mischievous twinkle in her eyes says she's trying to shock me. Grace walks to the counter, and I force my eyes to stay firmly on the ceiling to keep from staring at her ass, my fists tightly closed with the effort.

She returns and hands me a can of Coke. In her other hand, she's holding a white mug, and I catch a waft of alcohol as she brushes past me to sit in a booth to our right.

"I guess that's not Coke."

"Nope." She pops the 'p' and drinks deeply from her mug.

"Does your mom know?"

"Well, hello there, Mr. Good Boy." She swallows another sip, shrugging as her gaze drops to the dark liquid in her cup. "She's otherwise preoccupied."

Staring at her closely, I see moisture gather in the corners of her eyes. She wipes it away abruptly with the back of her hand, then gulps down more of whatever she's drinking.

I was right. Something's going on. And I'd be lying if I said the look on her face, pain and sadness mixing in her big eyes, didn't feel like a kick to my stomach.

*What's upsetting you so much, Grace?*

# ten

## Sol

"HEY, IS EVERYTHING OKAY?" I ASK HER IN A LOW VOICE, hands twitching to reach out and touch hers to soothe her pain. I doubt she'd appreciate my touch, even if it was meant to comfort her.

"It's going to rain tonight. I can feel it."

I'm so confused at the abrupt shift of conversation that it has me wondering if I've imagined her words altogether. Is she drunk already?

"What?" I squint at her, trying to gauge where she's going with this.

"I love it when it rains in the summertime. There's something so magical about it." She tips the mug against her lips once more, throat bobbing as she empties it into her mouth, then sets it on the table. "Have you ever kissed someone in the rain? Like in the movies?"

Holy queen of randomness—

She jumps to her feet, all thoughts of kisses and rain forgotten, and grabs my hand. "Come on, Sol. Let's dance."

Still reeling from the unexpected turn of conversation, I need a few seconds to catch my breath. Plus, my head is still stuck on the 'Have you ever kissed someone in the rain?' part of her question because now I can't stop imagining her full lips on mine and wondering how they'd feel.

She seems to sense my confusion. She stops tugging my hand, seeing as she can't move my big body with her tiny hands. She curves a finger in the hoop of her earring instead. "What? Is the offer of friendship no longer on the table?"

I have a feeling if I open my mouth, I might end up saying something highly inappropriate, so I just nod, hoping she understands the offer is still on the table.

She stretches her hand out to me again, fingers wiggling impatiently. "Let's dance, then. I'm offering you an olive branch. You better take it because it might not happen again anytime soon."

Thoughts of our lips fused together finally clear out from my mind at her words. "You don't know what you're asking for, Grace. These babies"—I point at my feet—"might look nice, and sure enough, they walk all right, but they're weapons of mass destruction when it comes to dancing."

What I don't say is that after a day in the sun working on the gazebo, I'm also pretty sure the smell coming off me will make her eyes water. I cringe at the thought. I'd rather she not be forced to deal with the scent of my sweat so early on in our newly formed friendship. If ever.

She snorts so loudly, a rather unladylike sound, and the fact she doesn't even look concerned about it is such a huge turn-on. "Show me what you got, Mr. Good Boy."

I sigh and stand, setting the unopened can of Coke on the table. "I think I should leave—"

"Just one dance," she rushes out. "I'll try not to corrupt you too much, I promise." She looks up at me innocently, but her lips twitch, fighting a smile.

I roll my eyes and smile. I study her for a heartbeat, knowing full well I should really book it out of here. Like right this second. But the thought of dancing with her is like a siren song, and everything else fades as the loud thumping in my ears grows louder. My only motivation right now is to keep that mischievous look on her face. And if that means showing her just how bad of a dancer I am, then so be it.

I'd been so focused on her I didn't notice the songs had shifted from fast to slow while we'd been talking. But now here I am, standing in front of Grace and wondering what to do with my hands. And legs. And hips. And eyes because they might try to stray below her neckline and get a good look at her—

I swallow hard and clear my throat.

She takes my hands and places them on her waist, then puts her hands around my shoulders, hugging my neck as best as she can. We're a little awkward, but she feels amazing against me as though my hands were built to rest on her like this.

I shouldn't be feeling happy about this. I should step away. Instead, I press closer, her soft body curving into my hard one.

She looks up at me, and even though she has this dazed look telling me she's not quite sober, I can't help being sucked into those rich maple-syrupy depths.

I'm so *fucked*.

I'm about to mutter a quick, *"I can't do this, Grace,"* under my breath, but the second she shifts closer and her head hits my chest, she relaxes in my arms, and the words fly out of my head.

Wow. She's so short. I knew she was, but this position makes our height difference that much more obvious.

Especially when her stomach is literally brushing against my crotch.

I groan inwardly, wondering if she can feel how hard I am, or if she's ignoring it to spare me the embarrassment. If I don't get my body under control and stop the lustful thoughts, she'll be herding me out of the diner door.

The second she drops her gaze to my chest, I exhale, relieved. I look around us and find Debra watching, and I can't tell whether she's curious or happy.

"Is your mom okay?" I ask Grace.

She stiffens but stays in my arms.

"She's just having a bad week. Bev and I thought this little party would cheer her up."

I'm dying to ask her what's going on, but I have a feeling she would find it intrusive. So I say, "I think it's working. She looks much better than she did this morning."

Grace doesn't say anything. I focus on swaying my body without moving my feet until the song ends. I drop my hands and hastily stumble away from her, tugging my T-shirt down. My whole face feels like it's on fire. Being this close to her affects me more than I expected.

It hits me then.

I'm not sure I can be friends with Grace without wanting to touch her, without wanting *more*. I'm sweating from just holding myself back.

"Are you leaving?" she asks, surprised when I take a step toward the door.

"Uh . . . yeah. I'd better go. Ivan and MJ are waiting for me back at the apartment." My voice sounds shaky, and I clear my throat, darting a gaze over her shoulder at Debra, Beverly, and Mark, who are now seated in a booth. Their heads are down, and they seem focused on the large piece of paper—a seating plan for Beverly's wedding. "Thanks for the dance. Tell Bev, Mark, and your mom thanks, as well."

Abruptly, I turn around and slip out the door like a coward and jog to my car parked two blocks away. Before I even unlock the door to my truck, fat drops of rain begin to pelt the ground around me, and one hits my cheek as I look up at the darkening sky. I hop inside my car and shut the door, then lay my head on the headrest, mouth opening with a sigh.

I need to keep my distance from Grace for both our sakes. If I don't, I'm worried I'll act on my fantasies, and that would ruin everything.

Ivan is going to shit his pants when I tell him what happened. I can already see him laughing and saying, *"I told you so."*

I jam the key into the ignition and push my foot on the gas. The rain is coming down hard now, making the wipers sway like crazy. Grace's words flash inside my head.

*It's going to rain tonight. I can feel it.*

*Have you ever kissed someone in the rain?*

And I'm back to imagining how it'd feel to have her lips moving against mine. My tongue caressing hers.

I groan and shove those thoughts in the back of my head, then force myself to focus on the drive home.

✠

On Friday, which is my normal day off from work, I make it a point to avoid Deb's Diner because I'm feeling restless. I feel like I'm coming out of my own skin.

I went for a run as soon as I woke up, but it didn't help. I needed something to distract me, which is why I'm waiting for Ivan's shift to be over. As soon as he walks out of the bed and breakfast where he works as a receptionist, I drag him to Scarborough with me to ride the go-karts. The fact that he doesn't press me for information even though he senses something is wrong makes me appreciate him more. But I'm sure it's only a matter of time before he asks.

Four hours later, we drive back to Portland, but I'm still

wound tight. MJ is waiting for us as soon as I park my truck outside our apartment complex. They're going on a date. She invites me to join them, but I'm in a shitty mood, so I decline the offer and spend the evening playing my guitar and watching YouTube videos. It's pathetic, really, since I'm the one who put myself in this position to begin with.

I think about calling my uncle for advice. As a priest, he's always had a good ear, listening carefully to people's problems and supporting them on their quest to finding solutions.

But I end up chickening out, feeling like I need more time to think about it myself before talking it out with someone else.

I head for the shower, my thoughts a jumbled mess, and before long, I'm rubbing one out. I'm more aggressive than I'd usually be with myself, hoping to ease the tension that has my body in its claws. I come hard with Grace's name spilling out of my lips like a prayer.

That night, I fall asleep with guilt and confusion as my bed companions, desperate for answers. But no matter how much I look for them, they're always still too far out of my reach.

# eleven

*Sol*

O N SATURDAY, I WAKE UP FEELING MORE IN CONTROL OF MY life. In fact, I'm ready to discuss it with someone. As I get dressed for Beverly and Mark's wedding, the need becomes pressing.

I'm watching as the bride and groom—now Mr. and Mrs. Steinman—finish their first dance when Ivan finally works up the nerve to ask about Wednesday. Quietly, I tell him everything that happened.

The party. The questions about kissing. The dancing. Me leaving like a coward.

He smiles and says, "I told you so," just as I knew he would. Overnight, I've managed to convince myself I've got everything under control once again and tell Ivan so.

That is, until my gaze veers to the left and I catch a glimpse of Grace walking across the lawn toward the gazebo where the wedding took place earlier. Her off-white, short-sleeved dress draws attention to her rich coloring, accentuating her curves all the way to her legs, where the dress stops a few inches above her knees.

She returns a few minutes later, carrying a large bag, and hands it to her mom, who looks considerably better than the last time I saw her. Standing side by side, the similarities between the two of them are staggering. Both are short with slightly round-ed faces and upturned noses. Debra's skin is a darker shade of brown than Grace's.

"You have it handled, huh?" Ivan asks, amused.

I whip my head around to look at him, unable to find a re-tort because he's right. Mentally, my tongue has been hanging out this whole time as I stared at Grace.

It's embarrassing really.

The song ends, and the newlyweds leave the dance floor, re-turning to their seats. The band starts playing "Sway" by Michael Bublé. Soon enough, the dance floor is once again filled with people.

"You should just go ahead and ask her to go with us to watch Sublime Chaos play."

"I thought MJ asked her."

"Yes. But I think it'd be more tempting coming from you."

I rub my palm down my face and stretch my legs in front of me, subtly watching as Grace is led to the dance floor by Beverly and Mark's twelve-year-old son, Sam. He's staring up at her with pure adoration as they start to move to the music.

*That kid has better moves than me*, I realize with a sigh.

"The worst thing she can say is no," Ivan adds after a beat, one brow rising to his hairline. "Right?"

I laugh under my breath and shake my head. Ivan's wrong.

The worst thing she can say is *yes*. And it terrifies me.

God, she looks so sexy swaying her hips like that—

"Dude," Ivan says, laughing. "You look about ready to eat her right here and now."

"What?" I turn to him, brows set in a frown.

His gaze darts to my lap, then back up to mine. "Seriously? What are you, thirteen? We're at a wedding, Callan, and here you are getting a hard-on for some girl!"

"Shut up." I grab one of the linen napkins from the table and lay it over my lap.

"You need to stop thinking about her that way and actually do it, man."

"So I'm supposed to take advice from you now? Who are you, Dr. Phil?"

He rolls his eyes. "Yeah. I mean, aren't you exhausted? You're torturing yourself. You should sow your wild oats before you leave in September."

I drag my fingers through my hair in frustration. "Can we not have this conversation here?"

"Just looking out for you, dude."

I stare at him. He raises his hands in surrender, stands, and then backs away. "Just saying."

He heads toward the table where MJ's sitting, then ducks his head to kiss her forehead. She smiles sweetly up at him, and he sits on the empty chair next to her, tugging her on his lap. He looks in my direction and catches me watching them and mouths "Go," before moving his gaze from me to where I know, without having to look, Grace stands.

I search the hall for my uncle and find him sitting with a bunch of other guys from town. Our eyes meet, but then his gaze slides over to Grace as though he can read my thoughts, then back to me.

What's with everyone knowing exactly what I'm thinking about as if it's written on my forehead?

I force myself to look away from the knowing look in his eyes and back to the girl on the dance floor. My palms itch at the memory of us dancing together at the diner—my hands on her hips, her head on my chest—

My heart speeds up as I watch her move.

She dances as though she's made from wind and water, effortlessly and gracefully. I trail her with my gaze, my body following her as though she's a magnet and I don't have a choice but to obey the pull. She twirls and shimmies her shoulders, throwing her head back and laughing.

Her beautiful curls are secured on top of her head in a loose ponytail, swaying as she moves. I feel the urge to run my fingers through them just to see if they feel as soft as I've imagined on many occasions.

I have a feeling given time, Grace could be the kind of woman men make sacrifices for. She has the power to make a man forget his dreams and help her pursue hers just to see her happy. Just to be near her.

*I want to be near her.*

The thought washes over me, making me catch my breath. Well, I'll just have to practice self-control much harder.

I head down the hallway leading to the washrooms just as the song comes to an end. I walk out a few minutes later, intending to go back to my table. Laughter reaches me from across the room. It sounds light and fresh, like the beginning of spring. I inhale briefly to calm my nerves, and before I know what's happening, my feet are guiding me toward the laugh with one goal in mind.

Grace is standing at the bar with her back braced on the counter. I'd recognize her laughter among a thousand voices.

Her head is thrown back again, eyes closed. She's smiling like she knows something others don't. I'd give my left arm to know what she's thinking right now.

I watch her, unable to turn away from the sight. She's too addictive. Too fascinating.

Then she opens her eyes and tilts her head toward me.

"Hey, Father Callan," she greets, a playful glint in her eyes.

I find myself chuckling. "I haven't earned that title yet."

"Sol," she murmurs, then makes a sound in the back of her throat, almost a purr, sending heat straight to my dick. Is she doing this on purpose? Who is this person? It's like she has morphed overnight from a sullen teen to a tempting seductress.

Sucking in a deep breath, I watch her watching me with interest. She lowers her gaze, a rare smile touching her lips.

# twelve

*Grace*

"WANT A DRINK?"

Sol shoves his hands inside his black pants and nods. "Yeah. Sure." His voice, usually calm and deep, sounds rough, as if he just woke up from a deep sleep. He clears his throat and says, "Water, please."

"Water? At a wedding?" I tsk and sigh. "Did you know that drinking water at a wedding is considered bad luck for the newlyweds?"

His eyes go wide at that. "Reall—" He cuts himself off and scratches the back of his head, mirroring my teasing smile. "Good one, Grace."

God, I love teasing him. He looks awkwardly adorable when he's flustered.

I laugh. "So juice?"

He smirks. "Yeah, thanks."

After I place our order for two cranberry juices, we both fall silent, watching the bartender prepare our drinks. As soon as they're ready, we leave the bar area. I twirl the glass in my hand, scanning the room to avoid staring at Sol for too long.

I still don't know what to make of his abrupt departure last Wednesday. Maybe I did or said something to upset him. I hadn't been the friendliest when he first approached me that day, but I thought after my apology and our dance at Mom's cheering-up party, he and I were on the same page.

Apparently, I was wrong.

"So." I face him and lift the glass. "Cheers to the newlyweds."

"Hear, hear." He touches his glass to mine, then tips it into his mouth.

I sip from my glass, taking the time to study him from under my lashes. I inhale sharply when I realize he's staring at me.

*Busted.*

Color floods his cheeks, and his lips tilt upward at the corners as he pushes back the locks of hair from his forehead.

"So what's your verdict?" he asks.

"Cute."

His eyebrows dip thoughtfully. "You think I'm cute?"

I shrug. "I think so, yeah."

He exhales loudly. "Wow."

Judging by his expression, I can tell Solomon Callan has no idea the effect his striking sapphire eyes have on people, including me.

"Cute." He shakes his head and chuckles, then drinks from his glass.

"Is it so hard to believe?"

"You're the first person to ever tell me that."

"Seriously?" My eyes widen in disbelief.

He shrugs, dropping his gaze to his dress shoes, and murmurs, "Thanks."

He asks after a beat, "Want to sit down?" He points at four empty seats a few feet away.

I nod, heading that way, and feel him press his palm on my lower back. My body stiffens involuntarily. Not because his touch is unpleasant. Quite the contrary. It's unexpected and rather nice.

"Sorry." He draws his hand back immediately and shoves it inside his pocket.

"It's fine," I say, sitting down. "I was just surprised."

He sits down across from me and sets his glass on the table. His leg bounces as he watches the crowd and his finger *taps, taps, taps* a beat on his thigh.

"So what happened the other night? At the diner, I mean? You left in a hurry."

He opens his mouth to say something, then shakes his head and shuts it again, pressing his lips firmly together. "I was exhausted, I guess."

"Oh," I mutter, then take a sip of my juice. "I wondered if—"

"You broke your promise not to corrupt me too much?" He smirks.

I slap a hand over my eyes and laugh, embarrassed. "Yes. I wasn't exactly sober." My hand falls away from my face, and I hold it out to him. "I don't want to mess up this chance at friendship. So . . ." I trail off and wait patiently, hopefully, for him to meet me halfway.

His big hand engulfs mine in a firm handshake. My body jolts at the contact, and every part of me comes alive. I'm mesmerized by the veins on his forearm under the rosary bracelet, disappearing beneath the rolled-up sleeves of his white button-down shirt.

His gaze slides to our hands, moving up to rove over my face and settling on my lips. His mouth parts subtly, the tip of his tongue peeking out to lick his bottom lip.

Oh my God. How sexy is that!

"We're cool," he mumbles, probably not aware of his thumb brushing my knuckles, his touch feather soft.

I gasp and try to cover it by biting the inside of my cheek, but the goosebumps on my arms betray me.

He jerks upright, taking his hand with him. He blinks several times as though he's coming out of a haze. "Shit. I'm sorry."

"There's nothing to be sorry about."

His leg bounces faster, the air between us suddenly crackling with tension. The kind of tension that has my stomach dipping deliciously and my thighs tingling.

One week ago, I was certain no one had the ability to make my blood sing. To make goosebumps rise on my skin with just a smile. Then Sol came along and proved me wrong. When he walked up to my booth, offering his friendship, he shattered parts of my resistance.

He clears his throat and asks, "You're going to Brown in the fall, right? I overheard your mom talking to my uncle about it."

"Yes?" I say it like it's a question, then quickly cover it with, "And you're going to Saint Bernard's Seminary in Boston."

"Yes, I am." He sounds so sure of his decision.

A feeling I know far too well stabs my chest. I've always had a hard time being around people like Sol. People who seem so sure of who they are and what they want. That's never been me. I've been lost for as long as I can remember.

"You're frowning," Sol says. "Did I say something wrong?"

"No!" I blurt out, then clear my throat and glance back at him. "It's just that . . ." I bite my lip, wondering if I'll sound too whiny. I shake my head. "It's nothing. Are you excited about the seminary?"

"Yeah." He smiles, looking peaceful and content. "I've been looking forward to this since I knew I wanted to be a priest."

I'm trying not to feel like a loser here, but to be honest, it's getting more difficult by the second.

"You don't seem too enthused about Brown," he muses. "You can talk to me, Gracie."

Gracie.

*Gracie.*

He called me Gracie. My name on his lips sounds like a melody.

In his eyes, I see sincerity and patience. He's completely focused on me, and it makes me feel like I'm the center of his universe.

"You're going to make a good priest, Sol. There's just this vibe about you. People won't hesitate to pour their hearts out to you and confess their sins," I say teasingly, enjoying the subtle flush that appears on his cheeks. "No wonder Seth looks at you like you hung the moon."

I remember last winter when he took over the youth group at church. The way he spoke and his actions commanded everyone's attention in the room.

He doesn't realize it; that much is clear.

Sol shifts on his seat as if my words make him uncomfortable. "He's a great kid."

"Aw. You're blushing. It's adorable."

He rolls his eyes and rubs the back of his neck with his hand. "Can we not focus on me?"

"Am I making you uncomfortable?" I tease, nudging his leg with the tip of my peep-toe heel.

"Would you stop if I said yes?"

I push my lip in a pretend pout. "But teasing you has just become my favorite thing to do."

Sol laughs, the sound deep, warm, and joyful. So alive and unguarded. "I'm glad you're having so much fun at my expense. Change of topic. Let's talk about *your* sins, or whatever it is that's bothering you." The mood shifts from playful to serious. I blow out a breath, pondering if I should tell him. Maybe telling someone will help untangle my thoughts.

"I'm not sure of who I am. Who I want to become. What I really want to do at Brown. Some days, I think I've figured it out, then the next, doubt creeps in, and I'm back to square one. That's why I want to take a year off. Take time off to think about what I really want to do in college for the next four years of my life. For the rest of my life, really. But so far, I'm still just as clueless. And now in a few weeks, I'll be heading to Brown, and I'm . . . *scared*."

"I think it's normal for you to feel that way. We're all a little lost, Grace."

"I'm eighteen. I should have figured this out by now." I bite my lip, twisting my fingers as the familiar worries and nervousness creep inside me. "Did you always know you wanted to be a priest?"

He laughs and shakes his head. "I wanted to be a magician."

I sit up straight and lean forward. "Really? Can you do tricks or something?"

"A few, yes. Like this one." He reaches his hand behind my ear, and when he pulls back his hand, he's holding a penny between his index and middle finger.

I press my lips, fighting a smile. "A *penny*? I could have sworn there's a twenty back there."

His shoulders shake with laughter. "Looks like my tricks need a little brushing up."

His eyes narrow into slits as if he's trying to remember something. "It started out when my teacher in middle school asked the class what everyone wanted to be when we grew up. I just knew, I guess. It's like there's this pull in me. Like God was speaking to me. Then Seth came along. He was really messed up in the head over some stuff that happened at his church back in Baltimore. Thinking about anyone else going through what he did . . . I was even more determined about the path I'd chosen.

"Every time when I hear about some of the negative stuff happening in the Catholic Church nowadays, I feel even more certain this is who I'm meant to be. People have lost faith in the church and forgotten the good things, and I want to change that. I know I'm just one person, and I'm probably being foolishly optimistic, but I believe it takes faith, no matter how small, to move a mountain. Last summer, I traveled to Peru with a few guys from church for a home building mission sponsored by the diocese. It was a life-changing experience." He pauses, determination and passion shining a bright fire in his eyes.

I nod, remembering his uncle talking about it during Mass.

"That trip reaffirmed my sole purpose for the path I'd chosen. Dedicating my life to being God's instrument in spreading hope and faith." Then his expression turns somber.

"After my mom and dad passed away, I was a wreck. I carried so much hate in me. Luke was . . . he was just amazing."

"I'm so sorry about your parents, Sol," I whisper, leaning forward and placing my hand over his, hoping to comfort him.

"Thank you." His gaze drops to our hands, but not before I see a slight shimmer in his eyes. He clears his throat, but his voice cracks a little when he says, "I'm better now. Really, I am." He sounds as if he's trying to convince himself. "Besides, you told me everything would be okay, and it was."

*Wow.* "You believed me?"

"How could I not?"

I'm elated by his words, but at the same time, my heart hurts for him. I feel selfish and ungrateful. This boy lost his parents, but he survived and managed to sort out his life.

I sigh and run the tip of my finger around the rim of my glass.

"Isn't it weird that we never really talked after that day in your uncle's office?" I ask.

"Yeah." He huffs out a laugh. "I wasn't brave enough to approach you."

"You talked to other people, though."

He looks at me from the corner of his eye, then looks forward. "They weren't you."

*What does that even mean?*

A hand touches my shoulder, interrupting my thoughts, and I turn around to find Mom. She splits a glance between Sol and me, and her eyes light up. It's so weird to see her responding to Sol that way even though she's spent most of my teenage years protecting me. She warned me about boys and their ability to break hearts. I'm grateful she had Beverly's wedding to keep her mind off things. She looks relaxed, like she's enjoying herself. But I know from experience that even though she seems happy now, it won't last. The next few days are still going to be rough on her.

"Looking really handsome, Sol. Doesn't he, Gracie?" Mom says, and I force a grin on my face.

Sol smiles up at my mom. "Thank you, Ms. Miller."

Then he aims his infamous half-smile at me, and I feel it everywhere.

*What's wrong with me?*

His smile shouldn't affect me like this. Clearly, the wedding atmosphere has gone to my head. Everything seems magnified and romantic.

I force my mind back to my surroundings just as Sol says, "I love what you did with the wedding, by the way."

"Oh, thank you." She squeezes his shoulder, then faces me with her eyebrows raised even though her twitching lips make it clear she's fighting a smile. "At least someone noticed."

I roll my eyes and laugh. "He's right; it's perfect. But you know that already."

She huffs and shakes her head. "Have either of you seen Collins?" Lines of worry etch on her forehead. "He's supposed to be out here taking pictures of Bev and Mark."

I stand. "I can help you find him if you want."

"I'll help, too." Sol's on his feet with his hands in his pants pockets. And with that, the two of us start our search.

"Oh, hey, listen. I've been meaning to ask you if you want to go to the concert with me. MJ told me she invited you, but I wanted to ask you if you want to go with me, um . . . *us*? Unless you have other pl—"

"Yes. I mean, no. I don't have other plans." I take a deep breath to calm my nerves. "Yes, I'd *love* to go to the concert with you, Sol." With a soft smile, I add, "It's a date," surprising myself. I haven't gone on a date since I broke up with Gavin.

His eyes widen slightly. "A date, huh?"

I laugh nervously. "It doesn't have to be. I just thought you meant, um, do you? Want it to be a date, that is?"

"I guess, yeah. I've never been on a date before."

*No way.* "How is that even possible? You're hot and—"

His brows shoot up. "You've called me 'cute' and 'hot' in the span of one evening. You're doing wonders for my ego, Gracie."

I don't think I'll ever get over the way he says *Gracie*.

I laugh. "Don't let it go to your head. Okay, we need to split up to find Collins faster before my mom goes into full-on panic mode."

"Good idea."

I start to walk away but stop when Sol's strong, warm fingers wrap around my wrist, turning me around to face him.

His eyes roam over my face for a few seconds before he lifts a hand and tucks a loose lock of hair behind my ear. My gaze falls to the onyx rosary beads of the bracelet around his wrist. Before he has a chance to pull his hand away, I reach up and run a finger across the bronze cross pendant pressing gently on the veins of his inner wrist. It seems to sparkle and shine with life.

Unable to hold back, I trace a finger along one vein. He sucks in a breath and goosebumps spread up his arm.

"*Gracie.*" He breathes my name hoarsely. He sounds like he's in pain. I lift my gaze to his, and what I see there makes me lose my breath.

Blue fire burning in those gorgeous wide eyes, mouth slightly parted on an exhale.

Heat crawls up my cheeks, responding to the way he's looking at me. "Um." I take a step back, out of his reach. "Sorry."

He steps closer, eyes looking even more fiery than before. "Don't be. It felt nice."

The tips of his ears redden at his admission, but it doesn't diminish his looks. Instead, it makes him more human and not the solemn, untouchable boy-angel who sits quietly in the front of church every Sunday during Mass wearing the black and white vestments reserved for altar servers with his hands folded in his lap.

"See you in a bit, Gracie." He brushes a finger along the back of my hand, then walks away.

I stand there, rooted to the spot, my feet too heavy and my heart beating too fast as I watch him walk away. The spot where the tips of his fingers had lingered for a few seconds burned as though he'd imprinted his very essence onto me.

Who knew quiet Sol had a touch that singed like fire?

I head in the opposite direction, smiling wide.

# thirteen

## Sol

AFTER WE FOUND COLLINS, GRACE AND I SAT DOWN AND chatted for a few minutes before Debra asked Grace to help her. Beverly and Mark left for their honeymoon at the end of the reception, so as much as I enjoyed hanging out with Grace, we had to part ways at some point.

Once I'm back at the apartment, I slump back against the front door and run my fingers through my hair. The confidence and elation I'd felt when I was around Grace is fading fast as nervousness quickly sets in.

I stride into the living room, glancing around the open-floor plan. The apartment is close to the rectory. It's big enough for two teenage boys learning how to navigate the world—as my uncle put it when he talked me into leaving the rectory.

I duck my head around the door to Ivan's room. He's sitting on a bean bag on the floor, his tongue sticking out at the corner of his mouth and fingers jerking as he presses the buttons on his controller. Beside him, MJ looks determined as she tries to beat him at the race car game they're playing.

For just a second, I entertain the thought of talking to him about Grace but change my mind, deciding to talk to Luke instead. I need guidance, the kind only he can offer. He always has the right answers.

It's obvious they haven't noticed me as they continue to yell at each other, eyes fixed on the TV screen. I head for my room while pulling my phone out from my back pocket and dialing Luke's number. He answers on the third ring.

"Hey." He sounds distracted, most likely working on his homily for tomorrow's Mass. I hear papers shuffling and my uncle muttering under his breath.

"If you're busy, I can call back later."

"No, it's fine. Give me a few minutes. I'm almost done."

"Yeah. Of course." I kick off my shoes, climb onto the bed, and prop my head on a pillow. My eyes automatically find the faded pink flower pinned on the corkboard above my desk. I never got rid of it because, for me, it represented hope when I desperately needed it. Plus, it reminded me of Grace.

I stare at the ceiling and start to count the cracks webbing across the white surface while waiting for my uncle to finish whatever he's working on.

"All done. What's up?"

"I need some advice, Luke." After a breath, I add, "It's about Grace. I asked if she wanted to go with me to a concert, and she said yes. It's like a date or something."

I pause once again, waiting for that final piece of information to sink in.

"I see."

"I'm . . . this is weird. I shouldn't . . . never mind." I swing my legs over the side of my bed and blow out a breath.

"Solomon?"

"Yes?"

"Take a deep breath, son."

I do as I'm told, then blow it out through my mouth. "You're allowed to have fun and hang out with kids your own age, including girls. Besides, it's just a show, right?"

"Yes," I say with conviction. I cover my mouth with my hand to stop myself from spilling out what's bothering me before I'm ready to share.

"Okay. Good." A pause, then, "Remember what we talked about on the day I rented the apartment for you?"

"Yeah?"

"After living with me and a bunch of old dudes at the rectory since you moved to Portland, I wanted you to be around people your age and explore more options out there."

"I loved living at the rectory. It was the only home I knew back then. I'm glad Mom and Dad appointed you as my legal guardian."

Luke lets out a weary sigh and clears his throat. Then he says in that priestly voice of his, soothing and patient and understanding, "There's nothing wrong with wanting to give the other life a chance."

I swallow the guilt choking me. "Then why do I feel like I'm betraying Him every time I think about Grace?"

"First and foremost, you need to remember you're human and feeling guilty is normal. Only you can decide what to do with it. You already know my thoughts about starting the seminary in the fall. You have such a good heart, a heart that is so open to love despite everything that happened in your past. You care too much, and you love too much. It's not necessarily a bad thing. Have I told you about Annabelle?"

"I don't think so. No. Who's she?"

"When I was seventeen, I fell in love with a girl," he says, and I sit up straighter, curious. He hardly ever speaks about his personal life. At some point, I thought he'd been born a priest. "She was new at my school, a quiet little thing."

"Was she pretty?" I ask, smiling, hungry for more details.

"Very beautiful." He chuckles. "She had long red hair and this amazing body . . ." He takes in a long, trembling breath. I've never heard him sound so unraveled, so passionate, other than when he's preaching during Mass. "Her eyes held me captive from the second we met. Green and wide, always filled with humor. She and I were crowned king and queen at prom that year. I loved her with everything that I was for as long as I could. But then the time came and . . . I broke up with her after prom."

I frown. "Why? I mean, you loved her."

He sighs, sounding exhausted. "I was afraid . . . I don't know. I was torn between her and what I thought God wanted me to be."

Silence follows his admission. Does he regret his choice? Does he miss her?

Unable to stop myself, I voice my questions. He doesn't say anything for a few moments. And when he speaks up, it's with an impassive voice. "I did what I had to do. What was right for me."

"What does that even mean?"

"Just be sure this is what you want to do, Sol. What was right for me isn't necessarily right for you. I don't expect you to do as I did, and no one can force you to make any decisions. Just know that."

I nod even though he can't see me, leaning back against my pillows, and stare at the ceiling.

"Solomon?"

"Yeah?"

"I'm very proud of you."

I grin, basking in his words. Then I remember what I wanted to ask him the second he mentioned his ex-girlfriend. "So did you, like . . . have sex?"

He clears his throat. "No."

I try to process that piece of information. "So, you're still a vir—"

"You do realize you're asking your uncle, who happens to be a priest, about sex, right?"

I laugh. "Okay, okay, fine."

We chat for a few more minutes. By the time I end the call, I feel lighter. I toss the phone on the nightstand and strip down to my boxers, then climb in bed. I fold my arms behind my head and wait for sleep to claim me.

*Thump.*

*Thump.*

"Yes, Ivan, *yes!*"

That snaps me out of my thoughts. Realizing what I'm hearing, I groan. These two are going to be the death of me.

*Thump.*

"Yes, kitten."

Kitten? I gulp down a snort.

*Thump.*

"Give it to me."

*Oh, God*, I think, before quickly apologizing for using the Lord's name in such an instance.

Lying on my side, I clutch the corner of my pillow and press it around my ears. A desperate attempt to block out the sounds of Ivan's bed hitting our shared wall. Still, I can hear the muffled sounds through the fabric of my pillow. I throw the useless thing aside and bang a fist on our connecting wall.

"Tone it down, would you?" I yell in frustration.

"Go to hell!" Ivan growls.

Asshole.

I snatch my phone from the nightstand along with the headphones, slap them on my head, and scroll through my playlist. I tap the screen and "Think About You" by Guns N' Roses blasts into my ears, efficiently blocking out the moans and groans coming through the wall.

Finally.

I flop back on the pillow and close my eyes, letting the lyrics roll around in my head.

The image of Grace at the wedding, dancing and laughing, flashes inside my head without warning. The thoughts have me sweating and my body aching.

I flip on my stomach, pressing my pelvis into the mattress to curb my raging need. But my hand sneaks down my stomach, fingers lifting the elastic band of my shorts, and I push them down my thighs. I'm so hard, and my body is coiled tight, begging for release. I grab my hard length, stroking my palm up and down.

Shit.

*Shit.*

I yank my hand away from my pants, breathing hard. I squeeze my eyes shut as guilt cuts through me. I can control myself.

Cold shower.

Definitely a cold shower will help.

I swing my legs over the side of the bed and bolt for the bathroom. I turn the water to cold and hop in, closing my eyes as the water hits my skin.

Fifteen minutes later, I'm lying in bed, listening to my favorite relaxing meditation music through my headphones.

# fourteen

*Grace*

SUNDAY MORNING, MOM AND I ARRIVE AT ST. PETER'S CHURCH. I'd be lying if I said I wasn't more than a little eager to see Sol.

It's funny how you can know someone for years and observe them from a distance but live your lives on parallel lines. Then one day, they walk up to you, and words are finally exchanged. And it hits you that someone has been missing in your life all along without you even knowing it.

And now all I want—no, *need*—is for him to notice me sitting in the congregation.

I watch Sol as he performs his usual altar server duties next to Father Foster. Sol's eyes subtly scan the crowd. The second they meet mine, one side of his mouth hitches up slightly. I glance around to check if anyone else noticed, then face forward again when I realize I'm the only one who did. Maybe because I'm massively obsessed with his cute half-smiles.

He bites his bottom lip between his teeth and looks away. I look down at my hands folded in my lap, pressing my lips together to fight a smile.

When it's time to offer the sign of peace, Mom leans into my side and whispers in my ear, "What's going on between you two?"

"Nothing," I mutter too quickly.

"Really?" She pauses. "That seemed like more than just a friendly smile to me."

My gaze whips up to the front of the church just as Sol walks toward the first row, shaking hands with the people sitting there. I realize with much regret that I should've dragged my mom to sit in that row. His eyes drift in my direction once more, lips pulled at one side in a subtle, crooked smile. It's kind of weird because he hardly ever smiles during Mass.

"Doesn't look like nothing to me, sweetheart," Mom whispers, pulling me out of the web of fascination I'm wrapped in.

"Mom . . . we're just friends."

The heat of my mom's stare burns the side of my face. I ignore it. I can't look at her. If I did, I know I'd end up telling her everything. The thing is, there's really nothing to tell.

The hairs at the back of my neck tingle in awareness. I twist around, my eyes scanning the crowd, and freeze when I notice Gavin's brown ones staring back at me.

What the hell is he doing in church? He hardly ever attends mass, so this is quite a surprise. And not a good one.

My stomach hurts as if someone punched me. I press my palm to my stomach, hoping to push back the pain.

Church is my haven. I hate that he's here. It feels like he's sullying the place.

I shake my head and face forward again, my hands clenched into fists on my lap. I hate him so much. God, forgive me, but I really do hate him. I wonder how long it takes for this feeling to fade.

Maybe never? Maybe it's just one of those things in life that never really goes away. They remind us to guard our hearts and make sure the next person we give it to will protect it as if he or she is guarding the Holy Grail. Until then, mine is safely locked away behind a steel cage.

The rest of Mass goes well. I don't turn around to look at him again, but I feel his eyes on me every second of the fifteen minutes.

When Mass ends, everyone heads outside. I search for Sol from where I'm standing, trying and failing to be subtle about it.

My mom is a few feet away, talking to some members of the congregation. She's smiling and laughing despite the past few days being a bit rough for her. She's doing better as time passes.

"Hey." That familiar voice has me spinning around, almost losing my balance.

Gavin fucking Bachmann. And he's extending his hand in my direction in what I believe is an attempt to steady me.

"Don't touch me," I whisper angrily.

He pulls his hand back, frowning.

"What are you doing here?"

He glances around before returning his gaze back to me. "Attending Mass, like every other person here." He smirks, and I want to punch his face.

I clutch my purse tighter and force a smile. "Well, good for you." I turn to go, but he grips my bicep, causing my whole body to tense. I could easily dislodge his hand from my arm, but I wouldn't want to make a scene.

"I said don't touch me."

"Grace. Come on, don't be like that. Can we forget about high school for a min—"

"Fuck *off*." The words are low, meant for the two of us only. I'm about to pry his fingers off my arm the way I learned in self-defense class years ago when a familiar voice interrupts us.

"What's going on here?"

I whip my head around to find Sol standing behind me, eyebrows furrowed. He looks at me, then at Gavin. His gaze drops to where Gavin's hand is still gripping my arm, and his nostrils flare, his eyes bright with anger.

"Get your hand off her."

Sol sounds calm. The only things betraying what he's feeling are how his hands are now curled into fists and the way his body is locked tight as if he's ready to go to war.

Gavin laughs, the sound grating in my ears. "This doesn't concern you, Callan." When Sol stays exactly where he is, eyes drilling into Gavin's skull, Gavin's eyes narrow, moving between Sol and me, and he says, "Wait. You two? Really?" He looks incredulous. Neither Sol nor I speak. "Since when are would-be priests allowed to bang chicks? I can't say I blame you, man. She's—"

"Walk away, Bachmann," Sol grits out, stepping forward and partly shielding me from Gavin. "Before we make a scene in front of everyone."

"I can handle him, Sol," I say quietly. "People are starting to stare."

"Or what?" Gavin scoffs, not even bothering to look at me. "You're gonna strangle me with that rosary in your pocket? Oh, wait. Maybe you're going to hit me again to teach me a lesson. Which one is it?"

Wait, *wait* a damn second. Sol hit him? My Sol? When? Why?

Oh my God!

I'm about to voice all these questions when Gavin opens his big mouth and laughs as if he just told a funny joke, eyeing me with interest.

"Let me guess. You didn't know, huh?" He thumps Sol's shoulder and winks. He freaking *winks*. "Brave Knight over here confronted me at the school parking lot after we broke up to your avenge your honor. He almost broke my nose with his giant fist.

He didn't get suspended, thanks to me for not reporting his ass to the principal," he says, directing a sneer at Solomon. "Well, Callan. There goes your pristine reputation."

I think back on the time after the incident. Gavin showed up in school with dark bruises around his nose and under his eyes. He told everyone he'd hurt himself while trying to tackle one of his team mates during football practice.

Oh, my gosh.

Sol continues to stand there, unmovable as a mountain, his jaw twitching as he stares Gavin down. Sol's almost a foot taller than Gavin, so he towers over him easily. His usually peaceful demeanor is replaced by anger as it pours off him in waves. I've never seen him like this. I'm still trying to wrap my head around this whole revelation.

Gavin drops his hand and steps back, glaring at Sol. "Wouldn't want Church Boy to get into a fight in front of the Lord himself, now would we?" His lips curl into a sneer before he stalks away.

Sol whirls around and dips his head to meet my gaze. He reaches forward as if he wants to touch me but freezes. "Are you okay?"

"I'm good. Thank you for standing up for me." I give him a smile, but he doesn't smile back. Instead, his eyes leave mine and trail after Gavin, his jaw clenched tight. "He wouldn't have done anything to me. Not in front of everyone. Besides"—my smile widens into a grin—"I can handle him."

He eyes my petite frame doubtfully, the crease between his eyes deepening. "How?"

"I've got a few tricks up my sleeve." I wink at him playfully, hoping to ease the concerned look in his eyes.

He sighs and rakes his fingers through his tousled hair, which seems to have a mind of its own. "I gotta go. Luke's having some guys over for lunch at the rectory. He needs help with some stuff." He studies me, really studies me, taking in every feature of my face before asking, "Are you sure you're okay?"

Gosh, he's so sweet. "Yes. I swear, I'm okay."

He nods. "All right. I guess I'll see you around?"

"Sure."

He looks like he wants to say something else. Instead, he shakes his head and walks toward the rectory in long, powerful strides.

I watch him until he disappears around the corner, then walk over to where my mom's still chatting with one of the parishioners, oblivious to what just happened.

"Are you sure you'll be okay?" Mom asks me as we head for our car a few minutes later. She's leaving for Port Elizabeth for a three-day meditation retreat later this afternoon.

"I'll be fine."

"What about the diner?" She bites her bottom lip worriedly.

I roll my eyes, which makes her smile. "Mom, please don't worry. I literally grew up in that diner. I know my way around it with my eyes closed. I'll manage."

Just before we get inside the car, she hugs me tight.

"Was that Gavin back there?"

I pull back and meet her gaze with a chuckle. "You never miss anything, do you?"

She rolls her eyes playfully as if to say, *are you seriously asking me that.* "You're my daughter. I notice *everything.*"

I take her in. Her skin glows under the midday sun. Her dreadlocks are tied in a low bun, bringing her cheekbones and jawline in stark focus. It hits me all over again how beautiful she is. How blessed I am to have this woman as my mother.

"Sweetheart?" She nudges my shoulder to claim my attention.

"Uh, sorry," I say, remembering what we were talking about before my mind wandered. "I have no idea what he wanted."

"Sol swooped in like a gallant prince to the rescue." Her brows shoot up, and I remember her words during Mass.

"I would've easily handled Gavin," I declare vehemently.

Her eyes fill with pride. "I know. Come on, let's go home. I'm starving."

Warmth fills my chest at her words. I love that even though she's concerned, she trusts me enough to give me space and let me handle my own shit, but I know I can always go to her if I need to talk.

"Mom, hang on a second." I tug her hand before she can walk farther. She stops and turns to face me. "You know you'll never lose me, no matter what, yeah?"

Her eyebrows bunch into a frown. "I do."

I watch her closely when I say, "It's just that, um, the other day, I overheard you telling Bev you thought you were going to lose me and, well. . ." I leave the sentence hanging, hoping she'll open up to me.

"I'm sorry for worrying you, sweetheart. I was not myself and"—she takes my hands in hers and laces our fingers together—"let's just enjoy today. We'll talk, okay?"

"Okay." I can't help the disappointment knotting my stomach. But at the same time, I don't want to upset her now that she's doing so much better even though there's no way I'm going to let this go. "I'll hold you to that."

Dread flashes across her face before she pushes it back, nods, and smiles.

After lunch, Mom heads to the diner. Feeling restless, I sprawl on the couch and scroll through the TV channels. Of course, there's nothing interesting on TV. Before Sol, I was satisfied with being alone. Keeping my own company. But now I need . . . more. I'm practically hemorrhaging desperation as the need to have someone to hang out with burns a hole in my chest.

I grab my phone from the coffee table and scroll through my contacts, pausing when MJ's name pops on the screen. And before I can talk myself out of it, I tap her name and take a deep breath, then press the phone to my ear.

She answers the call on the fifth ring.

"Hello," she greets in a tired voice.

"MJ? Grace here." I pause. When she doesn't say anything, I clear my throat, feeling nervous all of a sudden. "Did I call at a bad time?"

"Sorry, I'm a little distracted." In the background, I hear the sharp crackle of an intercom, followed by a woman's voice paging a doctor. "I'm at Mercy Medical Center visiting my grandmother. I brought her in this morning."

She sounds completely drained, the complete opposite of the upbeat girl I officially met two weeks ago. I really don't know her well, but the thought of her at the hospital, most probably on her own worrying about her grandmother, has me shooting up from the couch.

"I could drop by to keep you company, um, and visit your grandmother . . . is it okay?" I squeeze my eyes, hoping I'm not overstepping, and add softly, "That's what friends do, right?"

She doesn't answer for a few seconds. I'm about to tell her to forget I offered when she says, "I'd love that. Do me favor? Could you grab me a coffee from Fisher's Gold? I need my fix. The one at the hospital cafeteria isn't cutting it."

I grab my purse and car keys and hurry toward the door. "Sure. How do you want it?"

"Ask the barista for a red eye. I need the extra shot of caffeine."

"Got it. Please text me her room number. I'll be there soon."

"Okay," she murmurs, sounding relieved.

MJ is sitting in the waiting room area when I arrive. She stands up and dashes in my direction, practically falling into my arms. I lean forward and place the bowl of chicken soup and coffee paper cup on the nearby table, then wrap my arms around her shoulders.

"Thank you for coming," she says, stepping back and wiping the tears that have sprung in her eyes. "I feel like I'm going to go insane from worrying about her."

"What happened to your grandmother?"

"Pneumonia. They've put her on a ventilator, and it's fucking scary seeing her like that." She sniffs. "She's sleeping now. I needed a break, so I came to sit out here."

She sits down on one of the black leather couches and motions me over to sit next to her. I do as she asks me, setting my purse on my lap.

"Do your parents know?"

She nods. "Mom will be here this evening." She glances at me with tired eyes and smiles. "Now that you're here, please distract me, or I might end up bawling again. I never thought I'd hear from you."

"I planned to call you at some point—"

"Really?" She laughs. "You looked so overwhelmed after I left your booth that time at the diner."

I roll my eyes and smile. "I called you today, didn't I? Where's your phone?"

She digs it out of her pocket and hands it over. I save my number in her contacts and give it back. "You have my number now. Which reminds me, you didn't ask for my number in return when you gave me yours."

She watches me cautiously as she says, "Honestly, I was scared. It took me a lot of guts to approach you. You're a little intimidating, you know that? Anyway, you never hang out with anyone. You seem nice, and everyone needs a friend. Giving you my number was a way of letting you know I wanted to be your friend, so I left the ball in your court after that."

I nod to let her know I understand her reasoning and settle deeper into the couch. As I'm sitting next to MJ, the hopeful feeling I felt the other day at the diner returns.

"What do you do for fun?" she asks.

"Well, let's see. Cliff jumping, origami, swimming, working at the diner—"

She snorts. "You call working at the diner *fun*?"

"So exciting, right?"

"Yeah." She rolls her eyes with a laugh. "Anyway, once Grandma feels better, I'll show you my version of fun."

"Which is what exactly?"

"Patience, little grasshopper. You'll see."

# fifteen

*Grace*

MONDAY TURNS TO TUESDAY, AND SUMMER GETS HOTTER and hotter. The diner takes up most of my time and energy, pushing thoughts of Sol and school to the back of my mind for later. Beverly and Mark return from their honeymoon, which is a relief. As soon as Beverly walks in through the diner's doors on Wednesday morning, she grabs me by the shoulders and gently pushes me out the door, telling me to take the rest of the day off.

I get in my car and drive around without any destination in mind. Tomorrow's Lemon Raspberry Cupcakes Thursday at the diner. I could go home and get a head start on those, but I prefer to make them in the evening so they're still fresh the following morning.

One hour later, I find myself parked in front of Joe's Auto Body Shop, where Sol told me he worked when we talked at Bev's wedding.

The scene from Sunday after Mass pops in my head, Gavin's words still fresh. I still can't believe Sol punched him. I'm so confused. That image doesn't really fit with the Sol I know.

A few people walk in and out of the shop, but I can't see him anywhere. I'm still wondering if I should go in or drive off when he appears at the door of the workshop. I sit up straight, my eyes trailing him as he heads toward a white car parked under a tree shade just outside the shop. He pops the hood up, then turns the cap on his head backward before disappearing underneath. When he's done, he starts heading for the workshop but stops in his tracks, turning around abruptly. He scans his surroundings, his brows lifting in surprise when he finds me watching him. He immediately changes direction, covering the distance between us in long strides.

Suddenly, my mouth feels dry, and my heart is racing as I take him in. The navy blue trousers he's wearing are splattered with oil, giving him a rough look that fits him more than I'd like to admit. I roll down my window as he gets closer. My lips crack into a smile when he stops in front of my door, mirroring my expression.

"Hey." He glances right and left as if scouting the area for something, before facing me again. He turns his cap around to face forward. "I feel like our roles have been reversed."

"Yeah?" Shit, I sound breathless. Definitely not good. I really don't want to scare him off. He already looks nervous as is it. "How's that?"

Phew. My voice has gone back to normal.

"Stalker becomes the stalked."

"Ha! Don't flatter yourself, Solomon," I say, rolling my eyes at him.

A few drops of sweat roll down the side of his face. He removes his cap and wipes the sweat from his forehead with the back of his hand before putting the cap back on. He smells like gasoline and oil and boy-man.

"What's up? Aren't you working at the diner today?"

"Bev's back. She ordered me to take the rest of the day off." My gaze drops to the white tag on the front of his navy blue

T-shirt. It says Joe's Auto Body Shop in bright red letters. "I was just driving by the garage, and . . . well, here I am."

His hand reaches up and tugs one of my braids, rubbing the strands between the tips of his fingers. The back of his fingers brush my shoulder as they fall away. I jolt in my seat as the burning sensation of his touch ricochets all over my body.

*Oh my gosh.*

"I, uh, I should let you get back to work." I grip the wheel with one hand, then use the other to turn the ignition key.

He studies my face, his features turning gentle. "Give me thirty minutes. Then I'll be yours for the rest of the day."

He walks back into the garage without waiting for my answer. I can't help the way my gaze follows him, taking in the way his shoulders look, strong and sure, then my gaze drops to his ass, framed nicely in his work trousers.

Leaning my head back on the headrest, I blow out a breath and close my eyes, smiling. A hot breeze blows into the car, making the air inside the small space more stifling than before. I bunch up my T-shirt and tie a knot at my midriff to get some relief, then settle back in my seat.

I startle awake some time later to the feel of someone gently shaking my shoulder. I blink several times to clear my vision. Sol, now wearing a gray T-shirt and shorts, flashes his usual smile at me, causing my stomach to dip delightfully. I must have drifted off to sleep while I waited for him.

He opens my door all of a sudden and scoops me up from my seat, causing me to squeal. My arms flail around before clasping his neck for support.

"Put me down, you dork!"

He laughs, seemingly having gotten over the nervousness from before. "Nope." Holding me with one arm, he leans back inside the car and rolls up the window and grabs my purse, kicking the door shut with his foot when he's done. "We'll take my truck. Your car will be safe here."

"Where are we going?"

"You choose," he says as he heads toward his truck. "Have you eaten already?"

I nod.

Sol sets me on my feet, then opens the passenger door. He looks at me thoughtfully, then at his truck, no doubt realizing I'm too short to climb the darn thing. Laughing softly as he shakes his head, he grips my hips and lifts me, settling me on the seat. Standing back, he waits as I buckle my seat belt with shaky fingers because *oh my God!* Sol is too sweet.

He rounds the car and hops into the driver's seat, then twists his upper body to face me. "So where to?"

I bite my cheek, considering my choices. "Can I drive?"

He barks out a laugh. "No way. You look like you're about to fall asleep. In fact, you *were* sleeping." He watches me closely. "I could take you home—"

"Ranger's Cove," I blurt out.

He blinks, then says, "What?"

"You asked me where we're going."

"Okay." He starts the car, then looks at me. "Ranger's Cove it is then."

I nod, smiling. I can't remember the last time I felt this relaxed. Happy. It's surreal. A few minutes into the drive, I reach over and pinch his bicep.

"What the—" He frowns while rubbing the offended spot. "What was that for?"

"Just making sure this is real."

His eyes leave the road for a second to look at me. "Oh, it's real. You're sitting in my truck, and I'm trying my best to appear cool and calm about it." Too soon, the mesmerizing ocean of his gaze returns to the road.

"Oh." *Oh.* "You don't have to pretend with me. Just be you," I say quietly.

He sighs and rubs his forehead with his hand. "What are we doing, Grace? What am *I* doing?"

"We're just hanging out. Don't beat yourself up, Sol."

He seems to consider this for several seconds, then he nods. "Cool."

We drive for a few more minutes in silence. I study his profile with as much subtlety as I can muster. His features seem calmer now, carefree even. One of his hands steers the wheel while the other hangs loosely on the leather, his fingers tapping the wheel rhythmically.

"So what's at Ranger's Cove?" he asks, bobbing his head to whatever song is playing inside his mind.

I pull my legs onto the seat and rest my chin on my knees. "My mom and I used to go there when I was a kid. It's one of my favorite places."

"It's always been just you and your mom?"

"Yes." There's a strain in the word. I don't want to discuss my mom or the man who was never a father to me. "What song is playing in your head, Sol?" I tap my temple for emphasis.

His mouth curves into a smile. "'Smells Like Teen Spirit.'" He points at his phone on the dashboard. "Put it on the docking station and check the playlist. It's on there somewhere."

I do as I'm told. The song starts playing through the speakers.

"I like it. You have good taste. Clearly, I underestimated you."

He chuckles. "So you thought I had bad taste in music? Is it because I want to become a priest?"

I nod, slightly embarrassed. "Sorry." I laugh awkwardly, settling back in my seat. "I thought you listened to whatever priests or seminarians listened to, to stay focused. Chanting songs or something."

"Are you stereotyping me right now?" he points out, sounding amused.

"Oh, crap. I totally am. I didn't think about it—"

"Relax, Grace. I'm only messing with you. But yeah, I save those for when I'm having a particularly, um, trying day."

I want to ask him what he means by that, but then it occurs to me that he could be speaking about sex. Sol's an eighteen-year-old guy. And from what I've seen and read about boys and their wild hormones, well, he must be very good at self-control.

"Are you going to miss it when you go to the seminary?" I ask before I can stop myself.

"Miss what?"

"Hanging out with your friends? Freedom?" I pause, then add, "Sex?"

He chokes and starts coughing, his cheeks flushing red. "It's not like I'm going to prison." His index finger starts tapping a fast beat on the steering wheel. He's nervous now. "You can't miss what you've never had, I guess."

And I don't need to ask to know he's talking about sex.

My legs slide down the seat as I twist my body to face him. "You're a virgin?" How is that even possible?

"Yes." He shifts in his seat uncomfortably, pinning me with a frown. "Why are you so surprised?"

"Because . . ." I start, then stop myself when his frown deepens. "I mean, the other day you admitted you'd never gone on a date and now this. You can't seriously tell me girls haven't thrown themselves at you."

"I've had a few offers." He shrugs. "I wasn't interested."

He's looking at me intently before returning his eyes on the road, and I'm afraid to read what's behind that look.

"Oh." I purse my lips. "Wow." Well, look at that, a guy who values virginity. "Okay. Please don't take this the wrong way."

He gives me a wary look.

"You have this angelic vibe going on, but then you smile like you did back at the garage and bam! It's . . . I don't know, there's a little bit of wicked hidden under there, somewhere." I shrug nonchalantly.

He chuckles. "You make me sound so badass. What about you, Gracie? Got any ounce of wicked in you?"

I glance out the window and bite my bottom lip. "Do you believe the rumors about me?" I face him again. I need to see his reaction to my question.

Humor drains from his face. "No."

I pull my legs back up and hug them to my chest. The memory of that night after the pep rally flashes inside my head, haunting me. I wince, shutting my eyes.

Taking a shaky breath, I say, "Gavin and I, we'd been going out for a few weeks and he'd been hinting about us having sex. Then after the pep rally, we started fooling around in his car. It got heavy pretty quick. At first, I didn't think too much of it. I was a lot more innocent and trusting back then, so I just went along with whatever he was doing.

"But when he became too intense with his touches, I realized his intentions. I got uncomfortable, so I stopped him and demanded he take me home. Which he did, but he was pretty pissed about it. He called me a cock tease." I swallow the lump now blocking my throat, then whisper, "'The apple doesn't fall far from the tree. Like mother, like daughter.' That's what he said before he grabbed my arm and dragged me out of the car. He left me standing outside my apartment, confused and hurt, and drove off. I thought—I thought he loved me."

I take a deep breath, remembering how my mom had

freaked out when I entered the apartment, crying with my clothes in disarray. "Nothing happened, but—" I stop talking and stare ahead. "When I arrived at school the next day, rumors were already circulating that Gavin and I had sex the night before and that he dumped me because I was sleeping with other guys. I shouldn't have let them victimize me like that. Naturally, everyone believed him without a second thought, and I became the school's official slut."

I bite my cheek and exhale. "Lithium" by Nirvana fills the silence. Eventually, I add in a small voice, "So, yes, I'm still a virgin, too."

At some point during all this, he'd parked his truck on the side of the road.

From the corner of my eye, I see Sol's hand move. He reaches for me, and his long fingers circle my neck, pulling me toward him.

At first, I resist, too embarrassed to move.

What if he pities me? I don't want his pity. Or anybody else's, for that matter.

"Come here," he murmurs in a soft voice. His gentleness is my undoing.

Quickly, my fingers unbuckle my seat belt. I move closer to him, burying the side of my face into his shoulder, fighting back tears. Gavin is not worth my tears.

Silently, Sol starts driving again, and we stay like that for the rest of the drive.

"What Gavin said after Mass . . . is it true? Did you really hit him?"

Sol's body tenses. I lift my head to meet his gaze, but he's staring straight ahead, jaw clenched.

"Yes."

His answer leaves me breathless for a few heartbeats. No

one has ever stood up or fought for me, other than my mom. "Why did you do it?"

"He hurt *you*, Grace. How could I not?" Sol's words are barely audible.

*Thud.*

*Thud.*

*Thud.*

That sound increases in volume and speed in my ears as his words play on repeat in my head.

Oh, gosh. "Thank you."

His chest rises as he inhales deeply. He doesn't say anything for several seconds. He sighs, then says, "I might not be a connoisseur on how to treat women, but what he did, it wasn't right."

Sitting here in Sol's truck, leaning into him like he's my anchor, I feel the heaviness that has been following me for three long years slowly melt away. Having Sol's hand cupped around my nape protectively breaks me and eases the pain in me at the same time.

I'd never told anyone other than my mom what happened that night.

But I didn't even hesitate with Sol. I trust him. And that both exhilarates and scares me.

# sixteen

*Sol*

WHEN WE ARRIVE AT RANGER'S COVE, I PARK THE TRUCK and jump out. My thoughts are still consumed by what Grace told me. I'm not one to hate. It goes against what I am and what I stand for. I've always been taught to forgive and be understanding. But Gavin? I could hate him easily. In fact, I think maybe I do.

*"Love your enemies and do good to those who hate you."* Luke 6:27.

For once in my life, I wish I could get a one-day hall pass to *feel* all the emotions I hold back. I bet my soul would be lighter for it.

"You okay?" Grace asks, tentatively touching my arm, and some of the tension melts away.

I nod, forcing a smile, unable to form words for fear of speaking what's really on my mind. We're here to have fun, and I don't want to be a killjoy.

She laces our fingers and tugs my hand gently. I follow her on a dirt path flanked by trees. Minutes later, we spill out into a small clearing with a view of the Saco River ahead of us. I've never been here before.

Beside me, Grace literally vibrates with energy the closer we get, increasing her pace, so I have to lengthen my strides to keep up with her.

We stop just as a group of guys our age are leaving, their hair and clothing wet. I lean forward, eyeing the water below, then glance at Grace. Her hands grip a rope I hadn't noticed before, and she's wearing a wide grin on her face. She kicks off her shoes and shakes her arms.

"What are you doing?"

"Rope swinging."

I suck in a deep breath, trying to slow my panicking heart. "Wait, it's almost a thirty-foot drop to the water. And you're not dressed for swimming."

She laughs, the sound reminding me of the beginning of spring. "It's not that high. I've done this before. But we could walk farther down this trail and jump off a twenty-foot cliff if you prefer." She adds the latter in a teasing voice.

"God, no." I shudder. "What kind of person jumps off a cliff for fun?"

She winks at me. "You have no idea what you've been missing."

She's crazy.

But she's also kind of awesome.

I watch anxiously as Grace tightens her hold around the rope with both hands. She looks over her shoulder at me, grinning wide, then looks back into the shimmering water below. She sprints forward, her bare feet gaining momentum as she nears the edge of the cliff. Then she throws her full weight into the jump, the rope swinging with her body. When she's about thirty feet above the water, she lets go and does a backflip before her body disappears beneath the surface of the water.

Leaning my shoulder on the nearest tree, I watch,

hypnotized and slightly light-headed as she repeats the process over and over. Eventually, she stands in front of me, water still dripping down her body and—

"Come on, Sol. Your turn." She nudges my shoulder with her hand, pointing at the rope.

But my legs seem to have lost the ability to move. I watch her as she squeezes the water from one braid, then the second. She looks really young without makeup. So beautiful.

My eyes veer down, and I groan inwardly. Her white T-shirt is plastered against her body, accentuating the outline of her purple bra. The exposed skin of her midriff looks so soft, my fingers itch to touch it. Shifting my weight from one foot to the other, I drop my eyes to her mid-thigh denim shorts, checking out her amazing legs.

Christ, I can't stop staring at her. My dick seems to have forgotten the little promise I made to myself, and he's suddenly very interested in being more than friends.

She coughs, and my head snaps up. The look she gives me makes it clear I wasn't subtle at all. She chooses not to comment on it, thank God. "So? Will you try it?"

I clear my throat to get rid of the tightness holding my voice captive. "No way am I dropping into that river."

"Oh, come on. It's *fun*! Wait, can you swim?"

"Like a fish." I turn away and eye the long drop down, shuddering. I don't mind heights, really. But plunging into that water . . . into the unknown—

"Do you want me to jump in too? Together, I mean?"

The thought of my body pressed against hers makes my breath stall. God, I want to jump her.

Uh, I mean, with her.

Jump *with* her.

"I'd probably crush you once we landed in the water."

She snorts. "Yeah, you would, you big giant."

I clutch my chest, pretending to be wounded by her words. "Way to go crushing my fragile ego, Grace."

This time, her shoulders shake in laughter, but I can't see her eyes or her mouth because she's staring at the ground, kicking dust with her foot.

"Fine. I'll do it." I give in just so I can see those stunning eyes leveled on me. "But if I die, I'll come back to haunt you."

All of a sudden, she leaps up my body and hugs me, arms and legs wrapped around me. Her entire front is plastered to mine. "You're going to love it!"

My body fires to life, and my brain's yelling, *"Oh my God. Her tits are just so round and soft against my chest. She smells like water and vanilla waffles."*

And *dear God*. I'm hard again.

I angle my hips to the side and wrap my arms around her, never wanting to let go. She gasps when I tighten my arms, burrowing her tiny body deeper into mine. My nose automatically presses into her hair, breathing her in.

She shivers. Goosebumps spread on her arms as she pulls back and grins. She plants her lips on my cheek in a noisy kiss. "Go get it, tiger." Her legs uncoil from my waist, and I bend my knees slightly, setting her on the dusty ground. She's staring at my chest now with a horrified look on her face. I glance down at my shirt and see a wet spot there.

"Uh, sorry. W-water from the river." She licks her lips, still avoiding meeting my gaze.

"If you say so," I tease her.

She buries her face into her hands and mutters, "Oh my God, Sol!"

Knowing she'll get more embarrassed if I laugh, I press my lips tight to stop myself from saying anything else. She's seriously the cutest chick ever. Two weeks ago, I would've never imagined I'd be here with her, laughing and watching her get flustered.

"Okay. Let's do this," I say before I lose my bravado. I kick off my shoes, then grab the hem of my T-shirt and pull it over my head. I stretch my arms while eyeing the long drop to the water below, and my heart beats faster.

"Having second thoughts?" Grace asks. My gaze cuts to her, and I catch her taking me in with her lips parted. My muscles flex in response as if she's actually touching me. When she notices me staring back, she rubs her hands over her cheeks and averts her gaze and mutters. "Okay, let's see how brave you are."

I stride forward and grab the rope, trying to shake off the shiver her intense perusal caused. I could easily get addicted to this feeling.

Within seconds, I'm taking deep breaths to calm my nerves. Then I sprint forward like I've seen Grace do multiple times, my heart racing and blood roaring in my ears. I'm definitely going to die while trying to impress Grace with my non-existent rope swinging skills.

I kick off the cliff, and then my feet are in the air, and I'm wondering why the hell I agreed to do this.

But as the adrenaline starts rushing through my system, the rope swings me back toward the tree line, and there's this moment where I feel invincible, free—until I hear Grace yelling for me to let go of the rope.

And I let go, close my eyes, and pray feverishly.

My feet hit the water first, then the rest of my body joins. Then silence. My arms start slicing through the water, and within moments, I'm at the surface, breathing hard. I glance up at the trees and see Grace jumping up and down while clapping her hands.

I swim to the shore and return to her side, grinning wide.

"You did amazing!" she gushes, hugging my waist as soon as I'm within arm's reach. "Wasn't that fun?"

My face finds the crook of her neck, hugging her back, smelling her hair. "It was kind of fun."

She giggles and steps back, hooking her arm around mine. "Want to try again?"

"Yes," I say automatically because rope swinging and seeing Grace laughing like this are my new high as everything else fades in the background, and I allow myself to have fun, like, really have fun for the first time in a long time.

✠

*Grace*

We're driving back to Portland after spending four hours in Ranger's Cove. For me, it's the most amazing four hours I've ever had. It's still hot out, so our clothes are almost dry.

I lift my legs and curl them under me onto the seat, sleepy but happy. "Thank you for today, Sol."

I can feel his eyes on me and a smile in his voice as he says, "I think I'm the one who needs to thank you, Gracie." He pauses. "Tired?"

"But happy," I counter, then glance out the window and squint, realizing we're not on the same route we used heading to Ranger's Cove. "Where are we going?"

"Just a little surprise." He sounds pleased with himself. "We're almost there."

Before I can open my mouth, I read a flashing sign that says Saco Drive-In. He makes a right and rolls down the road. He parks outside what looks like a snack bar.

"We're watching a movie?" I'm suddenly awake and looking out the window, excited. "I've never been to a drive-in cinema before."

He smiles at me, and it's so tender it steals my breath away. "I'm glad your first drive-in experience will be with me then."

I scramble out of the truck and stretch my legs. As I reach back inside the cab to grab my purse, Sol's hand covers mine, sending a shiver down my spine. He yanks his hand back as if the contact burned him.

"My treat." He flashes me that half-smile, then unfolds his long frame from the driver's seat. He rounds the Chevrolet and stands beside me. "Come on. Let's hurry so we can beat the line."

We head toward the snack bar where there's, in fact, already a line snaking around the little shop.

Ten minutes later, we walk out carrying two huge bags of popcorn and drinks. After settling back inside the truck, he weaves his way slowly toward the screen several feet away.

"What are we watching?"

"*Transformers.*" He points at the board listing the current movie showing. I didn't notice it when we drove in.

We're sitting on a pile of blankets in the bed of his truck when the movie starts. Despite the warm night, there's a light breeze rolling through the open-air field, causing me to shiver. Sol grabs another blanket and throws it over our legs, then slides his arm across my shoulders and tugs me close to his warm body.

"You okay?" he asks, his lips brushing my earlobe.

I nod into his chest, snuggling closer. "Today was perfect. Thank you for spending it with me."

His entire body swells as he inhales deeply. "Glad you're not bored of me yet."

"I'll be sure to let you know when I'm bored," I shoot back playfully.

He laughs. "Smartass."

"Jackass."

He pulls back to look at me. "Did you just call me a *jackass*?"

I shrug and blink up at him innocently. "I thought we were rhyming words."

He shakes his head, silent laughter rocking his body as he pulls me to him. "You're a nice little surprise, Gracie."

I can't stop the big grin from spreading across my face. These moments are what friendships are made of. These precious, rare moments filled with teasing each other and laughter are what I've been missing. We fall into a comfortable silence as we wait for the movie to start.

"When's your birthday?" he murmurs in a lazy, deep voice.

My heart flips inside my chest, and I don't know why. It's just a simple question that requires a simple answer.

The opening credits scroll up on the white screen in front of us, and I say, "Why? Are you planning on surprising me? Because I love a good surprise party."

"Good to know. Come on, out with it."

"March twentieth. You?"

"September ninth."

"Cool."

The movie finally starts, and I shamelessly snuggle deeper into his chest and sigh softly. With stars twinkling in the dark skies and Sol next to me, I'm in heaven. This is pure bliss. And I wish I could draw out this one moment into a thousand more. A thousand more filled with the scent of his cologne and summer and his strong arms holding me close.

# seventeen

*Grace*

I T'S ALMOST CLOSING TIME AT THE DINER, AND I'VE JUST FINISHED clearing the tables with MJ's help. She dropped by an hour ago to hang out since I was closing today. I'm totally grateful that she came, to be honest. I have someone to chat with as I finish my chores and prepare what I need to make tomorrow's muffins. We filled each other in on what's happening in our lives.

She walks in from the kitchen and climbs on the stool at the counter. "I hate to break it to you, babe, but Sol looks at you like you're a unicorn or something."

I huff out a laugh. "A unicorn?"

She waves her hand and says, "Or something."

"I *am* something." I bunch one of the napkins from the counter, scrunch it into a ball, and throw it at her. Caught off guard, she tries to duck, but the ball of tissue bounces off her forehead.

"Yeah." She snorts. "A terrible liar, for sure. Keep lying to yourself that you two are only friends."

I throw my hands in the air in exasperation. "There's nothing going on. Even if I wanted—"

The diner door swings open. A gust of hot air rushes in

right before Sol's long legs follow in all their toned and tanned glory.

"Abraca-freaking-dabra," MJ whispers. "He's like a genie. You call his name, and he appears."

"No kidding," I mutter, hoping I'm not drooling. Sol looks good enough to lick.

*What is he doing here?*

He seems distracted as he ambles in our direction, the navy blue T-shirt he's wearing emphasizing his pecs and broad shoulders. He digs his fingers through what looks like freshly washed hair as his gaze meets mine and stays there for several seconds. MJ clears her throat, effectively breaking the connection. I want to kick her in the shin. Or somewhere equally painful.

"Hey," he greets, his eyes bouncing between MJ and me.

"Well, this is my cue to leave, I think." She hops down from the stool and rounds the counter to give me a hug.

"You don't need to leave—"

She snort-laughs. With her arms around me, she whispers in my ear, "Really? If looks could kill, I'd be ash at your feet. The way you glared at me for breaking that smoldering stare between you two . . ." She steps back and adds in a much louder voice, "I need to check on my grandmother."

And with a sly wink, she grabs her purse from behind the counter and heads for the door with a small wave of her hand.

Sol slides onto the stool MJ vacated, one side of his mouth hitched up in an almost- there smile. My breath stalls, and my knees get this tingly feeling. I have to grip the counter to hold my weight up.

Oh, *my.*

"Hey." He steeples his fingers on top of the counter and stares at me. I can't tell what he's thinking as his gaze roves over my face and settles on my mouth. His teeth bite down on his bottom lip as we continue to eye each other.

*God*, he smells so good. I imagine crawling over the counter, pressing my nose into the hollow of his throat, and breathing him in. My cheeks heat at the thought.

"You hungry? We're about to close up, but I can whip up a snack real quick if you want." I cringe, hoping he didn't catch the breathless desperation in my voice.

"Sure!" he answers, sounding just as eager, then laughs. "I mean, yeah. I could eat. Need help?"

"Oh, well, you can just sit there and relax"—*looking all pretty just for me*—"or you could come into the kitchen and keep me company," I offer, suddenly feeling shy.

"Now that's an offer I can't refuse." He flashes a grin and climbs to his feet. "Is your mom around?"

I shake my head. "I'm closing alone today. Why do you ask? Are you planning to do something naughty? Like ravish me in the pantry?"

I was only kidding, but my own joke surprises me. I'm not usually this playful. Especially with boys.

Instead of laughing, however, Sol sucks in a sharp breath, and his eyes become smoldering blue fire. Scratching the back of his head, he coughs a little. "Jesus, Grace."

The knuckles on his other hand gripping the counter are white. I may have pushed him too far. All of a sudden, I want to push him a little more, just to see how far it takes for his control to break.

It's such a bold and bad idea. And for some screwed-up reason, I can't stop myself.

"On a scale of one to ten, how nervous are you?"

"Three, maybe," he answers. "I've gotten used to being around you."

I breathe through the excitement and anticipation swirling

in my belly as I head into the kitchen. After tying an apron around my waist, I start putting out the ingredients I need to make waffles. I pre-warm the waffle iron, but my senses are attuned to Sol's movements as he shuffles around on the other side of the door. I'm dying to know what he's doing. I mean, what's more interesting than waffles?

He says something, but it's muffled.

"What?" I ask.

"You play the guitar too?" He ducks his head around the door, sounding surprised. He must have found Mark's guitar.

"It's Mark's." I toss my ingredients in a bowl. "You play the guitar, right? How about you play something for me while I make these?" I blink up at him and smile sweetly.

He stares at me for several seconds, his eyes growing darker. His fingers curl around the doorframe.

"What?" I whisper, trying to breathe through the quivers ricocheting all over my body.

He's staring at me, like *really* staring at me. Need, hunger, guilt, and finally resignation cross his face, then he straightens to his full height. "You look cute."

Heat fills my cheeks. I lower my head between my shoulders to hide what I'm feeling. I'm not sure when my feelings went from liking Sol to desperately wanting to spend every second with him.

I don't know what to do with the multitude of emotions tearing through me. How is it possible to feel like this, like nothing else matters but this moment?

Frankly, it's terrifying. Is this how my mom felt for my dad—this indescribable, intangible feeling? No wonder it almost destroyed her when he left. There's no way someone could recover easily after feeling like this for someone else.

It's just not possible.

God. I need to stop this before I fall in too far. Sol and I aren't meant to happen.

I stare down at the bowl and shiver when his fingers sweep loose tendrils of hair from my temple. He secures them behind my ear gently, brushing my skin.

"You cold?" he asks in a whisper.

I can't tell if he's teasing me or genuinely wants to know.

I can't look at him, though, because I'm afraid my mind is just playing tricks on me.

No relationships, remember, Grace?

Why the hell am I thinking about that? Sol and I are *not* in a relationship. At least not the one my stupid heart craves. But sometimes a hopeless heart is just that—desperate to feel like it belongs to someone, beating in the same rhythm as someone else's.

He's leaning closer now, his chest brushing my arm. And I swear I feel his heart beating as fast as mine. I put the whisk aside and grab the bowl of beaten egg whites, but his fingers brush the side of my body before dropping down into the bowl. He scoops up some batter with his index finger and puts it inside his mouth. He makes an approving noise in the back of his throat.

"Vanilla and butter," he murmurs, smacking his lips. "You smell like vanilla waffles."

I snort, my cheeks heating. "How would you know that?"

He scoops another dollop of batter and licks it off his finger. "Back in high school, whenever you'd enter a classroom, the whole place would smell like vanilla waffles. I *love* vanilla waffles."

Oh my God. Wow.

With that, Sol walks out of the room casually as though he's just told me the weather forecast for the upcoming week.

I finish preparing the waffles with a wide grin on my face

while humming "Sweet Child O' Mine" by Guns N' Roses under my breath, then make a quick job of preparing a batter for some muffins. My ears perk up at the light strumming of a guitar as Sol tunes it.

We're soon sitting across from each other in a booth with a plate stacked with waffles. Sol sets the guitar on the seat next to him and rubs his hands gleefully as he glances around the table. Within seconds, he's piled a few waffles on his plate, adding a healthy portion of chocolate and ice cream on them. Then, he bows his head and makes the sign of the cross. He says a grace prayer in a low voice with his hands clasped together on the table. I watch him, fascinated by the movement of his full lips. He ends the prayer the way he started it. Praying before a meal has never looked so sexy.

Don't get me wrong. I try to remember to pray before my meals, but sometimes hunger overrides all thought.

Sol grabs his fork and knife and digs into his food like a starving man, shoveling huge chunks inside his mouth.

"So good," he says with his cheeks bulging.

I laugh, shaking my head, and fill my own plate with a heavy dose of maple syrup and vanilla ice cream. "Glad you like them."

We eat in comfortable silence, our eyes catching a few times.

"The last time I ate waffles with ice cream was . . ." He trails off, his eyes losing focus. Almost sad. "My mom used to make waffles every Sunday after church. We called it Waffle Sunday. It was the only day I was allowed to have ice cream and waffles and syrup. Then we'd snuggle on the couch and watch movies." He smiles wistfully into his now empty plate, shrugging. "Sorry for being a downer. This just reminded me of her." He waves a hand across the table.

"Sounds wonderful." I dig around inside my head for

something that'll cheer him up but come up empty.

He pulls out his phone from his pocket. His fingers fly across the screen before he hands it to me. "Here's my mom and pop. Most people say I look like my dad."

I study the image of the man who's an older version of Sol and a woman with black hair standing next to him. While Sol is a carbon copy of his father, he definitely got his eyes from his mom. "Yeah, you do." I hand him his phone back, give his hand a comforting squeeze.

"What about you?" he asks. "Your dad, I mean?"

*Ugh.*

Talking about my father isn't easy for me, but Sol opened himself up to me. Plus, he's looking at me as if he wouldn't mind spending the rest of the evening listening to what I have to say.

"Never met him," I say quietly, folding my arms across my chest.

The oven timer goes off, signaling that the muffins are ready, thank God. I excuse myself and head to the kitchen. Moments later, I slip back into my seat and swiftly ask, "Weren't you supposed to entertain me with your guitar skills?" I smile, but I doubt it reaches my eyes.

He studies me for a few moments. He nods once as if he understands my need to change the subject. "Sure."

Grabbing the guitar, he scoots to the edge of the seat, then cradles it in his lap. He loses himself in his own thoughts as he thrums the strings, trying to decide what song to play. Then he stands up, humming under his breath. I catch the familiar notes of "Sweet Child O' Mine" by Guns N' Roses. He lifts his chin, his mouth tugged up in that familiar crooked grin as he stares knowingly at me through his lashes. I sit up straighter, my eyes widening.

I want to ask him how the hell he knows I love this song, but the complete bliss on his face stops me. Right now, Sol looks like an angel with a wicked side but plays his guitar like a rock star, humming the lyrics as if each and every word is precious. I make a mental note to add this memory into my Beautiful Memory Jar when I get home.

# eighteen

## Sol

BY THE TIME I STRUM THE LAST NOTE OF THE SONG AND LOOK up, Grace is leaning forward, eyes shining, mouth gaping, the tiny gap between her two upper teeth peeking. If I keep staring at her face any more, I'm not sure what I might do, so I stand and stretch.

"*Wow*. That was incredible! Are you sure your calling isn't to be a rock star?"

"Thanks." I give her my back and head for the guitar case, wearing a grin on my face. "I'm not good with big crowds. I prefer to give private performances." I steal a glance at her over my shoulder.

"Oh," she murmurs, blinking rapidly, then drops her gaze to the table and nibbles the corner of her bottom lip.

I grin at her bowed head, thinking how cute she looks flustered. After putting the guitar away, I return to the booth.

"Where did you learn to play like that?"

"YouTube videos and tons of practice. Luke also hired a private tutor to teach me—a kid who was looking to make money while attending music school."

"Playing like that requires dedication. Can you sing too?" she asks, her eyes bright with hope.

I laugh. "Er, no." She deflates a little. "It's only fair, you know. I don't want to be greedy and hog all the talent."

This time, she bursts out laughing. "How very considerate of you." The laughter fades and she asks, "How did you know? The song, I mean. How did you know it's one of my favorites?" The wary look I haven't seen in days is back on her face.

"You hum it under your breath all the time. Even back in high school," I say, watching her carefully for any signs of freaking out.

"Oh," she says again, dropping her gaze to her hand fidgeting with the fork, and adds quietly, "I didn't think anyone ever paid attention to me. They certainly spent time talking about me, but it never felt like anyone really saw me."

I slide my hand across the table, wanting to touch her. To soothe the haunted look from her features. Instead, I curl it into a fist and place it beside hers. Taking a deep breath, I tell her the truth. "Whenever you and I are in the same room, you have my complete, undivided attention, Grace. You always have."

She gasps softly, and her eyes meet mine. We stare at each other in silence, but my skin prickles with a weirdly fascinating sensation.

"Can I ask you something? It's totally fine to say no." She adds the last part quickly. She smiles and looks at the spot over my shoulder, her fingers tapping a quick beat on the table. She looks vulnerable, her eyes wide, allowing me to see how nervous she is. I mean, how can I say no to her?

"Sure." I settle back on the seat and stretch my arms along the back of it.

"Can I . . . can I kiss you?" Her eyes snap back to mine, and she hurriedly adds, "I know you're heading to Boston in a few weeks and—" She sucks in a deep breath. "I *really* want to kiss you. I promise I won't try to do anything else. Just kiss you."

Holy. Shit.

I take a deep breath, letting her words sink in, and realize I'm breathing faster than normal. My gaze falls on her mouth, and I literally stop breathing because that *mouth*, God help me. It's like a gateway to a whole new galaxy where secrets and wishes are waiting to be unveiled.

I need to kiss her. I want to discover the universe beyond those full lips. I've been fighting the need to kiss her since I walked inside the diner and saw her wiping down the counter. But my brain is telling me it's a bad idea and kissing her will irrevocably change me. Change my life. I know I won't be able to come back from that. But the other part of me, the part that has a hopeless, desperate crush on this girl, just wants to drag her onto my lap and let her do whatever she wants.

"It's getting late. We should probably lock up and leave," she says in a small voice when I take too long to reply. She pushes her hair back before standing up and starting to stack our plates together. Her gaze meets mine briefly. "Look, I'm sorry I made this awkward. It's not fair to you—"

I reach out, curling a finger through the belt loops on her jean shorts, and tug. But she doesn't move toward me. Instead, her grip around the plates grows tighter, and she turns to leave.

"Gracie." I tighten my hold, forcing her to set everything back on the table and look at me. "Come here."

I pull her close while placing my other hand on her hip. Then, I slide both hands in the back pockets of her shorts, pulling her closer until all I can see is her face and her lips—so close to mine.

Her chest rises and falls quicker than before, and I realize mine's doing the same. We stare at each other. I wonder if she regrets asking to kiss me. That thought makes my chest ache. Right now, in this moment, with my face inches away from her boobs, I'd do anything for a chance to know what she tastes like. My fingers skim along her arm and bury themselves in her hair. She trembles against me, so I know she wants this as much as I do.

Earlier today after leaving work, I drove home. My mind was preoccupied, and I was restless, so after taking a shower, I got into my car. And somehow, I found myself parking the truck outside the diner. Maybe this is why I came here; I don't know. But I really want to find out.

"Do it." My voice is a whisper. I'm almost breathless with want. I want to yank her down and kiss her myself, but she looks like she's about to flee. So I let her come to me. "Kiss me."

She bites her bottom lip as she comes closer. I'm glad I'm sitting down because my knees are shaking with anticipation. Then her lips touch mine, her eyes on me the whole time. Need has my fingers tightening in her hair as she presses her lips more firmly to mine. Her tongue peeks out, running along the seam of my lips. I groan and shift on the seat to ease the discomfort in my shorts. My mouth opens, and the second her tongue touches mine, my body rattles with a shiver. This moment feels sacred. Like a blessing. It feels blasphemous and holy all at once. It scares me.

Tugging her into my lap, I fist her hair in my hands as I incline her head further, fusing our lips together more firmly. But our noses are in the way, and we have to find the right angle to stop bumping into each other. It's frustrating at first because I want her lips on mine and her breath mingling with my breath. Our heads finally slant in the right positions, and our lips fit perfectly. We both exhale in relief and groan at the contact.

Something in me breaks loose. Suddenly I'm pulling at her hair frantically, and my kisses become hungry and aggressive. I'm trembling and desperate and all I can think is I've never felt anything like this before, and I don't ever want to stop or let her go. I don't need to wonder if she's enjoying this kiss too. Her hands fisted in my hair, yanking me closer and closer are all the answers I need. She's pressing her chest into mine, and I swear I can feel her heart hammering. Neither one of us wants it to end.

We break apart and gulp for air, and my hands leave her hair, greedy to explore other parts of her, but they end up on her hips, pulling her further into me.

"More," I beg, because right now, that's all I can do.

Beg like my life depends on it. At this point, I feel like I'm about to go up in flames.

"Fuck yes," she murmurs between my lips, throwing a leg over my thighs and sliding closer.

I'm hard, so hard, I'm falling apart. My hips jerk, seeking contact with her body. Her hands cup my face, my neck, moving down my body and under my shirt. It's like they can't decide where to land. I'm almost coming apart with just her touch. Oh, God. I need to take control of this situation before I shoot my load in my pants.

My fingers find hers on my chest. I entwine them together and pin them on my lap. She whimpers but doesn't stop kissing me. It feels so good. Why was I freaking out before?

Her hips start thrusting back and forth, and she moans softly. She scoots back until my knee rests between her legs. Her sounds become louder the faster she grinds herself on me. She yanks her mouth from mine and buries her face into my neck, jerking faster, moaning louder, and breathing harder.

Is she doing what I think she's doing?

Oh, shit. I swear my dick's going to hulk out and rip my shorts apart. My boxers are already wet with pre-cum.

I release her and move to grab her hips, but before I do, her back arches, and she whispers my name with an "Ooh" and it sounds like "Sol-ooohh." It's the sexiest sound I've ever heard. I hold her close as she comes down from her orgasm until I feel her ass shift. She leans back, sweat beading her forehead, pupils dilated. She looks down at the spot between her legs and shuts her eyes tight as if embarrassed. I'm sure if her skin were a shade lighter, her cheeks would be blazing red.

I run my fingers through her hair, swallowing the emotion stuck in my throat.

"You coming apart like this for me is the most beautiful thing I've ever had the pleasure of seeing, Grace," I finally tell her.

She groans, burying her head in her hands. "I've never done anything like this before. Felt like this." Her words are muffled, but I still understand what she says.

I grasp her wrists and tug her hands away from her face, then lift her chin with a finger, leveling her eyes with mine. "Thank you."

The sound of a phone ringing startles us, breaking the looming silence. Her body jolts up, and she jumps out of my lap, stumbling to the other side of the booth. As soon as she has the phone in her hand, she answers it, pressing it against her ear.

I exhale deeply and scrub my palm down my face, not sure if I should be grateful or frustrated for the interruption. Will things change between us now?

Her soft voice pulls me out of my thoughts.

"At the diner," she says, peeking at me from below her lashes, a smile curling her lips upward. "I'm almost finished. I'll be home in twenty minutes." She nods as she listens to whoever is on the other side of the call—her mom would be my guess.

"See you in a few minutes. Bye." She ends the call and looks at me while pressing the phone against her lips.

Now the air is filled with a different kind of tension, awkward and weird. She's probably thinking, *What now?* Because it's the same thing I'm thinking. It's like we crawled inside a hole full of awkwardness.

My fingers play with the beads of my bracelet, and I flash her a smile. "Let's clean up so I can get you home."

"Okay." She looks relieved and jerks into action as if she'd been desperately waiting for me to say those words. She sprints toward the kitchen, shoving her phone inside the back pocket of her shorts.

For the next ten minutes, we clean up the kitchen and the booth in silence. I can't stop looking in her direction. Her curly hair falls around her shoulders in a rumpled mess, thanks to my eager fingers.

The cute, shy smile she sends me before resuming her work has me hopeful that she's more embarrassed than regretful. As for me, I could never regret anything that happened tonight. But that doesn't mean it doesn't scare the hell out of me.

# nineteen

*Grace*

FRIDAY MORNING, I ROLL OUT OF BED WITH A POUNDING headache. I feel like I slept inside a bottle of alcohol. But my mouth feels fine, and I don't remember drinking last night. Maybe I'm just drunk on Sol's kisses.

After he followed me home in his truck and walked me to my door, we tiptoed around a simple goodbye.

The kiss had been, in one word, phenomenal. It was like kissing in the rain with the sun shining overhead. Kissing Solomon Callan was like being swept away by an unpredictable storm. Then I came on his knee.

I was so embarrassed at first, but after replaying the moment over and over in my head, thinking about it, thinking how much I loved the feeling of absolute bliss rushing through me and the way Sol watched me with pure fascination and need at that moment, I decided I didn't have anything to be embarrassed about.

Four o'clock this afternoon finds me sitting in my usual booth at the diner, unable to concentrate on the task of researching courses and basically doing anything that could possibly help me narrow down what I want to do in college next fall. What I really want to do is throw my laptop across the room.

My mind replays last night over and over. At some point, I

check my phone to see if he's called or sent a text but remember we haven't exchanged phone numbers. I keep peeking out the window, hoping to catch a glimpse of him . . . but he doesn't appear. Eventually, my mom, who's been watching me like a hawk, walks over and sits across from me.

"How's the bookkeeping coming along?"

"Good, I think." I glance down at the laptop guiltily and close the document. I'm not ready to tell her my thoughts yet. Not until I have concrete plans. "I should be done in an hour."

She laughs softly, and my eyes meet hers. I can't help but notice how much happier and more relaxed she looks since she came back from the retreat.

"You're going to have a stiff neck if you keep twisting like that to look out the window. Let me guess. Sol?"

My cheeks grow warm. "Not everything is about him these days, Mom." I ease the harshness of those words with a reassuring smile before returning my gaze to the laptop and pretend to type.

"He's in Boston."

My head snaps up at the words.

"What?" Why would he go to Boston this early? Unless what happened yesterday scared him off.

"I dropped by St. Peter's to talk with Father about the food drive in fall. He mentioned Sol would be heading there today. He had to take care of some things before school starts."

My heartbeat slows down.

"You two have been hanging out together a lot recently." She eyes me closely. "Is there something going on?"

I shake my head a little too hard. "No. Just friends. I promise. Besides, that's what you wanted, right? For me to find more friends?"

She nods, still studying me. I squirm in my seat, feeling uneasy.

"I did. I still do. But I'm worried about you two. The way he looks at you, Gracie. It's not the sort of look you see on the face of a future priest. He looks at you with eagerness."

"Mom—"

"Just be careful, okay? I don't want to see you hurt again."

I nod, unable to hold her gaze for longer than several seconds.

Even though I knew well enough that he'd be leaving in a few weeks, I still chose to kiss him. It was a spur-of-the-moment thing. Between him telling me I smelled like vanilla waffles and playing my favorite song, something just changed between us. Something clicked as if pieces of a puzzle finally fell in place.

"One other thing," she continues. "I know you said you needed time. But you need to decide what you really want to do, Gracie. College starts soon, and we haven't even started buying what you need."

"Please, Mom. Not now."

"Yes, right now." Her jaw clenches, eyes narrowed. Then she takes a deep breath through her nose and out through her mouth, and I know she's trying to control her rising temper. "I've been patient with you. I've worked so hard to get you into Brown. And I know. I know I went about it the wrong way and did some things that made you resent me—"

"Stop, please." I squeeze my eyes shut, hating myself, hating that fifteen-year-old brat who despised her mother for things she didn't understand. "I didn't . . . I was stupid, and I didn't understand or see the whole picture until you told me what happened between you and your parents."

I open my eyes and find her watching me with a gentle expression. I bite the inside of my cheek nervously. "But I can't just do whatever you choose for me. Psychology was your dream. Going to Brown was your dream, Mom. Not mine. I love you, but I need to do this my way. And right now, I really don't think I'm ready to start college this year. I need time. *Please.* I need you to understand."

She opens her mouth to say something but seems to think otherwise. Instead, her lips tighten. She looks angry as hell, but at some point, I need to stand my ground.

Mom's eyes lower, and she slides her hand across the table over mine, squeezing once.

"I've been wondering," I say quickly, effectively changing the subject. "Maybe we can talk later tonight? About what you wanted to tell me a few weeks ago?"

She visibly tenses. Her hands shake above my own. Her reaction makes my insides tighten almost painfully. "I'm not . . . I still need some time, okay?"

"Okay," I mumble, somewhat relieved even though I'm the one who brought it up.

She stands up and smoothes down her apron before turning and walking away with her head down.

I roll my eyes, but the tears burning in them make it hard for me to appear as indifferent as I'd like.

Mom has been saving for my college fund for as long as I can remember. Then five years ago, her parents offered to contribute since I was their only grandchild even though the first time I met them was when they visited us the summer I turned thirteen. My mom hardly ever talked about them. It was the worst and the best summer I've ever had. Worst because I could feel the tension between Mom and my grandparents and best because I was so excited to finally meet them. My family.

Two years ago, they gifted me the Fiat on my birthday. At first, Mom refused to accept it, saying she didn't want to depend on them and give them the satisfaction of thinking she needed their help or charity. Eventually, she gave in after I cried and begged her for weeks. After that, my grandparents didn't put pressure on her about wanting to visit me. I have a feeling they wanted to, though, but after everything that had happened between them and my mom, they were handling the situation with care.

We talk on the phone from time to time, though.

I swipe the palms of my hands on my ripped jean shorts and inhale deeply. Shoving my earbuds into my ears, I scroll through my phone, picking a random song on my playlist. I pull the laptop closer, push any thoughts of college and Sol to the back of my mind, and get lost typing out my options.

The next time I look up, Sol is standing next to me, his thighs brushing the edge of the table. I glance at the clock on my laptop and realize I've been working for an hour straight. I look up again. His cap is pulled low, as always, and I can't really see his eyes properly. But from the way his focus is aimed solely on me, I know he's inspecting me closely.

"I thought you were in Boston."

He nods, tugging his cap a little down his forehead.

"So we should really exchange numbers," he declares, leaning forward and planting his palms flat on the table.

My eyes drop to those hands, those hands that touched me with so much adoration last night. Those beautiful hands—

"What do you say?"

My gaze snaps up to his. "Yeah. Sure! I mean, totally." I press my lips together to keep from rambling any more.

Sol grins, moving around the table and sliding into the seat across from mine. He pulls out his phone, then stares at me expectantly.

Oh, God.

We're doing this. We're really doing this.

# twenty

*Grace*

MY HEART IS BOUNCING AROUND IN MY CHEST THE WHOLE time Sol and I exchange our numbers. I wonder if he can hear how loud it's beating. Or the way it's trying to break free from its cage at the mere sight of him. Goosebumps spread up my arms when the tip of his index finger brushes along my knuckles as he tries to catch my attention.

"What time should I pick you up tomorrow?"

*Pick me up?* "What?"

"The show," he clarifies, uncertainty crossing his face. "Wait, you still want to go with me to the concert, right?"

Oh, crap. "Yes! I still want to go with you. In fact, I've been looking forward to this the whole week—"

"I can see that," he teases, then snickers.

I laugh, my gaze darting to the side, and see my mom watching us from the counter. Her words flash inside my head.

*Just be careful, okay?*

I look away, breaking eye contact, and return my attention to Sol, who's studying me with a concerned look. His gaze follows the path mine traveled seconds before.

"Everything okay between you and your mom?"

"Everything's fine," I assure him, forcing a smile. I never

thought smiling would feel this painful. I'm the opposite of fine. I feel awful thinking about my conversation with my mom and guilty for not wanting what she wants. "Seven o'clock."

Sol blinks a few times. "Seven o'clock it is, then."

I wink at him. With a smirk, he stands up and lifts his arms to stretch, yawning. His T-shirt rides up, exposing a taut stomach and the trail of hair disappearing into the band of his shorts. Curling my hands into fists, I look down at my laptop, my cheeks on fire. I remember my hands on his skin there. My thighs squeeze together as heat curls low in my stomach.

God. He'd felt so *good*.

"Ivan and MJ will meet up with us at Mike's Bar on Wharf Street," he says. "Wear something pretty." Did his voice deepen at that, or is it just my imagination?

I look up and see Sol standing there, one leg bouncing as he watches me from under his cap. I wish his eyes weren't hidden behind locks of hair and that hat. "Leave the cap at home."

He laughs, giving me a two-finger salute before saying, "Got it. See you tomorrow, Gracie."

He says my name like it's a naughty little secret between us.

I bite down on my bottom lip as I watch him walk out of the diner, then focus back on the keyboard in front of me. I let the smile I was fighting so hard to conceal spread across my face.

Why must he become a priest? It's like dangling an apple in front of a very hungry horse, knowing very well he can't reach it. Eat it. That's how I feel every time I look at Sol; like I can look or maybe touch and kiss him if I'm lucky enough. But in the grand scheme of things, he doesn't belong to me. And to be honest, me and the Big Guy up there are on good terms. I wouldn't want to piss Him off. He's gotten me through some really tough times. Besides, Sol will leave eventually. And I still need to be right with God when that happens.

I sigh. At least I know what he tastes like. What his kisses and that almost-there smile feel like on my lips. The memory is imprinted in my brain forever.

Shoving the earbuds back in my ears, I force myself to focus on the work in front of me, trying to ignore the butterflies fluttering inside my stomach in anticipation.

✠

My room looks like it was attacked by a tornado. Clothes and shoes are scattered everywhere in my attempt to find something to wear and from the frustration and anger that have been building since my mom and I argued. She approached me again on my way out of the diner. I could see how desperate she was to try and understand why Brown wasn't my choice. Emotions were high, and words were wielded like swords, cutting deep and leaving gaping wounds in their wake. I said some really awful things to her; my mom, my best friend. I told her if she wanted me to go to Brown so badly, she could go herself. Maybe having me instead of following her dream had been a mistake. She winced with every blow, her face crumbling with every word I hurled at her. I don't know what got into me.

God.

What am I going to do? Why am I ungrateful and self-centered? I wonder who I inherited those traits from. Definitely not from my mother because she's the most selfless person I've ever known.

I feel like everyone is moving forward with their lives while I'm standing still, waiting for the world to nudge me in the right direction. Sometimes, I feel like I'm holding my breath, afraid that if I exhale, the world will slip from under my feet, sending me plummeting and I'll never get up.

The thought of calling Sol and telling him I won't be going with him tomorrow momentarily fills my mind, but that would mean spending the rest of the evening in my room with my wild thoughts, seething and pitying myself.

I groan and press the heel of my palms to my eyes, pushing back the tears of frustration threatening to fall. I want to punch something, tear something apart. What's wrong with me?

I drop my hands from my face and inhale deeply through my mouth.

Sol. So determined and patient and good. But . . . is he really just a friend? I'm not so sure anymore.

I want to kiss him again, feel his hands on my hips, even though my brain keeps screaming that it's not a good idea. I shouldn't get my hopes up.

*It's just a little flirting and having fun. Nothing serious,* I tell myself.

*Do you believe your own lies?* I inwardly ask, remembering how good it felt to come apart in his hands.

I shake my head. No more lustful thoughts of Sol today. Or at least for the next few minutes. I stop pacing and sit on the edge of my bed. Dropping my head to my hands, I wonder if:

a) My mom is right, and I was lying to myself when I told her Sol and I are just friends.

b) Maybe I could eventually enjoy and appreciate psychology and criminal justice and finally become a profiler.

*Her* dream.

I take deep breaths.

I need to get out of here. I glance at the clothes on my bed, but nothing seems appealing to wear. I need something new, something to perk me up a little.

I grab my phone from the nightstand and quickly text MJ, asking her if she has time to go dress shopping with me.

There's one truth in my mind: I'm trying to impress Sol. I want to please him.

I can't deny that and won't even try.

## twenty-one

*Grace*

W E WIND UP INSIDE A LITTLE BOUTIQUE IN OLD PORT. MJ asks me what I'm looking for, and I tell her I have no idea. When it comes to shopping, I wing it. My fashion decisions mirror my life choices. I can never settle on a specific style.

Subtly, I take in MJ's outfit, admiring her sense of style. High-waisted black shorts, white tank top that shows off her flat stomach, and a pair of red and blue ballet flats. Her chestnut brown hair is tied in a loose bun at the base of her neck. It hits me how stunning she is. So stunning I feel self-conscious standing next to her.

She catches me staring and smiles confidently. I notice two of her lower teeth aren't straight, and I'm stupidly relieved. At least she has a flaw.

"What?" she asks.

"You're beautiful," I tell her.

"Yeah?" she asks, with a pink tinge to her cheeks. "Thanks."

I nod and feign indifference, but my lips are twitching, fighting back a smile. "It's disgusting, actually."

She blinks at me, probably gauging how serious I am. Then she laughs. "Bitch, please. You're so sweet-looking it's giving me a toothache."

I snort out loud. "Come on, help me find something to wear."

We head toward an aisle full of dresses. MJ plucks a few from the rack with efficiency as if she does this every day. She dumps them in my hands, then points me to the changing room. "Try this one"—she points to an olive green off-the-shoulder dress—"and put those beautiful shoulders on display."

"Are you always this bossy?" I grumble, stepping into the room the size of a shoebox and stripping off my shorts and T-shirt to slip on the dress. I study my reflection in the mirror, tugging up the drooping neckline.

Hmm. If it were to dip any farther, I'd end up being the showstopper instead of part of the audience.

"You have no idea. Just ask Ivan." She giggles, and from the mischievous gleam in her eyes, I'm certain we're talking about completely different things.

I push back the curtain and step out, sweeping a hand down my body in flourish. She eyes me up and down critically, tugging the dress here and there.

"Not sure how I feel about this." I point at my chest where the swell of my boobs is literally saying hello to MJ. "I'm trying to impress, not tempt."

She laughs, ushering me back inside the room. "Let's see the next one."

A red halter dress catches my attention. My mom likes to quote one of the greatest fashion icons, Bill Bass, "When in doubt, wear red." I do exactly that, then stand back and look in the mirror. It fits snugly around my chest down to my waist, then flares out.

"Speaking of impressing . . . you and Sol . . .?" MJ starts saying and trails off.

"What about it?" I ask, smoothing my palms over my hips, loving the way the light material hugs my figure, stopping mid-thigh.

"Are you two together *together*, or just together?" she says. "Messing around."

Definitely messing around. All I know is I love kissing him. I love that he sees *me*. It's hard to believe someone finally can see me when I've made every effort to be invisible.

"Nothing has changed since the last time you asked me."

"Huh." She's silent for a moment. "I wonder if Sol has gotten that memo yet."

I duck out of the changing room and stand in front of my new friend, arms spread to the sides. "He's definitely gotten the memo. In fact, he's pretty much the one issuing the memo." I spin around slowly. "What do you think?"

"Wow." Her mouth drops open. "*Wow*. That boy will fall from grace as soon as he lays his eyes on you."

I choke out a laugh. "What?"

"Those hips are going to kill him."

I bite my bottom lip and study my reflection again. "Maybe I should get another dress?"

"What? No!" she protests. She eyes me up and down. "I gotta say, I find your hips very disgusting."

"Oh, shut up." I laugh at her use of my earlier words, my cheeks burning at her compliment. It's been a while since I bought myself something pretty, and I really love this dress.

I pay for the dress, and we leave the shop. When we reach the spot where our cars are parked, I hug her, thanking her for agreeing to go with me, then we part ways.

Driving home, I feel particularly blessed for Sol and MJ. One month ago, I didn't have friends. Now I have two, maybe three if I'm counting Ivan. He and MJ come as a package. I mean, that can't be pure luck, right? I believe they've been put in my life for a reason. I'm really looking forward to finding out what it is.

# twenty-two

*Grace*

"Wow."

That's the first thing Sol says as soon as I open the door. His eyes move from my hair pinned atop my head with curls falling down my shoulders to the red dress. They linger a little too long on the curve of my hips before moving down to my white Chucks. His Adam's apple bobs as he swallows. "You clean up well, Gracie."

"You too." I'm literally drooling, taking in the casual gray V-neck T-shirt that does wonders for his shoulders and arms, camel-brown chino shorts and black Chucks. I want to eat him up.

"Come on in. I'm almost ready," I say, hoping my thoughts aren't showing through my eyes.

Curling a hand around the door to stop myself from touching Sol, I step aside to let him in. His gaze darts around the small hallway, taking in the walls decorated with pictures of my mom and me. He looks up, and a smile curves the corner of his mouth. "You still make these, I see."

"Yeah. How—"

"Told you. I noticed every little thing about you. I also remember when you showed the kids at weekend camp at church how to make them. You impressed the heck out of them."

My cheeks flame red, and my heart expands in my chest.

*Oh, my. Sol.* I clear my throat.

"Do they symbolize anything?"

I nod. "The paper cranes represent hope and peace. Have you heard of *Sadako and the Thousand Paper Cranes?*"

He shakes his head, his eyes lighting up with renewed interest.

"For my eighth birthday, my mom bought me *Sadako and the Thousand Paper Cranes* by Eleanor Coerr. It's a story about this girl, Sadako Sasaki. She discovered she had leukemia when she was eleven years old, a product of radiation poisoning from the bombing on Hiroshima. According to Japanese tradition, if you fold one thousand paper cranes, you'll be granted one wish.

"Her wish was to live in a world without nuclear weapons. She only managed six hundred forty-four paper cranes."

The brightness in his eyes dims. "That's really sad."

I nod. "Her efforts didn't go to waste. The rest of her classmates folded the rest. She was buried with one thousand paper cranes. Later, when I really got into origami, I did more research on it and found out that she in fact folded about thirteen hundred cranes and not six hundred forty-four as mentioned in the book. There's a monument of her at the Hiroshima Peace Memorial Park. I'd like to visit it one day, you know."

He flashes that almost smile at me and murmurs, "Hope and peace. It's a beautiful story. A bit dark, but beautiful regardless."

He takes a step closer, eyes of blue fire and lips parted. He stops abruptly and shoves his fists into his shorts pockets and clears his throat. "We better get going before Ivan bursts a vein."

Shaking off the shivers hijacking my body, I mutter, "Right," then rush to my room to grab my purse.

Several minutes later, we're heading out of the building

with Sol's palm pressing on my lower back. I can't help but lean back, absorbing his warmth. I know how dangerous it is to allow myself to enjoy his touch, but right now, I can't seem to think of any reason it's such a bad idea.

We arrive at Mike's Bar with a few minutes to spare. I glance up at Sol as we walk through the parking lot, suddenly feeling a little nervous. It's been a while since I socialized in a big crowd, and I'm a bit rusty. What if I'm not good at small talk? What if I make a fool of myself? What if I embarrass him?

I'm so caught up in my own thoughts, I don't realize Sol has slowed down until he tugs my arm. I turn to look at him, catching the crease on his forehead.

"You okay?" he questions, taking a step forward.

"Yes," I answer too quickly. "I mean, yes, I am. Why do you ask?"

"You seem a little tense." His eyes dart down to my sides, and I follow his gaze to my clenched fists.

"Oh." I flex my fingers. "I'm fine. I'm just—" Before I can finish the sentence, a crackling sound fills the air, drowning out all other sounds.

Sol visibly flinches, his eyes wide and alert as they dart around, scanning our surroundings. His chest rises and falls with quick breaths. He meets my gaze again, and I see an emotion I've never seen before. Fear.

"What's wrong?" I ask, bridging the gap between us. Panic stirs in my chest as my gaze splits between his now-pale face and searching for the source of his agitation.

He doesn't answer. Instead, he looks right, then left, and exhales deeply before bending to his waist with his hands braced at his knees. He shakes his head as though he's ridding himself of something awful.

"You're scaring me, Sol." I rest my hand on his shoulder and squeeze gently. "What's going on?"

He straightens and covers his mouth with one hand. "I thought . . . I . . . that sound . . ." He trails off, a haunted look on his face. He's looking at me but not really seeing me. It's so fucking weird. Then slowly, his face fills with color and light returns to his eyes. "I'm okay. That sound brought back some memories. I'm fine now."

He gives my hand on his shoulder a little squeeze and flashes me a tentative smile. "Come on, let's go. We don't want to keep Ivan and MJ waiting."

"Are you—?"

"Grace?"

I'm a little taken aback by the bite in his tone. It takes me a few seconds to reply. "Yeah?"

"I don't want to talk about it."

I nod and say, "Okay. Cool. No problem."

*Whatever. Message received.*

I start walking toward Mike's Bar, fast, increasing my pace when I hear his loud footfalls behind me. He calls my name. I ignore him and continue marching forward. Something is building inside my throat, gaining momentum by the second. It's anger. No, it's more than that. It's a mixture of anger and hurt.

Abruptly, I spin around, causing him to stumble back to avoid crashing into me.

I follow him, poking his chest with my finger, my breathing erratic with irritation. "I don't know what's going on with you, but you have no right to snap at me like that."

He raises his hands, palms facing me in a sign of surrender, his eyes wide with shock. "I'm sorry, okay? That's what I wanted to say to you, but you kept walking away from me." He pauses, lowering his head to meet my gaze. "I'm sorry. I didn't mean to talk to you like that."

My hand forms a fist, and I press into his hard pecs, glaring up at him. "But you did. Look, I'm worried about what just happened, okay? It's fine if you don't want to talk about it. I get it. Just don't try to bite my head off for caring about you."

"I remember you doing the same when I tried to befriend you."

I look at him, shocked and annoyed. "I—"

He sighs, shaking his head. "Sorry. I shouldn't have said that. I just . . . it's the Fourth of July. I don't have good memories of this day." He pauses, fixing those intense blue eyes on mine, looking remorseful. I want to ask him what he means by that, but I don't want to push him. "Thank you for, uh . . . caring about me."

His chin tips down slightly, smiling that stupid smile that makes my stomach do incredible things.

Damn it. Does he have to look so cute?

I roll my eyes, fighting a smile, and force my quivering knees to cooperate as I give him my back and pretend to be pissed off at him.

"Don't be mad at me," he pleads as he falls into step with me.

I look up at him. I can't help it and sigh. "You make it impossible for me to stay mad at you."

"It's my charm, isn't it?" he asks with a full grin now. My heart beats a little too fast, and I'm breathless.

Instead of answering him, I shake my head and laugh. His warm hand moves down my spine and rests on my lower back as he steers me toward the bar.

When we approach the door, Ivan and MJ are waiting outside. A few people are scattered near the entrance, either smoking or chatting.

Ivan is the first to spot us. He jerks his chin in our direction, and MJ turns to look at us as we approach. Sol's hand falls away from my back, and I want to beg him to put it back there, but I don't. I focus on a sullen looking Ivan, then at MJ, who is grinning wide at us.

"Finally," he grumbles, straightening to his full height but doesn't let go of MJ. "You guys took your sweet time getting here, huh?"

"Stop whining. We're here, aren't we?" Sol shoots back playfully, slapping his friend's back with his hand.

Ivan mumbles something under his breath as he herds his girlfriend inside the bar. I follow them in with Sol trailing me.

We stop at the foot of the steps in the basement, and I glance around the small room packed with people from wall to wall. My body buzzes with excitement, and I push the memory of the argument with my mom to the back of my mind. I haven't been to a party or a concert in forever, so I'm really looking forward to this. Maybe it will be the push I need to get out there more and enjoy life instead of spending my days at the diner and my nights at home, watching pointless TV or baking within an inch of my life or counting cracks in my bedroom ceiling.

Ivan waves at someone across the crowded room, then turns and nods for us to follow him. Sol's hand slides down my arm and entwines with my fingers before he shoulders his way through the mass of bodies. He's a head taller and bigger than most people in here, so it's easy for him to navigate his way to where his best friend is leading us.

We halt at a table near the raised stage. Sol hooks his arm around my waist and brings me forward to stand in front of him. Just when I think he'll drop his hand, his grip holds me tighter.

"Guys, this is Levi, my roommate at James Fredricks College." Ivan jerks his thumb at a guy with shaggy dark blond hair and gray eyes. He's standing next to a stunning blonde, one of his arms around her shoulders.

We shake hands while Ivan makes introductions.

"You already know who you'll be rooming with?" I ask.

Ivan nods. "Both our dads have known each other for years. So when we realized we're going to the same college, Levi's mom called in a favor from a friend on the board of trustees, and the rest is history."

"That's pretty cool."

MJ asks each one of us our drink preference, then she excuses herself and heads for the bar. Levi says something about checking if his brother needs something and takes off to the backstage.

According to Ivan, Levi's big brother, Jethro 'Jet', plays the drums for Sublime Chaos, which is the reason Levi is in town. He's from Northford, Connecticut, and he lives a few miles away from James Fredricks.

Since Fredricks is one of the colleges I'm looking into applying to for the next fall intake, I make the most of this opportunity.

"Hey, Ivan. I'm thinking of applying to a few colleges that offer a business degree. Maybe you could help me with some information?"

Ivan's eyes widen slightly as surprise registers on his face. He and I haven't talked a lot in the past, other than when I'm taking his order at the diner. He's probably shocked I said more than five words.

"Yeah, of course." He grins at me. "Wait, I thought you were going to Brown?"

"I changed my mind."

"And your mom—"

"Stop it with the questions, Ivan. She doesn't like it," Sol says from behind me, and there's a hard, unmistakable edge to his voice.

Ivan's eyes flicker above my head to meet Sol's. "Protective much?"

Sol's chest rumbles with a growl, and when I twist around to look at him, I find him scowling at Ivan. He looks at me and clears his throat as he attempts to school his features. I can't stop the smile on my face from breaking free.

"It's okay," I whisper.

He stares down at me and licks his lips, but he doesn't say anything. MJ returns with the drinks, shoving two sodas in our direction and then hands Ivan a Coke. The lights dim and a large spotlight centers on the stage as the band, made up of three guys and one chick, steps onto the stage.

They begin playing a cover of "When September Ends" by Green Day, and the room explodes with cheers and people start singing along. They follow that with a few more covers and then some of their own songs, which have a pop-rock quality to them that I find I really like.

After the first break, Jet grabs the microphone and flashes the crowd a dimpled smile. A sigh sweeps across the basement.

"I'd like to call my brother on stage." He shields his eyes from the bright spotlight aimed at the stage with one hand and searches the crowd. "Levi, where are you, bro?"

Levi detaches himself from the blonde he's with and jogs up on the stage. Standing side by side, the resemblance is eerie. Twin dimples on both their cheeks, straight blond hair falling over their eyes.

They do the one-arm hug thing men love, then thump each other's backs.

"If it weren't for him, I wouldn't be here today," Jet says, ruffling his brother's hair. "I thank him for pushing me to start this band with Jax, Will, and Fig over there." He jerks his thumb to the lead singer, guitarist, and the second drummer respectively.

"Want to show them what you got, baby bro?" Jet asks Levi, who shrugs. Then he turns to look at his bandmates and nods, before shoving the microphone in his brother's hand. He jogs back to the drums and resumes his position. He taps his sticks three times, and the beginning of "Livin' on a Prayer" by Bon Jovi fills the room.

The two brothers belt out the lyrics, their voices deep and husky in that rocker style that has everyone screaming and goose-bumps forming on my arms. It doesn't take long for the crowd to join in, me included. Soon, we're all jumping up and down, drunk on the lyrics, hands in the air and heads bouncing. By the time the song ends, I'm sweating and tipsy from the music.

Levi takes a bow and then waves while flashing those dimples to the crowd, before handing the microphone to his brother. He hops off the stage and shoulders through the crowd while accepting high fives. I can't help but wonder why the hell he isn't a part of the band. With a voice like that, he could go places.

"That was amazing!" MJ shouts in my ear, and I nod, my throat clogging with emotion.

The band starts playing the next song, and I'm lost once again in the vibrancy thrumming in the air.

When they finally take a break, I take a few seconds to breathe in the cigarette-perfume scented air. I don't care that my lungs are probably covered in soot from the smoke or my clothes will smell like I slept inside an ashtray.

Being here with my new friends, dancing and singing off-key, for the first time in a long time, I feel happy. I feel like I belong.

Sol shifts restlessly behind me every few minutes, so I turn around, intending to ask him if he's okay, but he beats me to it when he leans down, his lips brushing the shell of my ear, and asks, "Want to get out of here? I want to show you something."

"Sure. I need to use the bathroom first, then we can go."

His hand on my waist squeezes gently before dropping away from my body. I miss it immediately. The warmth, the re-assurance of his touch.

Sol says something to Ivan, then gives MJ a side hug before turning to face me. I wave a goodbye to Ivan and MJ. She wiggles her eyebrows playfully, and I remember her words from yesterday at the shop. Heat fills my cheeks.

"Stop it," I mouth, widening my eyes for emphasis.

She just grins and waves me off, mouthing back, "Enjoy, babe."

Once again, Sol leads the way through the crowd with me in tow, ducking every now and then to avoid being smacked in the face by a flailing hand. We make it to the small hallway, and he points out the sign for the washrooms.

# twenty-three

*Grace*

WHEN I STEP OUT OF THE BATHROOM, I'M DISTRACTED BY thoughts of how much I enjoyed the evening and wondering what Sol wants to show me when fingers wrap around my bicep from behind. My body tenses, and my muscles lock in place as my fight or flight response kicks in. I spin around lightning fast while reaching up and grabbing the hand with both of mine. Then, I twist the wrist attached to that hand. A painful groan reaches me as my assaulter's body doubles forward and my leg thrusts up, landing a swift kick on the stomach or groin. I'm not sure which because I'm too busy trying to disarm whoever it is.

"What the fuck?" a familiar voice grinds out. "Jesus."

I jump back and stare in horror at the blond-haired boy now bracing himself against the opposite wall, doubled over to the waist.

"Oh my God. Levi?" I step closer cautiously. "I'm so sorry. I didn't know it was you."

He lets out a low moan, clutching his lower stomach with his hands.

Not quite the groin area. Thank God.

His head lifts, and he squints at me through the bangs falling over his forehead. "What's wrong with you?"

"What's wrong with *you*?" I shoot back, my worry fading fast. "You should know better than to grab girls that way in a crowded bar's hallway."

He props his hands on his hips and attempts to straighten to his full height, but freezes, biting down his bottom lip in pain. I shift my weight from one foot to the other nervously.

"Did I . . . uh . . . you know, are you going to be okay?"

He stares at me with his chin dipped and chuckles or coughs, not sure which. "Well, my balls are cursing you right now, but sure. Yeah."

Oh. So I did, indeed, hit the groin area. Not the lower stomach. *Ouch.*

"Grace?"

I spin around and come face-to-face with Sol, a concerned look taking over his features. "What's going on?" His gaze darts back and forth between Levi and me, then back at Levi. "Are you okay, man? You look like you might pass out."

Levi points a shaky finger in my direction. "She's tiny and dangerous, this one. She should come with a warning." He attempts to smile but ends up grimacing. "I shouldn't have crept up on you like that. I'm sorry. I just wanted to tell you I have a prospectus of Fredricks and a few other brochures in my car that you might be interested in. Ivan told me you were planning on applying there. Thought I'd check if you wanted me to grab them for you."

"Oh," I mutter, feeling even worse. "That's really nice of you. Maybe you can pass them along to Ivan later, after, um, everything is back to normal? He can give them to me."

He nods. "Of course."

"Again, I'm really sorry."

He waves me off with a hand. "I'll live."

"Okay. It was nice meeting you, Levi."

This time he grins, and I notice how ridiculously cute he is. "It was quite interesting meeting you, Grace."

Sol's body stiffens next to me, then he mutters, "Come on, let's go." He jerks his chin to Levi. "Later, dude."

Outside the bar, he pulls me to a stop. Then he leans forward, aligning his body with mine and caging me between the wall and his large frame. He tucks a finger under my chin and tugs it up to meet his gaze.

"I can't believe you handled Levi like that."

"In my defense, he grabbed my arm. I didn't know it was him."

He flashes a grin down at me. "It's quite sexy."

I roll my eyes and laugh. "I told you I can take care of myself."

"Remind me never to mess with you." He pulls his hand back, sliding it down the side of my arm, and links our fingers together. He leads us back to where he parked his truck.

As usual, Sol waits until I'm buckled in my seat before heading to the driver's side and hopping in. Once he drives away from the bar, the silence between us remains. I had fun tonight, and I feel lighter and . . . happy. I've missed this, hanging out with friends and chatting about everything and nothing. And now I have something to look forward to. I can't wait to get my hands on the pamphlet Levi promised to pass along to Ivan.

I mentally check that off my list, then sigh happily.

"Where are we going?" I ask, eager to know where he's taking me.

His hands flex on the wheel, his gaze focused straight ahead. "It's a surprise." He tosses me a smirk before concentrating on the road again.

He leans forward, one hand leaving the wheel, and turns

on the radio. He settles on a station playing a heavy metal rock song.

I watch his profile as he bites his bottom lip, gaze focused ahead, forehead creased.

"What's wrong?"

He purses his lips thoughtfully. "He didn't hurt you, did he?"

I blink, wondering what he's talking about. "Who?"

"That guy, Levi. You said he grabbed your arm."

Oh. "No, he didn't. I guess I'm a little neurotic. I'm not used to people grabbing me, so I panicked."

His head tilts in my direction, and his blue eyes study me intently. "I don't like him."

I laugh all of a sudden, hoping he's joking. But if that muscle pulsing in his jaw is any indication, he's dead serious. "You don't even know him."

"He looks sketchy."

"'Do not judge, or you too will be judged,'" I say, quoting Matthew 7:1. "Are you supposed to judge someone before getting to know them? Isn't that like a sin or something?"

He shrugs. "I'm not a saint." He pauses, then adds, "You really have me pegged for a non-sinner, don't you?"

It's my time to shrug. "I don't remember ever seeing you do something bad in school or around town. But I've seen you do good things for the community, Sol. Several times. You're like this perfect guy—"

He shakes his head, his brows bunching into a frown. "I'm not perfect."

I'm about to open my mouth and tease him, but the troubled look in his eyes stops me.

"I'm . . . sometimes I feel like I'm hiding behind a wall. I feel things. I want things I probably shouldn't want."

"Oh?" I raise a brow. "Like what?"

He's quiet for a few moments as he switches gears, and I can't help but watch his hand at work, the muscles in his thigh tensing and shifting as his foot pushes down on the gas. His lips are pursed as a little frown forms between his eyebrows. I wait, giving him time, sensing that he's troubled and working something out inside his head.

The car slows to a stop, and I jolt upright. Looking out the windshield, I realize we're parked in front of an amusement park. I look to my right, taking in the way the lights from the surrounding buildings reflect on the Atlantic Ocean nearby. Old Orchard Beach is beautiful during the day but breathtaking at night.

"I haven't been here in so long." I smile, turning to face Sol.

He flashes me a full grin, looking considerably better than he had a few minutes ago. "My uncle used to bring me here when I was a kid. I'd live on the beach if I could. I love it here."

He's quiet, taking in the sight in front of us, and I'm eating him up with my eyes, the way the street lamp where we are parked illuminates his face.

He flicks his wrist to look at his watch, then glances out the window again. "It's almost time," he mutters, exhaling deeply.

"Time for what?"

"The fireworks." Sweat beads his forehead as he looks around like he's trapped and can't get out. "Fourth of July, remember?"

"You don't like fireworks?" I ask, trying to figure out why he looks scared. Then why did he bring me here?

He nods, then shakes his head. "Reminds me of the day my parents died. We were driving home from watching the fireworks on a Fourth of July."

Understanding dawns on me, my mind going back to the way he snapped at me earlier. He was hurting, and I didn't have the slightest idea what was going on with him. I shift closer, reaching forward and tugging his hand in mine, and whisper, "I'm so sorry."

He exhales loudly, then chuckles nervously. "I usually prefer staying home on the Fourth of July, but I wanted to bring you here today. You enjoy watching the fireworks, right?"

"Yeah. I mean, sure. But you didn't have to do this for me."

He shrugs, his gaze shifting to the space above my shoulder. "I want to. I have to get over it at some point."

"This is not something you just get over, Sol," I say softly. "And it's okay."

He presses my palm to his cheek. "You're here with me. It makes it better."

Those eight simple words crash into me like a storm. I scoot forward and pull him into a hug. "Thank you for bringing me here."

He pulls back and kisses my forehead like he always does. I'm addicted to his touch, no matter how fleeting. I savor and treasure each one.

We sit in silence when the fireworks start going off. Out of the corner of my eye, I see Sol flinch every time the crackling sound pierces the air, and my hand squeezes his a little tighter in comfort.

He tugs my hand, reclaiming my attention. What I see in his face has my heart beating wildly. He's studying me so intensely, it's giving me goosebumps on my arms.

"What is it?"

Instead of answering me, he gets out of the car and kicks his door shut. Within seconds, he's rounding the front of the car and opening the passenger door. He holds out his hand for me.

Intrigued and more than a little breathless, I unbuckle my seat belt and put my hand in his, allowing him to help me out.

As soon as the door slams shut, he pins me against the car, holding my face in his hands. His scent mixes with the scent of the rolling sea, creating a delicious elixir I'd love to bathe myself in forever.

His gaze roams my face as though he's memorizing every feature, and I can't tell what he's thinking.

"What is it, Sol?" I repeat the question, starting to get worried.

"Have you ever wanted something so badly, then something that's in complete opposition to that initial longing comes along, and suddenly, you find yourself forced to choose between the two?" He inhales slowly, then releases my face and shoves his hands inside the pockets of his shorts.

Disappointment crashes into me, but I tuck it inside my chest and fall in step with him as he leads the way toward the beach, watching the last of the fireworks disappearing into the dark sky.

I wanted him to kiss me. I want to kiss *him*. Why can't I take what I want? It's not like I'll be kissing him for the first time. But I have a feeling I need to tread carefully this time.

*God.*

*Have* you *gotten the memo yet, Grace?* I ask myself because *holy shit.* My heart's already invested in this boy, and every part of me wants to cling to him and never let go.

# twenty-four

*Grace*

AS SOON AS WE HIT THE SHORE, SOL KICKS OFF HIS SHOES AND stands barefoot in the wet sand. His eyes squeeze shut, and his head falls back. He gives out a low, satisfied groan as a wave crashes gently around his ankles. That sound, no matter how innocent it is, is my undoing.

I study his profile, taking in the way the lights from the pier play across his features. A sigh slips through my parted lips. Sol makes my heart trip over itself and my lungs fight for precious air. I don't even want to think about how soon he's leaving.

As if he can hear my thoughts, his eyes fly open. He turns to look at me with mesmerizing eyes, and I lose my balance. His hand darts out to steady me even though I wasn't in danger of falling.

I'm only falling for him.

"Whoa. You okay?" he asks, his eyebrows lowering in concern.

"Yes," I mutter quickly, giving him a nervous smile. "Thanks." I should move away, but his hand on me feels like an anchor.

His touch loosens, then pauses as if he doesn't want to let go just yet. After another wild thump of my heart, he releases me. He leans down to pick up his shoes from where he dropped them, letting them dangle on the tips of his fingers.

"You should try it." He jerks his chin toward my toes.

I'm about to kick my shoes off when I remember the state of my toes. I shake my head. "I'm good."

He smirks. "I don't believe you. You want to do it."

"Oh?" I raise a brow, eyeing him. "What makes you think that?"

"You're looking at my feet longingly. Unless . . . you have a foot fetish." His eyes widen, mouth falling open. "Do you have a *foot fetish*?"

"Oh my God, *no!*" I laugh. "Chipped nail polish."

He looks down. "I bet your toes still look cute regardless."

"You're so good for my ego. I think I'm going to keep you," I joke, kicking off my shoes and bending down to pick them up. When I straighten and look up, his gaze is on mine.

"Keep me?" he asks in a low voice that sweeps down my spine like a caress.

"I mean, I didn't mean keeping you like a pet or something. It's just—"

All of a sudden, he laughs the kind of laugh that comes from deep within his stomach, shaking his entire body. I forget I'm horrified by his suggestion and just stare at him, trying to remember the last time *I* laughed that hard. These moments with Sol are worth everything, so I steal them and tuck them in the pockets of my heart for later.

He notices me staring, and his laughter dwindles to a stop. His eyes, Lord, his eyes soften, heat replacing the humor.

"You're so cute when you're flustered," he says with a chuckle, but I'm still watching him, mesmerized. "You're staring, Gracie."

I snap out of the hypnotic moment. "I love the way you

laugh. It's beautiful."

He scratches the back of his neck, his mouth quirking to one side. I'm certain he's blushing, too. "Thanks." His voice is a husky whisper.

We walk along the beach in silence, lost in our own thoughts.

"What's your story?" Sol asks over the lulling of the crashing waves. "Tell me something about yourself that you haven't told me before." He pauses, unhurried. It feels like forever is ours at that moment. With a soft voice, he continues, "Tell me, who is Grace Miller?"

Dread is quick to make a nest in my throat, and it feels as if I'm choking on my own memories and emotions. Talking about myself is not something I like. In fact, I hate it. But I understand his eagerness to get to know me, the real me, because nobody wants to befriend a brick wall. In my core, I know there's nothing malicious about his intent. He's genuinely intrigued.

"Um, yeah . . ." I cough, trying to think of something, anything, to say, and when my mind goes blank from the anxiety, I laugh nervously. "I don't know. I'm not that interesting, I guess."

He shakes his head. "Quite the contrary. You've had my attention from the second I first saw you. Believe me, you are interesting. You intrigue me."

I shake my head and inhale a shaky breath. "I grew up here. I'm terrible at making life decisions, and I love baking, love making origami . . ." Damn it, that all sounded really lame. I scramble to find something more interesting to say. "I love cliff jumping."

He grins at me, probably remembering our day at Ranger's Cove.

"And I love kissing you."

His grin grows even wider as he pushes the locks of hair off his forehead. He didn't wear his usual baseball cap, like I asked. "You do?"

I give him a shy smile. "I do."

Those two words hang in the air between us. A breeze blows softly across the shore, sweeping the words up to the stars. A familiar shiver runs down my spine as I lift my nose, breathing in the scent of the sea. But there's a new scent mixed in. I smile happily, and his eyes seem to sparkle at that.

"It's going to rain soon," I announce.

He steps in front of me, and I stop abruptly. "How do you know? I've been wondering how you knew it was going to rain ever since that time when I was leaving the diner."

"Can't you smell it in the air?"

He shakes his head, his forehead creased in a frown. "What does rain smell like?"

"It's earthy, fresh. I can't really describe it. According to my mom, my great grandmother had the same . . . gift. Well, that's not the right word. But you know what I mean."

"Are you sure you're not supposed to be a scientist?"

"God, no. I wish." I laugh. "I'm not too fond of science." Looking into the distance, I say, "I've always been able to tell when the weather is about to change."

"Superpowers, huh?" He shakes his head, smiling. "You're badass, you know that, right?"

"I am, aren't I?" I toss him a smile.

"Charming, Gracie." He chuckles, shaking his head. "I mean, the way you accept a compliment. Very *graceful*."

I swat his shoulder with the back of my hand. "Ha! Ha! Very funny." I roll my eyes playfully at him. "Are you looking forward to sharing a room in the dorms with someone you've never met before? What if he ends up being weird or snores? Or likes to walk around naked?"

He huffs a laugh, but his gaze turns somber as he glances down at our ankles, deep beneath the surface of the water. "Yes, actually. Well, not the naked part." He chuckles. "I'm excited and nervous. But living with people who have the same goal as I do is going to be great for me. Have you decided what you want to do?" he asks, swiftly changing the topic and tilting his head to look at me. "In college, I mean."

I shake my head, crossing my arms around my middle, gaze focused on the ocean ahead.

We watch the way the green, blue, and yellow lights from the pier bounce on the undulating waters in silence, both lost to our thoughts. It looks magical, as though I could just wade over there and be swept into a different world. But, like most things, it's just an illusion.

I look at him. "You know when you're a kid and never thought you'd be required to make decisions because your mom or dad would always make them for you? Then suddenly, you're eighteen, and there's this pressure bearing down on you. Everyone wants to know what you want to do. Which college you'll go to, what your plans are . . ."

I press my right foot into the wet sand, digging deeper with my toes. "It's . . . that's when you start realizing you're not a child anymore. That the little bubble of innocence and bliss you'd been living in up until that point has well and truly been popped." I sigh loudly. "My mom and I argued before I left the diner today. I said some really mean things to her, Sol. I was such a bitch. She's been doing her best to protect me my whole life, and what do I do? I bitch and moan like a spoiled brat."

"What happened?" he inquires, frowning.

I tell him everything. How I want to choose my own path and not the one my mom has already decided for me. How I need more time to figure out who I am and what I like. And how I love her, but I need to live my own life.

"Can I say something?" he asks.

"Of course."

"Your mom wants the best for you, which is perfectly understandable. She loves you, and that's why she says and does the things she does. Out of love." He scrutinizes me intently, as if gauging my reaction. What he sees must make him comfortable or something because he continues to talk. "But you have the right to follow your own dreams. And if you make mistakes along the way, you'll learn from them. From what I've seen, you two are very close. Maybe you need to sit down and really talk? Tell her how you feel. What do *you* want to do?"

"I don't know. She's my best friend, too, so I don't want to hurt her. I think seeing me struggle to find my path makes her want to push me toward hers even more. I've toyed with the idea of going for business maybe. I've worked most of my life at the diner, helping with some business management stuff, and I really enjoy it."

He steps toward me, bringing his face closer to mine. "Yeah? Then do it, Grace. Whatever you choose, make sure it's something you want." He's speaking with so much passion, it makes me feel like I can do anything.

"Why do you have to make so much sense?"

He drags a hand through his hair. "I've been there, so I know what you're going through."

"It feels good to talk to someone who understands." I smile softly, but I can't stop thinking about the pained look on Mom's face. "My mom is everything to me. She's so brave, Sol. One of the bravest people I know. And wise.

"I remember when I was seven years old, back in elementary school, and we were on the playground during recess. All of a sudden, one of the black kids stood in front of me and frowned. He put his hand next to mine and asked me why my skin was lighter in color than his. He asked me if I was white or black."

I shake my head, remembering how confused I was by the end of the day. "That evening, I asked my mom why my skin was different than hers. I asked her if I was black or white. Do you know what she said to me?" I don't wait for his answer because I'm too swept away by the memory. "She told me I was whoever I wished to be. That beneath our skin, we all bleed red."

"She's pretty amazing, Gracie."

"She's the best." I hear wonder in my own voice. "She's my hero."

"Good." He bumps my shoulder with his. "We need more of those nowadays. If you want to talk to her, I can take you home."

I shake my head. "I'll do it tomorrow. She and I need a few hours to calm down."

"Of course." He drags his hand through his hair, then asks, "Okay, you have got to tell me how you handled Levi. I'm dying to know."

I cut through the air with a slanting stroke with the side of my hand and yell, "Karate chop!"

His lips twitch, his eyes dancing with amusement, and his eyebrows hit his hairline. "Good to know. I'll keep that in mind." He winks at me. "Let me guess. Your mom made you take classes?"

"Yep," I say, popping the "p." A small laugh slips through my lips. "She signed me up for self-defense classes when I was ten years old."

"Great thinking on her part. Not everyone you meet has good intentions these days. Better to be safe than sorry."

We walk in silence, our hands brushing lightly. I squint at the ground and try to make out the shape of our toes covered in water while gathering the courage to open up to him.

From of the corner of my eye, I notice him watching me.

He swallows hard before tossing his shoes aside and taking a step forward. His arm slips around my waist, turning me to face him. He pulls me flush to his body, making me go up on my tiptoes. His forehead touches mine, and his air becomes my air. The rapid beating of his heart mirrors mine, and I wonder, for just one second, if our hearts are telling each other what our mouths can't.

"I try so hard to stay away from you, but like a boomerang, I keep coming back to you. What have you done to me, Gracie?"

# twenty-five

*Grace*

HIS WORDS STEAL THE OXYGEN FROM MY LUNGS, AND THE steel bars around the cage housing my heart liquefy a little.

"Bewitched you with my womanly charms?" I joke, closing my eyes and brushing my nose against his.

"You sure did." He chuckles softly but turns somber fast. "I don't know what to do."

"I do," I say, pressing my lips on the edge of his mouth, forcing myself not to go farther. If he wants this, then the decision has to be his. "Maybe we should stop spending too much time together. I can't even begin to imagine how difficult this is for you."

He swallows, his gaze veering off to my left shoulder, probably considering my words. "Maybe, yeah." His arms tighten around me for just a few beats before they fall away.

Stepping back, he grabs his shoes and hands me mine. We continue walking, the air between us sparking with tension. How does someone come back from a revelation like this?

I clear my throat and attempt to form my thoughts. As much as I enjoy spending time with Sol, the constant tugging of the invisible thread connecting us becomes too much sometimes. It's like we're two magnets, drawn to each other the way only oppo-site poles can. We pull apart, but the magnetic field between us always draws us back together. It's inevitable, like the rising and setting of the sun.

I sigh. Time to change the subject.

I've never told anyone about my father. Maybe talking to someone else other than my mom will help ease this hurt, this feeling . . . as if something is missing in my life. I need to get it out before the words roll back down my throat and churn acid into my stomach.

"When I was six, my mom finally told me—after I bom-barded her with questions about my father's whereabouts—he left before I was born. So cliché, right?" I laugh, but it sounds bitter even to my own ears. "My mom was eighteen. She was due to start her undergraduate program at Brown University, but then, I happened. My *father*, whoever that person is, packed and left town, leaving my mom alone and pregnant.

"Growing up without a father wasn't easy, I won't lie. Every night before I went to sleep, I'd get down on my knees next to my bed and pray to God he'd bring him back into my life. I'd write letters to Santa, asking him for one thing only—my dad. Every Christmas Day, I woke up early, hoping to find my father sitting in the rocking chair by the window, waiting for us." After a moment of silence, I add, "It never happened."

I shake my head and smile at the memory of the five-year-old version of me, so hopeful and innocent.

"I watched other kids bring their parents to school events. Sometimes, my mom couldn't get time off from work. She had just gotten this new job as a maid for some rich guy, and she didn't want to risk losing it. So I had no one there." I shrug. "I don't care what anyone says; my father is nothing but a coward who didn't stick around and accept his responsibilities."

Suddenly, I'm feeling hot. Furious. I'm wearing too many clothes, and I'm sweating, and I need air. I knew I resented him, but now, this emotion inside me feels bigger.

"Come here." Sol tosses his shoes aside, reaches for my arm, and pulls me to his side. He wraps his arms around me, holding me tight. "God, Gracie. I'm so sorry. I had no idea," he murmurs into my hair.

"Same here," I mutter into his chest. "I mean, all that stuff just poured out of my mouth . . . I had no idea I'd bottled up so much inside me."

"How do you feel?"

I pull back and meet his gaze. "Slightly better. It's just—you see now where my mom is coming from. She sacrificed everything for me, her dream to attend college. Her parents wanted her to *take care of the problem* so she could move forward with the plans they had for her, and when she refused, she was completely on her own after that. Without a second thought, she withdrew whatever little savings she had and moved to Portland."

I squeeze my eyes shut and open my heart, letting the words bleed out of it. "Bev and her mom, Regina, helped my mom a lot when she moved to Portland. We moved out when I was about three years old, despite Regina insisting we should stay until my mom got back on her feet. I guess she didn't want to overstay our welcome.

"From what she told me later, she'd underestimated how challenging it would be being a single mom with no college education and an extra mouth to feed. Some of my earliest memories growing up were of various men, different ones every night, coming and going from our house. I must have been around four or five years old. She tried to shield me from her . . . activities, but it wasn't easy. We lived in a one-bedroom apartment. I slept in the bedroom, and she slept on the couch in the living room.

Then she got the job as a maid, and it kept her busy. I knew it wasn't normal for men to walk in and out of our house, mostly during the night. Bev's mom would pick me up from daycare when my mom couldn't, and we'd spend the afternoon baking at her house.

"Regina passed away a couple of years ago after contracting pneumonia. According to the doctors, her body became resistant to antibiotics and it finally gave out. She was like a grandmother to me."

I inhale quick breaths and squeeze my eyes shut to ease the ache in my chest. When I open them again, I find Sol taking in my features, and whatever he sees there has him cursing under his breath. His fingers cup my nape.

"What happened to your grandparents?" He practically spits the words, his nostrils flaring.

"I've only met them once. They visited us the summer I turned thirteen."

"And . . .?"

I finally smile. "They're a little snobby."

He chuckles.

"They opened a college fund in my name after the visit." I sigh, pressing my forehead to his chest. "Maybe they did it out of guilt for throwing out their daughter. I don't know. My grandmother calls me every once in a while. I have a feeling they miss their only child, but they are too proud to admit it."

He clears his throat. "You know dads are supposed to be there for their kids and take care of them, right?"

"I do."

"Yours doesn't know what he's missing."

I bump the side of his arm with mine and murmur, "That's really sweet. Thank you."

The image of my mom, looking tired and worried, flashes

inside my head, and suddenly, I want to go home and check on her. I lift my head to look up at Sol. "Please take me home? I need to talk to my mom before she goes to bed. She and I have this thing we do whenever one of us is pissed off with the other. We promised to never go to bed angry."

He kisses my forehead. After brushing the sand off our feet as best as we can, we slip on our shoes, and then he takes my hand in his. We start walking back toward the car. I didn't realize we'd wandered so far from the parking lot, so it takes us longer than I'd imagined to get to his truck. Sol keeps throwing cautious glances in my direction as if he's afraid I might disappear.

"What do you want?" I ask, attempting to break this weird vibe around us.

He stares at me, eyebrows creased. "Right now? Well, I want to take you home so you can talk to your mom."

I shake my head. "Earlier, you said you want things you have no business wanting." My voice shakes on the last word, but I forge ahead, feeling brave all of a sudden. "What do you want? You never said."

The frown deepens. "It's not important."

We stop in front of his truck.

"I don't agree with that. You are important. So whatever it is, is important, too. What do you *want*, Solomon Callan?"

He rolls his eyes and ducks his head down, but I see his shy smile as he shoves his hands inside the pockets of his shorts. He stares down at his feet still covered in sand. For just a few seconds, I wonder if he's going to answer my question.

Then he takes a step forward, pulling his hands from his pockets, and rests them on my hips. He lifts his head just a little and stares at me through his lashes, smiling softly. We just stare at each other, hearts wide open.

And for just an infinite second, I pretend we're two people

standing on the edge of forever.

"I want—I want you. I want to kiss you just like that night at the diner." He inhales sharply. "I see you everywhere. Even when I'm on my knees praying to God, I see you. It's as if you're that missing beat in my heart. I don't know. It sounds stupid. I can't really explain it. All I know is that it's you. It's always been you."

I blink up at him, my mind processing those words, but I think my brain cells are either fried or swooning because I'm still stuck on 'It's always been you.'

And then, the impact of his words hits me. His feelings echo mine, but I'm not about to admit that to him. Instead, I hike on my tiptoes and press a kiss on the side of his mouth. He inhales sharply, and his hands tighten around my hips as he murmurs, "Gracie."

And that voice, the way my name sounds on his lips, half groan, half whisper, seals the deal for me.

Holy crap. I'm *so* screwed.

# twenty-six

*Grace*

"**K**ISS ME, SOL," I WHISPER, CUPPING HIS JAW IN MY hands. "Forget for just one second you are you and I'm me. Let's pretend we are two people standing under the stars reveling in this magical moment. This is our safe space. No one is watching us. *Kiss me.*"

His forehead is bunched in a frown as indecision dances in his eyes as he stares at my mouth. Then it's like a switch has been flipped inside him. He makes this sexy sound similar to a growl and mumbles, "Maybe Ivan was right. I need to get you out of my system. Maybe I'll be able to move on after this."

And with that, he grips my hips tighter and walks me back until my backside hits the front of his truck. My back arches as I lean onto the hood, his body following mine as though we're caught up in a dance only our bodies know.

My dress bunches around my hips when I swing my legs up and wrap them around his waist. His narrow hips fit perfectly between my thighs, and the bulge in his shorts presses down on me. He shifts and *oh my God*. Oh, my *freaking* God! He hasn't done anything yet, but I want everything. I don't know what it entails, but I want it so badly.

His hand moves up to grasp the nape of my hair, his fingers

knotting around the strands as though he's afraid to lose control, then he watches me, his mouth pulling into that almost smile. His head lowers, and just before his lips meet mine, he *smiles*. Then he's kissing me hard, letting his mouth rest on mine for several seconds. And when he starts moving it, my hands grab his shoulders, scared I'll float away if I don't hold on tight.

My eyes fall shut on their own. Our groans fill the nightly sounds. My body writhes on top of the hard surface as I try to get closer to him. The hand on my hip slides up and under my back, and he lifts me as though I'm made of clouds, hugging me close. Lips still locked, he starts walking, and my eyes flip open. Within seconds, he's already made it to the back. He breaks the kiss to catch his breath. I suck in a lungful of air, again and again.

"Come on," he rasps, opening the backseat door and setting me down on the faded leather. I have no idea how he managed to dig out the keys from his pocket and open the door, but I'm grateful for it.

I scoot in, legs like jelly and my heart racing inside my chest. There's no way I'm going to stop him, despite telling him we should try staying away from each other.

Sol follows me inside and shuts the door. He shifts and turns until his large frame is on top of mine in the small space. Then without warning, we're all over each other. Hands and mouths, tangled limbs, racing hearts. We're gasoline. We're fire.

I reach down, brushing my fingers along his waistband, tentatively moving my hands to the front of his shorts. He sucks in a deep breath, closing his eyes, and swallows hard. Feeling brave, I snap open the first button and tug down the zipper. I glance down as my hands push the shorts over his hips and dip into the—

*Tap, tap, tap.*

The insistent knocking on the window yanks me back to

reality. Sol scrambles to cover me with his body even though I'm still dressed, then looks over his shoulder.

"Jeez, guys. You realize anyone can see you, right?" the guy yells, jerking a thumb to the lamp next to the car.

"Shit," I mutter, sitting up while Sol hoists himself up and pulls up his shorts. "Sorry."

He waves his hand. "Keep that shit behind closed doors." Then he turns and strides away to join a group of guys a few feet away.

Laughter bubbles up my throat. I slap a hand over my mouth, but the sound slips out anyway. Sol's hands pause, and he looks at me, his face still flushed, and his lips swollen from the kiss. He shakes his head and chuckles. When he's done and the laughter fades, we watch each other, acknowledging what almost happened.

Disappointed spreads through my chest, but at the same time, I wonder if it was a blessing in disguise. Lust makes people stupid and reckless. He would've probably regretted it later. How can I live with myself after that?

I force a smile and say, "Saved by the knock, huh?"

Sol exhales and steps out of the car without a word, slipping into the driver's seat. I follow him out and join him in the front.

# twenty-seven

*Sol*

TENSION CURLS AROUND MY SHOULDERS AND NEED BURNS A hole in my chest. I grip the wheel tight to stop my hands from shaking. I'm still reeling from the kiss and what almost happened in the truck at the beach.

Oh, God. I was so close. So close to having sex with her. And I'm not sure what disturbs me more; the fact we almost lost our virginity in a truck, of all the places, or the fact that I can't stop asking myself, *what if* I chose her?

I blink several times to clear my vision from the memory, then glance at Grace before returning my gaze to the road. Her eyes are closed as she sings along to Destiny's Child's "Independent Women" on the radio. She's a terrible singer, and judging by that cheeky smirk of hers, she knows. I hold back from saying anything. I need to calm the raging boner in my shorts, hoping it will get the message and lie low for a while. I focus on muttering a Hail Mary under my breath.

The song ends, and I hear her sigh as she wiggles on her seat as if she's trying to get comfortable, then settles down.

I focus on what she told me at the beach.

Now I understand Grace a bit better. Understand the insecurity I see in her sometimes, and how she often steers away from uncomfortable conversation.

I don't know what happened between Debra and Grace's father, and I don't have the right to judge. I just, I don't know. I guess, I wish Grace's father would have stuck around. I was lucky enough to know mine up until the accident. And I'll always be grateful for that.

"Okay, Grandma," Grace says, amused, touching my hand to claim my attention, then points at a parking spot across from her building. "Park over there."

"Grandma?"

"You were driving so slow I aged ten years by the time we hit the outskirts of Portland."

I cut the engine and lean back in my seat. I run my hand through my hair. "I'm sorry."

"You're distracted." She licks her lips nervously, fiddling with the strap of her purse. "Is it . . . is it what we almost did?"

My fingers unbuckle my seat belt, and I shift on my seat to face her. My gaze roams her face in the dimly lit space, taking in every feature. Something uncoils in my chest, something warm and contagious. I'm shivering, which causes my hands to shake a little. I feel like I'm catching a fever as heat burns through my veins, setting every part of me on fire like poison.

I take deep breaths to calm myself as I try to understand what my body is telling me.

"You okay?" Grace is asking me, reaching up and pushing back the ever-present locks of hair on my forehead. "Talk to me." She's pleading now. I'm a dick for making her worry. I need to figure out what's happening to me before I scare her.

The answer to what I'm feeling hits me, the impact jolting me upright on the seat. Her eyes whip back to me, alarm clear in her face.

"Wha—"

"I-I love you," I blurt out clumsily. Shit, how embarrassing is this. I laugh awkwardly. "I always thought if I ever got to say those words to someone I wouldn't sound like I'm spitting them out. But they really didn't come out smoothly." I shake my head, inwardly hitting my head against a wall. "I—"

She slaps a hand over my mouth, cutting off my words, her eyes wide and unblinking. "Don't say it."

She drops her hand, shifts on her seat, and looks out the window. "God, Sol. Why, *why* did you say those words?" she whispers with a shaky voice.

And the Insensitive Jerk Award goes to Solomon Callan. Why can't I stop making things difficult between us?

I sigh, placing one hand on her shoulder and turning her around to face me.

"I know I'm giving you some mixed vibes, and I'm so sorry about that. It's just that I can't keep it inside anymore, Gracie. I feel like I'm going to explode and . . . please say *something*. Anything. I don't care if it's to tell me to shut the hell up or tell me to go jump off a cliff and never show my face—"

"Shut *up*." Her voice trembles, and her eyes shine with tears.

I blow out a shaky breath and laugh. "That works."

"You're leaving soon, Sol."

I don't say anything because I don't know what to say.

"Yet here you are, telling me you love me."

I nod, lifting a hand and wiping the tears at the corner of her eyes with my thumb. "I'm sorry for upsetting you. I—"

She presses a finger against my lips. "Let me say this, please. I know I'm supposed to encourage you to follow the path you've chosen," she says, "but you changed me. You made me believe there's good in the world. I just want to be selfish for once in my life and not let you go."

This need to have both Grace and follow my calling is

killing me. I can't keep doing this to both of us.

I sigh wearily and drag my fingers through my hair. "Come on, let me walk you to your door."

She looks out the window for a few seconds, then straightens her shoulders and slings the strap of her purse over her shoulder. With one last unreadable look in my direction, she unlocks her door and jumps out.

I join her on the sidewalk, and we cross the street just as fat drops of rain start falling around us. Soon, we're surrounded by sheets of rain.

When we get to her door, she unlocks it and steps inside, then turns to looks at me. "I really had fun today, Sol. Thank you."

I nod. "Same here." *Until I told you I loved you and scared both of us.*

She waves, her lips curling at the corners. "Good night."

"Good night, Gracie."

As soon as the door closes behind her, I walk back to the truck, hoping the rain helps clear my head. I'm just about to open the door when a small hand wraps around my elbow. I spin around, my eyes growing wide at the sight of Grace.

My fingers move without my permission and tuck the locks of hair behind her right ear. She licks her lips, and my eyes drop to her mouth. I swallow hard, moving my hand to cup her cheek.

"Sol," she whispers.

"Grace," I breathe.

She squints up at me through the rain, locks of hair plastered on her forehead. "Are you going to kiss me again?"

"I don't know. I don't think I should."

"Have you ever kissed someone in the rain, Solomon Callan?" It's the same question she asked me at the diner before, the look on her face soft, grounding me, grounding my heart, which seems to have grown wings inside my chest.

I'm a complete mess, and I have no idea how to control my feelings for her. Especially when she's looking at me like that.

I inhale the earthy scent surrounding us. *Rain does have a smell*, I realize. Taking her in, I smile. Even with her hair curling rebelliously around her head and mascara running down her face, she is the most beautiful girl I've ever seen.

I shift my body to face her. "No. Never."

"Me either." She hikes up on her toes. "But we're about to change that."

Her mouth presses against mine, her warm breath on my lips. The tip of her tongue tentatively licks my bottom lip, and I come undone. My hands land on her hips and yank her to my body. Then I'm kissing her, inhaling the scent of rain and vanilla waffles as fire licks my veins, scorching my skin from the inside out. And I can't get enough.

We break apart for air moments later, panting, foreheads pressed against each other. She makes a soft, satisfied sound that has my body firing up. It sends shivers down my spine, their thrill sinking into my very bones.

"My mom's going to kill me. She warned me about you, you know."

I stiffen. "She did?"

"Yes. She's just worried that we're getting into something that will break us once you go off to seminary."

"She's right, you know."

Grace shrugs. "Not everyone is lucky enough to experience something magical in their lifetime."

I lower her to the ground and hug her close to me. "Good night, Grace," I whisper into her hair.

"Good night."

She extricates herself from my arms and skips to the door,

that damn dress sticking to her body like a second skin. I groan under my breath and squeeze my eyes shut. I need a cold shower pronto.

I hop inside the truck. As I slide onto my seat and jam the key into the ignition, I think about the evening. One day, I'll look back on this day and remember Grace made it more bearable, distracting me from thinking about my parents.

Then tonight's events hit me hard. My chest tightens, and a lump forms in my throat. Shame and guilt sit heavy in my stomach; the promises I've made to God, to Seth, my uncle, and to my mom and dad whenever I visit them at the cemetery, they all flash in my head. I press my clenched fist onto my thigh until a throbbing pain echoes all over my body. It doesn't loosen the thickness blocking air from getting past my throat.

I lost control. Most people don't understand why I'm rigid about having sex, given that I haven't even started the seminary yet, but it all comes down to principle, I guess.

I've been very keen about a vocation to the priesthood for years. As much as I was fascinated with Grace since I met her when I was ten, sex was never something I really thought about. Sure, I got aroused often, like every hormonal teen everywhere. But I knew what I wanted. I knew the endgame.

And now, in just a few weeks, I'll be heading to the seminary. I need to sort myself out. Soon.

# twenty-eight

*Grace*

MY HANDS FLY TO MY CHEST, A SHRIEK BURSTING FROM MY lips as I catch movement near the window in our living room. A second later, light spills across the space. I blink several times to focus on the shadow—my mom, sitting in the rocking chair, holding her phone in one hand.

"Oh gosh. You scared me, Mom."

She stops rocking and observes me. Her forehead is lined with worry, and her eyes look tired. She looks like she hasn't slept in weeks, which makes me feel even more guilty about our argument earlier today. Or maybe—maybe she's sick. Panic seizes my heart, propelling my feet forward.

"What's wrong?" I rush forward and drop to my knees in front of her. "Are you feeling okay?"

She rolls her eyes. "I'm fine, sweetheart. I wanted to talk to you before I went to bed."

I sigh, relieved. "Me too. Let me get out of these wet clothes first. I'll be right back." I shuffle out of the room.

I return minutes later with a towel wrapped around my wet hair and sit down on the couch, then turn to face her. I'm caught between dread and relief, wondering how this conversation will go. I clear my throat of the lump of nervousness blocking my airway. "You go first."

She examines me for a long time and sighs. "I realized I'm turning into my parents when I try to force you to do what *I* want and not what *you* want. I'm sorry, Gracie."

I clasp my hands on my lap to keep them from fiddling with the edge of my T-shirt. "I'm so sorry for saying those things about you. You didn't deserve that, and I wish I could take them back." I pause, carefully considering my next words. "I just want you to understand that we both want different things. Remember that time when you told me I could be anyone I want to be? This is me choosing my own path. I'm not afraid to make mistakes. That's what life is all about, right?"

She nods again, her mouth twisting into a grin. "Your grandparents are going to be pissed. They hoped you'd choose to go to Brown, like they did. They actually met in college. Your grandfather's side of the family attended Brown. So, you can imagine their disappointment when I couldn't attend." She chuckles softly, but there's no resentment or bitterness in her expression.

"Honestly, I care about what you think. Not them." I take a deep breath and continue. "I know I could apply for spring intake, but I'm not ready. I *need* to be ready first, Mom."

"Grace." Her voice is stern, her expression stubborn. "You can't be serious—"

"Mom, please. My choice, remember?"

Her expression clears, and she nods. "Next fall. What are you going to do in the meantime?"

"Open a lemonade stand and advertise the hell out of it," I joke.

My mom laughs. "Remember that time when you were six and you insisted on making your own lemonade the way Regina taught you, then sold it to everyone on the block?"

"I was good, wasn't I?" I laugh, remembering how young

and optimistic I was.

"You had a good marketing strategy, and it helped a lot. Plus, your cute little face and adorable eyes won everyone over."

Silence falls around us as we think about the past. I remember how much I enjoyed coming up with the plan to sell the lemonade. Maybe there's something to this memory after all.

I tuck my legs under me. "Are you sure you're okay?"

"Just tired." Her forehead creases, and she seems troubled. But I know my mom. She won't discuss whatever is bothering her until she's ready. We are very similar in that way. "Nothing a good night's sleep can't cure."

We stare at each other for a few moments: me, weighing the truth behind those words. Her . . . well, she's just assessing me. I can't crack that look on her face, and it makes me nervous.

Her next words stop me short, the disappointment in her features making me panic. "I saw you and Sol out the window. He's leaving, Grace. How are you two going to walk away from this when he leaves?"

My mind is in chaos as I scramble to find a viable explanation, but all I can come up with is, "Are you spying on me now?"

She stares at me, chin raised, lips flat in an unyielding line of disapproval.

"I just . . . I really enjoy spending time with him."

"Did you have sex with him?"

"What? No!" I groan under my breath, heat splashing across my cheeks. "We're just hanging out. I promise."

She nods and then tries to cover the lingering doubt with a frown. "Sex is, um, it's just one of those things that is special, you know. You have the power to decide who you give yourself to. You need to be sure."

"I know, Mom. Jeez. I'm not going to have sex with him, okay?"

She sighs wearily, rubbing her hands down her face. After a deep inhale, she stands up and heads for the TV console. "Hey, want to watch *One Tree Hill*? I really want to know what happened after Nathan and Lucas fought."

I grin wide and nod, appreciating her peace offering. Of course, I know what happened after the fight between Lucas and Nathan. I've watched every episode of *OTH* more times than I can count, but for her sake, I let her believe I'm eager to see what happens too.

We settle on the couch to watch, but my mind, my body, my thoughts, every single part of me tingles at the memory of Sol's hands and mouth on me.

But mostly Sol's words.

*I love you.*

# twenty-nine

*Grace*

THE WEEK GOES BY QUICKLY, AND BEFORE I KNOW IT, IT'S already Thursday. Sol and I haven't seen each other as much as I would have liked. In fact, it seems as though we've hardly seen each other at all. I text him, and he texts back, but he seems distracted. His responses are made up of a maximum of five words. I wonder if I'm being too needy, and old insecurities begin to resurface.

Maybe now that he's had the time to think about what I said, I've scared him away? Or maybe he realized what he said and is giving me an out. If I were in his shoes, I'd probably be freaking out, too. Sol and I are just two hearts gravitating toward each other, regardless of the odds stacked against us.

*Ugh.*

I'm driving myself crazy. I hate feeling like this, which is the reason why I avoided getting involved with anyone after Gavin.

I sigh, shaking my head to disperse those thoughts, and concentrate on finishing serving breakfast at the diner.

At eleven o'clock, I hang up my apron and then drive to St. Peter's Church for my weekly confession. This has always been my little ritual on Thursdays, a source of comfort.

MJ and I planned to hang out at her place later today. I

figured since I was trying to put myself out there and make friends, spending more time together and getting to know one another would be a good place to start.

I'm sitting in the third row of the church, trying to untangle the chaos in my head. I don't know what I'm feeling right now. It's not love. It's more than that.

More lethal. Potent.

It flows through my veins, infecting my blood with its poison. I'm not even sure how I'm still breathing. I should be dead. Instead, I'm sitting here, looking over my shoulder at the main entrance every few seconds like a forlorn lover waiting for her love to return home from war. The worst thing is, the antidote for this poison is the one person I shouldn't be fantasizing about. The person I shouldn't pin my hopes on because he will never be mine, but my heart, my stupid, desperate heart is already invested in him. Building castles in the air and dreaming of happily ever afters.

I force my gaze back to the front and stare ahead at the altar, waiting for confession to start. Something bumps my thigh. The scent of motor oil and cologne slams into me. My head whips up, and I come face-to-face with Sol's blue eyes.

"Hey," I whisper. After a few minutes of simply staring at each other, butterflies take flight in my stomach.

"Hey you." His mouth tips up at the side, my favorite smirk making an appearance, but it's shadowed by apprehension. Is he nervous?

God, he looks so hot. I've missed that beautiful face of his.

"You lining up for confession too?" I ask, hoping my face hides what my heart is feeling. I don't want to get my hopes up again, only to have him disappear like he did the past few days.

He shakes his head, his eyes darting around us before returning to me. His leg is bouncing, and his finger taps a frantic beat on the pew in front of us. "Can we talk?"

"*Now?*"

"Yes? Look, I know I've been an ass the past weeks—"

I laugh and shake my head as if it was nothing. "You don't owe me anything, Sol."

"Yes. Yes, I do." He drags his fingers through his hair. "Come on. Please? Just five minutes."

"Fine." I stand, pressing my palms down my black and white plaid dress to stop them from shaking. I'm dying to touch him.

He nods. "This way." He grasps my bicep and tugs me to the side, then all of a sudden, he changes direction and heads for the confessional booth.

"What are you doing?" I whisper in panic.

I catch a glimpse of Mrs. Grinsberg's white head bowed—one of the church patrons—clutching a rosary in her knobby hands. Three other patrons are sitting nearby—one sitting in the front row, and the other two sitting several rows behind.

He tosses me a look I can only describe as roguish before reaching the confessional door, opening it, and shoving me inside. He looks around the church one more time before joining me, squeezing his large frame into the small space.

Oh my gosh! "What's happening? I thought you wanted to talk."

He shifts around until we're standing front to front. I have to pull my head back, back, back to see his eyes. Damn freaking giant.

"Confession starts in a few minutes, so I need to say what I came here to say before my uncle walks in."

"Make it quick. Like really quick." My heart is racing so fast inside my chest I'm wondering if it's going to trip on itself.

"You didn't say it back."

"Say what?"

"That you love me. So I was kind of wondering if you feel the same about me, or—" The sound of heavy footfalls echoing on the other side of the door freezes his words on his tongue.

"Or what?" I ask when the sound fades.

"Or if I'm just your boy-toy."

My mouth drops open. "My *boy-toy*?"

His eyes twinkle with mischief and mirth, and seconds later, I slap both hands against my mouth to keep the laughter inside.

"You're insane," I finally say, then chuckle under my breath. "Is that why you stayed away?"

He shifts his body, then pulls me flush against him.

"Partly."

I stare, my heart in my mouth, waiting for him to continue.

"Having to leave you behind when I go to Boston . . . The thought of breaking your heart terrifies me, Gracie. I don't want to hurt you, yet I can't seem to stay away from you either."

"You got cold feet." There's a loud thudding in my ears, and I shake my head slowly. "My heart's safe. I'm not the one in love, remember?"

I'm lying through my teeth, hoping to save my pride and escape potential heartbreak.

His eyebrows crease, lips pursed as he carefully studies me. And then, like the sun parting through dark clouds, a huge grin replaces that stormy look on his face.

"What?"

"Oh, sweet Gracie. The way you deny your feelings for me, it's cute."

"Wait, what?"

"This." His hand palms the back of my neck, yanking me to him. Before I know what's happening, his mouth is on mine, destroying my defenses and igniting me.

My body grows tight. Everything fades, and all I see and

smell and hear is Sol's ragged breathing. A surprised but delight-ed moan escapes me as I sharply tug his hair, my heart pounding in my ears.

And just like the first time we kissed, my body is overloaded with all these feelings; shiver after shiver racing down my spine, heat, so much heat surrounding me, burning a trail through my veins. All he needs to do is light the fuse, and I'll go off like a bomb. When it comes to Sol, my body has only one reaction—combustion. And from the way he's hungrily kissing me as though he's about to go to war and might never come back, it's obvious how much I affect him in return.

One of his hands grips my thigh as the other travels up to my breasts, holding one deliciously tight. His tongue sweeps along the seam of my lips, and I open up for him, desperate for his taste. He groans low, exploring my mouth. I moan in re-sponse, tasting mint on his tongue. Sol is all hands and hard body as he pins me to the wooden wall behind me.

When did he become this brave? This naughty? Holy shit, he's so sexy and hot.

"Oh my God, oh my God!" I pant against his lips when I pull back to catch my breath and common sense starts trickling in. "What are we doing?"

Pulling away, his head falls back as his eyes squeeze shut. He murmurs in a rough voice, "We're talking."

I huff out a laugh as he lowers that sinful mouth of his to mine once more. "No, *no*. Get out before your uncle comes."

He blinks as if he's trying to clear his vision. As he steps back, his hands fall from my body, and just when I think he's leaving the confessional box, he drops to his knees in front of me. His palms move up my bare legs, pausing around my knees and squeezing gently.

His dark head moves, and he presses his lips on the skin

above my right knee. "What am I going to do about this? Us? It took all my strength to stay away the past couple of days, and I just couldn't hold off anymore. I had to see you."

My fingers sink into his messy hair and tug, forcing him to look up at me. I don't answer his question because the answer hurts too much.

Footsteps echo outside the booth, followed by the sound of a throat clearing. Whoever it is stops and greets someone in a low, calm voice.

Father Foster.

Sol's eyes widen, reflecting the same fear wreaking havoc inside me.

This could end so badly for both Sol and me. He puts his finger to his lips and mouths, "Shh." I nod, unable to hear anything above the thudding in my ears.

Luke is just wrapping up the conversation when Sol's hands swiftly push my dress up. My gaze flies to meet his just as he leans forward to whisper, "I won't let us get caught, okay?"

Swallowing hard, I nod again.

Without warning, he hooks two fingers around the waistband of my panties and tugs them down.

"What the heck are you doing?" I whisper in a shaking voice. When did he become this naughty? This brave?

*Ohmygodohmygod.*

His trembling hands hesitate, uncertainty filling his features. Then he rolls his shoulders as if he has made up his mind about something, excitement and fear fighting for power in his eyes. "A souvenir," he murmurs.

Caught off guard, my hands grip his hair tighter as he lifts one of my legs and then the other so I step out of my panties.

He pulls back as he bunches the cotton material in one hand and mouths, "See you outside."

The wooden door on the priest's side of the booth creaks open, then shuts with an echoing sound, reverberating through the old church and snapping me out of my shock. Sol slips out of the booth at the same time, so the sound of the door closing behind him is masked by the echo. I drop to my shaking knees on the kneeler.

On the other side of the mesh window, I hear fabric rustling, followed by Father Foster clearing his throat. He says something, but my brain is full of white noise. My hands make the sign of the cross on autopilot, and I fall silent. My throat is tight, and my heart beats fast. *Oh my God!*

Sol and I are *so* going to Hell.

Father Foster clears his throat again, pulling me out of my thoughts, reminding me of my surroundings.

"F-Forgive me, Father . . ." I trail off when my voice shakes.

My gaze sharpens on the mesh separating us. His head is bowed, his focus on something beyond my line of sight.

I take a deep breath and start again. "Forgive me, Father, for I have"—the image of Sol and me kissing like our lives depended on it, then his hand moving under my dress and pulling down my underwear flashes inside my head—"sinned."

*Shit. Shit. Shit.*

I'm going to kill Sol.

I force myself to focus on what Father Foster is saying, but it's just a jumble of words. I say something, I don't know what, just something about the sins I've committed this week, which seem to have multiplied in the past five minutes. But I don't confess the more recent ones. He gives me my penance, and I start to stand. The box has gotten incredibly small all of a sudden, and I'm thankful to be finished. Until Father Foster speaks once more.

# thirty

*Grace*

HE ASKS ME IF I'LL BE HELPING MY MOM WITH THE UPCOMING food drive.

"Yes," I whisper, wondering if Sol is still waiting for me on the other side of the door.

"You and my nephew," Father Foster continues, and all thoughts of Sol freeze inside my head. And I'm wondering why, why, why he feels the need to be so chatty today of all days. "He's a good boy."

"I know." *Good boy, my ass.*

Sol is all kinds of bad when he wants to be. I don't even know what has gotten into him today. He's acting so different. Bolder than usual.

"He seems to like you very much."

I'm about to ask him if Sol told him that, but I quickly press my lips together and wait for what's coming next.

"I assume you feel the same way about him?"

"Yes," I murmur. "I mean, he's a very good friend."

He doesn't say anything for several seconds. It's the kind of silence that speaks volumes. He doesn't believe me. "He hasn't withdrawn his application to the seminary yet."

I clear my throat and try to hide how nervous I am. "Do you, um, disapprove of Sol and me spending so much time together?"

"Most spiritual advisors would disapprove, yes." He pauses, inhaling deeply. "As his mentor, I should be steering him away from anything that keeps him from focusing on his goals to be ordained. But as his uncle, I want only what's best for him. Clearly, he's quite taken with you. The only time I've seen him this passionate about something is when he's talking about how much he wants to follow in my footsteps."

Air is suspended between my lungs and throat as I wait for him to continue talking.

He sighs, and I can see movement on the other side of the mesh. I think he's covering his mouth or dragging a hand down his face. I can't tell exactly.

Finally, I take a deep breath and close my eyes, feeling as conflicted as Sol. My thoughts drift to the boy waiting for me outside this booth; his kindness, the way his eyes light up when he sees me, his smile, his relentless pursuit to be my friend . . . and I know, I know I'm in love with him.

"What do I do?"

"Unfortunately, he has to decide which path to follow. Which loss is more bearable."

I nod, acknowledging the truth in his words. Fleetingly, I wonder if I'm ready for whatever choice he'll make.

I shudder and shake my head, pushing those thoughts away.

Father Foster hums under his breath like he always does, indicating the end of my session. So I grab my purse and stand, almost running out of the booth, clutching my dress to my legs to keep the cool breeze from hitting my lady bits. I join Sol on the pew and do my assigned penance, then add an extra prayer for good measure. When I'm done, Sol leaps to his feet from the bench. Any lingering thoughts and doubts about Sol and me fade away as he laces his fingers with mine and leads the way out of the church.

We don't stop until we're outside in the parking lot next to his truck.

"Holy shit!" I breathe out, the impact of what we did flashing in my head. "You're insane. You know that?"

He opens the door to the passenger seat, grips me by the waist, and hoists me inside. My butt lands on the warm seat, reminding me I'm not wearing underwear. Because he took them.

"I'm not enjoying the breeze, Sol. I need my underwear back," I tell him after he joins me inside the car.

"Answer this first, and you can have them back." He slants a smile in my direction. "You more than just like me. True or false?"

My traitorous mind goes back to our moment inside the confessional box, and I squirm as heat pools between my legs. "True. I more than just like you, Sol."

"Good." He fishes my panties from his pocket and holds them out to me. He eyes the white cotton material in his hands. "Really pretty."

I snatch them from his hands, my face on fire, and slip them back on, then straighten my dress.

"What's going on? I've never seen you like that, Sol."

He holds my gaze for several seconds, then shakes his head as if he's trying to clear it. "I don't know. I came here to talk to you, but then I—" He sucks in a deep breath and shakes his head again. "Even the sanest person is prone to moments of insanity. I wasn't in the right frame of mind. I'm really sorry."

"It was kind of hot." I squirm in the seat, heat gathering between my legs just thinking about that version of Sol. "I *really* liked it."

His mouth twists in a crooked smile, but it doesn't reach his eyes, which seem a little troubled. We drive into town, chatting about everything and nothing. I'm still riding the high of doing something so scandalous and not being caught.

When my phone beeps inside my purse, I pull it out and check my messages. There are three messages from MJ, and she wants to know what time I'll be at her place. Shit. I completely forgot we were supposed to be hanging out after confession.

My gaze darts to Sol just as his briefly meets mine, and my pulse quickens at the lingering heat in his eyes.

"What?" he asks.

"MJ and I were supposed to hang out later. I promised her I'd go to her place after church."

"We could eat lunch, then you could hang out after?" he asks. "There's this Chinese restaurant I've been dying to try out."

I nod and quickly type out a text to MJ, letting her know I'll be at her place in about two hours.

Sol parks outside the restaurant, then jogs to my side and opens the door for me. He holds out his hand, and I put mine in his, allowing him to help me out. He slams the door behind me, then he's moving forward, invading my space. I stumble backward until I feel the hard metal of the passenger door digging into my shoulders and back. My line of sight is filled with him and only him as he subtly leans forward, wide shoulders blocking my view, blue eyes watching me intently, and lastly, his scent surrounding me. All I want to do is press my nose into the crook of his neck and breathe him in until I'm drunk on his scent.

"I really want to kiss you, but I'm afraid I might not stop if I start," he murmurs.

"Do it. I'm not going to stop you. I have zero willpower when it comes to you, Sol."

"I shouldn't be leading you on like this. There are about ten million reasons to stop doing this before it gets even messier, but I can't remember what they are right now—"

When I slam my mouth onto his, it takes a moment for him to recover from my attack. He groans, his other arm sliding up to wrap around my back, holding me so close I can feel every single hard plane of his chest and abs. The metal of the car behind me digs into my back, but the pain is completely obliterated by the sensations his mouth creates in my body.

And as I'm sinking deeper into him, a voice in my head yells at me to stop and take a step back. Spare the heartbreak and save my sanity. But my heart, my reckless, stubborn, hungry heart shuts it down as my need for him takes over. My feelings for Sol have no pride.

He pulls back a little, brushing his lips on the corner of my mouth as he tames the stormy kiss. "Still starving?" His voice is rough, sending heat pooling in my belly.

"Yes," I murmur, smiling. "I could survive on your kisses alone, but I need to stock up on energy."

His body shakes with laughter. I'm about to step away from his arms when I feel them tighten around me. "Just . . . let me hold you for a few minutes. I need to, um, calm down."

I was so consumed by his mouth that I didn't notice what was going on south.

A few minutes later, his fingers lace with mine. He kisses the back of my hand before leading us toward the restaurant.

"Wait!" I grab his bicep, stopping him. Then I point at the shop next to the restaurant with the words *Aunty Rowena Palm Reading Services* flashing in neon blue and green. "I've always been curious about this. I want to see what they're all about."

"Babe," he drawls, and I *melt*. It's the first time he's called me that. It's a simple word, but it just makes me feel special. "Are you serious?"

"Yes. Come on." I pull his arm and he lets me.

Inside Aunty Rowena's shop, we're greeted by the scent

of burning sage and a different smell I can't put my finger on. Within seconds, a woman wearing a flowing gown and a head-scarf seems to glide into the room. She's wearing red lipstick, and her lashes seem too long to be normal. When she smiles, I feel warmth in my chest.

"Welcome to Aunty Rowena's Parlor." She waves her arms elegantly. "What can I do for you?" Her gaze is on me now.

"I was wondering . . . well, I'd like to know my future." I cut my eyes to Sol. He rolls his eyes, his lips twitching. "Ignore him. He already has his future figured out," I tell Aunty Rowena.

She smiles politely at him before turning to face me again. Nodding, she ushers us through a doorway that has green and orange sheer curtains for doors. After silently gesturing for us to take a seat at the reading table, she walks across the room and lights up what looks like a bunch of dried-up twigs. She walks around the room, waving them in the air.

When she's done, she comes back to the table and takes a seat. She asks me to place my hand in hers. A look of concentration fills her features. Her fingers trace the lines etched in my skin, her frown deepening.

"Do you see anything?"

She nods but doesn't say anything. I fidget on my seat, uneasiness creeping down my spine.

Sol puts his hand on my knee and whispers, "Maybe we should go."

Aunty Rowena's fingers tighten around my hand, but still, she doesn't say a word.

I shake my head and mouth, "Just a few more seconds."

Eventually, she lifts her gaze to mine, and goosebumps erupt on my skin. Her gaze roams my face carefully as if she's unlocking a certain part of me I didn't even know existed. I'm starting to freak out. A few minutes ago when Sol and I walked inside this shop, it was purely for fun. Now I feel trapped as a chill grips my heart in its icy claws. I can't shake it off.

"This line here." She points at one of the lines on my palm, the thick one. The life line, I think. "You'll enjoy a full life, a life full of love and family." Then she traces the two lines on the side of my hand. "Two hearts, one soul. I see two men in your future. You will be forced to make very difficult decisions. Decisions between life and death. Decisions between the two men in your life."

The hairs on the back of my neck rise. I pull my hand back and laugh nervously. "Two men? I doubt that."

Her gaze cuts to Sol, then back to me, smiling patiently. "I'm only telling you what I see, child. Your future has yet to play out." She pulls out a piece of paper from a drawer and scribbles something on it, then slides it in my direction.

I look at the sum on the paper, dig out a couple of ten-dollar bills, and set them on the table as I stand. "Thank you," I mutter as I turn and trail Sol out the door.

Sol wraps his arm around my shoulders and tugs me close as we head to the restaurant next door, but I'm no longer hungry. I'm still thinking about what she said. About decisions between life and death and what that could possibly mean. Decisions between two men . . . I'm already feeling the weight of losing Sol pressing down on me, and it hasn't happened yet.

"I don't believe her," he announces confidently. "No one has that kind of power to tell the future. Only God knows what he has planned for you."

I nod, desperate to believe him. I've never been one to believe fortune telling or superstitions, but something was so eerie about the way she was looking at me. Aunty Rowena's words have already burrowed themselves inside my bones, and I can't seem to dig them out.

# thirty-one

*Grace*

"**D**UDE. DID YOU JUST FART?" MJ ASKS, LIFTING HER head and turning to look at me.

"Oh, shut up," I pant, trying to breathe through this awful yoga position. My legs are spread, my butt is sticking up in the air, and my fingers are wrapped around my ankles. "I can't believe you talked me into doing this. I swear this pose should be banned."

She snorts, shifting positions effortlessly and standing on one leg while the other is stretched in front of her. Her hands move forward to grasp the sole of her foot. She rests her head on her knee. "Come on, lazy butt. We're almost done."

I straighten and attempt to imitate her, but I lose my balance and fall on my backside with a squeal. "Ack. I *am* too lazy for this shit," I moan, stretching flat on my back on my mat, watching MJ execute her pose perfectly.

After leaving the restaurant, Sol dropped me off at St. Peter's to collect my car. Then I drove to MJ's place, still thinking about Rowena's words. The second I walked inside MJ's apartment, she seemed determined to carry out some sort of initiation to social media. Apparently, she looked me up on Facebook but couldn't find anything. I thought she was going to faint when I told her I didn't have an account. So the first thing we did was set one up, then I added her, Ivan, and Sol to my friends list.

The thing is, I had an account up until sophomore year, but I deleted it after breaking up with Gavin. I couldn't stand seeing all the mean posts and comments circulating on my friends' timelines. Besides, the friends I'd made in the time he and I were together turned their backs on me, so I had no interest in being social after that. The pain wasn't worth it.

"Sol is right, you know. No one has that kind of power to predict the future," MJ says, interrupting my train of thought, referring to what I told her while she was setting up my Facebook account. I tuck my arms beneath my head and face her. "But I'd be freaked out if I were in your shoes and someone told me that. I mean, decisions between life and death? Who wants to hear that when they're, like, eighteen?"

She straightens to her full height and wipes the beads of sweat from her forehead with the back of her hand, then effortlessly lies down on the mat. I wish I had that kind of grace.

She winks at me. "Wanna make out?"

The change of subject jars me, and I blink rapidly. "W-what?"

She grins saucily. "You're staring at me like you want to jump me."

"Wait, *what?*" I'm still trying to catch up with this turn of conversation. "I am?"

She bursts out laughing, clutching her middle with her arms. "Oh, God," she says between hiccups, then points a finger in my direction. "You should see your face."

I chuckle, appreciating the sound of her laugh, thinking how much I'm enjoying her company. She sounds so carefree and happy, and it's infectious. "What if I'd said yes?"

"Well, we'll never know now, will we?" She laughs, then flips onto her stomach and reaches for her phone from the table we pushed to the side to make more space for our yoga session. She murmurs something about texting Ivan back as her fingers fly over the keyboard. She tosses the phone on her mat, then flops onto her back again.

"Sol and I kissed in church today," I blurt out.

There's a long moment of silence. "You did *what?*"

The memory of Sol's heated eyes, wicked mouth, and naughty hands sends heat pooling in my belly. I rub my thighs together and smother a sigh. I'm so lost in that flashback my eyes shut and I imagine him on top of me, shirt and pants off, his hard length grinding between—

"Grace!" My eyes fly open, and I find MJ watching me curiously. "You can't just tell me you two kissed in church and then leave me hanging like that."

I press my hands on my heated cheeks. "We kissed." I take a deep breath. "In the confessional box."

Her mouth gapes, her eyes wide.

"I know. It was super-hot. I've never seen him like that. Is it wrong I loved it? I mean, we were in church. Who makes out in church?"

Her mouth closes, and she clears her throat. "Okay, back up a bit. Are we talking about the same guy here? Church boy? Our perfect, innocent man-child? Solomon Callan?"

I nod, remembering the way he pulled down my panties with the playful glint in his eyes. A shiver runs down my spine. "Believe me, he's far from innocent."

"Wow. That's so *scandalous.*" She laughs, clapping her hands, but suddenly stops, her eyes going wide. "If Luke finds out . . ."

"Sol left as soon as his uncle entered the other booth."

She grins wide. "So you two finally admitted your feelings for each other? This calls for a celebration. Brandy or tequila? Or weed? I have a small stash Ivan left here a few days ago."

I laugh. "Why am I not surprised?"

Just then her phone starts to ring. She grabs it from the table and swipes a finger on the screen to answer. Her whole expression turns soft, and I know she's talking to her boyfriend. I stand and head to the kitchen for a glass of water.

She ends the call a few minutes later and jumps to her feet. "Forget the tequila. We're going out."

"Oh. Where?" I ask, setting the still-full glass on the counter.

"Fisher's Gold." I blink at her, not comprehending. "It's a coffee shop downtown. They have karaoke night every Thursday."

"I can't sing to save my life."

"That's the whole point of karaoke. It's supposed to be fun." She takes my hand, grabs two glasses and a bottle of brandy. Then we head down the hallway to her room. "I need to change, then we can do our makeup."

"Is this what you meant by your version of fun?"

"Yep. Plus, it will take your mind off what that woman said."

"So you and Ivan are pretty serious?" I ask while she's changing into a slinky black dress.

I glance down at what I am wearing: denim skirt, my mom's short-sleeved, white chiffon blouse—I haven't done laundry this week—and white Chucks. And decide I don't look too shabby for a karaoke night at a coffee shop.

MJ shrugs. "I think so, yeah." She hands me one of the glasses, then plops down on her mat. "His mom doesn't approve, though. She wants him to find himself a Korean girl."

I frown. "Why?"

"To stick to his roots, I guess. I don't know." She tips her glass and gulps down the brandy.

"But that doesn't seem fair, considering his mother didn't stick to her roots."

MJ sighs, her face falling. "It's exhausting sometimes."

"Everything will work out. I just know it. I mean, how can someone not love you?"

"Aw, I love you too, babe." She smacks a kiss on my cheek. After deciding we're taking my car, we head to the spot where my Fiat is parked.

"By the way," she announces. "Levi's meeting us there. I'm just letting you know so you can prepare yourself, since, you know, you kicked him in the family jewels the other night."

# thirty-two

*Sol*

FTER PARTING WAYS WITH GRACE AT ST. PETER'S, I DROVE back to the auto shop to start working on Beth's car. I ordered the parts I needed to fix it, and they were being delivered this afternoon. Grace's worried face flashes in my mind. She still seemed anxious about that woman's palm reading. I hope she doesn't let it get to her. I make a note to text her later to check on her.

Seth is driving his bike up and down the deserted road. As soon as he sees me, a big grin replaces the ever-present solemn look on his face. I'd completely forgotten I promised him he could watch while I did the brake work on his mom's car.

"Hey, Seth. Have you been waiting long?"

"I just got here."

"Great. Come on, let's get started."

My boss, Joe Soltz, is lounging in a wicker chair that has seen better days, sipping beer from a bottle. His favorite auto magazine sits on his lap, his thumb ready to turn to the next page. He lifts the hand holding the beer in our general direction in greeting, before glancing back down. He doesn't bat an eye when his gaze cuts to Seth. He's already used to Seth's impromptu visits. Plus, Joe knows I'm careful when Seth is around.

Joe is a sixty-year-old, quiet guy, no drama. Happily married to the same woman for thirty years. He has five children. He first took me in when I was fifteen with an itch to learn to repair cars. Next to playing soccer at Winston High, this was my favorite thing to do. I enjoyed fixing things just as much as I loved being part of the Mass.

Seth trails behind me as we enter the shop, dragging his feet, head bowed like he's afraid of looking people in the eye. It's one of his tells whenever he has something on his mind.

"What's going on?" I ask,

"Mom spoke to Father Foster about me, you know, getting baptized. I was kind of wondering if you'd like to be my godfather."

"Yeah? That's awesome, man."

He flashes me a bright smile. "Is that a yes?"

I nod. To be honest, there's nothing I wouldn't do for Seth. He's grown on me over the years.

"Awesome." He brings his fist up and waits until I bump it with mine.

"All right. Let's get to work so your mom can have the car back to cart your lazy ass around."

He guffaws and yells, "I'm not lazy!"

Before long, Seth and I are wearing coveralls—well, Seth's borrowed coveralls are wearing him instead—and are neck deep in motor oil while "Hotel California" by the Eagles blasts across the garage.

A few hours later, we clean up and head out. I'll do final touches tomorrow, then do a test drive before Beth comes to collect it. I load Seth's bike into the back of my truck and usher him in the passenger seat. My phone vibrates inside my pocket, and I pull it out, swiping the screen to read the message.

Ivan: *Dude. It's karaoke night at Fisher's. Wanna hang out?*

The time on my phone indicates it's 6:10 p.m.

"Hey, I'm heading to Fisher's after this. Want to come with?" I ask Seth.

He glances at his wrist watch. "Sure. I have a friend coming over to my house in about an hour from now, so I won't stay long."

Joe's working on a blue truck at the front of the shop when Seth and I emerge from inside the workshop. I pull out of the parking lot and wave at him as we drive off.

I park the truck a few blocks away from Fisher's Gold, lock the doors, and then head to the coffee shop. A guy who looks like he dropped from the Renaissance era is yelling into the microphone, swiping his dark hair from his eyes as he belts out the lyrics from "R.E.S.P.E.C.T." by Aretha Franklin. Seth chuckles and shakes his head.

"Think you sing better than that dude?" I tease him, ruffling his hair.

He rolls his eyes. "Sign me up."

I laugh, scanning the almost full room for my friends. And what I see freezes the laughter in my throat. Levi is sitting between MJ and Grace. His blond friend from the concert is nowhere in sight. My hand bunches into a fist, and I growl, "Come on, Seth."

Grace laughs at whatever Levi is saying. My stomach churns with acid because that same laugh aimed at *him* is the same one that makes my heart race.

"Er, Sol?" Seth calls from beside me. "You okay, bro?"

"Yeah. Why?"

"You kind of look like you're ready to barf."

I glance down at him and grimace. "My stomach feels kinda funny. It will pass."

"Yo, dudes." Ivan waves us over. Three sets of eyes turn in

our direction. Grace's eyes widen in surprise, then a wide grin follows. The smile on Levi's face disappears fast, replaced by a dip of his eyebrows.

I nod my head at him in greeting; one of my brows goes up as if to say, "Do you have a problem, man?"

His gaze shifts to Seth and he reaches his hand across the table, introducing himself to Seth. "Levi Carter."

Seth shakes his hand and mutters, "Seth Kruger." He pulls back his hand and thrusts both of them inside his shorts pockets.

With the introductions done, I usher Seth to sit on the only available chair at the table next to Ivan, then grab one of the only free chairs from a nearby table and set it next to Seth.

After ordering a mango smoothie for Seth and an iced coffee for me, I sit back and try to relax. Ivan tries to pull me into conversation, but I can't stop eavesdropping on the conversation across the table.

Ivan and MJ high-five each other when a woman at the temporary stage calls their names. They head toward her and grab a microphone each. As usual, they sing "Alone" by Heart.

I steal a gaze to my right at Levi, and my jaw clenches.

What is she telling him? What is he telling her? And the moment my eyes fall on her lips, the scene at the confessional booth flashes inside my head.

Seth elbows me in the ribs, and I wince, ripping my gaze from Grace.

"What?" I snap at him, then immediately regret my tone. "What is it?"

"You like her?" Seth asks, forcing my attention back to him.

I cough once, clear my throat. "She's just a friend."

"But you like her more than a friend. I see the way you're looking at her." His eyes bore into mine accusingly.

I pinch the bridge of my nose with two fingers. "No—I

mean, yeah. I've known her for a very long time and she, um, I . . ." I trail off. I can't lie to him about my feelings for Grace. I've done enough lying the past few weeks to last me a lifetime.

"I thought you wanted to be a priest," he asks, disappointment filling his features.

"I do."

"Yeah? Is that why you're looking at her like you want to, I don't know, kiss her or something?"

*Oh, God. Am I that transparent?*

"Look, why don't you finish your drink, then we can talk outside, okay?"

He pushes his chair back and stands up. He stares at me for several seconds, then shakes his head, turns and shuffles toward the door, shoulders stiff and hands shoved in his shorts pockets. The look of disappointment on his face plays on a loop in my mind's eye, and I panic. I've let him down. I've let myself down. I need to talk to him. I have no idea what I'll say, but I can't let him ride his bike home in anger.

"Hey. Everything okay?"

I glance up to find Grace standing next to me.

I push my chair back and get to my feet. "Everything's fine." My voice comes out much harsher than I intended.

Grace flinches and takes a step back. "Okay! You don't have to bite my head off."

I sigh wearily. "I'm sorry." I glance out the window where Seth is pacing in front of Fisher's Gold, his fingers linked on the back of his head. "I need to go talk to him."

My gaze cuts over to Levi, then back to Grace. She's probably much better off with him or someone else than hanging around a conflicted jackass like me.

I open my mouth to tell her exactly that, but snap it shut as I remember something my uncle used to tell me when he started mentoring me. *Your words have the power to comfort, break, or encourage someone. So be very careful what you say.*

"Hey, could you let Ivan know I took Seth home?"

She nods, watching me with those beautiful eyes that say so much, yet so little. And I know without a doubt, that's the part of her I'm going to miss the most.

Seth is no longer pacing outside Fisher's Gold. I scan the area and catch a glimpse of him already stalking toward the spot where I parked my truck. I jog after him, my mind racing through different excuses, anything, to explain to this boy who let me into his life and trusts me. But all I see is the way he looked at me before he fled the coffee shop.

He stops at the back of the truck and unlatches the tailgate rear door, then clambers onto the truck bed.

"Seth, wait!"

Seth stops long enough to send me a glare over his shoulder, then grabs the handlebars of his bike. He drags it across the bed, then hops down from the truck and proceeds to try lifting it up.

I grip one of the bars with one hand, halting his progress. "Can we talk?"

"What's there to talk about?"

"You can't ride your bike home like this. You're angry and besides, it's getting dark." I loosen my hold, then ask again in a softer tone, "Can we talk?"

"I can't talk to you right now." The bike jerks as he tries to pull it out again, then grunts in frustration. "Just leave me alone."

I rub the back of my neck. "Okay, fine. Just let me drop you home."

"Why do you even bother?"

I wait until he meets my gaze. "Because I care. You're like a brother to me, Seth." I let my walls down and lay myself bare. "I *care*."

His nostrils flare as his lips press in a thin line. Just when I think he's going to shut me down, he exhales, his eyes filling with tears.

"I still don't want to talk to you," he mutters as he releases the bike and shuffles around the truck. I sigh in relief when I hear the door open and shut a few seconds later. I dig out my keys from my pocket, bracing myself before joining Seth in the front seat.

I yank the cap from my head and toss it on the dashboard, then drag my fingers through my hair. How do I start explaining to him about the connection I feel when it comes to Grace? Would he understand, despite his past experience with the Catholic Church? I'd promised to be the change. And what does that make me? Admittedly, I was thirteen, and I didn't understand that I could ever feel what I feel for someone, anyone, as I feel for Grace.

But I have to try.

"Can I say something?"

He continues to stare ahead without acknowledging me, his arms crossed on his chest and one leg bouncing,

I forge ahead. "I never make a promise I can't keep. Despite what you saw back there, I'm still pursuing this path."

His gaze cuts to me, still doubtful. "What about her?"

"I like her very much," I admit. "But that's it."

A lump forms in my throat. I swallow the lie, forcing it down until it settles in my gut, heavy and nauseating.

He looks out the window. I choose to stay silent and give him time to think about what I just said as I continue to drive.

By the time I drop Seth outside his building, he seems calmer. I'm about to drive off when he taps the window on the passenger side. I lean over and roll down the window.

He clears this throat, his eyes averted to the space above my shoulder. "Uh, I'm sorry. I didn't mean to go psycho on you."

"Warn me next time, man." I chuckle, despite the brick in my stomach.

He laughs. "Sure thing."

✠

*Grace*

"So, are you two, like, together or something?" Levi asks.

I blink twice, then take a deep breath to keep my shit together. I drag my gaze from the door as it closes behind Sol and face Levi. He studies me with curious gray eyes.

"It's complicated," I mutter, reaching for my glass of water and gulping down its contents.

"Isn't he like—"

I set the now-empty glass on the table and face him again, a ball of irritation burning in my chest. "How is this any of your business?"

He blinks several times, obviously taken aback by my snappish tone, and says, "I was just wondering—"

"Well, stop, okay?" I turn my attention to the stage just as Ivan and MJ finish singing the song "Alone." "You don't hear me asking about your girlfriend or whatever."

He averts his gaze to the couple now heading in our direction and scratches his head, looking suddenly uncomfortable. "We're on a break."

I raise my eyebrows. "I see. So you decided to put a four-hour drive between you two?"

Those soulful eyes return to me. With his shaggy dirty

blond hair and that look on his face, he reminds me of a tortured artist. "Something like that."

MJ plops on the chair next to me and throws her arms around me in a tight hug. "I'm so high on singing." She glances around and frowns. "Where did Sol and Seth go?"

"They left. You guys were amazing!" I gush, hoping to steer her away from her question. Subtly, my gaze darts to the clock on the wall where the coffee-making machines are located, wanting nothing more than to go home and wallow in misery.

I should ignore the pain burning worse than heartburn in my chest, but Seth's words keep replaying in my head and the look on Sol's face haunts me.

"Maybe you and Levi should sign up to sing."

I shake my head, give her a quick hug, and stand up. "I think I'll head out, too."

She searches my face, understanding dawning in her eyes. "Call me later?"

"Sure, yeah." I smile and grab my purse. After waving good-bye, I leave Fisher's Gold and head to the spot I parked my car. Inhaling deeply, I breathe out frustration and chaos to clear my head. To be honest, I don't think I have enough strength to dwell on any thoughts of Sol.

I scroll through my phone and tap Adrenaline playlist on the screen, then hit play. Thoughts of Sol and Seth are pushed in the back of my mind as "Shut Up And Drive" by Rihanna blasts through the car speakers.

I know the time is coming when I'll have to be strong enough to let go of Sol. I need to prepare my reckless heart, and I need to do it soon.

# thirty-three

*Grace*

AFTER THAT DAY SOL AND I KISSED IN THE CONFESSIONAL,
followed by him showing up with Seth at Fisher's
Gold, we haven't really talked again. I left a few
minutes after he stalked out of the coffee shop, despite MJ, Ivan,
and Levi protesting. I have no idea what's going on with Sol.
Every time I hold the phone in my hand ready to call him, I set
it back on the table, choosing to give him time to sort himself
out. Like I said at Old Orchard on the Fourth of July, spending
less time together might help. Not being able to talk to him or
see him hurts like a bitch, but if it makes things easier, then I'm
staying away.

On Saturday morning, I walk into the kitchen dressed in
my sleeping shorts and a T-shirt to find my mom leaning on
the counter. Her favorite mug full of steaming coffee is on the
counter in front of her, clutched in her tight grip. Beverly usually
opens the diner on Saturday, which means Mom will be closing
later.

Mom jolts upright when she sees me, her hands knocking
over the mug.

"Shit," she mutters, turning around and grabbing some paper towels from the roll next to the sink.

I watch as she cleans up the mess, noticing how her hands tremble.

"Morning, sweetheart. Did you sleep well?" she greets belatedly, tossing a smile over her shoulder at me, but instead of her usual genuine happy smile, it looks strained.

It's obvious she's trying hard to look cheerful but failing miserably.

"Yes." I lean against the laminated counter, fold my arms over my chest, and watch her, wishing I could read her. "Mom, you'd tell me if something was wrong, right?"

Her body visibly tenses. When she doesn't answer me after several seconds, I step closer and rest my hand on her shoulder.

"You'd tell me, *right?*" I repeat, my stomach churning with worry. I've never seen her so unnerved.

"I need to talk to you about something."

"Sure." Trepidation forms a lump in my throat as I follow her into the living room.

I sit on the edge of the brown couch and fold my hands in my lap to stop them from shaking. I don't know why I'm shaking, but her tone worries me.

Mom steps in front of me and lowers her small frame to the coffee table, then reaches forward and takes my hands in hers. I can't stop looking at our joined hands, marveling at how much hers have worked tirelessly to provide me—us—with food and safety. Gratitude spreads through me, warming my chest as I raise my eyes to meet hers, and her tired, wet eyes soften.

"I love you so much. You're a miracle, Gracie. *My* miracle."

Tears burn the corners of my eyes, terrified of what she's about to say. "You're scaring me, Mom."

Was I right last night? Is she sick? Oh my God. Is she dying? How would I survive without her?

For as long as I can remember, I've always feared being

abandoned. Some nights I'd wake up from a nightmare screaming and scrambling out of bed in a panic. I'd dash into the living
room where my mom slept on the pull-out couch worried she,
too, had left me like my father had left us. I was convinced the
feeling would eventually go away when I grew up, but I guess I
was wrong.

Mom's hands squeeze mine gently, and she murmurs in the
same calm voice that made everything better. "Breathe, Gracie.
Just breathe." She repeats the same words until my breathing
has calmed.

"I need to tell you some things about me. But first, I hope
you forgive me for what I'm about to say. I did what I did to
protect you because I thought it was the right thing to do." She
swallows hard, then clears her throat. "I still think it is."

I nod and brace myself for whatever she's about to say.

"It's about your father. He didn't leave like I told you. He
and I were never together, nor were we in love." She stares down
at her lap and blinks several times.

"He didn't? Where is he?" I ask, my heart beating faster than
it was before.

"I-I don't know, sweetheart."

I wipe my sweaty palms on my sleeping shorts, then place
them back in hers. "Just tell me, Mom. I'm eighteen. I can handle
it." My words are much braver than what I'm feeling.

"When I was eighteen, something happened to me." She
pauses, the muscles in her neck moving as she swallows. "I'd just
graduated from high school almost a month before, and one of
the guys from school threw a party. Sort of a get-together. I'd
gotten a ride from my best friend to the party. So when I realized
it was past my curfew, I went to check if she was ready to leave,
but she was too drunk to drive. And she wasn't in a hurry to
leave anyway. So I left, opting to call a cab."

Her gaze drops to our hands but not before I see tears gather at the corner of her eyes.

"There was construction on the road leading to my house, so it was closed temporarily for repairs. The driver dropped me off about one block away from my house, so I had to walk the rest of the way. A man appeared out of nowhere as if he'd been waiting for me and—" She sucks in a deep breath.

*No, no, no!* It can't be true.

My heart is beating so wildly, it's about to burst through my chest. I know what's coming even though my brain is refusing to accept it. I know what she's about to say, but I can't find the words to stop her because I think I'm going to throw up.

"I tried to fight him, but he was stronger than me." She closes her eyes, her features twisting in pain as if she's going through the same thing she did eighteen years ago. "I tried to get away, but then he threatened to kill me, and I could see it clearly in his green eyes that he meant it."

Bile churns in my stomach, boiling up my throat. I thought I could handle hearing the story, but it turns out I was wrong. I slap a hand over my mouth and bolt for the bathroom. Vomit spews before I even reach the toilet, and I fall to my knees. My head hangs over the porcelain as tears burn a trail down my cheeks. Just when I think I've nothing left inside me, I throw up some more. Acid burns my throat from throwing up.

I feel a presence next to me before my mom joins me on the cool marble floor and puts her arms around me, hugging me tight. I cling onto her as she rocks us back and forth.

I can't stop crying. I'm not breathing right. I need fresh air. I need to leave this house and just go. Run. I don't know. I just want out. Disbelief has given way to rage. I'm so angry, my body feels as if it's about to splinter open.

I wiggle out of her arms and jump to my feet.

"Grace—"

"What happened to him?" I wipe my hand under my nose, trying hard to hold it together. Hatred like I have never felt before burns through my veins in spades. "Did the police catch that . . . *monster*?"

She nods, her red-rimmed eyes begging me for something. I don't know what. Never in my eighteen years on this earth have I ever thought I'd be calling my own father a monster.

A coward? Sure. But a rap—I can't bring myself to say it. To even think the word.

My heart breaks in a million pieces, and I can't catch them all quickly enough before they crash to the floor and break in a million more.

Shattered pieces of hope all around me. If I try to move, they'll cut through the soles of my feet and leave scars I don't ever want to bear.

I can't believe this.

I can't. I can't. I can't.

"He was in prison until eight years ago."

I greedily suck in air to feed my lungs, to clear my head, to clear the anger rolling like a tsunami, then close my eyes, trying and failing to stop this feeling, this ugly feeling of betrayal, from consuming me. Because what happened to my mom is bigger and much worse. The pain thrashing inside me breaks loose.

"You told me he abandoned us when you were pregnant. I hoped and prayed he'd come to his senses and come home. I held on to the idea of a man I thought you'd loved. I believed I wasn't enough for him, that I wasn't worthy."

"Gracie," she says, voice low, appalled and saddened at my words. "You're more than worthy. It's him who isn't. I wanted to tell you, but I was so ashamed. I was trying to protect you."

I swipe my cheeks with my palms, the need to flee so strong.

But the way my mom is looking at me, so terrified, I'm glued to the spot by the fear in her eyes.

"I'm so, so sorry."

"God, Mom. *Please* stop. Stop apologizing for something that was out of your control. It wasn't your fault, okay?" I throw my arms around her, hugging her tight.

My words are her undoing, and the dam breaks. This strong woman, my best friend and protector, has kept this secret for eighteen years. How did she not break from the weight of it all?

I kiss her hair as pieces of my life start to fall in place; the self-defense classes, birth control pills, her trips to Port Elizabeth every year for the meditation retreat, how sad she gets every June. Her telling me that sex is one of those things that gives you the power to choose who you want to give yourself to. She wasn't given a choice. It all makes sense now.

"Thank you for telling me. I know it was very hard, but I want you to know I'm glad you told me."

We end up on the couch, holding each other. Once she falls asleep, I untangle our bodies, grab a blanket from her room, and cover her. Then I scribble a note for her to let her know I needed to get some air and not to worry. I'll be back soon.

I quickly change my clothes, favoring jeans shorts and a baggy T-shirt, then stumble to the door and shove my feet into a pair of sneakers.

Once I'm outside, I forgo the elevator and descend the five flights of the stairs while blinking hard to keep the tears at bay. Once I reach the lobby, I dash out the main door and into the light of the early morning, the pieces of my broken heart trailing after me.

# thirty-four

*Grace*

I'M NOT SURE HOW LONG I'VE BEEN WALKING; ALL I KNOW IS THE sun is already glaring in the middle of the clear blue skies. My feet are numb, and sweat beads on my forehead.

I glance around, trying to pinpoint where I am, but all I see is the sea on my right and a row of buildings on my left. My throat is parched, and my mouth feels weird. Like it's full of sand.

Someone yells my name, but I'm too tired to look for who it is. The person calls out again followed by the sound of tires crunching softly on the gravel. A car door opens and slams shut, then a tentative, "Grace?"

I stop and look over my shoulder. Ivan jogs in my direction, his face a mask of concern.

"Jesus. Where the hell have you been?" He drags a hand through his well-groomed dark hair, his usual calm demeanor gone. "Are you okay? Where's your cell phone? We've been trying to reach you."

I run my fingers through my disheveled hair. "I'm fine."

He eyes me up and down. "You don't look fine."

I shrug weakly and give him my back as I turn to inspect my surroundings with detachment.

"Your mom's worried sick. Come on, get inside the car so I can take you home."

I shake my head and force my feet to take a couple of steps forward. I'm not ready to go home. I need time to get my shit together.

He curses under his breath, and I hear footfalls crunching gravel behind me, then a hand gently tugging my wrist. "At least hop in and get out of the sun."

We walk back to his car. He waits until I've snapped my seat belt on, then slams the door shut and jogs around the car and slides onto the driver's seat.

"How did you find me?"

"Luck, I guess." He restarts the car and slowly drives away. "Your mom called Sol to check if you were at our place. He got worried and called me. We split up hoping to find you quicker. We've been looking for you for the past four hours."

I've been gone that long?

"Sol's worried out of his damn mind. You're going to drive that poor boy crazy one of these days." He cracks a smile but quickly clears his throat and looks away when I don't return it. Then he pulls out his phone from his pocket. "I'll shoot him a text to let him know you're okay."

I haven't seen him in so long, and I'm not sure if I want to. Not when I'm such a mess.

"Where are you taking me?"

"I need to run a few errands before midday. I could take you to our place."

I cringe, wondering what Sol must be thinking of me. Did my mom tell him what happened? I don't think I could face him right now.

"Is MJ home?"

He shakes his head. "She left for New York this morning

and won't be back until Monday."

I sigh, closing my eyes. "I could stay in the car while you run errands."

"No can do, Grace. Look. I'm taking you to my place, all right? If you don't want to talk to him, then you won't need to, but please, your mom needs to know you're okay."

I nod begrudgingly, allowing my body to sink back into the seat. I'm physically and mentally so exhausted that my mind shuts down, lulled by the soft music drifting from the car speakers.

A gentle shake of my shoulder jolts me awake.

"We're here," Ivan says, holding the car door open.

Then he leads the way toward their apartment complex.

Ivan lets us in with his key, then stands back so I can walk in first. I'm still blinking, trying to get my eyes accustomed to the lighting in the room, when strong arms close around me. My body tenses, and I don't return the hug immediately. Then the distinct scent of oil and that special smell that only belongs to Sol fills my senses, comforting me. I sigh into his chest and wrap my arms tight around his waist.

"You're okay," he murmurs while stroking my hair repeatedly with his fingers. Ivan announces that he's leaving and will be back later and closes the door behind him. "I thought I was going to lose my mind, Grace."

"I'm so sorry for worrying you," I mutter into his chest.

Sol pulls back and takes me in, concern furrowing his brows. "When did you last eat or drink anything?"

"Last night, I think." Or was it this morning? Did I even drink any coffee?

He sighs before leading me into the living room and ordering me to sit down. He heads to the kitchen and returns with a bottle of water and hands it to me before leaving the room.

"Could I use your phone? I need to let Mom know I'm okay."

"Sure." He pulls it from his pocket and gives it to me. "I'll be right back."

"Sol? Is she okay?"

Hearing her voice and the concern dripping from her words causes a lump to form in my throat, and my eyes burn with tears.

I clear my throat to stop my voice from shaking. "Mom?"

There's a long pause filled with uncertainty before she says, "Sweetheart?" She sounds almost scared to speak now. "Are you okay?"

Am I okay? Not really. I'm still trying to process everything. I don't answer. Instead, I say, "I'm so sorry for worrying you. I needed air, and I lost track of time."

"It's okay. You're all right, and that's all that matters."

I press my eyes shut to keep the tears at bay as questions burn the tip of my tongue, but I hold them back. I don't really feel comfortable asking them on the phone. Instead, I ask, "Are you . . . can we talk?"

"Yes. Of course," she answers, sounding hopeful. "Come home whenever you're ready, sweetheart. I'll be waiting for you."

I nod. "I love you."

After telling her I'll see her soon, I end the call.

Moments later, Sol walks in carrying a large plastic dish filled with soapy water and a towel in one hand.

"What are you doing?" I ask when he crouches on the floor and takes one sneakered foot in his hand.

"You've been walking in the heat wearing these"—he taps the shoes—"for hours. Just want to make sure everything's okay."

"I can do that—"

His hand tightens on my ankle, his eyes meeting mine. "I'll just take a quick look."

He's being too sweet. And didn't he, like, disappear on me for days on end? I can't find the energy to ask him or be mad at him. I let him check my feet, carefully peeling off my sneakers.

He starts to clean my feet, working diligently without lifting his head to look at me. He doesn't ask me what happened. My breath is caught somewhere in my throat, and once again, tears fill my eyes as he continues to take care of me. Sol is going to make a wonderful priest, and that fact makes my heart hurt even more.

"Everything looks okay," he murmurs, examining my feet after drying them with the towel. "But you need to put your feet up for a few hours to keep the swelling down."

I reach for him, running my fingers through his hair, urging him to look at me. He does, and the worry in his eyes sucks all the air out of my lungs. "Thank you."

He stands and nods, then strides out of the room, taking the towel and plastic dish with him. I gulp down some of the water, not realizing how thirsty I am until it's empty.

"I'll whip up something quick for you to eat," Sol says as he reenters the living room and heads to the kitchen. I want to tell him not to bother, that I'm not hungry, but I don't have the energy to stop him.

I nod, closing my eyes and letting my head fall on the back of the couch.

The next time I open my eyes, Sol is sitting on the couch next to me. He sets a plate on my lap and another bottle of water on the table. "Eat, then we can talk. Uh, I mean if you want to talk about what's going on. Or I'll take you home, or you can stay here. Just let me know what you want to do, okay?"

"Thank you." He's being so sweet, and it's taking all my strength not to crawl in his lap and let him hold me. Instead, I take a small bite of the sandwich just as my stomach growls loudly. "I didn't realize I was so hungry," I say between bites. "This is really good."

He smiles, but it's bleak and worry lines crease his forehead. I polish off the rest of the sandwich in silence. I feel his gaze on me every few seconds, and the silence is just getting awkward.

Sol takes the plate and sets it on the table, then scoots closer, lifting my legs and resting them in his lap. Then he grabs his phone and headphones from the table and hands me one of the earbuds. He shoves the other one into his ear. Within seconds, hard rock music streams into my ear.

"Sweet," I say, appreciating that he's still not pushing me to talk. "Who's this?"

"12 Stones." He taps his screen a few more times, then sets his phone down between us. "This one is titled 'World So Cold.' They've gotten me through some very difficult times."

I squeeze his hand in thanks, then stare at the ceiling, going over the conversation with my mom in my head. I can't even begin to imagine what she went through, the moment . . . that moment when she felt trapped. God.

A shudder wracks through me. I try to push that memory from my mind and focus on the lyrics of the song playing.

"Why do people do bad things?" I ask rhetorically. "Why do some people hurt others?"

The couch dips as he shifts his weight, and I feel the intensity of his concern from his eyes on me. I turn to meet his gaze head-on.

Inhaling deeply, Sol entwines my fingers with his. "Sometimes I think it's a cry for help. Maybe no one was there for them when they needed help the most. Maybe they needed some sort of guidance to set them on the right path. I don't know. I wish I knew the answer, Grace."

"Or maybe they were born evil." My tone is dark and biting.

"No one is born evil."

I mull over his words, when suddenly I feel like I've been sucker-punched. What if I'm carrying that gene, and it's transferred to my kids or something?

Oh my God.

Pulling my feet from his lap, I bolt upright and bury my face in my hands. God, please let this not be the case.

"What is it?" Sol asks from beside me.

I'm not sure I can face him right now or tell him what's going on. I can't bear seeing disgust or pity in his eyes.

"Talk to me, please." He grasps my hands and gently tugs them down to reveal my tear-streaked face. "Tell *me*."

Even though my vision is blurred with tears, I see the lines of worry on his face, and my resolution melts away.

"Today my mom opened up to me for the first time ever. I can't remember how many times I've asked her who my father is, but now I wish I had never insisted on knowing." The song ends and the next one starts, filling in the silence and giving me the time I need to collect my thoughts. I have no idea where to start telling him what happened to Mom. Will he look at me differently? I sure as hell feel different, dirty, guilty.

"She was eighteen when it happened. *Eighteen*, just like me." I take a deep breath and slowly stumble through my words and tell him what happened eighteen years ago. By the time I'm done, I'm exhausted and still angry. The thing is, I'm not even sure if I'm angry with my mom or the man who brought so much pain in her life.

Sol's eyes are filled with pain, and he's breathing hard. He reaches for me but freezes, watching me as if asking for permission. I nod and tug the earbud out of my ear and toss it next to the phone. He does the same with his and shifts closer. I fall into his arms, sinking into him as his arms wrap around me.

"I'm so sorry, Grace. So sorry."

This time, I don't cry. I don't think there are any tears left in me. We stay like this for a little while longer, me soaking in his comfort and him holding me tight as if he's trying to transfer all the pain from my body to his.

He pulls back but doesn't drop his arms from around me. Then he shifts our bodies so he's lying down on his back and I'm on top of him with my head on his chest.

"I know you're hurting. Your mom is pretty special, you know. She didn't give you up like someone else might have done. She loves you, Grace. So much."

His words, the same words that have been filling my every thought, cut me deep and I feel like I'm bleeding from the inside out. At the same time, the truth settles in my chest, offering me the peace I've craved since I fled our apartment.

"She does," I whisper. "Now I understand why she had me take self-defense classes at such a young age and put me on—" I slam my mouth shut before the words can come out.

"Put you on what?"

"Um, birth control pills." The words pour out in a rush as heat fills my cheeks. "She took me to see her OB/GYN when I was fourteen. I thought she was just being overly conscious about that kind of stuff."

Sol's arms squeeze me a little, letting me know he's following the conversation.

"Everything makes so much sense now, but . . . part of me wishes I was back to the times when it didn't. Knowing hurts so much more than I ever thought it would." Eventually, my eyes grow heavy with sleep, and with the steady beating of his heart against my ear, they fall shut.

# thirty-five

*Grace*

I JOLT AWAKE, MY HEART RACING INSIDE MY CHEST FOR NO APPARENT reason. I glance around and find Sol sitting across from me, watching me.

"Hey," he greets in a husky whisper.

"Hey." I glance down my body, noticing the sheet covering me.

"You seemed exhausted. I didn't want to wake you."

I nod, throwing back the sheet. "What time is it?" I ask, sitting up on the bed.

He checks his watch. "Seven-fifteen in the evening."

"Oh, gosh. You missed Mass because of me."

"I'm staying with you for as long as you need me. I called Luke to tell him I won't be attending today."

"That's really sweet of you, Sol. I should go home and talk to my mom."

He stands up and stretches, his T-shirt riding up. I yank my gaze away because I have more pressing matters than drooling over his abs. "I'll drop you whenever you're ready."

"Sol?"

He twists around to look at me, his tousled hair standing around his head. He pushes back the locks of hair on his forehead, and those piercing blue eyes come into view.

"Thank you for everything."

At last, that crooked smile appears, and the world tips sideways. I didn't realize how much I missed it until now. "You're welcome, Gracie."

He leaves the room, returning moments later with my shoes. After I slip them on, I stand, wincing as pain shoots from my feet, then mask it with a cough when Sol turns to look at me.

"I'm ready."

He heads to the front door, and I trail after him, not liking this strange tension between us one bit.

Once we're on our way, he darts a gaze in my direction, then back to the road. His hands flex on the wheel.

"Listen. I know I've been MIA the past week or so. I—I'm not in the right headspace."

"You couldn't pick up the phone and tell me that? Or text me? Isn't that what friends do?"

He purses his lips, and the urge to press mine to his makes me squirm in my seat. Damn, lust has no shame.

*Like seriously, Grace. Abort those thoughts right the fuck now.*

"I'm sorry," he says in a soft voice.

"Yeah. Sure."

We drive in silence the rest of the way. When he parks the car in front of my building, I face him and find him studying me.

"Thank you for this, Sol."

He nods. "Call me if you need to talk or just anything you need, okay?"

I smile and get out of the car. "Don't be a stranger, okay?"

He waits until my mom buzzes me in before driving away, a rock the size of Texas sitting heavy in my chest.

The moment I walk inside the apartment, I know my mom has been keeping herself busy the past few hours while I was away. The floors look shiny; the ever-present dust on the book-shelves is now gone. The kitchen counter spotless.

I raise my brows at her, and she just shrugs as if to say, *I had to keep myself busy.*

We end up sitting across from each other on the couch in the living room. My hands are clutching a pillow tight in my lap just to give them something to do. She's leaning forward, red-rimmed eyes watching me warily. I want to hug her and tell her I'm fine. That she and I are okay. But I need to know the answer to one question that has taken precedence above all others.

I clear my throat to relieve the lump of nervousness lodged in there. "Did you . . ." I'm not sure I can get the words out of my mouth. My stomach is already roiling with panic. As much as I want to know the answer, I'm also terrified. But if I don't ask, I'll never know.

My life has been an equation of unknown variables. I don't want to live like that anymore. I need to stop feeling lost, fearing the unknown.

"You can ask me anything, Gracie. *Anything.*" She smiles, understanding clear in her eyes.

"Did you consider other options? Like adoption or . . ." *Abortion.* I can't bring myself to say that word out loud. It's just so final and brutal.

As if she can read my thoughts, she quickly says, "Getting rid of you like that was never an option. It never crossed my mind to walk into a clinic and do it. Plus, I come from a family of staunch Catholics. Mom and Dad would have arranged for an exorcism if I'd considered it." She laughs, shaking her head.

Then she inhales deeply, the hand resting on her knee form-ing a loose fist. "After your grandparents realized I was pregnant, they took over and started making arrangements.

"Mom arranged for adoption through an agency. Everything

was going so fast, and I was still reeling from what had happened and was going through therapy. I let my parents take over completely because I felt like they knew what was best for me. When I was eight weeks pregnant, Mom accompanied me for my first prenatal visit. I was lying on the bed during the ultrasound, confused and tears falling down my face, feeling lost, when she started pointing out where the baby was; the little arms and legs, head, then I heard this fast *thump, thump, thump* coming from the little screen."

A brilliant smile breaks across her face, and her eyes shine with tears. I suck in a deep breath and hold it, waiting, waiting, waiting until my lungs burn, desperate for air. But still I wait for her words.

This feels like the moment I've been waiting for. The moment when scattered pieces of my life come together to form a larger picture. Sometimes we go through life, floating aimlessly with no destination in mind, looking for some kind of sign, a life-altering moment that will shake you to your core and give you purpose. I guess this is mine.

"You resembled a tiny bean, and you were wiggling a lot. And I was just lying there staring at the screen in wonder. And just like that, I *knew*. Everything became clear. I didn't feel lost anymore. I knew what my purpose in life was. So I looked up at your grandmother and said, 'Mom, I'm keeping this baby.'"

Air whooshes out of my mouth and nose, followed by a low sob. I bury my face in my hands, my shoulders loosening as relief sweeps through me. Even before Mom told me what happened, I knew, deep in my heart, that she'd fought her parents to keep me. But hearing the story unties the knot in my stomach I never knew existed.

There's a sound of fabric crinkling and then the couch dips as a weight settles next to me. Then I'm being pulled into a tight embrace.

"Shh, sweetheart," Mom says. "No one tried to take you away from me after that. I wouldn't let them."

Twisting my body around, I bury my face into her shoulder and wrap my arms around her waist tightly. She strokes my hair over and over.

Eventually, I lift my head and look into her eyes, and this huge ball of gratitude grows with every passing second. And when I feel like my chest is about to rip open, unable to contain my feelings, I say, "Thank you for keeping me."

She smiles, her bottom lip quivering and eyes gleaming with tears as she wipes my tear-stained cheeks with her thumbs. "You're my little angel. My blessing."

We don't attend Mass the following day. Instead, we snuggle on the couch and just talk and watch videos from when I was a toddler. My baptism, when I lost my first tooth, birthday parties, my First Holy Communion, and my graduation. We laugh at the ones Mom took the first time I learned to roll from my back to my belly and when I attempted my first steps. Growing up, I used to give her a hard time whenever she whipped out the camera to take photos and videos. But now, now I'm grateful for these memories.

By the time I go to bed, I feel like I'm ready to take control of my life. I know how I got here. I know exactly what it took for my mom to bring me into this world. And I want to prove to her, despite everything, she can be proud of her daughter. If I can be half as strong as my mom, I'll consider myself blessed.

# thirty-six

## Sol

I HAVEN'T SEEN GRACE SINCE SATURDAY WHEN I DROPPED HER OFF at her place. After talking to Seth, I realized I was being selfish. What kind of person makes promises and gives hope, then rips it away when temptation strikes? I didn't want to be that kind of person.

I still don't, but I need my friend back.

She hasn't called or sent me a text. When I realize I almost messed up an oil change, something I've done so often I could do it with my eyes closed, I know my head is not in the right head-space. I finally cave, and after speaking to Joe, I take the rest of the day off. My breathing picks up, anticipation buzzing through me as I climb into my truck and drive to Deb's.

As soon as I park my car, I'm hurrying toward the diner in long strides. The little bell above the door tinkles as I step through it. My gaze quickly scans the room and lands on Grace refilling the pastry display case. I lick my lips and flex my hands, nervous all of a sudden. It reminds me of the way I felt several weeks ago before she and I became friends, and I don't like it. But I'm not going to let it stop me.

I stride toward her, pull the stool from under the counter, and sit down, then prop my elbows on the Formica counter.

Grace finishes stocking the display case and stands up. Our eyes meet. Hers grow wide, and then a huge grin splits across her face.

"Hi!" She rounds the counter and wraps her arms around my waist in a hug. I wasn't sure what to expect when I walked in here.

The anxiousness I was feeling seconds before melts away, and I wrap my arms around her, pulling her tight against my body.

"Hey." I lean back slightly, my gaze roaming her face, noticing the dark circles around her eyes. "You doing okay?"

She starts to nod but seems to change her mind and shakes it. Her honesty jostles something inside me. Warmth fills my chest, and I hug her to me again. It's such a great thing to know she doesn't have to hide whatever she's feeling from me.

Even with the dark circles around her eyes and the haunted look in their depths, she's beautiful. Not just on the outside. Grace is beautiful in every way.

From the corner of my eye, I see Beverly standing next to a booth with a notepad in hand, ready to take the order from a family of three. I notice Debra walking toward me, and I quickly drop my arms from around her daughter. After she told me that her mom warned her about me, I've been more careful with the way I handle myself, especially in front of Debra.

A smile splits Debra's face when she sees me. And even though she looks as tired as her daughter, she somehow looks much more at peace.

"Hey, Ms. Miller," I greet her, returning her smile.

"Sol." She stops, facing us from the other side of the counter. Her gaze moves back and forth between Grace and me. "Why don't you two take a seat in the booth over there? I'll get you both something to eat."

"Actually, I wanted to ask you if I could borrow Grace for a few hours."

She hesitates for several seconds, then turns her attention to her daughter. "Could you take the order at table five before you leave?"

Grace nods and does what her mother asks. As soon as she's out of earshot, Debra turns to me.

"I don't think that's a good idea, Sol." Her voice is low, but I hear the worry mingled with a warning. "She cares for you, much more than as a simple friend. I see the way she looks at you, and the way you look at her . . . things won't end well when you leave."

I shift on my feet, suddenly very nervous "We both know our boundaries." I pause, wondering how far I should go with this conversation, and I decide to be honest with her. "She means a lot to me, too, Ms. Miller. The last thing I want is to hurt her in any way." I hold her gaze, hoping she can see the sincerity in my eyes. "I completely understand your concern. If you tell me to stop hanging out with her, I will."

Those words hang between us as she studies me with narrowed eyes. Then she takes a deep breath and steps away from the counter.

"You're a good man, Sol. And I trust you. I couldn't ask for a better friend for her. She's changed so much the past few weeks. She smiles and laughs more, and I know it's because of you. Thank you, Sol."

My throat closes up. Guilt assaults me as the past few weeks flash inside my head. I don't deserve her praise and trust.

Unable to form words around the lump in my throat, I force my lips to smile, then exhale the pent-up breath when she turns and grabs the white and pink apron hanging from a nail on the wall just as Grace returns. She rips the paper with the order from her notebook and hands it to her mother, then unties her apron and hangs it up.

"Ready?" She swings around to face me, her eyes brighter than when I walked in.

I nod and stand from the stool. After saying goodbye to Debra, I lead Grace out the door and toward my truck, the scorching sun causing sweat to break out on my forehead.

"Where are we going?" she asks as soon as we're buckled in.

"Uh . . ." I rub my stubbled jaw, realizing I don't really have a destination in mind. When I decided to drive by the diner, my only intention was to check on how she was doing. Then I saw her—her tired eyes and slumped shoulders—and suddenly, I wanted to see her eyes light up like that time we drove to Ranger's Cove. I clear my throat. "How about we just drive until we see something interesting?"

"So no plan in mind?" She smirks, squinting to keep the sun from her eyes. "You're such a rebel."

"Oh, shut up." I laugh, the knot that has been tightening in my stomach since the conversation with Debra finally loosening. Being around Grace, being able to laugh like this, melts something inside me every single time.

With my fingers curled around the wheel, I glance at the rearview mirror to make sure it's safe to pull out of the parking spot before driving away.

We've been driving in silence for a few minutes when I flick my gaze in her direction, taking in how peaceful she looks. "Everything okay between you and your mom?"

She sighs. "Yeah"—she rubs her forehead—"I think. We haven't argued or anything. Something has changed. It's been a little awkward being around each other." She sighs again.

"It's understandable, considering what she told you. But I'm sure everything will go back to normal eventually."

"I keep wanting to apologize to her for . . . everything. Honestly, it's exhausting. I miss that easiness she and I had, you know. I *need* things to go back to the way they were."

Seeing her so torn sends pain scorching through my chest. I take the next exit and pull over on the first street I see. Once parked, I reach over and take her hand in mine.

"You two will get through this. You just need time, okay?"

Tears shimmer in her eyes as her gaze bounces all over my face as if trying to decipher the truth in those words. Finally, she nods. "We've been talking about going to therapy together."

"You have? Whose idea was that?"

"Mine," she whispers as if she's not sure if it will work. "I just hope it will help."

I lean across the console and pull her in my arms without a second thought. She comes willingly, tucking her face into my chest. "Everything will be okay, Grace. You'll see." I kiss her hair before pulling back.

She wipes her face with her palm and gives me a tentative smile.

"Don't underestimate your strength, Grace. I know you. You'd move Heaven and Earth to make it work."

She starts to shake her head, but I give her hand a gentle squeeze to stop her.

"Your mom is the only parent you've ever known. You two share a bond stronger than the pain *he* made her—made you both—go through."

She nods, lifting her chin in determination as if ready for a battle.

"Good." I restart the truck and then toss her a smile, the one I know she loves, before pulling out of the spot and driving away.

We've been driving for a while when I see the arcade up ahead. Excitement courses through me. I haven't been there in a long time. It's time to rekindle some good memories. My mom and dad used to take me to the arcade back in Boston every Saturday afternoon.

"Ready to have some fun?" I point at the green building with different colored lights flashing.

"I've never been to an arcade before," she says, sounding unsure.

"There's a first time for everything, Grace Miller." I grin at her.

After finding a parking spot, I jump out of the truck and jog to the passenger door to open it for Grace. She hops down and swivels around to face me, moving closer.

"Have I thanked you for being my friend yet?"

"Y-you don't need to do that."

She steps closer until our toes touch, then slips her arms around my waist. My entire body shudders as air rushes out of my mouth. And then, she just hugs me, and my arms move of their own accord because this is Grace. When it comes to this girl, I can't resist her, no matter how hard I try. But this time, I've mastered control. I won't let my mind wander like before.

The world falls away, and for these few seconds or minutes or hours, it's just us. Then Debra's words flash through my memory, making me lose my breath for an entirely different reason. I'm about to take a step back when Grace snatches the cap off my head and plops it on her own, stands on her tiptoes and presses a quick kiss to my lips. She spins around and skips away, leaving me frozen on the spot, my stupid rebellious body a riot of nerves and hormones.

"You coming or what?" she asks over her shoulder, and I find myself grinning wide, despite the chaos her kiss left inside my head.

My Grace is back, and I couldn't be happier.

Dear God, help me. Please give me the strength to resist her.

I sigh, trailing after her while plowing my fingers into my hair and muttering a prayer under my breath.

# thirty-seven

*Sol*

FTER OUR TRIP TO THE ARCADE, GRACE AND I HUNG OUT AT her place for an hour. We were just chatting when she suddenly opened up to me, telling me she was worried her children would end up being like the man who fathered her.

Pain stabbed in my chest just thinking about her future without me, and my own panic threatened to swallow me alive. I pushed that image out of my mind and told her I couldn't imagine her children being anything other than honest and loving and kind, just like her and Debra. And as we continued chatting, I saw a fierce determination settle in her features, and I knew any child of hers would be lucky to call her their mother. She'd do anything for the people she loves.

On Sunday after evening Mass, I put away the alb, then head to Luke's office. His back is to me when I enter. He seems distracted as he stares at something out the window.

I sit down in my usual chair across the desk and stretch my legs in front of me. "You okay?"

He looks over his shoulder at me, and an uneasiness creeps into my chest at the concern darkening his features. Walking away from the window, he settles in his chair and watches me carefully for several seconds. Instead of answering my question, he asks, "You ready?"

I frown. "Ready? Ready for what?"

He drags his fingers through his brown hair, and I notice he has more silver now than he did a few months ago. "You haven't withdrawn your application to attend the seminary, so I assume you've made up your mind?"

I swallow hard and nod. "Yes." Going away to the seminary, putting some distance between Grace and me, is what I need to completely clear my head.

His eyebrows rise slightly. He covers his mouth with one hand, looking thoughtful. "So, Grace?"

Not this again. "What about her?"

Both of Luke's brows shoot up, and something in his eyes shifts. Disbelief, maybe? I'm about to call him out on it when he says, "You two at the confessional a few weeks ago . . .?"

I snap my mouth shut as heat burns my cheeks and ears. Shit. How does he know I was in there with Grace? I got out before he entered the booth. And why did he wait so long to ask me? Maybe he was waiting for me to tell him?

My brain scrambles for an excuse, any excuse, but it's pointless. My fingers dig through my hair, the need to hide from his knowing eyes overwhelming. Why did I leave my cap in the truck?

"Um, about that, I'm really sorry—"

He lifts his hand and stops me, his expression stern. I've never seen him like this before. It's terrifying. "I'll ask you again, son. Think carefully. Are you sure this is what *you* want?"

My eyes fall shut as the full weight of the decision I've been avoiding settles heavily on my shoulders. What I feel for Grace and my desire to serve God in the only way I know and ever wanted clash together. I know who I am when I'm with Grace, but without God, without finding out if He's truly calling me to serve him, I don't know who I am.

"I've thought about it, reflected and prayed, Luke. I'm ready," I declare confidently, hoping he doesn't hear the lies weaved in those words.

"All right," he says, and I can't tell what he's thinking. "I'll have the final papers for tuition signed and ready. Orientation is scheduled for next week, yeah?"

I nod. "I'll spend the weekend there. I plan to visit Mom and Dad and also check on the house, just to make sure everything's running well."

I was never able to bring myself to sell it or even rent it out. It's the place where I grew up for the first ten years of my life, and there are so many memories in that house. Sometimes, when I miss my parents, I like to drive to Boston and visit with them at the cemetery, then spend a few days in the house and watch videos of the three of us. Other than the church, that place is my haven.

After leaving Luke's office a few minutes later, I head to my truck in the parking lot, trying to breathe through the panic tightening its hold around my throat. I'm meeting Ivan and MJ at the apartment, just to hang out and have fun. I whisper a prayer under my breath, asking God to ease the ache in my heart. That my heart won't pine for her like it did before, like she's the missing link that completes me.

# thirty-eight

*Sol*

SUNDAY AFTER MASS, I HEAD HOME AND SLIP ON MY FAVORITE faded running shorts and T-shirt, then join Ivan at the Xbox. We've been playing for a half an hour when a knock on the door has me pausing the game. Ivan groans, running his fingers through his hair. "I was this close to beating you, man."

"Er. Dream on, dude. Are we expecting someone?" I ask, cutting a glance to MJ. She grins and winks at me, while shoving her current project inside a plastic bag. She's taken up crocheting as a new hobby, courtesy of her grandmother.

"Yeah. Grace. I thought she could use a little cheering up after, you know . . ." she explains, scrambling off the couch and skipping to the door. "Put away the toys, boys."

After MJ returned from visiting her parents, she and Grace talked about what happened while she was away.

I drop my controller on the table and stand just as I hear the front door open. I'm really glad they've gotten close. Grace needs people like MJ. People who'll readily offer her genuine friendship. At least she'll have someone else she can talk to when I'm gone.

Within seconds, MJ and Grace are walking into the room,

arms around each other, Grace with a plastic bag in her free hand.

I'm about to move toward her, but end up freezing on the spot as I take her in. My dick went from sleeping to "Hey there, gorgeous. Wanna play?"

She changed from the beige dress and heels she was wearing during Mass. Now she's wearing white shorts, a hot pink T-shirt, and low-heeled white shoes. A large, striped bow tie decorates the front. Her dark curls fall beautifully down her shoulders, and dear Lord, her lips are painted in a red lipstick that outlines her full lips perfectly. Every single thought I've ever had about her— the thoughts I'd safely locked away inside that little box in my head marked 'Gracie'—comes slamming back with a vengeance. Every single kiss we've ever shared flashes inside my head. I can't stop staring at her lips, or the way those shorts hug her—God help me.

*Stop stop stop. Don't backslide now,* I reprimand myself. *You're better than this. Remember what you told Debra at the diner about never wanting to hurt Grace in any way.*

She trusts me. She thinks I'm a good man.

I want to deserve her trust. I want to prove to God, to myself, and to Debra that I'm the person they believe me to be.

I shove the thoughts about Grace out of my head.

"Hey," I greet, watching as she walks over. "I didn't know you were coming over."

"Thought I'd drop by with this." She lifts the plastic bag, smiling shyly, and that little gap between her teeth makes my knees weak. MJ grabs the bag from her, and she flashes me an impish grin as she heads to the kitchen.

Grace throws her arms around me in a hug. I can't help it; I pull her to me. This close, she smells so good, like fresh waffles and Sunday morning, the memory of sitting between my mom and dad as we ate brunch after church.

I look where MJ is pulling takeout boxes from the bags, then glance down at Grace, grinning wide. It's like Christmas and my birthday all rolled into one. "You brought waffles?"

"Waffles Sunday. I thought we could eat brunch together because you're leaving. I mean, I should have called . . ." She twists her fingers nervously.

"Shush, Gracie. Just because I'm leaving doesn't mean you can't stop by whenever you want. We were friends before, before things got weird, remember?"

She nods, hiking on the tip of her toes and kissing my cheek. "We'll always be friends, no matter what. *Always*, Sol." Then she walks away and tosses her keys and purse on the coffee table and heads for the counter. Her scent lingers, teasing me, reminding me what I'll be leaving behind.

I remind myself she's better off being with someone who's clear about what they really want, not doing things half-assed. Sometimes loving someone means letting them go, no matter how much it hurts, because you know you are not good for them.

With that decision in mind, I join my three friends in the kitchen, making sure to keep a healthy distance between Grace and me by staying on the other side of the counter.

We end up taking the food with us in the living room where MJ suggests we watch a movie. After we all agree—or rather MJ and Grace—to watch *10 Things I Hate About You*, MJ and Ivan end up on the loveseat. Grace grabs a pillow from the couch before her friend can protest and tosses it on the floor. She plops down cross-legged and digs into her waffles and ice cream with vigor. It's a treat to watch her eat.

Finally, I settle for the ugly green plastic chair Ivan bought from a flea market downtown last spring and take a bite of my food. The movie starts, and from the corner of my eye, I see Grace kick off her shoes and wiggle her toes. I can't stop staring at her toes. They look adorable. I'd totally kiss them and—

*Oh my God.*

*Kiss her toes? What on earth is wrong with me?*

Why the heck am I thinking about her toes?

I sigh, scooping another bite into my mouth, and force my gaze to the screen just as one of the female actors—I'm not good with names—rips a poster from the wall. On my right, Ivan and MJ are feeding each other waffles and whispering to each other. If they start calling each other *kitten* or any other name, I'm out of here.

At some point, I find Grace watching me with heat in her eyes, but she bites the corner of her mouth and quickly looks away when our gazes meet. Then she sets her plate on the table and stands. Grabbing her pillow, she walks toward me. Then she's arranging it at my feet and tugging my hand, urging me to join her.

I start to shake my head, letting her know it's not a good idea, but she mouths, "Please. Please," and whispers, "Come sit with me."

And I do because I still haven't learned how to say no to her. I mean, it's not like she's asking me to touch her boob or something.

Seconds later, I carefully wrap my arm around her shoulder. She sighs, burrowing deeper into my chest. I haven't held her like this since the time she left my apartment after the revelation. I'm not sure if she wants me to, if she's comfortable with me touching her. It's just, I don't want to overstep.

I squeeze her shoulder to get her attention. When her gaze meets mine, I ask, "Is this weird, you know, after what your mom . . ."

She quickly shakes her head. "No. I was worried it would be weird for you."

"I-I missed my best friend," I finally admit, kissing her hair. "Cute toes, by the way. Pink looks good on you."

She giggles. "Now who has a foot fetish?"

"Should we leave you two alone or something?" Ivan asks, setting their plates on the table and standing up while pulling MJ to her feet. He drags her toward his room, tossing me a wink from over his shoulder.

Chuckling, I roll my eyes at his persistence, like a dog with a bone. He still doesn't get it.

Settling in my arms and letting out a sigh, the tension in Grace's body melts away slowly. "Are you going to miss me?" she asks.

"Of course, I will."

She's quiet for a few seconds. She lifts her hand and runs her fingers through my hair. She opens her mouth to say something, then stops, a frown on her face.

"What is it?" I ask her.

"I can't stop thinking about you. Us," she says in a low voice, eyes on the floor as though admitting it makes her weak. Or maybe she's ashamed?

She bites her bottom lip and inhales deeply. "I've been think-ing. Um, I know we almost did it in your truck . . . and I haven't stopped thinking about it. Do you think we could, I mean, do you want to. . ." She clears her throat and coughs twice, her hands wandering up my chest in cautious light strokes, then down my abs. They stop on my thigh, causing every nerve in my body to stir eagerly. I understand her meaning even without her saying it out loud.

My heart races in my chest, my pulse thudding in my ears. I

drop my arms and jump to my feet. "No, Gracie."

She nods, looking resigned, and mutters, "Okay."

"What I mean is—"

"Forget it, okay? I just thought . . . Sorry I asked. I don't know what's wrong with me. I know you said—"

I raise a hand in the air, cutting her off, not in the mood to simply *forget it.* "Why did you offer it if you're going to take it back?"

Why am I pissed off anyway?

She sits up on her knees, her eyes dark with irritation. "I'm sorry, okay? Jeez. What's gotten into you?"

I stare at the TV screen, wondering where this conversation went wrong. Sure, Grace is spontaneous. And sometimes, she says whatever is running inside her head. I should be used to it by now. But sex?

"So you'd give up your virginity just like that?" I scoff, crossing my arms over my chest. God, I'm an asshole. When did I become this guy?

She leaps to her feet and props her hands on her hips. "You think I haven't thought this through? You think I'd just do away with it like I'm scratching an itch?" She inhales deeply, her nostrils flaring. "You think, after all this time, after *refusing* to give it up to Gavin and whoever else thought I was easy, asking you if you want to have sex is no big deal? As if it meant nothing?"

Okay, so I didn't think this through before accusing her.

Holy shit. She's so pissed.

She whirls around all of a sudden, storming to the spot where she left her shoes. After slipping them on, she grabs her keys and purse from the coffee table and twists around to glower at me. I brace myself for the torrent of words I'm sure she's ready to throw at me, given that fierce look on her face.

Instead, she shakes her head and walks out of the apartment.

The sound of the door slamming reverberates inside the small space, and the ferocity of her anger still crackles in the air.

I take a step forward, ready to follow her, but instead, I sit my ass back on the couch. I drop my head in my hands, confused by my own reaction.

I open my phone to send her a text, but every time I go to type, words fail me. Eventually, I settle for a piss-poor *I'm sorry.*

She doesn't reply.

I don't blame her. When I first thought out this little plan about becoming Grace's friend, I guess I underestimated how complicated everything would be later.

I yank the cap from my head and throw it on the couch, then bury my face into my hands. What the hell am I going to do? Regret churns inside my stomach as sweat beads my forehead.

We can't part like this. I need to talk to her.

God, what a mess.

I dial her number and press the phone to my ear. The call goes to voicemail after five rings. I try again, and the same thing happens. On the third try, I wait until I hear the beep, then say, "Grace, I'm so sorry. I should have explained myself better instead of biting your head off." Inhaling deeply, I forge ahead. "I meant to say that doing it is not a good idea. I have a feeling if we do it, I won't be able to get you out of my system. And I need to see this through. I can't do that to us, Grace. Please call me when you get this, okay? It's okay to be angry with me, but please, *please* don't shut me out."

I disconnect the call and storm to my room. After changing into a pair of running shorts and a T-shirt, I grab my cell and headphones and head out for a run.

# thirty-nine

*Grace*

**I**'M SORRY.

Guilt knots in my belly as I stare at those two words.

It's been four days since I stormed out of Sol and Ivan's apartment. The thing is, I can't stop thinking about him. And I can't stop the ever-present weight on my chest, pressing and pressing until I feel like I'm suffocating. I drop my head in my hands as another wave of guilt washes over me, causing my hands to tremble.

God, I feel so stupid. It wasn't fair to ask him to have sex with me. I realized that the second the words left my mouth. But I couldn't go back and apologize. I was so embarrassed. I didn't want him to hate me. When I'm around him, it's like my brain short-circuits.

What if he does, though? He wouldn't say sorry if he did, right?

I shake my head to get rid of that thought.

I took a chance with him. It was stupid. And now I know sex wasn't the way to go.

My feelings for him cloud my judgment. And the fact he's leaving for Boston makes this emptiness in my chest even more tangible. All I want to do is hold on to him in any way I can.

When I'm close to him, I can't think straight. I desperately want his mouth on mine, his hands on my body. Is it even normal to feel like this? Should I be repulsed by sex after what happened to my mom?

I shake my head. No, what happened to my mom was horrible. This, this is sex. And it can be beautiful. With Sol, I know it would be.

I've been going in circles, like a dog chasing its own tail, bouncing between accepting his apology and spending the last few days before he leaves with him, and ignoring his text. He'll leave, find new adventures in his journey with God, and forget about me. Staying away is a win-win situation for the both of us. We won't need to say goodbye.

I hate goodbyes.

Sighing, I inform my mom I'm heading to Casco Bay Culinary Institute to sign us up for their weekly cooking class. Two nights ago, I found a flyer stuck between the wipers and the windshield of my car advertising the newly opened institute. I thought it would be a great mother-daughter bonding experience on top of the therapy sessions.

I leave the diner and head for my car when a hand grasps my bicep. My body tenses and I spin around, my foot raised, ready to slam it down on whoever touched me, but the scent of motor oil and sunshine fills my nostrils.

"Whoa! It's me, Gracie."

And just like that, the tension melts away from my body. I should be worried Sol has that kind of power over me, but right now, I'm too busy drinking him in like he's water and I'm parched.

"You shouldn't sneak up on people like that."

He looks offended. "I wasn't sneaking up on you. I thought you heard me walking up to you. I even called your name."

"Well, I didn't."

"Obviously." His lips twitch as he stares down at the foot that almost knocked him on his ass. His forehead creases slightly with a frown. "Look, can we talk?"

Panic grips my throat once again. It's as if I don't know how to be around him anymore, yet I want nothing more than to fall into his arms. "Right now? I kind of—"

"I just need a few minutes. I'm driving to Boston tonight for orientation. Can we talk in my truck? I have to go to the apartment to change my clothes before leaving. I can drop you back here when we're finished talking."

I nod reluctantly and allow him to steer me toward his truck.

We drive in silence until he cuts his eyes to me and says, "Aren't you going to confession today? You're the only person I know who attends confession every week."

"Not today." I find myself smiling at him. I can't help it. Not when he's looking at me with such gentleness. "The sins I would've confessed didn't quite happen," I say pointedly.

"I'm sorry I was an ass. I shouldn't have said those things to you."

I sigh and twist my body to face him. I pull one leg up, tucking it under me. "About what happened . . . I'm so sorry for putting you on the spot. It wasn't fair to ask you that." Unable to hold his gaze, I drop mine to his fingers drumming a quick beat on the wheel. "Your friendship means everything to me, Sol. I don't want to lose it."

He's quiet for a few seconds. I can feel the heat of his gaze on my face before he returns his focus to the road. "I didn't want to leave knowing you're still pissed at me. I won't be able to live with myself, Grace."

"I was angrier with myself, I think."

He pauses. "We'll still be friends, right?"

Friends.

"Yes." I smile, hoping I'm good at hiding the desperation overwhelming my heart.

"So we're good?"

I make sure he's looking at me when I say, "Of course."

I look out the window and realize we're parked outside his building already. And when my eyes move back to him, he's carefully assessing me. Then he murmurs, "Good," and turns to open his door, hiding his eyes from me.

By the time I unbuckle my seat belt, he's already opening the passenger door for me. He's such a gentleman. Why, oh why did he have to go and be a priest? I jump out, and we head for his apartment.

Once inside, he kicks the apartment door shut with his foot, then unlaces his sneakers and throws them to the side. He straightens to his full height, his hands clenching and unclenching at his sides.

"I'm really going to miss you, Gracie. Are you going to miss me?"

"Of course. You're my best friend."

He steps closer, the heat coming off his body wrapping around me. "Really?"

I step back, not because I'm afraid of him, but because he's just so overwhelming and intense. Especially when he's staring down at me the way he is right now. As if he wants to throw me over his shoulder and march off to his cave, beating his chest and growling, "Mine."

He bridges the distance between us, caging me to the wall, and I forget to breathe.

"What are you doing, Sol?"

He drags his fingers through his hair, then braces that

same hand on the wall next to my head as if he's trying to hold his weight up. He leans down, bringing his mouth to my ear, his nose into my hair, and inhales deeply.

"Ah, vanilla waffles. God, I could take a bite out of you right now, Gracie," he whispers.

# forty

*Grace*

THE EDGES OF HIS TEETH SKIM ACROSS THE SKIN THERE, THEN bite down, but not hard enough to break the skin.

I gasp. I squeeze my eyes shut as desire rushes through me, and my skin tingles as warmth pools in my belly. Too much heat and need slam into me all at once. I don't know what to do, but apparently, my body knows what it wants as it arches forward, pushing into his chest.

I whisper, "Sol."

I'm trying to remember why I'm here, but my brain is foggy. My fingers clench around his T-shirt and push him away. I suck in deep breaths. His head dips down, his mouth following mine, undeterred. "I thought—" I shake my head to clear it. "Aren't you supposed to be getting ready for Boston?"

"Yeah. Of course." His chest rises and drops fast, conflict and need darkening his gaze. His eyes, looking into mine, say everything his mouth doesn't, splitting me in half. I'm a ball of agony, hope, desperation, and *love*. So much love for this boy. He blows out air through his mouth and drops his forehead to my shoulder. "You're right. I'm sorry."

Those words combined with his husky voice cut through me. My fingers climb up his back and tangle in his hair. "Me too."

He lifts his head and kisses my forehead, then takes a step back. "I gotta go change." He jerks his thumb over his shoulder. "We good?"

I nod and force a smile. "Yes."

He gives me a brief smile before heading to his room down the hall. His bedroom door closing sounds like the ending of something that could've been beautiful. Something left unexplored.

At the thought, pain stabs my chest. I've never wanted anything or anyone as much as I want Sol.

# Sol

I grab the edge of my T-shirt and yank it over my head, then bunch it in a ball in my hands. I take deep breaths to calm myself because I'm shaking with need and frustration.

I need to get her out of here before my body finally caves and begs her to let me take her.

All of her.

And for her to take all of me.

She's my curse and my temptation, and right now, she's the escape that could save me from this hell I've been locked in since I knew what it felt to want someone.

Grace Miller will be my hardest goodbye, but to preserve my sanity, I have to say goodbye today. The sooner the better for both of us.

I toss the balled-up T-shirt in the hamper next to the door, then grab a clean dark blue one. I've just slipped my right arm in the armhole when I hear two knocks at my door.

"Hold on a sec," I mutter as I slide the T-shirt the rest of the way and tug it down my stomach. My heart races when I open the door and find Grace standing there, arms crossed around her midriff. "Almost done," I say, leaving the door open and crossing the room to grab the folder with signed paperwork.

"Um . . . so I was thinking we just have, like, one life to live, right?" she announces.

I stop at my desk and look over my shoulder. "Unless you're a cat or something, then yes. One life." I chuckle at my own joke. "What is it, Gracie?"

She laughs nervously. "Well, I have a suggestion."

"Can we do this in the car?" I grab the file and stride back to the door. She steps in my path and places both hands on my chest. Peeling the folder from my grip, she carefully lays it on top of the dresser before meeting my gaze with heat and pure need. Tension coils in my groin.

"Nope. I think we'd get arrested if we did it in the car." She giggles, her eyes dropping to my chest. "God, I think something's wrong with me. I just apologized to you less than ten minutes ago, yet here I am, asking you the same thing—"

"*Grace*." I bridge the distance between us. "Look at me, *please*."

She lifts her head. Her eyes are wide, and fear and need are warring in them when they meet mine. Her lip trembles slightly, and I know it's taking her a lot of courage to say whatever she's about to say.

"Just one more question before you leave. If you were given only one chance to do whatever you want, what would that be? Don't think about tomorrow or whatever. Think about the present."

"You," I say without thinking, the word coming out as naturally as breathing. My hands slide down to grip her hips and tug her flush against my body. That part of me I've been holding back breaks free as her scent surrounds me.

God, I want to kiss her so much.

"I want to put my mouth on your skin and explore every part of you with my hands. I want to feel you. Really feel you. I want to love you." My gaze roams her face, and I swallow hard, the possibilities of the things she and I could do flashing inside my head. "The way you deserve to be loved."

She's breathing fast now, eyes wide and almost black, bottom lip trembling. "Then do it. Do everything you just said."

My pulse thuds in my ears, and my vision blurs with want.

*No, don't do it, Solomon.* I shut my eyes tight, praying for control. *Maybe this is a test. Maybe—*

"Are you sure? It won't change what happens next, Grace. I'll still leave for Boston."

"I know," she whispers, nodding. "But I'd rather have you only once and have this experience to cherish than wonder how it could have been every single day for the rest of my life. My first time, Sol, I want it to be with you. No one else."

I shift my weight from one leg to the other. "But wouldn't you rather give it to someone who'll spend the rest of your life with you?"

"No." She shakes her head. "I want to have a piece of you with me. Something that is ours only, forever."

Everything grows fainter and fainter, and my vision goes blurry with want as this powerful desire consumes me whole. The need I've learned to control has broken loose.

Suddenly seized by a craving so fierce I'm practically vibrating with it, I hoist her up my body. I cross the room to my bed and lay her down, my frame draping over hers. My mouth captures hers, and the second our tongues touch, we both groan in relief.

"Finally," she whispers into my mouth, but I kiss her words away and replace them with soft, desperate moans.

If heaven has a sound, this must be it.

# forty-one

*Grace*

OL'S LARGE BODY COVERS MINE, PINNING ME TO THE BED AS HIS hips roll, creating a friction between us. My hands are moving, touching him everywhere, unable to get enough. Sinewy muscles, broad chest, chiseled jaw, his back, his arms. My fingers finally have the freedom they've been craving, and nothing's going to stop them.

I grab the edge of his T-shirt and yank it up, up, up, but his arms are in my way and his hands are consuming every part of me with firm touches, leaving imprints on my skin.

"Take this off," I order him.

He sits up on his haunches, grabs the edge of the T-shirt, and pulls it over his head, then throws it on the floor. His shorts and boxers get the same treatment. Then he's kneeling in front of me, looking glorious. My eyes trail down his shoulders, his chest, down to the fine line of hair on his lower stomach. And finally, his hard length.

He glances down at himself, then shyly at me, his cheeks flushing red. "I—um . . . well, is it okay? I mean—you know."

"It's beautiful," I say quickly, hoping to ease the discomfort so clear on his face. "I've never . . . seen one before, so—"

His eyes widen, hopeful. "You never, you know, saw—" He

coughs nervously. "Gavin or whatever?"

I shake my head, biting my lips to keep from smiling. He's so cute. "We mostly just kissed and never wandered anywhere below the waist."

The awkwardness disappears, and he smiles, and dear Lord, what a beautiful smile.

"Your turn." There's a tremor in his voice that wasn't there before as he leans forward and pulls me up so I'm sitting instead of lying flat on my back.

He settles behind me, and the sensation is alluring. I lift my arms as he pushes my blouse over my head. Then he throws it on the floor. He unhooks my bra, and it joins the rest of our clothes. His lips trace my spine, and his warm breath feathers my skin. I groan when his hands move to my butt and lift me, then proceed to remove my skirt. He turns me around, and I fall on my back, eager and nervous as he sits back. His eyes take me in, pausing for several seconds when they reach the space between my legs. When he meets my gaze again, his blue one is like the night sky.

He crawls up my body, and his tongue begins exploring me, my neck, my shoulders. He murmurs, "Sweet," takes my nipple into his mouth, and growls deep in his throat as he sucks on it gently. You'd think with him being so big, he'd be clumsy and awkward, but he knows how to work his body.

"Shit," he says, burying his face into the crook of my neck. "I can't . . . we can't do this."

"What? *Why?*" The latter comes out on a shaky breath. I can't believe this is happening.

"Because I don't have condoms. You could get pregnant and—"

"I'm on the pill," I say, relief pouring into me. "And we're both virgins."

His head snaps up, and his eyes blink as if he's trying to clear the fog in his brain.

He flashes me a grin then, lifting his upper body. "Thank God. I was about to run into Ivan's room and turn the whole place upside down."

He leans down, pressing his lips between my breasts, before raising his head and trailing shaky fingers down my stomach. They stop at my navel, circling once, twice, before moving down to my hips. His breathing picks up as they trace my skin there. My legs tense when his index finger soothes a path between my thighs. He lowers his head, and his mouth follows the same path his hand did. I'm sucking in air, shivering. His lips reach my navel, and my entire body feels like it's coming apart at the seams. My back arches off the bed as my body chases his teasing mouth.

I jolt upright when his warm breath tickles the skin between my thighs. "Wh-what are you doing?" I whisper or moan, I'm not sure. I feel him everywhere—his scent in my lungs, his touch in my bones, his thudding heartbeat in rhythm with mine as if we share one.

"I don't know," he answers in a husky voice. "Your body is my only guide. And right now, it's telling me you love what I'm doing to you."

My fingers sink into his hair and tug him up. "Come up here and kiss me."

He lifts his head and meets my gaze, that mischievous look I love so much shining in his eyes.

"You don't like it?" There's uncertainty in his voice, however.

"Oh, *God*. I do so much but—"

"Good." The confidence is back. His strong fingers grasp my thighs, and he parts my legs gently. "Lie back, Gracie."

I flop back on the mattress and cover my eyes with my arm. His head disappears between my legs. I feel a sharp bite on my inner thigh, and my gasp turns into a low moan when his tongue comes out to caress the skin, soothing the pain away. He murmurs under his breath as his nose touches the apex of my sex, and he groans deeply, the vibrations making my thighs shake.

"Please, Sol. I can't—I want *you*."

"You have me."

"No, *no*. I want you up here. Your mouth on mine and you, you inside me."

He presses another wet kiss on my inner thigh before shifting. He crawls back up my body, his hands brushing everywhere along the way. When he's hovering above me, his arms planted on either side of my face, he lowers his head and brushes his lips against mine.

"Are you sure?" he asks, his voice cracking with need.

I nod, licking my lips. My entire body is buzzing with want, burning with need. "*Yes*."

He looks down at the space between us and bites his bottom lip as he aligns himself with my entrance. Then he looks up and cups my face in his hands. "Promise me you'll never forget this, Gracie."

"I promise," I say, tears building in my eyes. I want to cry, and I promised myself I wouldn't, but this moment, this moment feels infinite. Like nothing can come between us.

## Sol

I run my thumb down her cheeks, gently swiping away the tear running down her soft skin. The look in her eyes, the naked want, is thrilling, but the tears coursing down her cheeks confuse me.

"You okay?" I ask, the tip of my dick only half an inch away from her heat. "We don't have to do this."

"I'm okay! Really," she counters, flinging her arms around my neck to hold me in place. "I'm just—this is a big deal. Plus, it's *you*, Sol. You." She smiles and kisses my mouth softly before dropping her head back on the pillow. "Love me," she says breathlessly. "Make me yours."

I don't need any more encouragement. I let go of her face and intertwine my fingers with hers. Slowly, I ease myself inside her, watching her watching me. Her eyes widen, and she winces, then cries out. I stop, jaw clenched, breathing hard.

"I'm *so* sorry," I whisper.

She feels so good, like coming home. And I wait, watching her body loosen as she relaxes, adjusting to me. I forge ahead, more careful than before, and when I'm fully inside her, we both exhale. If I could swear without inflicting God's wrath, I would because being this deep inside her means I can feel the brisk beating of her heart *everywhere*, and mine is galloping in perfect synchronicity. I thought I knew what love was when I blurted out the words back in July.

But now, I understand the true meaning of that word.

Love is when two hearts recognize each other's heartbeat, producing a beat sweeter than any music known to man.

God, she's so beautiful. What am I going to do without her? I push those thoughts to the back of my head and kiss her lips softly, then lean my forehead against hers as I start moving unhurriedly. My hands press down on hers as we find our rhythm, and our bodies move together seamlessly as if they've known each other forever. Forged to be united. I make her mine, my hunger for her ruthless, and my love selfish as I move inside her and make her my queen.

She's my first. And my last.

I'll always be her first.

That knowledge unlocks something inside me. I growl, my hips pumping faster. She moans, her legs coming around to lock behind my back. Her heels digging into my ass cause me to increase speed.

"I-I think I'm—"

Our breathing becomes rougher. I try to hold back, but I can't. My thighs are shaking, and my balls are tight. Then I'm coming inside her.

God. Oh, *God*. It's the most amazing thing I've ever felt.

"Did you come?" I ask, kissing her hair, combing it with my fingers.

She looks away as if she's embarrassed.

"Gracie?"

She shakes her head. "I tried, but I couldn't. It felt a little uncomfortable down there after, you know . . . but I hear it's normal the first time," she adds quickly as if trying to reassure me.

"I'm sorry." I feel like an asshole for not making sure she came too before following my own high. Realizing I'm smothering her under me, I roll on my back, taking her with me. I push away the impact of what I've done and just enjoy holding her close.

"I'll be fine, I promise. I'm just a little sore but being with you like this . . . it's the most wonderful thing I've ever experienced. Did you, um, enjoy it?" she asks hopefully.

Did I enjoy it? That question, I can't fully answer it without falling to my knees and just adoring her. Her body. "It was . . . it was perfect." I finally push out the words. "Thank you for trusting me enough to let me be your first. And . . . for being mine."

She kisses my chest, and I feel her smile on my skin.

# forty-two

*Grace*

THE FOLLOWING WEEK SOL AND I ARE HANGING OUT AT HIS place on Saturday afternoon with our legs tangled. One of his hands rests on my hip, while the other strokes up and down my arm lazily, the touch purposeful and steady. We're spending our last few hours together before he leaves for seminary.

My mind goes back to the second time we had sex a few days after he came back from orientation, after the soreness between my legs faded. He took such great care of me, making sure I orgasmed before he came. It's like once we gave ourselves to each other, we couldn't stop. Now I get why he said he was sure if we ever had sex, he wouldn't be able to stop.

My eyes close briefly at the memory of his hands and mouth on me, languidly as if he had all the time in the world. And my entire body sighs with the memory.

Sol has already packed his stuff, and he'll be leaving tomorrow morning. Mom was meeting with Beverly and her husband for brunch. I excused myself and told my mom I wasn't feeling too well. But from the way she looked at me, I think she knew where I was heading. We haven't spoken again about Sol. I've been avoiding that topic whenever I could.

Sol and I have been listening to music while lying on the bed. We mostly snuggle without saying much. My mind is chaos, and my heart is on a warpath, fighting heartbreak. I thought I was strong enough to watch him walk away, but over the past few days, I realized I'd been lying to myself.

"I love you," I murmur into his chest. "I just want to let you know. I love you, Solomon Callan. I didn't say it back that day, but . . . I could've. I was just scared. Still am."

He kisses the back of my head, and his hands tighten around me, but he doesn't respond. His chest rises and falls quicker now, his heart beating fast against my back.

Unable to stomach the silence, I say, "I-I wish things were different, you know."

He exhales shakily behind me.

"In another life, would you choose me?" I ask, knowing how unfair I'm being, but I'm slowly falling apart, and I don't know what to do other than be selfish.

"Yes."

"But not this life," I press. I knew what I was getting into from the beginning, knew his heart wasn't mine to keep.

Yet I still hoped.

"Gracie." His voice is hoarse. "I love you so much, but I have to walk this path. I just have to. I can't really explain it to you, but I feel like there's something bigger planned for me. I feel like I have a larger purpose to find in life."

A sob chokes in my throat. I cough to cover the fact that I'm about to break down and cry. All of a sudden, he sits up on the bed, shoulders stiff. He grabs his jeans from the floor and puts them on. I watch him stand, then sit back down on the edge of the bed, dropping his head in his hands, exhaling.

"Grace . . . Grace . . ." His voice drifts off as if he doesn't have the energy to talk, and my heart is shriveling inside my body.

He called me *Grace*, not Gracie.

His shoulders are hunched forward, the weight of his decision pulling him down. I'm not going to pretend I understand what he's going through, but I'm dying inside. I'm selfish, and I want him to choose me.

Stupid.

God, I'm stupid. I already knew where he stood. That he intended to pursue his dream of going to the seminary. Yet my heart, my body, everything in me got carried away, and now I've fallen so hard for him I can hardly pick myself up off the floor.

I kissed him first. And even though his heart wasn't mine to have, I knew there'd come a time when he'd have to choose between me and the call to serve God. I allowed hope to bloom in my chest, and with each kiss, it grew wings. With every touch, it took flight and soared, no longer a whisper in my ears but a roaring wind. I convinced myself he'd choose me. Love me enough to keep me. Now staring into his anguish-filled eyes, doubt washes over me. I'm shaking, waiting for the cards to fold and send me crashing down.

*Choose me*, my thoughts yell inside my head.

"Choose me," I say, surprising myself by how strong my voice is.

Maybe we were meant to be. Maybe I'm just like Delilah, and I'm Sol's downfall. Maybe I'm just a selfish person who wants more. Needs more.

Maybe—

His palm frames one of my cheeks as the other hand cups the back of my neck in a firm hold that feels possessive. His gaze meets mine like a tender embrace, his love shining like the sun. Then his mouth is on mine, pressing a soft kiss. My fingers find his hair and tug, pulling him closer. And before long, the chaste kiss turns into a hungry, all-consuming one. We're riding a sixty-foot wave of a kiss in an already turbulent ocean. It's hello and goodbye. My eyes close of their own accord, and I allow myself to sink into the feeling. Then we're both slowing down, our breathing ragged. My mouth skims his lips, his jaw, his cheek . . . memorizing his face. My eyes peel open when I taste wetness on my tongue and see tears streaming down Sol's face. With my thumb, I swipe them away just as piercing blue, blue, blue eyes open to meet mine.

"I'm sorry, Grace," he whispers. "I'm *so* sorry."

He digs the heels of his hands into his eyes, holding them there for a few seconds, his head down, shoulders rising and falling with each labored breath. Then he drops his arms to his sides and walks out of the room without a backward glance. My heart tells me to go after him, but my brain yells it's not a good idea. That nothing will come out of it.

Slowly, the cards fold and the foundation crumbles. I'm falling, shattering into pieces. I'm nothing more than heartbreak. Desolation smiles sadly as she opens her arms, welcoming me. I throw myself into her waiting embrace.

This isn't just a goodbye.

This is our end.

Swiping the tears off my face, I crawl out of bed and put on my clothes. Grabbing my bag from the desk, I leave Sol's room. I head for the front door, but the sound coming from things crashing on the floor from the bathroom has my feet freezing on the spot. My heart aches at the thought of Sol being in pain, and my legs guide me to the door. I press my hand on the wood surface, ready to push, but stop when I hear him muttering something fervently.

"Why, God? Why did you put her in my life, make me feel what it's like to be loved and to love someone so much? *Why?*"

A hushed sob rips through his lips. "I don't know what to do . . ."

Feeling like I'm intruding, I turn and leave without looking back. I can't make him choose me and make him regret his decision later.

# forty-three

*Grace*

*Three weeks later . . .*

DAYS BECOME WEEKS. I CAN'T SEEM TO GET MY SHIT together, and I miss Sol. I miss him so badly that half the time, I fiddle with my phone, typing out a text message to him and deleting it without sending. The saddest part of all is that I never got to properly say goodbye to him. And that hurts more than anything else.

I feel like a five-year-old, still trying to navigate the world and find my place in it. Time doesn't heal wounds. To me, time is an enemy. It doesn't stand still when you want it to. It keeps moving forward, even if you're still stuck in the same place. I haven't moved forward emotionally because my heart is in Boston, not inside my ribcage, where I can protect it.

My stomach ties itself in knots just thinking about Sol. I swear to God, everything makes me think of him.

If I go on like this, I'll go crazy. I need to move forward. I need to finally breathe, and the only way I can do that is by fixing that broken part of me. No one else can do it. I have to fix it myself.

Without giving myself time to think about it too much, I grab my car keys and head out. As soon as I'm inside my car,

I call my mom to let her know I've gone out for a drive. She doesn't ask me where I'm going, just tells me to be home by midnight. I know she worries about me. I see it in her eyes whenever she looks at me.

I can't tell her the truth, though, because she's going to try to stop me. Try to talk some sense into me, and right now, sense is the last thing I need. Not when I'm feeling like I'm cracking in a million different places, and the only thing that will heal those cracks is what I'm about to do.

Call it madness.

Call it recklessness or stupidity.

The heart is stupid and reckless and full of madness. And for once, my brain agrees with it.

My body thrums with anticipation as I swing the car onto I-95S. In desperate need of a distraction, I set my iPod in the dock and scroll through my playlist. "Just Like A Pill" by Pink thuds inside the small space, helping me momentarily forget the thoughtlessness of my actions.

✠

Almost two hours later, my navigation system announces I've reached my destination. I pull into the closest parking spot and glance out the window. The sun's already sinking behind the tall, red brick house. Now that I'm here, I'm not sure if driving all this way was such a good idea. The clock on my dashboard blinks 8:50 p.m.

My head falls to the steering wheel as I consider my options. When I finally look up, it's 8:55. If I want to make it back by midnight like I promised my mom, I need to make this quick.

I pick up my phone from the passenger seat. When I find

the name I'm looking for, I inhale deeply, then press the phone against my ear. Five rings later, the call goes to voicemail.

This is it.

This is a sign. I shouldn't be chasing old memories. I should make peace and move on with my life.

I swipe my face with the back of my hand. Why the fuck am I crying anyway?

I'm so angry with myself. Why can't I move on? Why am I so *weak*?

I throw my phone on the passenger seat, and I watch it bounce twice before clattering onto the floor. Then without giving it a second thought, I reprogram my navigation to home and drive away.

I screech to a stop at the first red light. I feel impatient to move, to race down the street and back home. Right now, even music can't distract me.

My phone starts vibrating on the floor. I squint at the screen, and my heart, which felt dead only minutes ago, sputters back to life as I see the name flashing.

I unhook my seat belt and lunge forward, snatching the phone and answering the call.

"Gracie." Sol's voice is rough like he's just woken up, and the way he says my name is like he's breathing in some much-needed air.

My eyes burn, tears streaming down my cheeks. I can't talk. There's this huge lump in my throat, and my hands are shaking so freaking much.

"Are you there? Gracie? Is everything okay?" He sounds a little panicky.

The lump in my throat lets up a little, and the only words that fall from my lips are "I'm sorry."

I hear something rustle in the background, followed by a

creaking sound, then a soft thud.

"What's going on? Where are you?" He's talking too fast now.

I glance out the window and realize the light has changed to green. I hear a horn coming from behind.

"Grace! You're scaring me!" He says my name louder to get my attention. I jerk upright in my seat.

"Stop shouting!" I yell back as I grip the wheel tightly and jam my foot on the gas. The car lurches forward. Startled, the phone slips from my hand as my fingers grasp the wheel.

I can hear him freaking out, but I need to get off the road without causing an accident.

When I'm safely parked on the side of the street, I retrieve the phone and press it to my ear.

"I'm here." I wipe my cheeks, then pull my feet onto the seat.

"Where is here, Grace?" he repeats in a tight voice.

"I-I don't know." I squint out the window, taking in the buildings flanking my car, then glance at the little screen on my navigation in front of me. "Buswell Street."

There's a long pause, then he says, *"In Boston?"*

"Yes."

"Why? I mean, what are you doing here?" He sounds so shocked.

I don't know how to answer that. My reason sounds really stupid and selfish in my head. So I say, "It was a mistake."

"What are you talking about?" He sounds exasperated, and I can picture him pacing and harassing his hair with his fingers.

"Um . . . I just wanted . . ." *Ugh. Just say it and be done with it.* "I needed closure."

This time, he doesn't say anything for so long I fear he's disconnected the call.

"Sol?" I say nervously, then continue talking. "I had to see you. I've been a mess the past three weeks. I haven't been able to move on because I feel like something's missing. I didn't get to say goodbye before you left. I just want to see you. To say goodbye face-to-face, then you'll never hear from me again. I swear to God—"

"Grace," he snaps, cutting me off.

"Yeah?"

"You drive me insane," he says, anger and concern cracking in those words.

"What?"

"When I saw your call, I was so worried. Then you answered the phone, and you weren't making sense. Do you have any idea how scared I was?"

Clearly, I hadn't thought this through. Shit. "I'm so sorry."

"Okay, text me the exact address where you're parked. I'll pick you up."

I start to protest, but he stops me.

"You're upset, and I don't want you driving in your condition. Text me the address, okay?"

"Okay."

God, I love him so much.

My Sol.

My best friend. The guy I'm in love with, who can never be mine.

After texting him the address, I rest my chin on my knees and wait. I don't want to think about how it'll feel to see him because my heart already aches from how much I've missed him the past three weeks. Every time a song plays on the radio or from my playlist, I picture Sol playing it on his guitar.

Abruptly, lights flash inside my car. A truck parks in front of mine, and a few minutes later, the driver's door opens and long, muscular, denim-clad legs appear. Then broad shoulders and a head full of unruly hair.

I'm frozen in my seat as I see Sol slam the door shut, watch as he makes the short walk between our two cars. He looks bigger and broader than I remember.

Random thoughts rush inside my head; that white T-shirt framing his chest and torso looks great on him. His jaw is clenched tight, and a muscle pulses furiously there. It's hot and scary because I've never seen him this pissed. But it's his mouth that has me breathing hard. His lips look ridiculously full and pink and so hot.

He reaches my car door and yanks it open. Then he just stares at me, and I stare at him, the air between us pulsating with energy.

He lunges forward all of a sudden and snatches me from my seat, dragging me out of the car. And then I'm in his arms, wrapped so tightly I can't breathe, but I don't care because I'd live like this, in his arms, forever. The warmth of his skin seeps into mine, and I feel alive and nervous and giddy and shaky.

He pulls back, his large hands on my shoulders. His gaze roams my face while his fingers trace the same path his eyes did.

"You're okay," he murmurs, finally cupping my face in his hands.

I nod, feeling guilty for being the cause of those worry lines creasing his forehead.

"We can't leave your car here." He looks at my car, uncertainty on his face. "I'm gonna drive my truck, and you follow me closely, okay?"

"Where are we going?"

"Somewhere we can talk." He plants a kiss on my forehead. "Get in your car."

I do as I'm told. He watches me until I'm buckled in my seat, then shuts the door and jogs to his truck. Within seconds, we're on the road. My stomach is like a roller coaster. I'm not sure what I'm feeling right now.

# forty-four

*Grace*

"WANT SOME WATER?"

"Yes, please."

These are the first words we've spoken since he picked me up. I'm starting to think coming here wasn't such a great idea. There's just too much space and no people to act as buffers.

He heads to the refrigerator and returns with a bottle of water. My throat is dry, and not because I'm thirsty. We're so close yet feel so far away. The need to reach out and touch him is breaking me apart, robbing me of my breath.

I gulp the water down greedily as he watches my every move intensely. When our eyes meet, he swallows hard and points toward the couch in the living room.

"It's a beautiful house," I say, totally sucking at this small chat thing. "This is where you lived with your parents before . . . Wait, won't someone at the dorms notice you're missing? Your roommate maybe?"

He just grunts, then says, "Turns out, we don't have roommates. Each of us has our own room in the resident halls. Right now, my fellow brothers are either in the common room playing video games or playing pool or foosball. No one will notice. And curfew is in two hours."

He sits down on the couch across from me, propping his elbows on his thighs, and continues to watch me with *those* eyes. It's so hard to read him right now. Other than the concerned way he looked at me when he showed up thirty minutes ago, he looks almost unaffected. Maybe he's already moved on with his life. I mean, he always had a clear goal in mind of which direction he wanted his life to go, even before I entered it.

I blink back tears and pretend to study every inch of the room. I feel lost more than ever now that I'm here in front of Sol, but he's a million miles away from me.

I set the bottle of water on the table and stand, heading to the fireplace mantle. There are three pictures inside silver frames. Two of the photos show a woman who is the spitting image of Luke, and the second frame has an older version of Sol. *His mom and dad.* In one of the photos, a younger Sol with his usual tousled dark hair and electric blue eyes grins widely at the camera. I reach forward and touch his face on the photo, my lips twitching into a smile.

"Why are you in Boston, Grace?" It's the raw need in his voice that makes me turn around to face him. Pure torment is etched across his features.

Inhaling deeply, I turn around to look at him, anxiety churning in my stomach.

"Aren't you happy to see me?" I hate how small I feel, how needy I sound. I'm beginning to realize love and heartbreak have no shame. I'd drop to my knees in front of him and beg him to just love me.

Hold me.

Just one more night. I'd do anything to feel his arms around me.

Sol shoves his fingers into his hair and tugs at the wavy

mass. "It's taking all my power to hold myself back right now."
He takes deep breaths and exhales slowly, his large frame shuddering with restraint. "Good God, Gracie." He whispers the latter in a vicious growl, and I don't know if he's pissed or happy I'm standing in front of him.

Nevertheless, I close my eyes and let that sound wash over me.

When I open them again, he's standing in front of me, so close. I don't move, though. Being this close to him is the cure I need for the venom annihilating every semblance of who I am.

"I'm sorry." I bite my bottom lip to keep it from trembling.

He sighs and pulls me in for a hug. "No, I'm sorry. I shouldn't have left the way I did."

At his words, my throat grows tight, so I bury my face into his chest and inhale his scent.

"But you did," I mutter into his chest. "You hurt me, Sol, and I fell to my knees. I can't stand back up, and I'm so fucking tired. Every time I think my legs are strong enough to hold me up, I *see* you everywhere I look. I feel you in here"—I press my hand to my heart—"and I trip and fall again."

"I'm so sorry," he murmurs into my hair. "I'm so fucking sorry. I was a coward. I couldn't stick around and say goodbye. I knew if I did, I wouldn't have left."

I lift my head to look up at him. "Would staying be so bad?"

"Yes. No . . . I don't know." He shakes his head, frustration coloring his features. "I have to follow this path. I just have to."

I understand he has to follow his dreams and see what God has in store for him. Sol's path in life had already been chosen for him. I mean, who can compete with The Guy up there? Sol might have been mine in summer—a gift I desperately needed—but not mine forever.

I lift my hand and smooth the lines marring his forehead.

"It's okay. I get it. I understand now."

He looks at me, eyes swimming in tears. "You do?"

I nod, pulling him down and pressing his forehead against mine. My chest feels hollow as though my heart has been ripped from it, leaving a gaping hole. This is what closure feels like, I guess.

I fall back on the balls of my feet and step away from him. "What time is it? I promised Mom I'd be home by midnight."

His eyebrows shoot up. "It's almost ten. There's no way you're driving back—"

"Sol."

He looks at me.

"I'll be fine. I promise. It's only a two-hour drive."

He scowls, his jaw set in a stubborn line.

"It's not my first rodeo." I chuckle, hoping to lighten the mood.

He stalks past me, brushing my shoulder with his arm, and I fucking shiver.

Oh, *God.*

He snatches his keys from the basket on the table and heads for the front door, grabbing the doorknob. He looks over his shoulder at me. "You coming?"

"Where are you going?"

"Portland."

"Please don't do this," I beg. "You'll miss your curfew, and someone will notice you're gone—"

"You're not driving in the middle of the night alone." His jaw clenches, his chin jutting out stubbornly. He stares down at his black shoes. I can't see what's going on in his eyes, but the second he lifts his head, I know I won't be able to deny him this. "Please, let me do this. If anything happens to you, God, I don't know w—"

"Okay," I say quickly, hoping to banish the look on his face. "Thank you."

His lips tip at the corners in a relieved smile. He opens the door and moves aside to let me pass. But before I can step out the door, Sol's strong fingers grip my bicep and yank me back. Then his nose is in my hair, inhaling deeply. He groans, whispering my name twice, then wraps his arm across my chest and hugs me from behind.

"What are you doing?" I whisper, closing my eyes as his nose brushes my neck, warm breath sending goosebumps over my skin.

His arm tightens, his body shudders. Pistons engage inside my body, ready to fire.

"Sol?"

"Just let me hold you for a little while." After a beat, he adds in a hoarse whisper, "Turn around."

I try, but he's holding me so tight I can't move. "Then let go of me."

"I can't."

I laugh. All of a sudden, our bodies are moving back, and the door's being kicked shut. He spins me around and cups my cheeks with one hand, while securing my wrists above my head with the other.

"What's—"

"Shh. No talking. No questions."

"Are you su—"

"Shut up, Gracie."

"But—"

He slams his mouth savagely over mine, silencing me with a searing kiss. It's hungry and needy and hot, and my back arches from the door, and my legs attempt to climb his large frame. He kisses me until my reservations melt away. Until all I see and feel and want is him.

A groan rumbles in his throat. His body presses mine into the door. And suddenly, as if he can't get enough, his hands slide down to cup my ass, and he hoists me up. Then he's spinning us around and heading past the living room and down a dimly lit hallway.

# forty-five

*Sol*

I TOSS HER ON THE LARGE BED, THEN STAND BACK AND STARE AT her small frame, still tight like I remember. I frown as my gaze travels from the darkish circles around her eyes, to her sunken cheeks, and down to her hips barely hugging her jeans. Guilt and regret twist painfully in my stomach.

"You've lost weight," I mutter.

She shrugs as if it's nothing, but to me, it's something. It's everything I miss about her. I loved her full body. I loved touching every part of it.

"What happened?"

"I've been trying out this new diet, and it's am—"

"Cut it out, Grace." I glare down at her. "What's going on?"

Her eyes move to focus on the space above my shoulder, and she's biting down her bottom lip. My heart starts racing inside my chest.

Is she sick? My uncle would have told me if she was, right?

*Right?*

No.

My uncle wouldn't have told me anything. Not when I clearly told him how I felt about Grace and that I'd appreciate if he didn't mention her in our conversations.

Grace is my undoing. Hearing her name makes me feel like I'm coming down with a fever only her touch can cure.

I could easily have chosen her over God. But I need to walk down this path and find out what God has in store for me. He fills this need in me that nothing else can. It's like a craving for more . . . I can't even explain it. All I know is that when I'm on my knees praying to Him, I feel the kind of peace I've never felt before, especially after spending the past three weeks with guys who have the same goals as me.

Grace deserves better, someone who'll dedicate their entire being to worshiping her like the queen she is. Not someone like me, someone whose heart is at war.

No. I don't want to destroy her life like that.

Yet here I am, three seconds away from doing something I shouldn't be doing.

"I don't . . . I can't eat or sleep, Sol," she admits. "I-I miss you so freaking much," she whispers, tears gathering at the corners of her eyes.

My hands clench with the need to scoop her up in my arms and comfort her. I inhale deeply to counter the pain in my chest and close my eyes as I remember how much of a wreck I was the first two weeks after arriving in Boston. I'd finally made peace with the decision I made, although the weight of missing her had settled heavily on my shoulders.

And now, now she's lying on my bed.

Eyes full of naked need and . . . love.

Body primed and ready for me.

I want to touch her so badly. I want to be inside her.

Before my brain can process my actions, I'm crawling up the bed and straddling her thighs.

I glance down at her T-shirt and smirk as I read the words, *Billy Ocean was my first love.* "Sorry, Billy," I murmur, bunching the ratty T-shirt in my hands and ripping it clear down the middle. "*I* was her first."

She squeals, then snorts. "You've ruined it. Mom's going to kill me."

"Just tell her the eighties called, and they wanted Billy back," I grumble.

She laughs, and the sound shoots straight to my dick.

"I missed that sound so much," I tell her as I scoot down and pull her Converse from her feet and throw them over my shoulder. I curl my fingers around the belt loop of her jeans and pull her forward. She gasps, her eyes wide with excitement and anticipation as I tug the zipper down, then yank the material down her legs. My gaze moves between her legs where she's covered by delicate white cotton, and I groan.

I'm panting and shaking with the need to put my mouth *there* and taste her.

"Look at me," she orders hoarsely.

My head jolts up to hers, and I swallow, my throat dry.

"I want to touch you."

"Then touch me," I breathe, spreading my arms wide.

She sits up and tugs the edge of my T-shirt up and over my head. I wait, my pulse thudding in my ears as I watch her take in my chest until her eyes pause on the spot just above my heart. Her gaze darts up to meet mine, then back to my chest as her fingers start tracing the words there.

"Grace, first & last. My beginning and my end," she whispers the words quietly. To others, the quote might not make sense.

She looks at me again, pressing her fingers to her mouth. "When did you get this?"

"A few days after I left," I say nervously. "I was a mess. I needed something that reminded me of you."

Plus, I was drunk on pain and guilt when I walked into the tattoo shop. I remember the feel of the needle as the tattoo artist imprinted that quote on my skin. Remember the ache and pleasure, knowing I'd have a piece of her imbedded in me forever, even if it was only her name.

She leans forward and presses her mouth to the center of my chest, then on the words etched into my skin. Her fingers skim my spine, and I feel as though I'm coming out of my skin as they slide to the front and pull down the zipper of my jeans. I brace my hands on the bed and lift my hips. She pushes the jeans down, pausing to wrap her small hands around my ass and squeezing it before pushing them the rest of the way.

Suddenly desperation claws in my chest. The air around us sizzles with want for each other. Then we're moving, pouncing on each other. Anticipation and need collide as soon as our bodies slam together. We're hands and lips and heat. Grace is the match, and I'm TNT. I'm two seconds from detonating. And then her tongue brushes mine, and I explode. Lights burst behind my eyelids. Passion sizzles in my blood.

My hand cups her nape, moving up and sinking my fingers into her hair, holding her in place. Weeks of need, weeks of missing her, pour into that kiss. She pulls back a little and mumbles *please, please, please,* before she smashes her mouth against mine, and this time, I'm the one begging her.

We break apart, coming up for air. My eyes slowly open, and I stare into her beautiful face. How can a body as small as hers hold so much passion? So much heat?

I'm about to mesh my lips with hers to continue kissing her when her eyes open. She dazzles me with a wide smile before pressing her fingers to her lips. My body shivers with the weight of that smile.

I want more. I want everything. *Now.*

"Enough playing around." I grab her hips and flip her to her stomach. I kiss her lower back along the spine, kissing the two small indents there before wrapping my body around hers. We both groan when I grind my hard length between her ass cheeks.

I gasp at the sensation, sparks shooting down to my toes. My grip around her tightens involuntarily, but the moan she lets out tells me she likes it. I thrust a few more times, our harsh pants filling the room like a carnal melody. I feel myself shake with restraint.

"Jesus, *Sol*," Grace cries out, wiggling beneath me, trying to get even closer.

This feeling, this indescribable feeling of being skin on skin with her, touching her, her scent so intoxicating and real loosens my body. My shoulders relax as the tension I've been carrying since I left Portland, left *her* without even saying goodbye, melts away. My hips pin hers down at the memory of how miserable I've been without her.

How far would I go to experience this feeling over and over again?

The answer nearly knocks me off the bed, and it worries me. She shouldn't be here in the first place. My body shouldn't be wrapped around hers like this. If my spiritual director ever got wind of this, I'd be thrown out of school before I could even blink.

Yet here I am, risking it all for a few minutes in heaven.

# forty-six

*Grace*

I LOVE HIS WEIGHT ON MY BODY, HOLDING ME DOWN BUT NOT crushing me. Feeling his heated skin on mine is everything I've missed and needed.

I sink my face into the pillow and bite hard as Sol presses a hot kiss on the back of my neck. His warm breath feathers the hair there, causing goosebumps to spread all over my arms. His hands leave my hips and slide between my legs, nudging them apart.

"Spread your legs for me, Gracie."

I do, almost crying in relief when a finger brushes my sex before sinking into the heat easily. I'm so wet with need, and knowing he'll be inside me soon makes my back arch. He slides his other hand flat on my stomach and presses gently, forcing my behind up. He growls, seeming satisfied with the position. He continues working his fingers inside me at the same time the hand on my stomach falls away. His body disappears behind me, but before I can complain, I feel the head of his hard length prodding my entrance. He seems to hesitate, and once again, the warmth of his body disappears.

I lift my head and glance over my shoulder. "What's wrong?"

He licks his lips, suddenly looking unsure. "I've only done

this with you . . . what I mean to say is—"

"Me too," I say quickly. "I'm still on birth control."

"Wider, Gracie," he pants huskily while nudging my legs, and I open, my thighs shaking with want.

He pushes inside me, pausing to ask me if I'm okay before proceeding inch by inch, making it last. Making it hurt so good. And when he's finally fully seated inside me, my legs give way from under me, unable to hold my body up. I slump forward, and his body follows mine.

"Are you okay?" he asks, kissing my shoulder.

I can only nod because what I'm feeling right now cannot be put into words. I don't even think there's a way to describe it.

He shifts his body slightly to the side to ease some of his weight off me. His fingers find mine above my head and lace together to form a loose fist. Then he throws a strong leg over my thighs. With his large body draped all over mine, I feel small yet powerful. He begins to move, his mouth kissing my neck as he plunges in and out of me. I push back to match his thrusts as the storm that has been brewing inside us both since he picked me up gains momentum, the violence of it taking me by surprise.

Sol seems different than during our first time. He's more intense, and he doesn't need to talk dirty to butter me up. His body does that for him. And I love it.

Our bodies stretch and twist, molding into each other. We ignite and burn, sweat rolling down our skin. I feel the edge of his teeth on my shoulder a moment before he drags them across my skin. His fingers slide up from between my legs and flatten on my stomach, pushing me flush to his body as he pumps inside me with vigor. I can feel my body eager to let go and just soar.

"I'm coming, Sol," I whisper, eyes squeezed shut.

Without a word, he groans and pants behind me as he

increases his pace, body coiled tight around mine. Unable to hold back anymore, I cry out his name, and my body shakes with release. I hear him cry out my name in response over and over in a rough voice, then his body grows tight as he chases his orgasm.

When we've finally come down from our high, he unlaces our fingers from the top of my head and shifts away, taking his heat with him.

Is he leaving?

Disappointment rushes through me, but then he grasps my hips and turns me around to face him, pulling the covers to our shoulders. He gathers me into his arms and just stares at me, his gaze roaming over my face as mine roams over his.

"What?" I ask, tracing the span of his shoulder with my finger.

His mouth curves into a one-sided smile. "What we just did, it was kind of amazing."

I smile, leaning forward and pressing a kiss in the middle of his chest. "It was, wasn't it? There must be something in the water around here because, dude, you have new moves."

He laughs and taps my nose with his finger. "Yeah?"

I nod, then roll away from him and lift myself on my elbows. "Have you been practicing? Wait, have you been having secret sex or something?"

He winks at me. "Jealous?"

My lips form a thin line as my stomach roils just thinking about him having sex with anyone.

When I remain quiet, he squeezes my hip and whispers, "I'm just joking. It will only ever be you, Gracie."

Then he swings his legs to the side of the bed, his words leaving me confused.

Before I can say a word, he looks over his shoulder at me,

his eyebrows dipped low. The enormity of what we've just done settles around us like a dark cloud.

"I have to get back before curfew."

My eyes roam his face, then meet his gaze. My breath stalls as I take in the emotion flashing across his features—love, need, confusion, hopelessness.

He glances at the clock on the nightstand. His eyes remain there. I have a feeling his intention is to keep me from seeing what he's feeling. "I want you to sleep here. Leave the key above the doorframe, and I'll grab it tomorrow."

"Thank you."

He sucks in a deep breath, returning his eyes to me. The desperation in them makes me want to crawl in his lap and hug him. I know what I have to do, though, but before I can open my mouth, he asks, "What are we going to do? About us. This. You and me."

"*Us?*" I blink at him in disbelief.

He scratches the back of his head, red spots coloring his cheeks. "You know what I mean."

I blow out a frustrated breath. "You chose *this*." I throw my arm out in a sweeping gesture in the general direction of the room. "You had me, but you chose to become a seminarian, Sol." My voice has risen now. And I know it's unreasonable and unfair to throw these words at him, but damn it.

I love him.

I want him for myself. But I don't want him if he's conflicted about what he needs to do.

I don't want to be second best. I want to be someone's first. Someone's always. Doesn't every girl deserve that?

My teeth dig into my bottom lip, and I take deep breaths to keep my temper in check as I study him—the worry lines marring his beautiful face, his usually sky-blue eyes now darkened with anxiety.

I crawl forward and sit next to him, letting my legs dangle over the side of the bed. His eyes fall to my chest and stay there.

"We can't do this again," I announce.

His whole body jolts as if he's been electrocuted, and his eyes fasten on mine.

"This is me letting you go, Sol." My fingers curl into my lap, and the feeling of my nails digging into my palms grounds me. Tears gather at the corners of my eyes, and I quickly drop my gaze to my hands. "I came here for closure, and I'm getting it."

I need to be strong and get through this, and looking at him, staring into those kind eyes of his that speak volumes without him saying a word, weakens me.

"I started this when I kissed you first, and now I'm ending it. We need to let go. Move on."

From the corner of my eye, I see his body shift, turning to fully face me. Then his thumb curves around my chin, and he tugs it up and exhales a long, shuddering breath that shakes his entire body.

"I know." He opens the clasp on the rosary bracelet from his wrist, tugs my hand to his lap, and swiftly puts it around my smaller wrist. "It looks good on you."

"I can't take this, Sol . . . I mean, isn't it like a good luck charm or something?"

His eyes are filling with tears as he lifts my hand to his lips and kisses the back of it. "I don't have anything to offer you other than this. Remember me. Remember *us*."

The tears I've been holding back finally fall down my cheeks. "Always."

He swipes the wetness away with a finger before pulling me into his arms. My front presses against his front, and I fight the urge to push him flat on his back and repeat what we just did moments ago.

Instead, I let him hold me, savoring this moment, the memory of his arms around me, the feel of his skin against mine . . . I let everything sink in. But this time the pain is not as violent as it had been when he left the first time.

After a while, Sol leans down and collects his clothes, putting them on. When he's done, he turns around to face me with a sad smile on his face. Tears shine in his eyes.

"Goodbye, Gracie." He leans forward and presses his mouth to my forehead. I feel the slight tremble of his lips as the kiss lingers for several seconds. Then he pulls back and shoves his balled-up fists into his pockets.

I nod and force a smile through the waterfall of hot tears. "Goodbye, Solomon Callan."

Then he walks out the door without looking back. I listen to the sound of his muted footfalls move farther away and finally the sound of the front door opening and closing.

I wait, for some stupid reason, hoping he'll walk back in and tell me he's staying.

God, will I ever learn?

I crawl back on the bed and pull the covers to my chest, then bury my face into the pillow, pulling in the scent of him.

Then I let myself fall apart, even though I promised myself I wouldn't.

# forty-seven

_Grace_

AUTUMN IN NEW ENGLAND IS SOMETHING TO BEHOLD. GOLD, yellow, and orange colors splash all around me, reminding me why it's my favorite season. But my mind is too preoccupied to notice the scenery. I dig my phone out of my handbag and scroll through my contacts, stopping on MJ's number. She answers the call after two rings. "Do me a favor. If my mom calls you to ask if I spent the night at your place, just say yes."

I've just left Boston, and I'm driving back home when panic suddenly grips me. I was so caught up in Sol, I forgot to let my mom know I wouldn't be home by curfew. I jolted awake around 1:00 a.m. covered in sweat and quickly typed out a text to my mom, then sent another text to MJ. When I didn't hear from her, I decided to call her first thing in the morning. Apparently, MJ is not a morning person.

"Why? Where did you spend the night?" MJ asks suspiciously, then yawns.

"Please don't judge me, okay?"

"I'll try," she mumbles, sounding like she's about to doze off.

"I drove to Boston to see—"

"Okay, I'm judging you." She sounds more awake now. "What the hell, Grace?"

"I just wanted closure." I sound too defensive, so I sigh and apologize, then say, "I had to see him, MJ. But one thing led to another . . ."

I hear the sound of sheets rustling, then a low moan, followed by a deep voice muttering, "Who's that, babe?"

Oh shit.

Ivan.

"Don't tell him!" I whisper urgently into the phone.

"Why? He's So—"

"Oh my God! Don't say his name!"

She huffs, and murmurs, "It's no one. Go back to sleep, babe."

Ivan groans and mutters something unintelligible, and seconds later, the sound of snoring fills the line.

"Where are you right now?" she asks in a low voice.

"On my way home. Just an hour away."

"I'll be waiting at Fisher's Gold. I need details," she grumbles, then adds, "and coffee."

She disconnects the call before I can respond.

I stare at the phone in the docking station for a few seconds before returning my attention to the road.

✠

MJ is sitting at the table near the window at Fisher's Gold, holding a large mug to her mouth as she takes a big sip. The chair next to hers is empty. I glance around the little shop to make sure Ivan didn't tag along, then sigh in relief when I don't see him anywhere.

As I make my way to where she's sitting, the scent of coffee and pastries slams into me, reminding me I skipped breakfast in my haste to get back to Portland.

"Hey," I greet her, pulling a chair out and sitting down.

Her head snaps up in my direction and she grins. "You naughty girl! Tell me everything."

Apparently, coffee makes MJ more agreeable and fun.

After ordering a breakfast fit for a king, I sit back and tell MJ everything. I'm grateful for her friendship because talking to someone about it all is exactly what I needed.

She eyes me and purses her lips thoughtfully. "He might be expelled if they know he's been fooling around."

I nod. "That's why I decided to end whatever it is that we were doing."

"So"—she licks her lips—"you've found the closure you were looking for?"

*No.* "Yes."

"Good. I know you miss him, and it will probably take a while for the pain to go away, but he's chosen his path. It's time to choose yours, too." Her voice is soft, her expression softer.

I really admire her no-nonsense approach to things. MJ is so grounded. I wish I were more like her and not the flighty, indecisive person I've been lately.

She cups her mug and brings it to her lips, taking a large sip of coffee, then sets it back on the table, keeping her hands around it.

She's right. I need to get my shit together. "Ivan and I are heading back to school tomorrow. He only drove me here to visit Grandma."

I nod again, trying hard not to feel like a failure.

*Breathe.*

I'll get through it somehow. I need to look for something to do before next year's fall semester.

MJ attends James Fredricks, as well, for the sports and recreational management program. Mom and I will be driving to visit Fredricks in two weeks, which I'm really looking forward to, especially now. I need to focus on my future.

For the first time in a very long time, a small spark of hope blooms inside my chest.

# forty-eight

## Sol

T HERE ARE ANGELS AND DEMONS AT WAR INSIDE MY HEAD, and the demons are winning.

I'm sitting across the table from Grace, the only person who has the power to silence the chaos in my head, and at the same time cause mayhem in my heart. I can't stop staring at her. Her lips highlighted in deep red lipstick, the way her rich brown skin glows when the soft lighting from the lamp above us hits at the right angle, her curly hair banded at the nape of her neck, displaying a heart-shaped face that makes me question my calling.

I should be heeding the advice of my spiritual director to remove myself from temptation. Instead, I'm wondering if she still tastes and smells like vanilla waffles.

I wonder if this is God's test of my loyalty to him. How long will my resolve hold before everything falls apart?

I'm home from seminary for Thanksgiving. Grace's mother, Debra, invited my uncle and me for dinner.

I should have politely refused the invitation and avoided placing myself directly in the path of wickedness, so close to the one person who makes me want to sin ten ways from Sunday. Instead, I accepted, then spent the next few hours alternating between meditation and praying feverishly to God for strength. Then I threw on a pair of running shorts and a T-shirt and went for a run, hoping the chilly November weather would help me focus.

By the time we left the rectory, I had steeled myself with resolve and patience and strength. That is, until Debra opened the door and stepped aside, inviting us into her home, and my eyes landed on Grace, standing beside the table with her hands clasped primly in front of her.

She smiled sweetly my way, and it hit me—coming here was a big mistake.

As we eat, conversation flows easily, but in my mind the same words keep playing, crowding my thoughts. *I hope my hard-on is not that obvious. God, give me strength to get through this dinner without embarrassing myself.*

It's hard to function when your mind is in turmoil. Hard to breathe when your heart is in your throat.

I'm not sure whether I love her or hate her. I don't know if it's myself I should hate for allowing her to occupy my mind, or if I should thank God for giving me the ability to love her so much that I've made an altar in my head of the memories we shared.

My gaze strays every so often to Grace. Hers briefly meets mine, sending a jolt of heat—*again*—straight to my groin before she looks away. Her eyes stay firmly on her plate as she lifts the fork to her mouth.

*Oh, God.*

Her sin-worthy lips part and close around the forkful of mashed potatoes, and I groan inwardly, picturing that mouth on me.

I quickly drop my gaze to my own plate and subtly shift in my seat, desperate for relief. I tug down my napkin on my lap, hiding the visible bulge in my pants. Squeezing my eyes shut briefly, I mutter, "Forgive me, Father. Forgive me, Father. Forgive me, F—"

"You okay?" Luke asks in a low voice.

My eyes fly open and my head makes an awkward jerk meant as a nod. From the corner of my eye, I see him assess me with those knowing eyes of his. Judging by the look he's giving me, the answers to his curious thoughts are written all over my face for the world to see. He turns away, frowning, and continues chatting with Debra.

*The heart is weak, greedy, and reckless. Selfish*, my spiritual director advised while staring intently into my eyes during our last session together before I left St. Bernard Seminary for Thanksgiving break. *Stay away from temptation. If something or someone leads you to consider sinning or to have impure thoughts, then it is wise to remove yourself from that situation.*

The words are clear in my head now, yet, here I am. Unable to remove myself from this situation without looking obvious.

I could drag her to her room.

I could kiss her.

I could—

*Stop.*

Guilt cuts through my conscience, causing my stomach to twist painfully. I shut my eyes tight again, trying to rid myself of those thoughts.

I don't even care at this point if I look like the veins in my forehead are about to burst with effort. If I don't block her out, if I don't block *Grace* out, my restraint will snap. When I close my eyes, it's easier to see the face of my spiritual director staring down at me with such disappointment at my thoughts. It helps. A little bit.

Even though my gaze is on the plate in front of me, I know

Grace is watching me innocently from under her lashes. I can *feel* her eyes on me. But they don't fool me. There's nothing innocent about the body beneath that pretty red dress. Everything about it is sinful and dangerous.

And no matter how hard I've tried to forget the feel of her skin against mine, both our smells mixed with the distinct smell of sex, it all seems to be imprinted in my very being. Those memories are a part of me. *She's* a part of me.

Two months ago, I renewed my pledge to God and myself. I promised not to let myself get easily swayed by memories of Grace. I purged all carnal thoughts from my mind. I was cleansed, and my faith and purpose renewed.

I was at peace, that is, until I found out where I'd be spending Thanksgiving dinner.

I wonder if today will be the day I break my vow.

My gaze lands on the bracelet I gave her when she was in Boston. The last time I saw her; the time we said goodbye at the house in Boston. Pride and joy rushes through me, seeing that she's wearing something I valued.

I never thought I'd see her after that. At least not this soon. When I decided to come home for Thanksgiving, I planned to do everything I could to avoid her.

Just then, the sound of the doorbell echoes through the apartment, taking me out of my thoughts.

"That must be Levi and Ivan," Grace says as she stands up from her chair.

Caught off guard, I jerk upright at the word Levi bouncing around inside my head. Ivan didn't tell me he was coming over when I spoke to him last night, so I'm a little confused as to the reason he's here. With *him*.

My gaze follows Grace as she heads to answer the door, my heart beating furiously in my chest.

"The boys and Grace are taking food to the homeless shelter downtown," Debra says, a proud smile on her face.

Grace returns a few seconds later with Ivan and Levi in tow. My best friend sits on the chair next to mine while Levi takes the seat next to Grace. He shamelessly pushes his chair so close to Grace's he's practically sitting on her lap, then slides his arm across the back.

The way he's looking at her . . . I want to wipe that flirtatious smirk off his face with my fist.

My hands curl into fists on my lap, and I have to force myself to look away. Anywhere else but at them.

*Ugh. Stop this, Callan. Where is all these coming from, huh?*

But I should know by now about Grace's superpower of waking up the Hulk in me.

Once pleasantries have been exchanged, Debra invites Ivan and Levi for dessert, then she stands up and walks to the kitchen.

Ivan nudges me on my arm with his elbow. "So how did it go?" he asks quietly, subtly nodding in Grace's direction.

I steal a gaze in her direction, and my nostrils flare in irritation when I notice the way Levi's upper body is twisted toward her, giving her all his attention. Ivan seems to sense the epic emotional state I'm currently in. He nudges me harder and whispers, "Stop this, man."

"What?" I turn to face him, feigning innocence.

"Whatever's going inside your head, just stop. Okay? It's not healthy." His eyebrows rise meaningfully.

I sigh wearily. "I know. I just didn't think seeing her again would be this hard. She seems happy . . ."

"There's nothing going on between them, I swear. So don't Hulk out, okay?" Ivan rushes to reassure me. "At least nothing I'm aware of."

I drag my fingers through my hair, frustration burning inside my chest.

I need air. I don't think I have the strength to sit here any longer because I can't stop looking at her like she's a glass of water and I've been trekking the Kalahari for the past three weeks.

Setting my napkin beside my plate, I push my chair back and excuse myself to go to the bathroom. I lock the door and turn to face the mirror, my fingers curling around the sink in front of me. I stare at my reflection while taking deep breaths.

*You can do this. Just go back out there, try and behave like a normal person, and attempt to contribute to the conversation for the next ten minutes. Then excuse yourself and thank Debra for the wonderful dinner, which you hardly even touched—and Grace for the stunning visual—then leave with your uncle.*

Easy.

Right?

The thought of spending even one more minute with Grace sitting directly across from me sends a tremor of need down my spine.

Flipping the faucet on, I splash cold water on my face until my skin feels numb. I turn it off and grab a few tissues and pat myself dry. I've been in here for too long. I'm sure everyone is wondering what's going on.

Taking a deep breath, I leave the bathroom and pause in the hallway, trying to listen to the conversation from the dining room.

"Hey," a soft voice whispers, and I jump ten feet high at that sound.

I spin around and come face-to-face with Grace. My heart pumps hard in my chest, and I'm sweating more than a sinner at confession.

I clear my throat. "Hey." I stare at her, trying to come up with a good conversation starter and end up saying, "You look beautiful."

A smile curves her lips, and she murmurs, "Thanks. You look"—she looks me up and down—"amazing."

We stand there, staring at each other. I should turn on my heels and join the others at the table, but there's this energy tethering me to the ground, and I can't move.

Finally, she sighs and turns to leave, and I panic. "H-how are you?"

Grace stops in her tracks and turns back to face me. "Good. You?"

Man, this is awkward. Instead of answering her, my gaze roams her face, so many questions flashing in my head. I don't even have a right to think about some of them, but I can't stop myself. I shove my hands in my pants pockets and rock on the heels of my feet. She sighs again, sounding defeated before turning around to leave for the second time. Something inside me snaps, and I pounce forward. I don't even know what I'm doing until I realize my fingers are wrapped around her wrist, and I'm dragging her to her bedroom.

Once we are inside the room, I release her arm and close the door behind me. Slowly, I spin around to face her. Her eyes are wide, and her chest is heaving.

"Are you crazy?" she hisses, her eyes darting around the room as if she's looking for an escape route.

She takes several steps back, keeping a healthy distance between us, and I find myself sighing in relief. Being near her activates that part in my brain that is only reserved for Grace. I have no idea what I might do if she's within arm's reach.

"What are you doing?" she asks softly.

Good question. What am I doing?

"Sol—"

"Are you happy? Are you, uh, you know, seeing . . ."

Understanding makes her eyes widen even more. "You can't be serious—"

"I know I don't have the right to ask, but just answer me, please. *Please*"

We stare at each other, the sound of our ragged breaths filling the quiet space. Debra's laughter drifts into the room through the closed door. Outside the window, the sound of a car honking fills the silence thrumming with tension.

"How can I entertain the thought of being with someone else when you're the only one I see? You're everywhere, and I can't shake you off, Sol. I can't . . . *I can't* . . ."

"I know what you mean, Gracie. I really do."

I lean back on the door and shove my clenched hands inside my pockets because they are shaking so badly with the need to just hold her.

"How am I still like this? Like my heart will burst out of my chest with what I'm feeling?" I mutter, shaking my head.

"Love is a bitch, huh?" she asks, her lips twisting in a bitter-sweet smile. "Welcome to Hell, Callan. Anyway, we have to go back before they come looking for us." She straightens, smoothing her hands down her dress, then throws her shoulders back.

Why am I more worried about losing her once we both go through that door than I am about being caught?

"Sol?" she asks, a frown on her face. "You actually need to step away from the door for us to leave this room."

"I'm not sure I can do that, Gracie."

"Why?" It's a breathless whisper.

"Because."

"That's not an answer."

Looking around the room, I breathe through my nose and

exhale through my mouth before focusing on Grace again. "I've tried so hard to forget this." I wave at the space between us. "Forget you, forget how you make me feel. In the two months we've been apart, I prayed. I promised God that if He gave me the peace I craved so badly, I'd dedicate my life to Him and only Him. I succeeded, living one day at a time. I was in control of my life and my emotions until I walked in this place and saw you."

She sucks a deep breath and crosses her arms on her chest.

"What are you thinking?" I ask, trying to read her but failing miserably.

"I'm waiting for your answer."

Shaking my head, I say, "Meet me in Old Orchard tomorrow afternoon at three o'clock."

She blinks several times, her mouth opening and closing. I'm so desperate to hear her response, every part of me is trained on her mouth, waiting. All of a sudden, her eyes fill with panic, and she grabs my bicep.

"Someone's coming," she whispers urgently, pulling me toward her closet, and shoves me inside before slamming the doors shut. The space is so small I have to curl my shoulders around me to fit without knocking the clothes off the hangers. In the eighteen years of my life, I never thought I'd find myself hiding inside a closet.

When I was fifteen, Ivan had this girlfriend whose parents were extremely strict. They were only allowed to hang out in the living room sitting across from each other. Then one day her parents weren't home. Ivan snuck into her room, but unfortunately, her parents returned before they could reach third base. He spent four hours in the closet, hiding, until her parents went to bed, and his girlfriend finally let him out. I imagine this is how he felt—trapped and scared. And slightly embarrassed.

I hear the sound of a door closing out in the bedroom.

Seconds later, light filters into the closet. I peel my body off the clothes and step out.

"My mom went to her room to grab some stuff. She's back in the living room now. Come on, hurry up!"

I stride to the door, but before I can exit her room, she grabs my wrist. I turn to face her.

"I'll be there." She drops my hand, and with a soft smile, she makes a gesture to let me know it's time I go back to the living room.

*I'll be there.*

I'm terrified and excited at the same time. I hate myself for being weak and greedy, but I can't stop feeling like I won the lottery.

God, I'm such a mess.

I return to the dinner table, forcing a reassuring smile when Luke looks at me oddly. Ivan frowns at me, his gaze darting in the direction I came from before settling on me again. I avert my eyes on the table to avoid the questions simmering in his. I hear Levi ask if he can help Debra pack the food to take to the homeless shelter. Grace doesn't come back until it's time for Luke and me to leave.

After saying goodbye to everyone and thanking Debra and Grace for the wonderful meal, we head to the truck.

That night, I get down on my knees next to my bed and pray. And for the first time in a long time, I don't have words to offer to God. My head is still full of thoughts of seeing Grace tomorrow. And when I climb between the sheets, I spend half the night counting the hours and minutes until I see her again.

# forty-nine

*Grace*

THE FOLLOWING DAY, I ARRIVE IN OLD ORCHARD TWENTY
minutes before three o'clock. I shiver and pull my
jacket tighter as a chilly breeze blows around me.
According to the thermometer in my car, it's nine degrees. The
temperatures are going to drop by nightfall.

Sol is already there waiting for me, though. He's standing a
few feet from the shoreline with his back to me.

I stop to take in his strong stature, marveling at the way the
black jacket clings to his broad shoulders perfectly, and the way
the dark blue jeans hug his backside is pure sin. He's wearing his
favorite cap, covering his short hair. He's been keeping it short
and groomed since he started at the seminary.

He looks over his shoulder as if sensing me, his eyes widening as though he's surprised I showed up.

"Hi," I greet him, coming to a stop in front of him. My
breath comes out in puffs.

"You came." His voice is husky, full of emotion.

"Of course. I said I would."

His lips quirk at one side, and my heart flips happily inside
my chest. My favorite smile. "Thank you."

I turn to face the ocean, watching the waves. We're standing so close, I can feel the heat from his body enveloping me. Another cold breeze sweeps across the water, and I visibly shiver. I step closer to his warmth.

"Better start talking before we freeze to death." I snag my bottom lip between my teeth, feeling worried. I spent the night tossing and turning in bed, wondering if he would regret asking me to meet him here. "And if you say asking me to meet you here was a mistake, I'm going to drown you."

His entire body shakes with laughter, and he wraps his strong arm around my shoulders, tugging me to him. I can't stop the blissful sigh that leaves my lips.

He kisses my hair. "I wasn't going to say that. I just wanted to see you again. Alone."

I duck my head and smile. His arm tightens, and I snuggle deeper, enjoying being like this more than I probably should. We start to walk slowly with no destination in mind. I revel in the silence. I know we should be talking about why we are here. I sense he wants to say something, so I give him time. I don't want to push him to discuss whatever it is that's bothering him, just in case it's not something in my favor. I know, I know. I'm such a chicken.

We've been walking for about ten minutes when the wind changes and the temperature drops further. He steers me back toward the parking lot and to my car.

He shifts his weight from foot to foot and tugs down the brim of his hat. "Maybe we don't have to stop this . . ."

I know what he means. This—us.

I shake my head, shrugging his arm off and stepping back. "We ended *this* the second you left for the seminary. We had closure when I drove to Boston to see you , Sol. Starting all over again will only end up hurting us. I'm trying to move on with my life." *Even though I haven't figured out yet how to do that.*

"You are?" He moves closer, invading my personal space. His Adam's apple bobs as his head lowers a notch, his gaze anxious and hopeful at the same time. He asks in a soft voice, "You don't miss me?"

If Sol is the sun, then I'm a sunflower. His words, the way he looks at me, pours warmth in me, making me thrive with false hope. I love and hate myself for being this person. Why am I wired this way? Why is it so hard for me to resist him, huh?

*Where is your pride, Grace Miller?*

All of a sudden, the knot of anticipation in my stomach uncoils. Anger burns through me, anger at myself. My inability to walk away.

I lift my hands and slam them into Sol's chest. Caught off guard, he stumbles back, his eyes wide with shock.

"You want to know if I miss you, huh?" I shove him with my hands again. This time he's expecting it. He doesn't move, but the startled look on his face deepens. "I miss you and I hate myself for it. Is that what you wanted to hear?" I lift my arms, intending to push him, slap him, punch him. . . I don't know. All I want is for him to feel the pain I'm feeling.

He grasps my wrists with his hands, then stares down at me. His mouth opens, but no words come out. He licks his lips, then tries again, shaking his head once. "Yes—no. I don't want you to hate yourself because of me."

I laugh, but it sounds bitter in my ears. "So what do you want?"

He stares at me for several seconds, drops my hands and steps away from me. My body sways, missing its anchor. I almost beg him to put his hands on me again.

*Almost.*

"I want you to be happy," he mutters.

"I *am* happy. Can't you tell?" I quip.

He eyes me doubtfully and says, "Um, you look pissed off."
Ugh.

"Look. You need to focus on being a priest and I need to—"

All of a sudden, his hands are gripping my shoulders and his lips mesh with mine, cutting me off. I didn't even see him move, which is quite a feat considering how huge he is. My hands move, ready to shove him away. Instead they curl around his jacket, because my knees feel weak and I'm afraid if I left go, I'll drown in euphoria.

The weird thing is that he's not even kissing me. Our lips are only pressed together. Yet, my heart is beating faster than before. I feel alive.

Oh, God.

Sol pulls back, still holding me as my resistance starts to wear off. "You and your mouth. You shouldn't put it anywhere near me when we're arguing."

He laughs. "Sorry." He doesn't look sorry.

We stare at each other for a few moments as our breathing normalizes. Sizzling chemistry or not, we're playing a dangerous game. My heart has already been a casualty of war once. Am I ready to risk it again?

No.

Yes.

*No.*

"But how can we continue?" My mouth opens and the words pour out. "When will I see you again?"

I sigh, the weight of what I'm asking for settling in the spaces between my soul. This imprudent, bold, stubborn, untamable soul of mine willingly jumping into the fire, just to feel the heat of the flames once again.

His chest deflates as breath rushes out of his mouth as if he's been holding it for a while. "I still haven't figured it out yet.

All I know is I've missed you so much, Gracie."

My eyes drift closed, and I blow out a long breath. I can't believe I'm considering this because it seems wrong, yet it feels right at the same time. The thought of not seeing him again makes my heart twist painfully in my chest. I suck air sharply and nod before I can change my mind.

"So I'll see you soon?" he asks, with hope in his voice.

"Yes. I mean, unless you change your mind once you get to Boston . . ." *God, Grace. What the hell are you doing?* "You won't change your mind, will you?" I ask as I get in my car. It's a plea. A warning.

He ducks his head into the car so we're at eye level and cups my face in his large hands. "No, I won't." He leans forward and smashes his mouth to mine in a quick, hot kiss. Then he pulls back. "Go on. I'll follow you with my truck."

"So creepy," I tease him and laugh when he looks at me confused. I roll my eyes and nod.

After he slams my car door shut, I watch him jog to his truck and jump inside. Within seconds, we're driving back to Portland.

When we arrive, I glance up at the rearview mirror and see Sol waving before making a left and heading toward the rectory. Once I get home, I start dinner for my mom, wondering when I'll see Sol again. That thought makes my heart beat faster. It's so wrong, but it feels right.

I think back to the day I drove to Boston, intending on finding closure and moving on with my life. Watching Sol leave was the hardest thing I've ever had to do. I thought I'd be okay and that time would heal my broken heart. What I didn't count on was what would happen if I ever saw him again. And then he was sitting across from me at Thanksgiving dinner, looking at me with those eyes that said everything his mouth couldn't. I felt a rush, the kind of rush I hadn't felt in so long. There was so much love and heat in them it took all my power to hold on to my cutlery. My blood roared in my ears, and my heart raced so fast in my chest I thought it'd rip through. It was the kind of high I'd been craving since he left for the seminary. I was addicted. I wanted more, and at that point, I would've done anything to keep feeling like that.

Then his lips on mine a few moments ago sent my craving for him and resistance colliding into each other. They crashed and burned, and the end result is a woman who's more than ready to accept the little slice of Heaven she can get from the love of her life. Pride and caution take a back seat. I'm a slave to my heart. Now I understand why some women willingly enter into a relationship with a man who is committed to someone else, yet they risk everything just to be with him. I never thought I'd fall into that category. Love makes us stupid. Love makes *me* stupid.

What does that make me? A sinner, a woman in love, or both?

# fifty

*Grace*

IT'S BEEN A WEEK SINCE THANKSGIVING. I STILL HAVEN'T HEARD from Sol, and I don't even know what's going on. His Facebook page hasn't been updated in ages. Did he change his mind? I shouldn't have gotten my hopes up because it only leads to disappointment.

Right after another school visit to James Fredricks with my mom, we drive home. Mom talks excitedly about driving me to college next fall, how happy she is that I've finally found what I want to do in college. For just a moment, my disappointment about Sol is pushed to the back of my mind, and I choose to enjoy this time with my mother. We've gotten so much better at communicating since we started therapy, so we're in a good place. She has been organizing a food drive with Luke for the past month or two. She seems to thrive on it.

Later on at home, I'm lying in bed in the dark, waiting for my mind to finally shut down so I can get some much-needed sleep, when I hear my phone beep with an incoming message. I fumble around in the dark and flip on the lamp. Squinting at the screen, my heart starts racing inside my chest as I sit up on the bed and read the words again.

*I miss you.*

I stare at the screen for a long time, a smile curving across my lips.

Me: *me too*

It takes a while for his message to come through. I start thinking he isn't going to respond when a message pops up on my screen.

Sol: *Can you get away on Sunday during the food drive? Meet me?*

Me: *Where?*

My weakness and love for this boy has no bounds.

Sol: *Capper's Harbor Inn at Portsmouth. On Maplewood Ave. The room will be under Thomas Schuster.*

Me: *What time?*

Sol: *2 p.m.*

Me: *Ok.*

Sol: *Ok.*

I hug my phone to my chest, my eyes closed as I plot how I'll sneak away to meet him without raising any suspicion. I have a feeling my mom will be busy at the food drive, so everything might just work out to my advantage.

My phone vibrates against my chest. I pull it up to check the screen.

Sol: *I can't wait to see you.*

Me: *Me either.*

And that seals the deal. I turn the lights off and lay my phone on my pillow just in case he texts me again. My heart is so full, and the elation thrumming through my veins softens my body, warming me all over. It's the sedative I need to calm my chaotic thoughts.

I close my eyes, smiling, and let sleep pull me under.

# Sol

Tomorrow, I'll hold Grace in my arms. I just have to be careful with the way I handle myself and not raise suspicion. The thought of someone finding out turns my blood to ice. But the thought of letting Grace go, especially after Thanksgiving, makes my stomach clench painfully.

I shift on the bed and lie flat on my back, my gaze trained on the ceiling. It's after eleven. It's dark, and everyone has already gone to sleep.

I've barely been holding on by a thread since Thanksgiving.

Why am I still struggling? Should I be pushing Grace away?

I keep asking myself these questions over and over, every single day. I wish I could talk to my uncle about it, but I'm scared of what he will think of me. Especially after the talk he and I had before I left for Boston.

I told him I had made my choice.

He doubted me. I could see it in his face, which only made me more adamant about it. Plus, I'd just left Grace on her bed, looking brokenhearted and so lost. I have never felt so confused in my life. If I was meant to be with her, then why had I felt so miserable at the thought of not serving God?

The past few weeks, I tried my best to hide the state of my mind. Classes went well, and I made sure to interact and participate in class, but I hardly ever hung out with the other guys during our free time. If anyone noticed how much of a wreck I had become, no one mentioned it. And I knew if the rector knew everything I've been up to since I started the seminary, I would be liable for disciplinary action. Even suspension.

I wonder what she's doing right now.

What if one day she meets someone who can give her

everything I can't? A family, children . . .

Jealousy burns through my veins at the thought of a faceless dude touching her like I want to, like I've done. Kissing her, *making love* to her. Then guilt pours through me, dousing the fire in my veins, leaving me cold. I mutter an apology to God and ask for guidance.

I don't know what kind of answer I'm expecting from Him because nothing happens. No illuminations as to which path I should follow or voice in my head telling me to obey the vows I made, only the sound of blood rushing in my ears and the feel of elation at the thought of seeing her tomorrow.

And I need to see her. I need to feel like I'm flying and soaring and whole, just like I did two weeks ago.

I have no idea when my thoughts stop taunting and torturing me, but when I wake up at seven o'clock the next morning, I realize I fell asleep somewhere between midnight and three o'clock.

Just one hour until Mass begins.

I leap out of bed and dash to the bathroom, glad to have it all to myself. I wouldn't want anyone getting nosy and asking me about the tattoo above my heart because it only belongs to me and Grace.

# fifty-one

_Sol_

LUNCH IS SERVED IN THE MAIN DINING ROOM AT TWELVE. I'M SO
nervous, wondering if my fellow seminarians can read
what I'm planning by just looking at my face. I force
myself to eat my food, then excuse myself and tell Gerry—
one of the guys I've gotten close to the past couple of weeks—
that I'm heading out for my pastoral assignment at the local
children's hospital.

Sitting inside the Toyota I rented for this purpose, I tug the
white collar from around my neck and shrug the black shirt off.
It's a warm, sunny autumn day outside, so I choose to leave my
jacket in the car.

Dressed in the customary black pants, a white T-shirt, and a
baseball cap pulled low on my forehead, I stroll inside Capper's
Harbor Inn.

Is she already here?

What if she doesn't show up?

My heart is in my throat as I head for the reception, tugging
my cap much lower to partly cover my eyes. My body is on high
alert. Whenever someone stares in my direction for longer than
three seconds, I break into a sweat, feeling as if they know me
and what I'm doing here.

The receptionist looks up and smiles. "Good afternoon, sir. How may I help you?"

I clear my throat and smile at her, throwing a little charm in that smile. She practically melts, blinking several times before looking down at the keyboard in front of her.

"I booked a king yesterday under Mr. Thomas Schuster." The lie comes out so easily, it startles and worries me.

Her fingers fly on the keyboard as she checks my details. "Yes, Mr. Schuster."

She looks up, her cheeks red as her eyes wander down my chest and over the span of my shoulders. I've been working out at the gym at school, mostly to purge out my frustration, and my body has been filling out quite nicely.

When her gaze meets mine again, she coughs a little, then twists around to grab a key card from a drawer to her left. She hands over the room key and informs me of the room's whereabouts.

"Have a nice stay, sir. And please let us know if you need anything." She stresses the last word, then scampers away, rubbing her red cheeks.

I turn and head toward the stairs.

Inside the room, I kick off my shoes and send Grace a text with the room number, then start pacing to ease the nervousness clinging to my body.

Ten minutes later, there's a knock on the door. I practically lunge for it and yank the door open. My breath catches in my throat as I take in the woman standing in front of me.

Lips slightly painted in red lipstick, long lashes made even longer with mascara, her curly hair falling around her shoulders down her back, and a pair of silver hoop earrings in her ears. She's wearing a knee-length black trench coat, black knee-high boots, and stockings.

*Grace.*

"Lord help me," I murmur under my breath just as she steps around me and heads inside. My mind goes wild, imagining what she's wearing under that coat.

She throws her purse on the nightstand and takes off her black coat, then tosses it on the nearby chair. I'm still standing at the door with my hand around the knob, watching her when she straightens and spins around to face me. She clasps her hands in front of her and shifts on her feet.

"How long do you have?" she asks.

I close the door and look at my watch. "A little over one hour."

"Good." She walks toward me, her hips swaying, and good Lord. I feel like I'm about to burst out of my pants. "One hour of you to myself."

I swallow audibly, my mouth dry, unable to get any words out.

This is what I wanted, yet I'm too distracted by her scent, her effortless beauty, and the sexy way she carries her body.

Tentatively, she puts her palms on my chest, then meets my gaze as if to check I'm okay with what she's doing.

I nod once to encourage her, and at the same time, I let my hand fall away from the doorknob. I bring both hands to her waist and squeeze, wanting to make sure she's really here.

Her fingers slide up and sink into my hair and tug.

"We have sixty minutes all to ourselves."

"Yes."

"I want you so badly," she murmurs as she pushes herself to her toes and kisses the side of my mouth.

Those words unlock the craving that has been building up for the past two weeks. I hoist her up and cup her ass as my feet swallow the distance to the bed and lay her down. My mouth is on hers, kissing her like I haven't been able to. Like I've wanted to do every single night when I lay alone in bed, jerking off to the memory of her.

My hands push up her dress until they find her bra and unclasp it. I bury my face into her chest.

"I've missed these babies," I murmur into her skin as I take a nipple into my mouth and suck it hard.

She gasps, and her legs wrap around my waist, holding me prisoner.

Her back arches.

I groan, grinding my hard length on the mattress. My fingers caress her body and push down her stockings along with her black panties. I kiss a trail down her stomach, brushing her navel along the way, to her inner thighs. I have never done this before, but I want to taste her now.

She sucks in a deep breath as soon as my tongue brushes her clit. I push a finger into her, working her until her whimpers turn into deep moans—music to my ears.

"You like that, don't you?"

"God, yes!" she screams.

I feel her hand in my hair, and just when I think she's going to pull me off her, she presses me down. With one hand under her ass, I lift her up and consume her. Taking in each of her little cries, her essence.

Then her body is trembling as I hold her firmly, my tongue and finger pulling the climax from her.

"Sol!" She shouts my name on a sob, and her tight body locks up and then loosens as she slumps down on the bed.

"Come here," she orders softly as soon as she comes down from her high.

I climb up her body. I'm so hard in my pants that I wince as my front presses down onto her stomach.

"I want to feel you inside me," she whispers, her hands sliding between us and fumbling with my belt.

Breathing hard, I watch her as she unzips my pants, then pushes them and my boxers down my thighs. I love seeing her like this, wanting me. As soon as her hands touch my stomach, all bets are off. I'm kicking my pants and throwing them on the floor, then grasping her arms in mine and pressing them to the mattress. She gasps in surprise, but her eyes are dark with need. I lower my body, and her legs fall wider to accommodate me. I release one of her arms and glance down where our bodies almost connect. Grabbing my dick, I align myself at her entrance, then meet her gaze with mine again.

Slowly, I push inside her, watching the way her eyes widen as I fill her. A moan slips out of her mouth when we're completely connected. Unable to hold myself up any longer, I collapse on top of her, making sure to angle my body to the side to avoid crushing her, then press my forehead against hers.

"You feel amazing," I murmur, pressing my mouth on hers.

"Move, *please*," she begs on a broken whisper. "I need you so much."

And I do, our breaths mingling and our gazes holding. I don't want to miss a thing, and from the looks of it, she doesn't either.

And when we come, it's explosive and earth-shattering. She calls out my name, and I shout hers. I roll to the side, taking her with me, and pull the sheets to cover our sated bodies.

"I've tried staying away from you, Gracie," I murmur against her head and kiss her hair. "I've tried so hard, but I'm physically incapable of letting you go."

She's quiet; the only thing that lets me know she's listening is her rapid breathing and the tightening of her hands around mine on her waist. Her heart is racing so fast I can feel it pounding through her back.

I check my watch for the time, then quickly set the alarm to go off in thirty minutes. I pull Grace flush against my body and circle my arms around her shoulders and waist. We spend the next few minutes chatting. I tell her about life at the seminary, and she tells me about going off to college. She's also thinking about taking a trip to see her grandparents to try to build a relationship with them before it's too late. Eventually, our time together runs out. We stand from the bed and straighten our clothes. We agree that I should go first, so after a scorching kiss to tide her over until the next time we meet, I leave the room.

Outside, I head for my truck. Guilt and resignation are my travel partners all the way back to Boston.

# fifty-two

*Sol*

AFTER THAT FIRST MEETING AT CAPPER'S HARBOR INN, Grace and I have been meeting mostly on Sundays whenever I could sneak out. God's day, ironically enough. It's the only day of the week where we didn't have a lot going on at the seminary, but I had to make sure I was back by six o'clock in the evening.

Today, though, I feel antsy. She seemed down the last time we met, so I promised her we'd do something fun together. And as usual, like every other time we meet, we choose a town that's far from Boston and Portland.

Grace and I spent an hour at a Christmas Market in Concord, which was fun and very addicting. By the time we are sitting down in a diner to grab some coffee, we only have about forty-five minutes to spare. We spend that time with her sitting next to me, her head on my shoulder, sipping coffee and eating apple pie.

When our time is up, I walk her to her car and wait until she's fastened her seat belt before leaning inside and taking her mouth in a fierce kiss like I always do. Lifting my head, I tell her I'll see her when I come home for winter break in two weeks.

I pull back and tuck a lock of hair behind her ear when I feel like we're being watched. I've had this same feeling every time, but it usually turns out to be nothing. I step back and glance around. As always, there's no one watching us. I shake my head and step back, then close the door. I wave at her as she drives away, then shove my hands inside my pants pockets and head toward my truck.

Two days before Christmas, I drive to Portland for winter break. It's twenty degrees outside. We had a light snowfall last night, and given the cold temperatures, the snow turned to ice. So the drive home takes almost three times.

I arrive in Portland at almost eleven o'clock and drive to the rectory. Luke is already asleep by the time I get there. I send a short text to Grace to let her know I arrived safely, then hop in the shower. When I get back to my room, I find her message waiting for me with a lot of smiley faces. After texting each other for a few minutes, we say good night and plan to meet tomorrow at St. Peter's Church for midnight Mass. The thought of seeing her excites me and scares me at the same time. This is the first time since I became a seminarian that we'll meet in public.

As soon as my head hits the pillow, sleep claims me, and I'm pulled under.

☩

The church is already full by the time Mass starts. I'm sitting on the sixth pew from the front, and Grace is two rows behind me. I know this because I felt the exact moment she entered the church; I felt her eyes on the back of my head as she slid onto the bench. When I looked over my shoulder, I saw her sitting next to her mom. Our gazes met and held. I felt high from the way she was watching me before she dropped her eyes to her lap. Dressed in a red dress, her face moderately made up, she looked stunning. I had to rip my gaze from her before anyone could see how much she affected me.

Throughout Mass, my thoughts remain on the girl sitting behind me. After Mass, everyone files out, and I join them, making sure to linger until Grace and her mom step into the aisle. After saying hello to Debra, I glance at Grace with a hello, hoping my face doesn't show what I'm feeling. As we fall in step, the crowd engulfing us, I let my hand move to the side, seeking her smaller one. Our fingers brush against each other, and I have to bite my bottom lip to stop the groan.

Before we walk out the door, she tugs my finger and whispers quickly, "Meet me here in thirty minutes. Driving my mom home first."

I nod subtly, then say goodbye to her and Debra. Shoving my hands inside my jacket, I take off toward the rectory to bide my time.

Inside my room, I can hear Luke moving around in his as he prepares to go to bed. And as soon as the house falls quiet, I slip out the front door, returning to the front of the church fifteen minutes later, unable to stay still. The grounds are deserted; the only movement is the slight sway of leaves as a cold breeze sweeps through.

Standing in the space draped in darkness on the left, I watch Grace as she walks along the line of the trees, making sure to keep her movements hidden by the shadows. She's changed into a black dress with a red jacket over it, the hood pulled down her head to cover her face.

She reaches the end of the line of trees, looks right and left, then dashes up the steps. I quickly grab her arm and yank her into the dark shadows where I'm hiding, spin her around, and crash my mouth on hers, swallowing her squeal.

We break apart and gulp for air, and I feel her shiver beneath my arms. "I've missed you. I want you so bad," I say, my voice rough.

"Me too," she whispers breathlessly, cupping my face and kissing me again. Our breaths become ragged, and I'm two seconds from pinning her to the wall and having my way with her. The more time we spend together, the more I need her.

"Come on, let's get out of here," I say, tugging the hood of my jacket over my head, then wrapping my arm around her shoulders. We step out of the shadows and hurry toward the parking lot, our heads bowed to keep the wind from our faces.

"Where are we going?"

I steer her toward her car, my gaze darting around us to make sure we weren't being watched. "I know this little place outside town that serves pancakes at all hours of the night."

Once we are settled inside her car, she backs out of the parking lot and follows my directions to the twenty-four-hour diner. We spend the next few hours in a booth at the corner, talking and kissing, eating pancakes and drinking coffee.

It's almost dawn when we finally leave the diner and head out to the parking lot where the car is parked, drunk on lust and need. As soon as I'm seated in the passenger seat, she crawls in after me and settles on my lap, then shuts the door. Then she's kissing me, and I'm kissing her back, thoughts of where we are or the fact that someone might find us flying out the window. Right now, it's just her and me and the hunger burning a hole through my chest. She pulls back and glances out into the still-dark, deserted parking lot before staring at me with dark eyes full of heat and mischief. Her fingers quickly unbuckle my belt and undo the buttons of my pants, causing me to suck air. Before I can say anything, she wiggles on my lap while lifting her dress and pulling down the stockings and panties. She lowers herself on my dick, and this time, I can't breathe.

"Oh my God!" I murmur, my eyes falling shut as heat rushes through me. "Shit."

"I just couldn't resist," she says, kissing my chin. "This is going to be quick."

I nod, gripping her hips and guiding her up and down. I'm distracted, excited, and terrified, my eyes darting out the window every few seconds. A deep moan pulls me back to the girl on top of me, and the world around us disappears as I watch her. Her groans are soft, and the way she's working my dick, I know I'm about to come. My hands grip her harder as she whispers that she's coming. She does, her body shaking, and her forehead pressed to mine. I follow her, flexing my hips and pushing myself deeper into her.

When we come down from the high, Grace lifts herself off me and rearranges her clothing, then crawls over the console and sits on the driver's seat. Still dazed and thrilled from what we just did, I tuck myself in and zip up my pants.

"Are you okay?" she asks, concern in her voice.

My fingers move to cup the back of her neck and pull her to me for a quick kiss that tells her how okay I am.

By the time we pull out of the parking lot, daylight is already filtering through the winter sky in the east.

# fifty-three

*Sol*

WINTER BREAK IS OVER, AND I'M BACK AT THE SEMINARY. During the break, we met whenever we could. Every time we parted, she walked away with my heart in her hands. I'm hopelessly addicted to being around her and talking to her.

It's getting much harder to give up Grace, yet the thought of abandoning my calling to be a priest is unfathomable.

Today, we're meeting at a small inn on the outskirts of Boston. Last night, I lay awake in bed, tossing and turning, thinking about where I wanted my life to go. We can't go on like this. I either have to drop from the seminary and be with her, or let her go.

Luke once told me sacrifice is the beginning of knowing what we are capable of. How strong we are. When we let go, we realize our own potential for growth.

I just hope by the time I arrive at the inn, I'll have made a decision.

When I walk inside the room, I find her sitting on the edge of the bed with her head bowed. The pounding in my ears grows louder and the fog in my head clears. Snapshots of the moments we shared flash in my mind like a movie. What started out as curiosity turned into friendship and more. Something I'm ready to explore.

She looks up, and the look of pure misery on her face sends me stumbling back a few steps. My stomach twists painfully and my thoughts scatter as panic freezes my muscles.

Something is wrong.

And before we can hug each other like we usually do, she stands up and walks around the bed to halts on the other side as though she can't bear being close to me.

She clears her throat and meets my gaze with tears swimming in hers. "I thought I could do this. But I—I can't, Sol. I'm not strong enough. I need more. I want all of you . . ."

I step forward, wanting to go to her but freeze when she lifts a firm hand to stop me. I shove my balled-up fists inside my pants pockets to stop myself from reaching out to her. Words form a lump in my throat, fighting to break free. To beg her to reconsider, because it's finally clear to me.

"Grac—"

She shakes her head furiously, eyes flashing with determination.

"I willingly gave you the power to unravel me because I loved the way it felt when you put me back together. I'm addicted to that feeling, and it's *destroying* me. Destroying us. I want more. I want to love you in the light instead of hiding what we feel for each other in the dark. I want to be able to walk with you side by side on the street without the fear of being discovered. I want so much, Sol. So much."

She pauses and wipes away the tears rolling down her cheeks.

"I'm taking that power back. I need to be able to move on and let you do the same. Our love, what we have shared the past few months, is beautiful and magical. I don't want to taint that.

I want to look back one day and say that I was loved, and I gave it right back."

My heart beats faster, and the pulse in my ears drowns my thoughts as I search for the right words. My mouth opens, and nothing comes out, no matter how hard I try.

"I love you," she murmurs. "But I had time to think. I don't know where my life is going. Being with you makes me feel like I'm on top of the world, but how long can this go on? I know you love me and you love God, but you can't have both. And I can't –I can't . . ."

She buries her face in her hands, and my heart literally breaks. I cover the distance between us and pull her in my arms, hugging her tight. I press my lips on her hair as hot tears fall down my cheeks.

"I'm so sorry for putting you in this position, Gracie. Listen—"

"Stop, okay?" She smacks my chest lightly with her fists. I feel each hit embed itself in my heart. "Just don't say anything. *Please.*"

My hands curl around her shoulders, ready to make her listen to me, but her quiet sobs stop me. So I just hold her.

We stay like this, our hearts shattering into pieces around us. I look back on the past few months, seeing how selfish I've been.

Without talking, she pushes away from me and grabs her purse and coat. She turns to walk to the door and opens it. Once she disappears out the door, desperation washes over me, and I jog after her. She's standing at the front desk, checking out of our room.

Once she is done, she slips on her coat and looks over her shoulder at me before heading for the main door. We can't part like this.

I trail after her just as she stops in front of her car.

"Grace!" I yell, my long strides covering the space between us. She turns around, and our bodies collide. My mouth crashes against hers, and we're kissing desperately, her hands tugging my hair and mine cupping her face, holding her in place. I'm memorizing this moment.

The kiss is over as soon as it started, and I'm stumbling back while she's opening the car door and getting inside the car. We stare at each other.

I'm about to open my mouth to tell her how much I love her, how much I understand her decision and I'm ready to give us a chance, how sorry I am, but she looks away and starts the car. Then she throws her shoulders back and pats her hair with both hands as if she's adjusting a crown atop her head.

Without another glance in my direction, she grips the wheel and drives off, leaving me standing at a crossroad. The weight of my sins presses down, down, down on my shoulders, and I feel like I'm suffocating.

My heart is at war. There are choices to be made, and I can't make them standing here. So I pull my cap from my back pocket and put it on, then head to my car.

I drive in the opposite direction. There's a gaping hole in my chest, and my hands are shaking on the wheel.

There are angels and demons at war inside my head, and I'm not sure which side is winning.

I wanted God. And I wanted Grace. I'd lost Grace, and I wasn't even sure if I had God.

*Disgraceful* (Grace Trilogy, Book Two) is now available.
Read on for the blurb.

I knew it was wrong, but I did it anyway. I fell for him.

*Hard.*

His half smiles and those blue eyes that pulled me deeper, threatening to drown me. But he was never mine to keep. Like all good and rare things, it came to an end. And I erected a wall around my heart to prevent suffering that pain again.

Dimples and gray eyes changed all that. He smashed through my defenses and stole what was left of my heart.

Until my past returns.

Now my heart is a war zone, past and present battling for my forever.

They say lightning doesn't strike the same place twice. I have the burns to prove that isn't true.

Who knew falling in love could hurt so much?

# about the author

Autumn Grey writes sexy contemporary romances full of drama, steamy kisses and happy ever afters. She loves reading stories with flawed and quirky characters, broody alphas and sassy heroines.

To keep updated with Autumn's work, follow her on:
Facebook:
www.facebook.com/AuthorAutumnGreyAG

Goodreads:
www.goodreads.com/author/show/7337710.Autumn_Grey

Instagram:
www.instagram.com/autumngreywrites

Website:
authorautumngrey.com

Bookbub:
www.bookbub.com/profile/autumn-grey

Join her list on www.authorautumngrey.com

# other books

Havoc Series Box Set

The Fall Back Series

*Fall Back Skyward*
*Breaking Gravity*

Grace Trilogy

*Desolate (Book One)*
*Disgraceful (Book Two)*
*Absolution (Book Three)*

# acknowledgements

This is always the hardest part for me to write. Hard because there are so many people who've supported me throughout the entire process while writing this story, and I'll unintentionally leave someone out.

This book wouldn't be what it is today without the help of the following people:

Sarah of Okay Creations—You blow my mind every single time. This cover is everything I dreamed of and more.

Stacey of Champagne Book Design: Your talent for making the interior of this book blows my mind. Thank you for being so patient with me.

My editing team: Marjorie Dumas-Gélinas (I can't thank you enough for helping me find the perfect image for the cover), Tricia of Emerald Eyes Editing, Emily of Emily Lawrence Editing, Jenny of Editing4Indies. Annette Brignac, Kaitie Reister, Astrid Heinisch, Zilpha Owens for proofreading the final version of this book.

Sarah Grim Sentz, Michelle Clay, Marley Valentine, Serena McDonald, Celesha Carillo, Maiwenn B, Jodi Prellwitz Duggan,

Selma and Sejla Ibrahimpasic, Malene Dich, Becca Zsurkán, Yahaira Martinez, Elizarey—Your constructive and honest feedback made this story even better than it initially was. I can't thank you enough for taking time to read it. Sarah, Celesha, Becca, Malene, Elizarey—my teaser-making queens. Thank you for all the beautiful graphics you made for this book.

The Minxes on Facebook, my favorite people on the World Wide Web. You ladies embrace my quirks and keep coming back despite my dorky ways. I love you! And Ninja Readers: Thank you for your unfailing support and friendships. So much love for you.

Special shout out to Malene, Becca, MJ Fryer, Sarah. A chance meeting on social media turned to friendship. Michelle Clay (No amount of words can describe how thankful I am for everything you've done for me, my rock), Marley Valentine, Maiwenn for the daily chats. For keeping me sane. Like Seriously. I had quite a turbulent year, but you ladies didn't falter in your encouragement. Celesha —My friend and my sister-ish. We live miles and miles apart, but when we chat it feels like we're so close. I can't wait to meet you next year in London. JeannineAllison—I'm addicted to our voice mail and GIF-ish chats. Selma and Sejla—my favorite twins—for the coffee and chats. You two have such generous hearts. You offer support before I ask which makes me adore you even more. I want to be you when I grow up. Your friendship and support means everything. Elizarey ( I'm quite convinced you're my sister, even though we've never met), Michelle and Annette for all your help in the Minxes and Ninja Readers groups, and for always touching base with me. And Dylan Allen for your constant friendship and reaching out to ask if I needed help days before the release of this book, even though you had a lot on your plate. Ann (forbiddenbooklover7 on Instagram), what can I say other than thank you for putting up with me LOL. You're amazing. Alexandra Seemann—Friends forever! You'll never know how much I appreciate and love you.

Give Me Books Team—It was amazing to work with you. Thank you for working hard to make this release a success.

To Bloggers and readers—thank you for tirelessly shouting out about our books and for taking time to read.

Join my reader group on Facebook for updates and fun:
Autumn Grey's Minxes
www.facebook.com/groups/350328071837578

Made in the USA
Monee, IL
20 February 2022